WELCOMING PARTY

He dreamed he was back in the shuttle on Gynos. His crewmen lay dead near the rear hatch. The shuttle's power had died, and it was very dark and very still. There were noises outside the hull.

The hatch started to open.

He was trapped, with no place to run, no idea what lay ahead. Faint light spilled in, just enough to outline the figures that stood on the other side, and beyond them the glowing walls of a passageway. There was not enough light to make out details, but it did not take much illumination to tell him what he was seeing was not human . . .

Look for these Del Rey Discoveries . . .
Because something new is always worth the risk!

DEMON DRUMS by Carol Severance
THE QUICKSILVER SCREEN by Don H. DeBrandt
A PLAGUE OF CHANGE by L. Warren Douglas
CHILDREN OF THE EARTH by Catherine Wells
THE OUTSKIRTER'S SECRET by Rosemary Kirstein
MIND LIGHT by Margaret Davis

MIND LIGHT

Margaret Davis

A Del Rey Book

BALLANTINE BOOKS • NEW YORK

A Del Rey Book
Published by Ballantine Books

Copyright © 1992 by Margaret Davis

Library of Congress Catalog Card Number: 92-97045

ISBN 0-345-37718-4

Manufactured in the United States of America

First Edition: January 1993

For Mom and Dad

Prologue

The ship's companion was dead.

The Quayla was damaged.

Chirith walked the corridors of his ship blindly, mind numb with shock. All voyages held hazards, but they had never anticipated such a calamity.

They had come here following the path an earlier deep-space exploration vessel, the *Itieth*, had taken. The vessel was long overdue and presumed lost. The Miquiri had few exploration ships, and all of those were on extended missions at the time the *Itieth* disappeared.

Chirith's ship, the *Nieti*, was the first to return to port. Though their own trip had been long and the crew was due for an extended leave, every adult on the vessel had voted to resupply and set out immediately to search for their sister ship. Only four had stayed behind: young males and females who were either approaching the age of mating, or had already passed through their first seasons without finding mates among the ship's company. They would travel to a more populated world and hope to find mates during their second seasons.

They did not know what had happened to the *Itieth*. Most likely she had suffered a malfunction, but she could have exited jump and found herself materializing in occupied space. Her star charts had come from an abandoned Ytavi ship—the same one upon which the first Quayla had been found. The charts had proved so reliable in the past that the Miquiri had come to trust them implicitly, using them to jump blindly into previously unexplored territory. But the charts were old. A rogue asteroid or comet could have appeared where nothing had been before. If the asteroid had struck a planet or a moon, the collision could have resulted in uncharted belts of space debris.

There were other possibilities. Contamination by deadly microorganisms encountered while surveying a newly discovered world was one; a violent encounter with hostile aliens was another. Whatever had happened, it was vital to determine the *Itieth*'s fate.

Her captain had planned a long jump from her last reported coordinates, pushing the ship to her very limits; Chirith decided to do the same. If a malfunction had occurred during jump they would not find her between here and her destination, no matter how long or hard they searched. He chose slightly different exit coordinates, however, hoping to miss any uncharted objects she might have struck.

The jump proceeded normally until the moment they should have returned to normal space. Instead, they came out into chaos.

Every system on the ship malfunctioned. None of their sensors or instruments worked, and they could not tell where they were or what was happening. The Quayla could not control the ship. In the end, all that saved them was momentum. The ship still traveled forward, even with her engines off, and they finally drifted out of instability into normal space. Only then could they start to count their losses. The *Nieti* had survived, but not all her crew were so lucky.

Chirith reached the end of the corridor. He opened the door to the chamber beyond and went in.

Death filled the assembly room. Bodies lay everywhere, covered by white burial shrouds. The living walked among the dead, searching for *akias*, mates, or children. Now and then, one would uncover a face the searcher had prayed not to see and emit a shrill, high-pitched cry of mourning.

Chirith saw Tirie crouched before one of the mounds at the center of the room. He went to her, knelt, and pulled back the white shroud, knowing what he would see, hoping against all reason he would be wrong. He was not.

Hinfalla. Ship's companion. Mate to Tirie. *Akia* to Chirith. Hinfalla had filled many roles in his life and had brought strength, honor, and grace to all of them.

He and Chirith had come to the *Nieti* on the same day. Both had been raised on trading vessels, but had turned their backs on their born-to families at the time of change, deciding they wanted different lives. Trade was profitable. Trade was safe. Trade was—boring. A berth on a trading ship was the ultimate prize for most Miquiri; for Chirith and Hinfalla, it was prison.

They had wanted to travel in unexplored space, seeking new

trade routes, new people and goods. Their families said they were mad. They said their wild blood would mature. It was mating they hungered for, not adventure. Chirith and Hinfalla had not listened. They had talked to everyone they met, seeking alternatives, seeking others who felt as they did. They found them among the crew of the *Nieti*.

They had been young and uncertain when they boarded the ship for the first time, terrified they had made the wrong decision. The *Nieti*'s crew had welcomed them warmly, accepting them as if they had been born to the ship. Despite that acceptance, they had suffered from doubts and homesickness and had turned to each other for solace.

Time had proved their decisions good ones, for they had found the challenges and stimulation they sought on the *Nieti*. They had both worked hard and prospered. When the ship's companion died, Hinfalla had taken his place. A few years later, Chirith had been chosen Tsiri—ship's leader. He had never expected to receive such an honor, and he was nearly overwhelmed by the decision. He knew Hinfalla's support had played a large role in his selection, but he also knew he would not have become Tsiri if he had not earned the respect and trust of his chosen family.

The years had been good to them, both of them. Until today.

Akia, my heart weeps for you, he said to Hinfalla's lifeless form. May your passage be swift, may your spirit return to bless us again.

Silence. Hinfalla did not reply. Hinfalla would never speak again.

A single note of mourning pierced the room. His? Another's? It did not matter. They were one in their loss, one in their grief. Tirie turned to him and buried her head against his arm. Her body rocked with sobs. He stroked her shoulder, wishing he had the right words to ease her grief. She had lost more than *akia*— she had lost her mate as well. Her loss far exceeded his.

After many minutes, her sobs slowed. She lifted her head.

"We cannot go on, Chirith," she said. "Hinfalla is dead. The Quayla is damaged and no one who lives can speak to it. We must return home. We have no choice."

"Yes," he said. His heart was heavy with sadness, his nostrils filled with the bitter stench of death and failure. With the ship and Quayla damaged, they could not go on. They would have to turn back. He gave Tirie a final pat on the arm, stood, and became Tsiri once more.

They would leave this doomed space at once.

PART ONE

The Dark Pilot

Chapter 1

They found him in Remedia's.

The bar lay at the end of a dark, grimy corridor that station maintenance must have ignored for years. The room was tiny, with just enough space for the self-service slot and five round tables that could seat two. A pair of men dressed in the tight black jumpsuits favored by the station's off-duty personnel sat at one of the tables, talking in low voices.

They looked up as Kiley and Jon Robert entered, their sudden silence at once hostile and suspicious. They had obviously come this far from the center of activity hoping to be undisturbed, only to have a crowd descend on them. One of them started to stand, but the other caught his arm and said something in a low voice. The man subsided, but he glared at the newcomers.

Kiley ignored him. Her attention was on a third man who sat at the rear of the bar, his body slumped forward over the tiny table. Drunk, she thought, disgusted. But there was only one glass before him and it was nearly full. He might only be sleeping, she told herself optimistically. More than one spacer short on money had spent the night in a self-service bar to avoid the cost of a room. There was only one way to find out. She started toward him, but before she could take a complete step, Jon Robert caught her arm and pulled her back.

"Kiley, wait!" he said in an urgent whisper. "I don't like the looks of this place, and if that's Lukas, we're wasting our time. We may need a pilot, but we're not that desperate."

"Aren't you being a little hasty? We haven't even talked to him yet."

"I don't need to. I can tell by looking he's not for us. Come on, let's get out of here. We only have three hours to clear port before they assess another day's docking fees, and it's going to

7

take nearly that long to run the preflight checks. We've wasted enough time already.''

"We're not wasting time!" she said sharply. "We agreed to hire a pilot. We've both been working double shifts to cover the bridge since Jon died. You're exhausted and so am I. One of us is going to make a mistake before long—a fatal mistake. And it won't be just you or me who pays, it will be everyone onboard: Holly, Lia, Reese, and any passengers we may be carrying. If you weren't too tired to think straight you'd be the first to say we've been taking an unacceptable risk.''

"We can manage a little longer,'' he said stubbornly.

"We can't, and even if we could, we need you back in the engine room. Holly's doing her best to cover for you, but she's no match for a freighter ten years past her life expectancy.''

"The ship's fine. She just needs a refitting.''

"And where are we supposed to get the money for that? A refitting will cost a minimum of five thousand credits. That's as much as we make in a good year, and it's been three since we had one of those! We need money, as much as we can make, as fast as we can make it. The only way we'll earn it is by staying out of port and making as many back-to-back runs as we can. If we can get full loads coming and going for the next few months, we might—just might—be able to afford a refitting by the first of the year. In the meantime, we need you in engineering, not on the bridge. Greg Lukas may not be much, but he has pilot's papers and he's available.''

"For a good reason—no one else will have him.''

"You don't know that,'' she returned impatiently, then changed tactics abruptly. "It isn't like you to be so unreasonable, Jon Robert. We haven't even talked to him yet. The least you can do is give him a chance. Besides, it's not as if we're signing him on forever. If he doesn't work out, we can find someone else at Aumarleen. In the meantime, you and I will both get a much needed rest. If you'd stop being so stubborn, you'd see how lucky we are he's available.''

"It's luck all right—*bad* luck. *He's* bad luck. You heard what his former crew was saying about him.''

"What? That he's a loner? That he has nightmares sometimes? So what? We're looking for a pilot, not a social companion. He has his papers and that's all that counts. The *Hilea's* crew may not have liked him, but I didn't hear one of them question his ability.''

"Only because you weren't listening. I'm telling you, Kiley, there's something wrong with him—wrong enough to make the *Hilea* dump him in midrun. He didn't just up and decide to leave the ship. Not on Demarker. Nobody in their right mind would have quit their job on a station so close to shutdown. He couldn't possibly have hoped to get work on another ship; there're no more scheduled to dock before pullout.''

''We stopped. Others probably will, too. No freighter's going to pass up an opportunity for a last-minute cargo if she has an empty hold. He wasn't taking such a great chance.''

''He was, and you know it. Talk about stubborn! You'd find something good to say about a heat wave in hell. Kiley, I'm telling you, he's trouble.''

''Not half as much trouble as I'm going to be if you don't let me go. I mean it, Jon Robert. Let me go, or I'll give those men something more interesting to watch than a family disagreement!''

For a moment she didn't think he would release her, but then his grip eased. She pulled free with a jerk and went across the room, not looking back to see if he followed. He would. No matter how fiercely he argued with her in private, he'd back her publicly when the time came. Their roles might have been reversed if he'd been willing to take Jon Senior's place as head of the family; then she'd have been obligated to obey his orders. But he had refused the position.

''I'm not Jon,'' he'd told them in a voice that shook at the first family meeting after their father's death. ''And I'm not captain of this ship. I'll fill in on the bridge as long as I'm needed, but I'm not the ship's captain and I'm not the right person to head the family, either.''

They'd tried to argue with him, but he had been adamant. ''If anyone's going to be head of family, it should be Kiley,'' he'd said. ''She's acting captain, and she doesn't mind making decisions.''

''Absolutely not!'' her sister, Lia, had shouted. ''If you won't be head, then Reese is the next logical choice. Kiley may be a good pilot, but she doesn't have the experience to make family decisions.''

''Neither does Reese,'' Holly shot back. Quiet Holly, who hadn't said more than ten words at a family meeting since she'd come onboard after marrying Jon Robert. ''He may be your husband, and he may know customs regulations backwards and forwards, but he doesn't know ships. Kiley does. She's practi-

cally run the *Widdon Galaxy* the last two years. Jon trusted her
and so should we.''

But Lia and Reese hadn't wanted her, and since she could not
vote on her own nomination they had been deadlocked, with
Jon Robert and Holly on one side, Lia and Reese on the other.
The sole issue they had agreed on in four hours of heated debate
was the need for a second pilot. Whether that pilot should be
Greg Lukas was another matter.

He didn't move as she approached his table, and her uneasiness returned. If she hadn't made such an issue out of giving
him a chance, she'd have turned around and walked out. Pride
was a terrible thing, she told herself. She'd back herself into a
corner this time, and there would be no easy way out.

''Greg Lukas?'' she asked, then repeated the words sharply
when he did not respond. He stirred and lifted his head.

Kiley took one look at his bloodshot eyes and slack face and
cringed inwardly. He was drunk, all right. Worse, he looked as
if he hadn't changed clothes or bathed for several days. He wore
a black flight jacket and the blue shirt and pants many commercial pilots adopted as a semiofficial uniform, but if wrinkles
were any indication, he'd done more sleeping than working in
the clothes. He had not combed his dark hair, and it needed
cutting. Heavy, dark stubble covered his jaw, standing out in
sharp contrast to his brightly flushed cheeks.

Jon Robert came up beside her. He started to make a scathing
comment about the pilot's appearance, then clamped his jaw
shut before he could say anything he would regret. It didn't take
years of living together to read his disgust, though, or the pointed
message he shot her: *Lukas might have papers, but that's all he
has.*

''Mr. Lukas, my name is Kiley Michaelson,'' she said crisply,
forging ahead when all she wanted to do was retreat. ''This is
my brother, Jon Robert. We'd like to talk to you.''

''Talk to me? About what?'' he asked, taking such deliberate
care to enunciate the words that she winced.

''We're off the freighter *Widdon Galaxy*, Lukas. We're short-
handed and need a relief pilot. For the run to Aumarleen,'' she
added hastily, catching Jon Robert's furious look. ''We understand you're available.''

''You want a pilot? For the run to Aumarleen?'' he repeated,
as if the words were barely sinking in.

''That's right.''

''And you're asking me?''

"Is there some reason why we shouldn't?"

He looked from her to Jon Robert. "Your brother can think of a few," he said, meeting Jon Robert's hostility with a surprisingly steady gaze.

"I can," Jon Robert replied, returning the look. The tension between them was almost palpable.

"My brother is not in charge of bridge operations," Kiley said firmly. "I am. We need a pilot. Unfortunately, the dockmaster's log only shows one on the station with intersystem certification: you. Unless you've signed on with someone else, that is?" she asked, eyebrows raised.

Lukas didn't bother replying.

"No, I thought not. You aren't likely to either, not with only one more ship scheduled to dock before pullout. What do you suppose the odds are you'll find an open berth between now and then? A thousand to one? A million to one? Not very good, no matter how you calculate them. I wouldn't like to be in your boots, Lukas."

"I'll find a berth."

"Will you? I don't think so. I really don't. And I doubt you do either. We can't offer much, but if you're willing to sign on as relief pilot, we'll give you transportation to Aumarleen in return. You won't have any money at the end of the trip, but you'll be in a busy port with ships coming and going daily. You shouldn't have any trouble signing on with someone else once you're there."

"You're offering me passage in return for piloting your ship?" he said incredulously, finally tearing his eyes away from Jon Robert's. "Standard pilot's wages are twice the fare a passenger would pay."

"That may be on Aumarleen, but this is Demarker. Like it or not, Lukas, we're the only job going. And we are going—in two hours and fifty minutes. The only question is, are you coming with us?"

Lukas didn't answer. His gray eyes had gone dark with anger, but there was something else in that look, something Kiley thought he'd rather have died than betray. Something so close to fear, her heart skipped a beat. Fear could make a man dangerous. More dangerous even than anger.

"Well, Lukas?" she prompted.

"What do you want? What do you really want?" he demanded, his voice little more than a hoarse whisper.

"Kiley," Jon Robert said, the warning low and urgent. She didn't need it; her senses had already gone on full alert.

"Only what I said," she told Lukas, deliberately softening her tone, trying to defuse the sudden tension. "We need a relief pilot. That's all."

"She's telling the truth," Jon Robert said unexpectedly. He was still watching the pilot, his eyes narrowed, but his expression had changed from hostility to speculation. "We'll give you passage to Aumarleen in return for your work. But we have to have your answer now. We don't have time to waste. Last chance, Lukas," he said in a louder voice, when the other man did not respond. He waited a moment, then shrugged. "Your decision, then," he said. "Come on, Kiley, we have to get back to the ship."

He took her arm again, drawing her away. She resisted, but he tightened his grip, then eased it just as quickly. He was trying to tell her something. But what? Not to say anything? Do anything? She started to argue, then stopped as she caught the urgent message his eyes sent.

"Come on!" he said, and she went.

"Wait," Lukas muttered before they had taken two steps. "Wait!"

They turned around in time to see him shove himself to his feet. He swayed and grabbed the table. "I've decided to come," he said roughly. "If the offer's still open, that is."

"It's open," Kiley replied. "But we have to hurry. You need to sign a contract before you can board the ship as crew. Is your gear close by? We can stop and pick it up on the way to the dockmaster's office."

"All I have is here," he said, reaching for a battered duffel bag beneath the table. He managed to bend over and pick it up on the first try, but it was touch and go. Jon Robert heaved an audible sigh and put out his hand.

"Let me take that for you," he said. For a moment, Kiley thought Lukas would refuse to relinquish his grip; then he gave in and handed the bag over.

"Not feeling very good," he mumbled.

"So I noticed," Jon Robert returned dryly. "Just try to hold on until you've signed the contract, will you? It shouldn't take more than a few minutes. You can get some rest once you're on the ship."

They had to walk five minutes to reach the elevator that would take them to the station's administrative offices. Kiley wasn't certain Lukas would be able to manage even that short distance as they started out, but he steadied as they walked and managed to keep pace with them.

There was only one clerk in the office. He rose without haste as they entered the brightly lit room and approached the counter.

"Michaelson off the *Widdon Galaxy*—right?" he said to Kiley.

"Yes," she replied.

"I suppose you're ready to leave?" He sighed. "I wish I was going with you, but I'm stuck here until pullout. Somebody had to stay and I was the unlucky choice. I've got to tell you, it's damned boring sitting here day after day, waiting for ships that never come. I don't suppose you'll be making a run back this way any time soon?"

"Not likely. We only stopped because we didn't have a full load out of Larabee. We heard Demarker was using independent freighters to haul out mining equipment the company decided to salvage at the last minute."

"Iverse Company wouldn't leave a drill bit behind if they thought it would pay to freight it out. For a while they were even talking about dismantling the station and hauling it out piece by piece. It didn't take them long to decide against that. She may have been state-of-the-art once, but she's well past her lifetime now, and it's been years since the company put more than a token amount of money into maintenance."

"They're just leaving her here, then? Floating in orbit?"

"That's what I hear. It's not as if she'll be a menace to navigation. With the mining operation on the planet shut down, nobody will have much reason to come this way. You may be the last independent ship to dock here. The *Hilea*'s captain has already cleared his ship for departure. They'll be leaving within the hour."

"We won't be far behind."

"Are you planning to take him with you?" the man asked, looking beyond Kiley to Lukas.

"Yes."

"Well, that's one less problem to worry about. I was afraid we'd be stuck with him until pullout. The dockmaster wasn't happy about the *Hilea* leaving him behind, but there wasn't much he could do. Is he going as passenger or crew?"

"Crew. We're hiring him for the run to Aumarleen. We'll need a contract—standard form will do."

The clerk nodded. He turned to the keyboard on the counter

and his fingers started typing. "Do you want the contract valid for a set number of days, or conditional on the end of the run?"

"Conditional."

"His position?"

"Relief pilot."

"And the payment amount?"

"List it as a working passage."

The clerk looked up at that. His eyes went from Kiley to Lukas and back. "He agreed to that?"

"Yes."

He took another look at Lukas, then shrugged. "I guess he didn't have much choice if he wanted to get off the station. Very well, I've listed payment as passage to Aumarleen. Is there anything else you want spelled out in the contract?"

"No. The simpler it is, the better."

The clerk finished typing and turned the screen on the counter around so Kiley could read the completed form. "I'll need your ID cards to verify your hand scans," he told her.

She pulled out her card and gave it to him. She scanned the document on the screen to be certain he hadn't made a mistake, then placed her hand over a square of glass on the counter. The clerk verified the match with her card, then handed her a light-pen. She wrote her name over the glass. The strokes showed up bold and confident on the screen, looking far more certain and controlled than she felt.

"Lukas, he needs your ID card and signature, too," she said when she finished. The pilot came forward and made a pretense of reading the contract, but she doubted he took in more than one or two words. His eyes had a glassy look that said he was holding on to consciousness by sheer effort of will. He placed his hand on the counter, palm down, then signed his name with painful deliberation.

"Anything else?" Kiley asked the clerk.

"That's all," the other man replied cheerfully. He swung the terminal back around and entered a process code. A printer hummed beneath the counter, then stopped. He reached down and pulled off the copies of the contract, handing one to Kiley and one to Lukas. "For your records," he said.

"Are we clear to leave now?" Kiley asked.

"You are. Just let traffic control know when you're ready to undock."

"Thanks," Kiley said with a smile. He'd been more helpful

than most station personnel she dealt with. "Good luck with your next post."

"May it be better than Demarker," the clerk said prayerfully, eyes raised to the unseen heavens.

"After you," Kiley said to Lukas, nodding toward the door. He looked worse than ever. She wasn't sure he'd heard her at first, but then he collected himself and lurched forward.

"Any problems?" Jon Robert asked as they rejoined him.

"No. The clerk's so bored, he acted as if we were doing him a favor by giving him something to do. I can't imagine being one of the last people left on a station this size. Just walking down these empty corridors is like being in a horror movie. I keep looking over my shoulder and jumping at unexpected noises."

"It's the echoes that get me. When it's quiet enough to hear your own footsteps, or a compressor kicking in two floors down, you start listening for sounds that aren't there."

"And then something skitters across the floor, so fast you can't quite see it." Kiley's shiver wasn't entirely an act. "I think we've been watching too many of those old movies," she said. "We'd better have Lia pick up something less spooky at Aumarleen. A nice tame love story, maybe."

"I know one. It's about a woman from Avalon who meets an alien from XXqst and together they explore the finer arts of interspecies communication."

"I've heard about that movie," Kiley said dryly. "Only they weren't exactly calling it a love story."

"I'm telling you, Kiley, it's a work of art."

"I'll bet. If you weren't—" She broke off suddenly as she realized Lukas was no longer keeping pace with them. He had stopped some three feet back and braced himself against the corridor wall, as if he could no longer stand upright.

"Jon Robert—" she said, but her brother was already moving. They reached Lukas just as his legs started to give way, caught him, and pushed him back against the wall before he fell. He didn't pass out completely, but his head rolled loosely to one side. Though Jon Robert took most of his weight, he couldn't hold the pilot alone. Kiley pulled Lukas's right arm over her shoulder and stepped closer to him to take some of the load, only to recoil at the abnormal heat radiating from his body.

"Jon Robert, he's sick," she said, sounding sick herself. "I thought he was drunk, but it wasn't that at all." Her voice started to rise and she had to force herself to remain calm. There weren't many spacers who didn't develop paranoia about contagion, and she was no exception. With each station they visited, they exposed themselves to untold bacteria and viruses. It didn't matter that controlling disease was one of the highest priorities on every station's list, or that there had not been a major epidemic in the past hundred years. The potential was still there, and the danger of infection was greatest for the spacers who traveled from port to port. Worse, not only would they be among the first infected, they would take the blame for spreading the disease as well.

"I don't think it's anything serious, Kiley," Jon Robert hastened to reassure her. "No one from the *Hilea* mentioned anything about illness among the crew. I'll give him an antibiotic when we get back to the ship, but my guess is he's just run-down and needs sleep. Adavic works on most everything and we have plenty in the medical supplies," he added, thinking ahead.

"But what if it's something more serious? Jon Robert, we can't take the risk he'll expose us all to some exotic disease!"

"Not sick," Lukas muttered, opening his eyes. He tried to pull free, but Jon Robert held him firmly.

"If you're not, I'd like to know how you explain your fever," he said. "You're burning up, man."

"Tired. Just . . . tired."

"You're more than tired. We have antibiotics on the ship; they should cure whatever's wrong, but first we have to get you there. Do you think you can walk if we help you?"

"I can walk," he said stubbornly, trying to free himself.

Jon Robert swore as the pilot's struggles nearly brought them all down. He tightened his hold. "Lukas, it's bad enough you're sick. If you're going to be belligerent as well, you can damned well stay here on Demarker. Let me help you!" he ordered as the pilot's knees started to give way again.

"Got a contract," Lukas said. His eyes were closed and he sounded delirious, but he wasn't giving in. "You have to take me."

"Not if you're sick, we don't. All we have to do is call station security. They'll put you in quarantine so fast, you won't have time to pass out."

"No!" Lukas gave a tremendous heave and managed to break free of them. He staggered to the middle of the corridor. But it wasn't anger that drove him this time. It was fear. Of being left behind? Or the mention of station security? Or just plain delirium? Kiley wasn't sure what triggered his reaction, but his panic

chilled her like an ice-cold shower. This wasn't fear bred of
guilt, it was the mindless panic of a man pressed beyond reason.

"Lukas, take it easy," she said, her breath coming unevenly.
"No one's going to leave you behind or call security. We wanted
a pilot and we still do. Jon Robert's a good medic. If he says
you aren't seriously ill, then you probably aren't. Let us help
you to the ship. You're only making yourself worse, fighting
us."

"I can walk on my own!" he insisted. He jerked away from
Jon Robert's extended hand and started down the corridor to the
elevator. Jon Robert grabbed his bag and caught up with him,
walking close enough to catch him if he started to fall again. He
didn't. Kiley didn't know how far down he had needed to reach
to find the strength to stand on his own, but he had found it, and
he rose a notch in her estimation in the process.

He boarded the elevator, rode up two floors, then crossed to
the dock security gate on his own. The uniformed guard cleared
him with a nod, barely looking at his card. Lukas summoned
up one final burst of energy and strode out across the vast,
deserted floor while the guard checked Kiley's and Jon Robert's
identification, then let them pass.

The outer station walls were transparent during the night cycle, and Kiley could see the *Widdon Galaxy* moored at the end
of the docking tunnel, hovering serenely against the star-filled
sky. She might not have been the largest or most modern ship
Demarker Station had ever berthed, but she was still beautiful
to Kiley.

She was smaller than the superfreighters that had docked at
Demarker when mining operations had run around the clock on
the planet below, but she still blocked a good portion of the sky
outside. Her hull gleamed black and silver—black for her solar
collectors and silver for the bands of sensor and monitor plates
that ran the length of her hull at regular intervals. The collectors
were useless during jump, but they gathered sufficient energy
to power the ship's environmental systems while they were in-
system.

A thousand years of discovery and innovation had gone into
her. The first two hundred of those years, humans had done
little more than explore their own solar system. They had sent
unmanned exploration vessels far into space, and they had talked
of building generation ships that would sustain life for the hun-
dreds of years needed to travel to the stars. Despite the uncertainty of finding habitable worlds, there had been no lack of

volunteers to crew the ships. Earth's population had grown until the planet could barely support the massive crush, despite global food-distribution programs. Earth held no opportunities, no hope for a better future—not for yourself, not for your children. There were plenty of people who would have seized any chance to leave, no matter what the risk, but in the end, that had proved unnecessary.

In 2164, at the age of nineteen, Stefan Svornak published the first of two papers that would change the course of human destiny. *A Proposed Modification to Ludendorf's Spatial Discontinuum Theorem* resulted in the most heated debate the mathematics and scientific communities had conducted in the past two centuries. The controversy was still raging when Svornak published *Theoretical Applications of Artificially Generated Discontinuum Fields*, a year later.

Thirteen years after the appearance of that paper, the first engine capable of twisting its way free of normal space and time was developed. In the thousand years that followed, humans virtually exploded off Earth. They found and colonized two habitable worlds in the first century. By 2334, sixteen more viable worlds had been discovered and plans for colonization were proceeding. By 2834, earth was so severely depopulated that the government and corporations were begging people to remain behind. Few listened. The center of civilization had already moved far beyond Earth, and humanity continued moving outward.

The new colonies were too busy growing to care about establishing a vast, bureaucratic regime to govern all the populated worlds. Still, some sort of extraplanetary control was needed, if only as a protection against the pirates that preyed on intersystem shipping lanes and occasionally swooped down on inadequately defended planets. The Consolidated Alliance of Planets Space Corps was born out of that need.

The Corps began as the international exploration agency that Earth formed to find and survey new worlds. Over time, its duties expanded to include the protection of recently established colonies. When the colonized planets decided a formal protection force was necessary, they turned to the agency.

After months of sometimes heated negotiations, the planets and the agency reached an agreement. The planets would provide the funds for the agency's continued operation, and the agency, now called the Consolidated Alliance of Planets Space Corps, agreed to police the shipping lanes between the worlds.

In return, the Corps received a mandate to continue acting as the primary vehicle of space exploration.

While the Corps provided protection, it was the traders who held human civilization together. They bought and sold goods and information, moving them from world to world. A good trader could retire rich; a poor one could lose all he or she possessed in a single transaction. The better ones founded large corporations that carried on operations after they retired or died. The corporations owned their own ships, hauling freight from one end of the known universe to the other, making deals so complex that only their computers fully understood the intermeshing transactions.

There were smaller, independent traders as well, who relied on hard work and instinct to turn a profit. Most did not have the resources to purchase their own ships, so they relied on private contractors to haul their goods—contractors like Jon Michaelson and his children.

The *Widdon Galaxy* couldn't hold as much cargo as the bulky, lumbering superfreighters the corporations built, but it took only one look at her long, sleek lines to know her designer, Charles Widdon, had loved ships and built them to last. The man who commissioned her had been a longtime admirer of Widdon, and they became close friends during the year the ship was being built. When Widdon died, just before she was completed, her owner named the ship after him. And when Jon Michaelson and his partner, Ty Kestel, pooled their pensions after leaving the Corps to purchase her, they let the name stand. They said it was only right that a ship that fine should honor the man who had designed her.

The two men had risked everything they possessed on the venture, but their investment had paid off. The *Widdon Galaxy* ran fast and lean, and she was able to turn a profit on runs larger vessels wouldn't touch. The profits had declined in recent years as the cost of maintaining her increased, but she still provided a living for Jon's children, as well as a home.

And she was home—the only home Kiley had known since she was eight, the only home Jon Robert and Lia had ever known. While Lia might chaff at the idea of remaining tied to the *Widdon Galaxy* forever, Kiley and Jon Robert wanted nothing more. It hadn't taken Holly many weeks to feel the same way. Jon Robert wouldn't have married her if she hadn't been willing to leave Endrun Station, but he had worried that she would find shipboard life claustrophobic. All of them had breathed a sigh of relief when she settled in easily.

Kiley walked faster as she neared the access tube leading to the ship's main hatch, eager to be back onboard. There was always a tiny fear at the back of her mind that the ship would leave without her. Reason told her it couldn't possibly, if only because she was the pilot. But the anxiety was an old one and deeply buried. She suspected she wasn't the only spacer to feel that way, but she'd never heard anyone else talk about the fear openly. Still, she'd seen Jon Robert touch the ship's hatch as he boarded, his fingers lingering just a second longer than necessary, too many times to believe she was alone in her anxiety.

She wondered if Greg Lukas ever felt uneasy when he was onstation. He certainly started up the access ramp eagerly enough, but he slowed as he neared the top. Either the slight incline was more than he could handle, or he was having last minute qualms. She lengthened her stride and reached him as he came to a complete stop.

"Problems, Lukas?" she asked. He shook his head, but he didn't move, nor did he look at her. His eyes were fixed on the dimly lit corridor on the other side of the hatch.

"We're almost there," she said, trying to sound both assured and assuring.

"Can't . . ."

"Can't what?" she prompted when he didn't continue. "What can't you do, Lukas?"

"Can't . . . make it," he said. Something flashed across his face. Despair? Shame? Desperation? Kiley didn't have time to identify the emotion before his eyes rolled back and he went limp. She grabbed his waist, but he was too heavy for her to support alone. For a moment she thought they were both going down, and then Jon Robert was there, taking the burden away from her.

"He's out cold," he said, inspecting the pilot briefly. He pulled Lukas's right arm across his shoulders. "We'll have to carry him the rest of the way."

"I'll get Reese."

"No!" he said sharply before she could hit the intercom button. "We don't want to let Reese or Lia see him in this condition. They have a tendency to overreact sometimes, and I can guarantee they won't agree to let him onboard if they so much as suspect he might be sick."

"We can outvote them."

"They could still place a call to station security. You know what would happen then."

"But they're going to ask if we found a pilot. What do we tell them?"

"That we did, of course, and that he's in his cabin, settling in. They know we have to leave in a few hours, and that it will take every minute of that time to complete the flight checks. They won't like waiting to meet Lukas, but they won't find it suspicious either. Come on, let's get going. I can't hold him forever."

Kiley repositioned herself, and together they half carried, half dragged Lukas onboard. He was nearly as tall as Jon Robert and it took both of them to maneuver his dead weight.

"Where are we going to put him?" Kiley asked when they reached the ship's main corridor. The bridge lay to their right. Straight ahead were family's quarters. The corridor ran for some distance on their left, terminating in the engine room.

"Across from you," Jon Robert said.

"In Jon's room?" Kiley said sharply, unable to keep the shock out of her voice.

"It's the closest cabin to the bridge. If we're going to have to keep an eye on him, we might as well save ourselves all the steps we can. Besides, I don't want to carry him any farther than I have to. He's heavy, in case you hadn't noticed."

Kiley still balked, but Jon Robert settled the issue by taking most of Lukas's weight and heading for Jon's cabin, giving her no choice.

They had cleaned their father's belongings out of the cabin the day after his death, but they couldn't wipe away the memories of his presence. Kiley took a shaky breath as they entered, but whether it was from pent-up emotion or relief at having made it that far without being seen by the others, she couldn't have said.

They tried to lower the pilot gently, but he slid out of Kiley's grip and fell across the bunk in a sprawl. Jon Robert caught his legs and swung them up, then straightened. "I'll get the medical kit," he said. "Will you go back for his bag? We can't leave it in the access tube."

Kiley half expected to meet Lia or Reese in the corridor, but they were nowhere to be seen. The duffel bag lay where Jon Robert had dropped it. She picked it up, vaguely surprised to find it wasn't heavier, then hurried back to the cabin. Jon Robert was already there. He had retrieved the medical kit and was pulling out a bioscanner.

"Help me turn him over and get him undressed, will you?" he asked.

He took Lukas's shoulders, Kiley took his feet, and together they turned him on his back. Jon Robert lifted him so Kiley could pull off his flight jacket and shirt. She tugged impatiently at the clothes, trying not to think about how much time this was taking. There was too much to do and too little time, but they had to get Lukas settled. Once they left port, they wouldn't be able to check on him until they were beyond the range of station traffic control.

"Take his boots off," Jon Robert ordered. She peeled them open along the sides and pulled them off. Dull and scuffed, they were as disreputable as the rest of his clothes. Jon Robert unfastened the pilot's pants and she helped him tug them off, leaving him in his underwear.

"That's good enough," her brother said. He picked up the scanner, unfastened the eight-inch-long wand from the side, and began a slow sweep of Lukas, starting with his head and going to his toes, covering every inch of his body. He watched the readings appear on the display, comparing them with the normal tolerances that were printed alongside.

"I'd have to run a blood test to be sure," he told Kiley when he finished, "but aside from the fever there doesn't seem to be anything serious wrong. His lungs are clear, his heart and circulatory system are functioning well within normal limits, and there's no sign of any enlargement in his internal organs. His estimated weight is on the low side, and the loss appears to be recent, but that might only mean the *Hilea* had a rotten cook or skimped on crew's rations. The adavic should bring his fever down within a few hours, and time should take care of the rest."

He reached into the med kit and pulled out an aqua-colored vial. He examined the label carefully, checking the dosage and warnings, then pulled out a pressurized injector and inserted the vial. "Wipe his arm off with this," he told Kiley, handing her a sterile swab.

Lukas didn't move as she cleaned a section on his upper arm. Jon Robert set the injector against his skin, then gently squeezed the trigger. He stood looking at the sleeping pilot a moment after he finished, worry dragging down the corners of his mouth.

"I'd feel better if we knew more about him," he said under his breath.

Kiley agreed. Lukas's skin might look alarmingly white against the dark spread that covered the bunk, and his ribs might be too prominent, but he must have used the *Hilea*'s exercise room regularly, for his arms and legs appeared well muscled, showing none of the loss of tone that resulted from prolonged periods in a low-gravity environment. Despite his illness, he didn't look helpless. Not in the least.

"You're worried he might be dangerous?" she said, voicing her own fear.

Jon Robert looked as though he was about to agree, then shrugged. "Maybe, but it doesn't matter now, does it? We're committed." He sighed. "Let's cover him up and let him sleep. We don't have much time left if we're going to make it out of port today."

Kiley helped him pull the blanket out from under the pilot. Lukas didn't stir. Jon Robert covered him, then headed for the bridge. Kiley paused at the door and gave the unconscious man a final look, wishing she knew whether she'd just solved their most pressing problem—or made the most disastrous decision of her life.

Chapter 2

Lukas woke slowly, head pounding, senses disoriented. He lay for a time without moving, aware he hurt, not comprehending why. He lifted his head, only to let it fall back immediately as the room spun dizzily around him. Closing his eyes, he held himself rigid, waiting for the nausea to pass.

When it did, he tried lifting his head again. The room didn't spin this time, but the walls had a tendency to waver disconcertingly at the edges.

He lay on a wide bunk at the side of a dimly lit room. A long wall abutted the bed to his right. A recessed shelf ran the length of the wall some six inches above his head, evidently intended as a storage space. Sliding doors above the shelf hinted at additional, concealed storage. Built-in drawers stretched from floor to ceiling along half the wall at the foot of the bunk, and a desk and chair occupied the rest of the space. A computer terminal sat in one corner of the desk, its screen dark. Air whooshed quietly through a vent on the wall, the sound reassuringly monotonous.

A faint line of light marked a doorway to his left. Controls for the door, room lights, and intercom were clustered next to the door in a luminescent square. Lukas craned his neck to look over his shoulder and made out a sliding door with a hand-sized depression on the wall behind him. A closet, most likely. Immediately to the left of that was the entrance to another room. Someone had left a light on in there, and he could see the corner of a sink and a mirror, and an opaque wall that he took for a shower.

His neck couldn't stand the strain any longer, and he let his head fall back against the pillow. Where was he? How had he come to be in this room? He had no memory of this place. None.

He shivered in the chill air and wished his head would stop aching long enough to let him think.

His last clear memory was his meeting with Captain Radaeus onboard the *Hilea*—the meeting that had ended with his dismissal. He had argued with the captain's decision, but Radaeus had remained adamant.

"I'm sorry, Lukas," the captain had said, "but the ship's surgeon released Commander Vryez for duty this morning and I've already placed him back on the schedule. You knew the duration of your job was conditional upon his return to duty when you signed your contract."

"No one said anything about dumping me on Demarker!" Lukas shot back, his voice rising in disbelief. "The station hasn't seen another ship in weeks. It won't, with pullout so near. I don't stand a chance of finding another berth!" And then, abandoning all pride, he had rushed on. "If you don't need me as a pilot, there must be some other job I can do. I don't care what it is, I'll do it. Just don't leave me stranded here."

"You won't be stranded. Your contract included a provision for passage back to Brekkan in case Vryez was able to return to duty before we reached our destination. I've already had the funds transferred to your credit card. If you find another berth before pullout, you're entitled to keep the money in lieu of severance pay. I know you're unhappy, Lukas," he added, not unsympathetically, "but that's the best I can do. You can file a protest with the dockmaster if you want, but I can tell you right now it won't be worth the fee."

"It isn't Vryez at all, is it?" Lukas said bitterly. "You could keep me on for the rest of the trip if you wanted to. It wouldn't cost any more than a return passage to Brekkan. If you're going to leave me behind, the least you can do is give me the real reason."

Radaeus stared at him, as if unable to believe he would address the ship's captain in that tone of voice. "You want the truth?" he said abruptly. "Very well, I'll give it to you. You're a good pilot, Lukas—damned good—but you have an attitude problem. You don't get along with the rest of the crew. The men say you're cold and aloof, that you go out of your way to avoid them when you're off duty. They don't like that. They don't like *you*. Worse, they don't trust you. That makes you trouble in my book, too much trouble to justify keeping you on, no matter how good you are on the bridge. You have one hour to pack, then I want you off my ship. Is that clear?"

"Yes, sir," he said.

He left without further argument, unable to face Radaeus any longer. He had guessed what the captain would say before he spoke, but the words still hurt. He had done his best to fit in. He really had. But his best hadn't been good enough, not on the *Hilea*, not on any of the other ships he'd served on in the past year.

He went back to the cabin he shared with two engineering mates and started packing. Emptying his locker had been easy, taking a total of five minutes. When you moved from ship to ship as often as he had, you didn't carry much. Running the gauntlet of stares that followed him down the long corridors had proved much harder.

He had thought the worst over once he put the ship behind him, but the stares continued to follow him. Wherever he went, from the dockmaster's office, to the station's single functioning commissary, to the few restaurants and bars reopened to serve the *Hilea*'s crew, the cold silences and colder looks followed. He took a room and decided to stay there until the ship left port, but the confinement drove him crazy. He couldn't sleep. He tried to, but he couldn't stop thinking about the endless days and nights that stretched ahead before the final ship arrived to carry off the last of the station's personnel. All that empty time, with nothing to do. He couldn't stand it. He couldn't!

Unable to remain still, he rose, repacked his few clothes, and left the room. He strode down corridor after corridor, taking elevators to nowhere, walking until he was too tired to stand up. He paid for another room, only to find himself staring up at the ceiling, wishing the nightmare would end. Waiting for the nightmares to start.

He left that room, too. He remembered a series of deserted bars selling self-service food and drinks, and miles of corridors that went on and on, but the images were cloudy and jumbled. He had the feeling something had happened at one of those bars—something unpleasant—but try as he would, he could not remember what.

The door swished and his eyes jerked open. Light spilled into the room from the corridor beyond and a man came in. He pressed the control panel on the wall, bringing the lights up. Lukas blinked in the sudden brightness. The newcomer was so tall that his head barely cleared the doorway. He had the wide shoulders and narrow hips of an athlete, a broad forehead, and a square jaw that narrowed at the chin. Thick blond hair covered his head, and his bright blue shirt matched the color of his eyes. He wore light brown pants made of some synthetic material that gave when he moved, adding grace to an already lithe walk.

"You're awake," the man said. His voice was as easy as his walk, his expression open. Still, the blue eyes that swept the pilot, then the room, missed nothing. Lukas had met men like him before, and he had no doubt that the deceptively easy manner would vanish at the first sign of trouble.

"How do you feel?" the man asked, crossing the room to stand beside the bunk.

"Fine," Lukas replied, his voice a harsh croak that belied his words.

The stranger grinned. "I seem to remember you saying the same thing on the way to the ship, just before you passed out. Tell me the truth. How do you really feel?"

"Ship?" he repeated, his heart missing a beat, then running wildly. He struggled to sit up. "What ship?"

"The *Widdon Galaxy*, of course." The man looked down at Lukas, his eyebrows drawing together. "You signed on for the trip from Demarker to Aumarleen," he prompted when Lukas showed no sign of understanding. "Don't you remember?"

Lukas shook his head in disbelief, then wished he hadn't because it started pounding again. With the pain came memories, however. He had been in a bar. A woman had come in. A woman and her brother. She had offered him a job.

"You wanted a relief pilot," he said slowly.

"That's right," the stranger said. No, not stranger. He had a name. Jon. Jon Robert, the woman had called him.

"You're Michaelson," he said, and the man nodded. "I remember you now. You and your sister."

"Kiley," he prompted.

"Kiley," Lukas repeated. She'd done most of the talking. "She's captain?" he guessed.

"Yes."

"I need to talk to her. Now!"

He had to get off the ship. He didn't know them, didn't know the ship. He must have been crazy to sign a contract with them. He tried to sit up, but the other man stopped him with a hand to the shoulder, pushing him back against the pillow.

"You're not going anywhere, Lukas. Not until that fever comes down."

"I have to talk to the captain," he insisted. "I have to get off the ship."

"It's a little late for that. We pulled out of Demarker two hours ago."

"No," he protested.

"Yes," Michaelson said. He grinned. "Don't look so worried. The *Widdon Galaxy* is a sound ship and we run a strictly legal operation. You're better off than you were on Demarker, whatever you may think at the moment." His eyes swept Lukas and worry clouded his expression again. "I've been giving you adavic to bring your fever down, but it doesn't seem to be working very fast. I think I'd better have another look at you."

He bent over and pulled a bioscanner out of a medical kit sitting on the floor next to the bunk. "I have to uncover you," he said, reaching for the blanket. Lukas grabbed the edge, but Michaelson pulled it away.

"The scanner won't pick up signals as well through the blanket," he said. "I know you're cold; I'll try to hurry."

Someone had undressed him. The air bit his bare skin, raising goose bumps. He stared blindly up at the ceiling as Michaelson ran the scanner's wand over his chest and down the length of his body, too miserable to be embarrassed by the stranger's scrutiny.

True to his word, Michaelson finished within two minutes and pulled the covers back up over Lukas's shoulders.

"Sorry," he apologized when they were in place, "but it couldn't be helped." He paused, still looking worried. "Your temperature is a degree lower than it was when we brought you onboard," he said, "but you aren't responding to the adavic as well as I'd hoped. Do you hurt anywhere? Anywhere at all?"

"My head aches."

"That's all?"

"Yes."

"You're sure?"

"Yes," he said sharply. He didn't want to talk. All he wanted to do was curl up in a ball and sleep.

"Have you ever had a fever like this before?" Michaelson persisted.

"No."

"Have you had any other signs of illness the last few weeks? Unusual fatigue, a rash?"

"No. Nothing. There's nothing wrong with me."

"Oh, there's something wrong," Michaelson returned. "I just don't know what. It doesn't look like anything serious, but

I think I'd better take a blood sample and run it through the analyzer to be sure.''

''You don't need—''

''I do,'' he said flatly, cutting off all argument. He rummaged in the chest and pulled out a wide, elasticized band that he fastened around Lukas's upper arm before swabbing the skin liberally with antiseptic.

''I haven't had much practice at this,'' he warned as the needle slid in, ''so I may have to try more than once.''

Lukas winced, but Michaelson kept on going until he hit the spot he was looking for. Dark red blood flowed into the needle, and he grinned. ''That's a relief,'' he said. ''It took me three tries the last time I had to take a sample. My technique must be improving.'' He released the band around Lukas's arm, slid the needle out, and taped a bandage tightly over the wound.

''I'll run this through the analyzer right away, but it will be a few hours before I get the results from the computer.'' He sealed the sample and set it aside. ''I'd rather not give you any other medication in the meantime,'' he said, more to himself than to Lukas, ''not unless that headache is really bothering you. You're in no danger, and I'd be taking a chance of doing more harm than good.''

''It isn't.''

Michaelson didn't look convinced, but he apparently decided to let the matter go. ''Are you thirsty?'' he asked abruptly.

Lukas hesitated. His head pounded and the light stabbed his eyes. He wanted Michaelson to leave. But he could use a drink of water. His lips were dry and cracked, and his tongue seemed twice its normal size.

He nodded, and Michaelson disappeared into the bathroom. He seemed to take forever coming back. Lukas couldn't understand what he was doing. He tried to sit up, but he couldn't even find the strength to raise his head, let alone his body.

''Here, let me help you,'' Michaelson said.

Only it wasn't Michaelson. It was something else. Something so horrible, his mind refused to see what his eyes beheld. He jerked up convulsively, trying to throw himself out of the bunk, out of danger, but something pushed him back down and held him against the pillow. He arched his back, fighting to tear himself free, but the pressure only increased.

''Let me go!'' he shouted.

Something hit his face—hard enough to shock him into a semblance of reason.

"Lukas, look at me. Look at me!"

He looked, and could have wept in despair as the room came back into focus. He was lying flat on the bunk, with Michaelson kneeling over him. The other man's hands gripped his shoulders, holding him immobile.

"Are you all right now?" Michaelson asked, watching reason return to his eyes.

He nodded, not trusting his voice.

"What's the matter with you?" he demanded. "It couldn't have been delirium, your fever isn't that high."

Lukas didn't answer. He couldn't.

Michaelson continued to stare at him, eyes narrowed. "Never mind," he said, dropping the matter abruptly. Too abruptly. He acted as if Lukas's violent response was of no importance, but Lukas wasn't deceived. Michaelson wouldn't forget what he'd done. He doubted the man ever forgot anything.

"I'll get another glass of water," Michaelson said, rising. "That one ended up on the floor."

It took all the strength Lukas had, but he managed to sit up before Michaelson returned. The blond man hesitated beside the bunk, as if uncertain what he would do, then he held out the glass. It was heavy; Lukas had to use both hands to hold it. He managed to drink a little, but his hands began to shake and water slopped over the rim of the glass.

"Let me help you," Michaelson said. He put his hand underneath the glass, taking most of the weight. Lukas bent his head and took another sip, then let go as the muscles in his arms gave out. Michaelson set the glass on the shelf beside the bunk.

"I'll leave the water here in case you decide you want more." He stepped back. "I have to go—we're close to jump. Is there anything else you want?"

"No."

"The intercom is set on voice-activate. If you do need anything, just call out."

"I'll be all right."

"Why is it, the more you say that, the less I believe you?" Michaelson replied with sudden exasperation. "I don't know where you got the idea that accepting help from others is a sign of weakness, but you'd better think again. I won't tolerate a crewman who can't admit to and accept his limitations, and Kiley won't either. If you aren't well, you're expected to say so. Is that clear?"

"Yes."

"I have your word, then? You'll call if you start feeling worse or if you want anything—food, drink, whatever?"

"If I need something, I'll ask," Lukas said, the words as distinct and precise as he could make them.

"Fine. I'll be back after we've jumped." Michaelson picked up the vial containing the blood sample and went to the door. "Try to get some sleep, Lukas," he said with sudden weariness, then turned the lights off and left.

Lukas pulled the covers tight around his shoulders and curled into a ball.

If I need something, I'll ask, he had said. He had known full well he would not, but it wasn't the lie that bothered him. It was the look in Michaelson's eyes just before the door closed. The look that said Michaelson knew he was lying.

Jon Robert turned the copilot's seat around, dropped into the chair with uncharacteristic heaviness, and swung to face the control board. He scanned the bank of softly glowing displays, taking in the ship's position, course, speed, and the status of the ship's environmental systems.

He's had too much practice reading the boards lately, Kiley thought guiltily. Before Jon died, he would have required several minutes to register all the information he now absorbed in a single glance.

"Sorry I took so long," he said. "Did Lia bring you dinner yet?"

"No."

"You still have time to fix something. Go ahead. I'll cover for you."

"I'll wait."

"Kiley, you need to eat," he said, taking his eyes off the boards long enough to look at her.

"Later. After jump. It's too close now."

"You'll just make yourself sick."

"I know what I'm doing."

"Do you? You look about an inch away from collapse to me. Refusing to eat isn't going to help."

"Jon Robert, back off!" she said sharply, and regretted the flare of temper immediately. "I'm sorry," she said with a sigh. "I shouldn't have yelled at you. You're right, I am tired. But I'm no worse than you, so stop telling me what to do. I'll have dinner later, after we jump."

She studied the string of calculations on the navigation plotting board once more, decided they would have to do, and pressed the accept key, feeding the jump time and coordinates into the ship's main computer.

They were accelerating rapidly now, less than ten minutes from transition. The ship swept forward, a faint vibration humming through her decks and hull as she gathered herself for the mighty thrust to come. Kiley's stomach tightened as excitement and tension jostled for position.

She controlled her emotions, burying them beneath a thick layer of calm, but she did not forget they were there, for they were the reason behind the years of training and hard work, the hours of boredom, the constant worry about money. In those last moments leading to jump and in that final instant of thrust when all life hung in the balance, she found the exhilaration and joy that made all the hours of boredom worthwhile. She would never have admitted it, because some truths were best left unsaid, but it was the sheer love of speed and power that kept her piloting ships, jump after jump.

"Ten minutes to transition," she announced over shipwide intercom. "Holly, are you set?"

"Affirmative, Kiley," the young woman replied. There was a breathless note in her voice; Kiley wasn't the only one who had to control her emotions.

"Lia? Reese? Are you ready?" she asked.

"We are, Kiley," Reese answered from their cabin. He betrayed no sign of excitement, but then he wouldn't. Reese never displayed emotion, not even during the most heated of family meetings.

"What about Lukas?" she asked Jon Robert, shutting off the intercom.

"He's sleeping," Jon Robert said.

"You checked on him before you came back?"

"Yes."

"How's he doing?"

"Better I think, but he still has a temperature. I'm running a blood sample through the analyzer."

"That's why you were late coming back to the bridge?"

"Yes. I'm sorry, Kiley," he apologized. "I know you wanted a break before jump."

"It happens," she said with a shrug. "He is going to be okay, isn't he?"

"Yes. I still can't see anything terribly wrong. I'll run the analyzer and bioscanner readings against the diagnostic tapes in the main computer, but I still think he's suffering more from exhaustion than any disease. A few days of rest and he should be back to normal.''

"Whatever that is."

"Yes."

"You think I made a mistake taking him onboard, don't you?" she asked, averting her eyes, pretending to scan the boards.

There was a long pause. "I don't know," he said.

The delay worried her more than any words he could have spoken. Not many people could match Jon Robert's inner certainty about himself and others. It was a knack he had, that ability to see people and know them instantly. Until today, she had trusted his judgment implicitly. In all the years she had known him, he had never been far wrong. He had even seen a good side to Reese at their first meeting.

It had taken her months to appreciate that Reese's coolness toward everyone but Lia could be an asset. If he did not respond warmly to others, neither did he antagonize them. He could talk to difficult customs and dock officials for hours and remain calm, though Jon Senior would have been shouting within minutes. He was honest, hardworking, and he did his fair share of the ship's work. He had no interest in piloting the ship, and virtually no natural ability, but he'd spent days after Jon's death doggedly learning sufficient navigational skills to bring the *Widdon Galaxy* into port if Kiley and Jon Robert should both be incapacitated.

She had been wrong about Reese. She had admitted as much to Lia once, with no small loss of pride. But she would have had much more to apologize for if she hadn't listened to Jon Robert's warning and restrained her more scathing comments after meeting him. Now she was hoping to hear Jon Robert say she hadn't made a mistake bringing Lukas onboard, that he wasn't going to be the problem she feared, but he wasn't offering reassurances.

"I'm pretty sure he'll take your orders and do his job," he went on. "I don't think you have to worry about that. He has too much pride to be anything but a model crewman."

"But? There is a but, isn't there?"

He hesitated, then said in a rush, "He's frightened, Kiley. I don't know why, but he's terrified. Worse than that, he refuses to admit he's afraid. I'm not sure he's admitted it to himself."

"You think he's in trouble? That he may have broken the law?"

Jon Robert thought, then shook his head. "No, not that. There's something about him—a sense of honor—I doubt he's done anything illegal in his life. He's like Jon that way."

"As if his preserving his integrity was more important than staying alive."

"Yes."

Kiley's hands tightened. Jon had not been an easy man to live with at the best of times. That some of his pride and integrity had rubbed off on his children hadn't made their lives any easier either.

"Well, if it isn't the law he's running from, what is it?" she asked.

"I don't know."

"But he is afraid?"

"Yes."

"That makes him dangerous, then," she said flatly, cursing herself for not listening to her brother from the beginning.

"Yes—but on the positive side, if he's as frightened as I think he is, he'll probably go out of his way to avoid trouble. He'll do his job to the best of his ability and spend the rest of his time trying to make himself inconspicuous."

"That doesn't sound so bad to me."

"It isn't, as long as he can control his fear. But if it continues to grow, or if he runs out of the energy required to continue suppressing it, he may come apart on us."

"As in explode?"

"He might, under the right circumstances."

"Do you think it's likely?"

"In the next four or five days? No, not really. But I think we'd better remain alert to the possibility."

"What should we do, then?"

"Don't pressure him, for starters. Don't ask too many questions, and don't worry if he wants to keep to himself when he's off duty."

"I won't, but what about Lia and Reese? How are we going to stop them from asking him questions? They won't settle for anything less than his life history, if I know them."

"I thought I'd leave that problem to you," Jon Robert replied. "He was your choice, after all."

"You don't have to rub it in," she said, then frowned. "We can't tell them to leave Lukas alone. That would just make them suspect something is wrong."

"Well, you'll have to think of something. Look at it as a challenge."

"More like an impossible dream," she returned shortly.

"Maybe, but we do have to keep them off his back. The very worst thing any of us could do is push him until he feels he's been backed into a corner with no escape. If he does start to unravel, that will be the most likely time."

"And it won't matter that we didn't intend to do that—or even that we have—only that he thinks we have?"

"Yes."

"I don't like this," she said vehemently. "I don't like this at all. I was trying to save our lives, not jeopardize them." She turned back to the control board, fussed with a key, then punched a display request and watched the ensuing data flow with blind eyes.

"Kiley, you didn't know," Jon Robert said quietly.

"But I should have."

"Maybe. Maybe not. We needed a pilot—badly enough to take him on. He may not have been a good choice, but he seemed better than none at the time. You weren't the only one who made the decision, you know. I could have refused to let him onboard. We're both responsible. Anyway, it's too late to go back. Just remember, he doesn't want trouble any more than we do. If we give him time and space enough to maneuver, I don't think he'll cause problems."

"You really have been on the bridge too much lately," Kiley said with a forced laugh. "You're even starting to talk like a pilot. Time and space to maneuver, indeed."

He laughed with her, but his eyes were serious. "Don't worry so much, Kiley. Everything will work out. It always does."

"I hope so." She looked at the board and opened the intercom. "Thirty seconds to transition," she announced.

Jon Robert's fingers hovered over the controls, waiting for her order.

She watched the seconds count down, then said, "Jump engines on."

After that, there was no time for further conversation. The ship's vibration changed to a deep rumble that resonated through her entire body. She took a deep breath and held it as the universe turned inside out and they twisted their way into the place that lay beyond time and space.

* * *

Someone was behind him. The hair lifted on the back of Lukas's neck. Primal instincts buried so deeply in his genetic structure that countless eons of evolution had been unable to erase them sent a surge of adrenaline rushing through his bloodstream.

He tensed, the muscles in his arms and legs coiling, preparing for sudden, violent movement. He restrained the urge, clinging to the irrational belief that whatever waited would give up and go away if he could just hold still long enough. He lay rigidly, taking shallow breaths until he thought his heart would burst from the tension.

And then, when he could stand the strain no longer, he turned over.

His heart stopped.

A creature stood over him, looking down. It had a long, straight body and a face like some ancient totem carved from wood. The head was too large for the rest of it. Huge black eyes glowered at him from under thick, baleful brows, and something that resembled tufts of hair or feathers covered its head and cheeks. It had no ears he could see, only slots at the side of its head. And its mouth—

Its mouth was a long, curved, wickedly sharp, yellow beak that jutted straight out from its face. The beak opened and a harsh, piercing sound came out. Its head went back, then flew forward, the beak coming straight toward him, driving down, burying itself deep in his chest.

Agony flared through every nerve in his body as the pointed beak plunged in, tearing past muscle, ripping through bone and cartilage. It grabbed his heart, then tore it free with a tremendous jerk. There were no words for the pain. It ripped through every nerve, the signal reaching his brain in one cataclysmic, utterly unbearable burst.

He screamed, the sound pouring out of his throat even as blood poured out of his chest. He was dead, yet the pain did not stop. It grew and grew until it was all that remained of him. He begged for mercy, begged for death, but the creature just threw back its head, opened its beak, and let his heart slide down its throat in a single gulp. It looked down upon him impassively. Then its head went back a second time, the bloodstained yellow beak pointing straight up before coming forward again, striking with blinding speed, going straight for his head.

His scream shattered the silence, ripping him from sleep.

He lay on his back, his heart thumping wildly against his ribs, his breath coming in great gasps. Sweat poured off him, drenching the sheets.

"Lukas, wake up!" someone was saying urgently.

Hands gripped his shoulders, shaking him. He opened his eyes and found a woman kneeling on the bunk beside him. She wore a yellow shirt and brown pants made of the same supple material as Michaelson's. On her, the fabric emphasized not size and muscle, but rather long, straight limbs and a slender waist. The shirt fit loosely, the collar open at her neck. She either had little interest in fashion, or she was more interested in comfort than appearance.

Her hair was long and dark. She wore it coiled at the back of her head, the braid looped round and round in a circle and fastened securely in place. Long, dark lashes fringed brown eyes flecked with green. She was not beautiful, but her bones were good. She might have drawn a second look were it not for the lines of fatigue that bracketed her mouth and eyes.

"What . . . ?" he said.

"You were dreaming," she told him, her voice cool and precise.

Dreaming? He blinked, then blinked again, trying to shake off the remnants of his nightmare. His heart slowed, and he took one breath, then another.

Color came back into the woman's face as he relaxed, and only then did he realize she had been frightened. Of him. He must have screamed aloud. He cursed silently. What must she be thinking of him? More important, why hadn't she asked about the dream? She must be wondering what would make a man scream like that.

"I had a nightmare," he said cautiously.

"Did you?" she replied, not sounding in the least interested. And then, as if realizing she was still holding on to his shoulders, she flushed and let her hands fall to her sides. Her sudden self-consciousness would have amused him under other circumstances. Or touched him—for there was something about her uncertainty that struck a sympathetic chord.

Despite her assurance, her aura of command, she was not invulnerable. She might command a ship, and tension and fatigue might line her face, but she was young, no more than twenty-four, twenty-six at the most. Whatever her age, she was too young to be captain of a ship, even a small freighter.

Unless this was a family ship.

My name is Kiley Michaelson and this is my brother, Jon

Robert, she had said. Brother and sister. He added that to the spacious cabin he had been given and knew he had to be right. The *Widdon Galaxy* was a family ship. No company would have hired Kiley Michaelson as captain, however exceptional she might be. There were too many older, more experienced pilots to be found.

If this was a family ship, there had to be more Michaelsons around. How many? Ten? Fifteen? Twenty? He swore silently. He could not possibly fit into such a closed group. If he'd been treated like an outsider on the *Hilea,* he would meet with infinitely more reserve and suspicion here. He couldn't believe they had taken him onboard at all. But then, perhaps they had assumed their closeness and numbers gave them security.

"Well, Lukas?" Kiley asked. She'd said something and was waiting for a reply. He stared at her blankly and she repeated her question.

"Are you feeling better?"

"I . . . yes," he said. And he was. The fever had broken, leaving him drenched in sweat. He started to throw the blanket back and stopped abruptly, remembering someone had undressed him.

She caught his arrested movement and the corners of her mouth twitched.

"You're decent enough," she said. And then, without giving him time to wonder how she knew that, said, "Just a minute. I'll get a robe."

She went into the bathroom and came back with a huge white bathrobe. Judging by the size, he guessed it must have belonged to Jon Robert—unless all the men on the ship were as big as her brother, a possibility that caused him several more moments of anxiety.

She tossed the robe on the bunk. "Go ahead," she said when he did not reach for it immediately. "I expect you could use a trip to the bathroom, and the bed needs changing if the sheet is as wet as it looks."

"I'll do it," he said quickly, but she shook her head.

"Lukas, you may be better, but I sincerely doubt you're feeling that good. No, don't argue," she ordered when he started to protest again.

The exhausted finality in her voice stopped him cold. He'd heard that tone before, from men who had been holding on to the ragged edge of control so long they couldn't remember how or why they had come to be where they were, only that they could not, dared not let go.

"All right," he said, his agreement surprising them both. He pulled on the robe, shoved back the covers, and stood up.

His legs wobbled, as if he'd been ill for weeks instead of a day, and he had to steady himself for a moment before he could stand on his own. Kiley started to offer a hand and stopped in midgesture as he jerked back. The contempt on her face spoke as clearly as words, though. *Go ahead then, do it yourself. If you think you can.*

He returned her look with one of his own, one that said he most assuredly could. He took one step, then another, and strength came back with each. She watched him, waiting for the first sign of faltering. When it did not come, she shrugged, turned around, and started to work on the bed.

She had finished changing it by the time he returned. She waited until he settled in, asked if he wanted anything to eat, accepted his refusal without comment, and left, all with a minimum of fuss that made Jon Robert seem like a neurotic mother in comparison.

It was only after she'd gone that it occurred to him to wonder why it had been Kiley Michaelson, captain of the *Widdon Galaxy*, who had checked up on him. There must have been any number of other family members with more time and fewer responsibilities who could have done the job. Why had she?

The question occupied him for some time before sleep claimed his body and mind again.

Chapter 3

"Permission to come on the bridge, Captain," a deferential voice said, startling Kiley out of her concentration on the boards.

She swung the pilot's chair around and found Greg Lukas standing in the corridor just outside the entrance to the bridge. He bore so little resemblance to the bleary-eyed man she'd talked to in the bar on Demarker, or the feverish one she and Jon Robert had undressed less than twenty-four hours before, that she had to look twice to be sure he really was Lukas.

He had showered recently and his dark hair was still damp. The dark stubble that had covered his cheeks and jaw was gone, though his skin looked slightly irritated, as if he'd had a mild reaction to the depilatory he used to remove his beard. His eyes were clear and bright, and his long legs gave no signs of unsteadiness. He was taller than she remembered—or perhaps it was only the way he held himself, shoulders back, chin up, standing so stiffly that he might have been at attention. His light blue shirt and navy pants appeared identical to the quasi-uniform he'd worn the night they met, but these garments were immaculately clean and pressed. He had tucked the shirt neatly into his pants, and his pant cuffs into supple, ankle-high black boots that shone as if they'd been buffed for hours.

If she had not seen the transformation herself, she would not have believed the disheveled man in the bar capable of such fastidious grooming. But even more disturbing than the change in his appearance was the quick perception and intelligence behind the steady gray eyes that met her appraisal—and returned it in full measure.

"Permission granted," she said, taking refuge in formality as she mentally scrambled to update her assessment of him.

"I'm surprised you're up," she added as he came into the room. "Jon Robert said you might sleep another ten or twelve hours."

"I'm feeling much better." He swallowed, then said stiffly, "I'm sorry for the inconvenience I must have caused. You needed a pilot, not an invalid."

"You don't need to apologize, Lukas," she said, cutting him off so his obvious embarrassment wouldn't spread to her. "It's not as if you chose to be sick. I'm just glad you're feeling better. Have you eaten yet?"

"No. I thought I'd see you first and find out when you wanted me to start standing watch."

"That's very conscientious of you, but are you sure you're up to working? Jon Robert—"

"I feel fine, Captain," he said, so convincingly she found herself conceding against her better judgment.

"Very well. We've all been working long hours and there's no denying we could use a break. Jon Robert and I have been alternating shifts, one eight hours long and the other four. Would that be a problem for you?"

"No."

"I'll take the first and third shifts. That would leave you on afternoons and nights. Is that agreeable?"

"That's fine. I assume you'll want to check me out before turning me loose. Would you like to do that now?"

"There's no rush. Jon Robert is due to relieve me in a few minutes so I can go to breakfast. Why don't you come along. I'll introduce you to the rest of the family, then show you around the ship afterwards so you can orient yourself. We can save the boards until your first watch."

"This afternoon?" he persisted.

"If that's what you want," she replied, surprised.

"That is why I'm here." He sounded so stiff he might have been the ship's captain and she the new pilot.

"Very well, this afternoon it is."

"What's this afternoon?" Jon Robert asked, appearing behind Lukas. "And who said you could get out of bed?" he asked the pilot.

"I wasn't aware I needed permission," Lukas returned, his chin coming up.

Jon Robert started to say something and stopped, going through the same rapid reassessment Kiley had made as he noticed the change in the pilot's appearance and manner.

"I guess you didn't, at that," he said. He turned to her, eyebrows raised. "Kiley?" A multitude of questions was contained in that single word.

"Mr. Lukas says he's ready to start work. I managed to convince him to have breakfast first, then take a tour of the ship, but he insists on starting this afternoon. That will free you up to man the engine room—provided you can manage one more full shift here?"

"Of course," he said, his attention straying back to Lukas. Kiley guessed he wanted to tell the pilot he should wait another day before starting to work, but the other man's cool gaze silenced him. Score one for Lukas, she thought.

The bridge could seat four—a pilot and copilot at the main boards, and two others at the backup communications and engineering boards. The chairs facing the main boards sat side by side. She stood and slipped out between them, vacating the pilot's seat for Jon Robert. He took her place and turned toward the main board, scanning the operative displays. The external monitors and scanners were off, useless during jump, but the engines and environmental systems required constant monitoring.

"Any alarms while I was asleep?" Jon Robert asked without looking up.

"Not one," she said. "The biggest problem I had was trying to stay awake."

"I was afraid of that," he said ruefully.

"Are you set?" she asked when he finished his first scan of the boards.

"Yes."

"You have the conn, then." She turned to Lukas. "After you." She gestured for him to precede her.

She took the lead when they reached the corridor and went down the wide passageway that led to the engine room at the aft of the ship. The first cross corridor led to their cabins. She passed that up and continued on to the next corridor, which branched off to the right.

"The galley is here," she said, going down the hall and stopping at the first door on her left. She pressed the control panel and the door opened with a swoosh.

The galley served as a food storage and preparation area. Transparent doors covered the walls straight ahead. Inside were bins containing frozen, freeze-dried, and dehydrated foods. An oven to heat meals and a refrigeration unit to store the fresh fruits and vegetables Lia grew in the hydroponic garden covered the short wall on the left. A long counter ran along the right-hand wall, a sink and several dishwashing units at the far end.

"I don't know how your taste in food runs," she said, "but we have most everything that can be dehydrated or freeze-dried. We have a hydroponic garden, too, so there are plenty of fresh fruits and vegetables to eat. There are dishes in the shelves over the counter and utensils in the drawers underneath. We usually eat straight out of the containers while we're on duty, but if you do use dishes or silverware, ship's rule is that you run them through the washer and put them away yourself."

"That's fair enough."

"We don't have set mealtimes because our duty schedules vary," she went on. "You can usually find a couple of us having breakfast about this time every day, but after that we pretty much eat when we can." Remembering what Jon Robert had said about skimpy rations on some ships, she added, "We have plenty of food, Lukas. Feel free to eat whatever you want, whenever you want."

She left him to look over the packets in one of the freezers while she pulled a melon out of the refrigerator. He settled on something promising to be scrambled eggs. She didn't know if he'd done much cooking before, but he didn't appear to have any problem reading the package label, adding water from the tap, and heating the resulting mixture the required thirty seconds.

"Ready?" she asked as he pulled the eggs out of the oven. He nodded and she opened the door at the end of the counter and entered the dining room.

Lia and Reese were sitting on one side of the rectangular table that filled the room, Holly on the other. They had been talking, but the conversation came to an abrupt halt as Kiley and Lukas entered. Kiley took a deep breath and plunged in.

"Lia, Reese, Holly," she said, "I'd like you to meet Greg Lukas. He'll be traveling with us as far as Aumarleen. Mr. Lukas, this is my sister, Lia Sybern, her husband, Reese, and this is Holly, Jon Robert's wife."

"Welcome to the *Widdon Galaxy*, Mr. Lukas," Holly said, her smile as warm as her red-blond hair. "I can't tell you how glad we are that Kiley and Jon Robert found another pilot. I was beginning to think I didn't have a husband anymore. We haven't had two consecutive hours together in the last month."

"I'm glad to be here, Mrs. Michaelson."

"Please, call me Holly," she said quickly. "We all use first names here; there's no reason you should be any different—unless you'd rather be called Mr. Lukas?''

"Greg will be fine," he replied with a smile. Kiley wasn't surprised that he smiled; few people failed to respond to Holly's warmth. What took her breath away was the way his mouth curved up at the corners, wide and generous. The lines of tension disappeared from his face and his expression relaxed for the first time since Kiley had met him. He was . . . devastating.

There was no other word for it. Holly and Lia thought so, too—Holly's smile brightened and even Lia's wary coolness eased noticeably. Only Reese failed to respond, a sure sign that Lukas's appeal had more to do with sexual attraction than personal charisma.

"Have a seat, Lukas," she said abruptly, refusing to respond to that smile. She sat in the chair next to Holly's, and he took an empty chair at the end of the table, leaving a space between himself and the others. He might appear confident, but he wasn't as relaxed as he wanted them to believe.

"Jon Robert tells us you came off the *Hilea*," Reese said as Lukas reached for his fork.

The pilot's hand froze, then continued moving. "That's right," he said noncommittally.

"Have you been working on freighters long?"

"About a year."

"And the *Hilea*?"

"This was my first trip on her."

"You must not have been very happy, to have left her at Demarker of all places," Reese said, then added very coolly, "or maybe it was her captain who wasn't happy with you?"

Kiley opened her mouth to intervene, but before she could speak, Lukas said calmly, "Captain Radaeus let me go because the pilot I was filling in for received clearance to return to duty. He'd had surgery and my contract ended as soon as the ship's physician released him from sick bay. It was just my bad luck that it happened at Demarker."

"But our good luck," Holly said, instinctively trying to ease the tension building between the men. "Is this the first time you've worked on a family ship?"

"Yes, it is."

"Well, you'll either love it or hate it," Lia told him flatly. "There doesn't seem to be any in between." Her tone left little doubt about the way she felt.

Lia could have been beautiful if she hadn't been so desperately unhappy. She had a heart-shaped face framed by honey-colored hair, enormous blue eyes, and a figure that drew appreciative looks on every station they visited. She could have had any man she'd wanted if she'd so much as smiled in return, but she'd forgotten how to smile after her mother Enorra died. She'd grown up too fast and taken on too much responsibility in her determination to look after Jon and Jon Robert. The result was a bitterness she had never quite overcome.

She had nearly succeeded after meeting Reese. She had not been attracted to him immediately, but he had loved her at first sight, and had pursued her with all the single-minded determination he possessed. His attention had irritated, then flattered her. Somewhere along the way, she had fallen in love with him. She was happier than she had been as a young woman, but the shadows had never completely disappeared. She loved Reese, and he her, but that wasn't enough. Nothing was enough so long as she remained chained to the *Widdon Galaxy*.

Sensing her misery, Reese put his hand on her arm, the gesture at once a warning and an attempt to comfort. "I doubt Mr. Lukas will have time for either love or hate," he said. "He'll only be on the ship a few days, after all."

"Unless Kiley talks him into staying longer," she said.

"Not even Kiley could be that persuasive," Reese replied. "The *Widdon Galaxy* can't begin to compete with commercial freighters when it comes to wages or prestige. I doubt Mr. Lukas will have much interest in staying on with us."

"He won't if you keep talking like that," Holly said, her uncharacteristic sharpness surprising them all. "Honestly, Reese, you'd think this was an inquisition the way you're carrying on. You seem to have caught us on an off morning, Greg." She turned to him with an apologetic smile. "Tempers are obviously a little short. Something to do with the lack of sleep, I suspect. Keeping this ship running with a crew of only five is just about impossible."

"Five?" Lukas was unable to hide his shock. "That's all of you? On a ship this size?"

"That's all," Holly answered. "There were six, but Jon Senior died last month. He was our main pilot and Kiley our backup. Since then, we've all been pulling double shifts. You can see why we're so glad to have your help."

"I'm beginning to." Lukas looked at Kiley. So they'd been desperate for a pilot, had they, and all the time she'd acted as if they'd done him a favor by taking him on.

You could have bargained—if you'd been in any condition to, she told him silently, her eyes steady on his.

Holly glanced at her watch. "I've got to get moving!" she exclaimed, gulping down the last of her juice. "Sorry to rush off, but Jon Robert will have my head if I don't finish running the monthly maintenance checks today." She looked at Reese. "Is that offer of help still open? It would speed things up considerably to have someone monitoring the instrument readings on the engineering board."

"It's still open." He heaved a sigh, gathered up his dirty dishes, and the two of them disappeared into the galley.

"I suppose I'd better get to work, too." Lia echoed his sigh. "If you'll excuse me?"

She left and the room suddenly seemed too big. Kiley ate the last of her melon and set her fork aside. "If you're finished, we can wash up, then take that tour," she said.

Lukas nodded. She expected him to make some comment about his wages once they were alone, but he didn't say anything as they put their dishes in washers, then waited for the units to rinse, sterilize, and dry them.

Kiley took him to the common room first. It lay on the opposite side of the main corridor, across from the galley.

"You're welcome here any time you're off duty and don't feel like staying in your cabin," she told him as he surveyed the comfortably worn chairs and long couches. "We have a fair collection of movies, music, and books stored on the main computer. You can use a headset if you want to listen to music here, or you can pipe it directly into your cabin. There are jacks for portable readers by the chairs and next to all the bunks in the cabins. You can access the books with them, or on any of the computer terminals. We've all added to the entertainment collection, and our tastes are decidedly different, so you should be able to find something you like."

After the common room came two more cabins, both empty.

"We take on passengers occasionally and they stay here," she said, opening the door to the first one and letting him glance inside.

The ship's hydroponics room was to their right. She took him into the garden and let Lia show off her collection of fruits and vegetables and the masses of flowering plants she cultivated as a hobby. She was happy there, as nowhere else on the ship, and she almost outshone the brilliantly colored blossoms as she pointed out the rarer plants she had collected on their travels.

Lukas praised her garden profusely and gave her another of those dazzling smiles. Lia softened appreciably, and Kiley almost groaned aloud. That was all she needed—Lia falling for Lukas, just because he complimented her on her plants. She and Jon Robert hadn't needed to worry about the pilot's reception—the real problem might be that he was greeted with too much enthusiasm.

How could we have been so wrong about him? she wondered as he charmed Lia effortlessly. Talk about overreactions. She'd never seen a man adapt so readily, with so little apparent effort, in all her life. Worst of all, he gave no sign of feigning his interest. His whole manner appeared so open, so genuine, not even her critical eyes could fault his performance.

"Your sister's garden is remarkable," he said after they left the room. "I've never seen so many different plants outside a botanical garden."

"Lia's spent years collecting them. There are some advantages to living on a freighter that travels from port to port."

He hesitated, then said diffidently, "You don't have much in common, do you? If I hadn't known you were sisters, I would never have guessed. You don't even look alike."

"No doubt because we had different mothers," she replied shortly, and started down the corridor, cutting off any opportunity for any further questions or comments.

The tour took almost an hour. She pointed out the ship's waste-recycling system, the exercise room, storage compartments, the engine room, and finally, descending a level, the four cargo holds.

"We have three full holds," she said. "We'll be stopping at Zyree tomorrow to off-load the medical equipment and supplies in number two. The remaining cargo goes on to Aumarleen."

"You seal the holds before departure?"

"Yes."

"But you could go in if necessary?"

"If we had to," she said. "You'd have to suit up first, though. Ship's regulations. Hold temperatures are set at zero Celsius unless we're carrying perishable freight. Depending on the cargo, we don't always circulate fresh air." She pointed to a control panel beside the door of number two hold. "You can always check the current conditions, but sensors can fail in an emergency, or worse, display false readings. Suiting up may seem like an unnecessary precaution, but we prefer to err on the side of safety."

"Always a wise decision," he said.

Was he laughing at her? Kiley gave him a sharp look, but he met her eyes without guile.

"That about covers everything," she said, "unless you have any questions?"

"No."

"Very well." She pressed the elevator button and they rode back to the main deck in silence. Lukas had kept pace with her during tour, but in the bright upper deck lights, he looked pale again. He's still not completely well, even if he tries to act otherwise, she realized, and was surprised to find the observation reassuring.

She ended the tour back in the main corridor. "I'm going to bed," she said. "Jon Robert will be covering the bridge until this afternoon. If you're still feeling up to standing watch, you can meet me there at sixteen hundred. Until then, you're free to do whatever you like. I don't know how it is on commercial freighters, but there are no unauthorized areas on the *Widdon Galaxy*. You're free to go anywhere onboard during your off-duty time. The only rule is: If the people around you are working, you either pitch in or stay out of the way so they can get their jobs done. Understood?"

"Yes."

She started to leave, but he stopped her. "Captain?"

"Yes?"

"Thank you. For showing me around," he added quickly when she raised her eyebrows. "And for taking me on. I—I do appreciate the chance you took on me."

"Chance, Lukas? We don't take chances. We don't ever take chances."

"No?"

"No," she said firmly and turned around again.

"Captain?"

She swung back with a sigh. "Yes, Lukas?"

"I'll be on the bridge this afternoon," he said, but his expression promised something else entirely.

"I know," she replied, responding to that other promise, if not entirely believing he could keep it. She sighed again. "I'll see you later, Lukas." She started down the corridor again. This time, he let her go.

Lukas stepped on the bridge at precisely 1600 hours.
Fourteen minutes and thirty-three seconds later he was han-

dling the control boards as if he'd worked with them every day
of his life. Kiley knew that was how long he took because she
had glanced at the chronometer before she began her orienta-
tion.

She had not doubted his capability after seeing him that morning, but nothing had prepared her for the way he absorbed the
displays and her instructions for calling up the myriad reports a
pilot had to deal with hourly. He looked, he listened, and after
one run-through could repeat back everything she had said word
for word. Either he had an eidetic memory or he'd seen so many
boards, in so many configurations, that this one offered no challenge.

He had started scanning the boards before he was all the way
down in the pilot's seat, and he had never stopped the entire time
she talked to him. She offered to activate voice reporting for
him—some people preferred to hear summaries of the reports
without having to wade through all the details—but he shook his
head absently. Kiley watched his eyes go from screen to screen
and decided she didn't have to worry. He clearly knew what was
important and what could be safely ignored.

Fifteen minutes into the shift, she simply turned him loose
and sat back, watching him run through every status check the
navigation, engineering, and environmental systems boards
could display. He had only two questions: the last time they had
updated the navigation charts and the password they used to
access the main computer.

"The last update was three months ago," she said, "and the
password is *Jon*, J-O-N."

He typed the letters, glanced at the monitor, then went utterly
still. "Kiley, that code accesses the ship's complete records. Her
maintenance history, the family's financial records, everything!"

"That's right," she replied equably. "I told you, Lukas, there
are no unauthorized areas on this ship. That includes the computer. What one of us knows, we all know."

"But some of these records are personal," he said. "Anyone
could call them up."

"They could, but they wouldn't. We don't read each other's
personal files."

"How do you know that? As far as I can see, you don't even
keep file access records. You wouldn't know if someone had
read them."

"They haven't."

"You can't know that. Not for certain."

"I can."

"How?" he demanded.

"I know my family. We may not always get along, but we do respect each other's privacy. None of us would open someone else's files. Even Reese and Lia don't read each other's personal records."

"But they could."

"They could, but they wouldn't," she told him. And then, when he still didn't believe her, "Lukas, are you going to read my personal files?"

"Of course not!"

"Well, neither would the rest of the family. It's a matter of trust. I trust them and they trust me. And now"—she looked straight at him—"we're trusting you. We can trust you, can't we?"

She had him. He started to say something, shut his mouth. Started again. Stopped.

"Lukas, whatever faults you may have, you are not devoid of integrity," she said quietly. "If I thought otherwise, you wouldn't be on this ship, let alone the bridge. You aren't going to read my personal files, any more than Jon Robert or Reese would."

"You don't know that," he said, as if those were the only words remaining in his vocabulary.

"I do. You wouldn't be so worried about file integrity otherwise. We have one password, Lukas. That's all we've ever used and that's all we need. Your being here makes no difference. Now, if you've finished looking things over, would you plot a course to Zyree from these coordinates?"

She fed him their post-jump position. He stared at the coordinates blindly, his mind still on the lack of computer security, then shook the matter off and went to work. Less than a minute later, he had a solution.

She checked his figures, not believing anyone could have arrived at an optimum balance of fuel and speed in so little time. But they checked out. She tried four alternatives anyway, searching for a better balance. She couldn't find one.

"You seem to have a knack for navigation, Mr. Lukas," she said at last. The admission didn't come easily, and she felt better when she heard him release a pent-up breath.

"Lay in your course on the main computer," she told him. "We may have to make a last-minute adjustment if the post-jump coordinates I gave you are off, but your solution will do for starters.'' She stood up. ''You're obviously capable of managing by yourself,'' she said. ''You have the conn until twenty hundred. I'll be back then to relieve you.''

Walking off the bridge and leaving him in control of the ship was the hardest thing she'd done since setting Jon's body adrift in space, but she did it.

Letting him bring the ship through jump the next afternoon was the second hardest. She sat in the copilot's seat, counting down the minutes until they returned to normal space.

''Thirty seconds,'' she said over the intercom, then turned to him. ''Ready, Lukas?''

He nodded and began pressing banks of switches in rapid succession.

''Shields up, all scanners on,'' he said. The viewscreens above the control board flickered, then went crazy as they tried to display the incomprehensible in livid shades of red, green, and blue. Whatever lay outside a ship during jump made no sense to the ship's scanners or visual monitors.

''Coming through . . . now,'' Kiley said. Her body turned inside out and light burst across the viewscreens above her head. She gasped, fighting to pull air back in her lungs, to focus eyes and mind. Lukas's hands were already moving.

''Jump engines off,'' he told Jon Robert over the intercom. ''Full reverse on main engines.''

Kiley lost the breath she'd managed to take in the sudden deceleration that followed. The ship lurched, close to rolling, and images of distant stars spun across the monitors. She reached for the controls automatically, but Lukas was already cutting back power to the starboard engine. The ship stabilized.

He was breathing faster than normal, and Kiley thought his fingers shook as he fed instructions into the computer to reduce engine speed, but that might only have been her vision blurring. She blinked, wishing just once transition would be easier coming out than going in.

''You might have warned me she pulls hard to starboard during rapid deceleration,'' Lukas said tightly when he had the ship on course and stabilized again. ''Do you realize the danger you put us in?''

''Didn't I warn you?'' she said. ''Sorry, I must have forgotten.''

''You? Forget? I don't believe that for a minute!'' he shot

back. "Not when it comes to this ship. I trust you found out what you wanted to know?"

"And what would that be, Lukas? That you can do more than memorize a control board within minutes, or plot a course in seconds? That your reflexes aren't impaired by transition? Things like that?"

"Yes, Captain," he said sarcastically. "Things like that." His mouth was set in a tight line and his shoulders were rigid with anger, but he hadn't forgotten himself so much that he took his eyes off the displays.

"I'm responsible for this ship, Lukas. If you couldn't handle her, I had to know now. Later would have been too late in a real emergency."

"I take it I pass?"

"If you have to ask that, Lukas, you aren't half the pilot you think you are."

He started an angry reply, worked through what she had said, and then his mouth quivered, perilously close to smiling. "I suppose I deserved that," he said after a moment. "Well, Captain? Is that the only test, or do you have another hoop or two you want me to jump through?"

"No more hoops, Lukas. Unless, of course, you'd like to show me how adept you are at docking maneuvers when we reach port tomorrow morning?"

"You actually trust me enough to take her into port?" he asked, not entirely joking.

"We'll reach Zyree on your shift. You might as well be the one to dock her. Unless you'd rather not?"

"I'd be glad to. I just thought you'd want to handle the maneuvers yourself. Most captains do."

"I think I can step aside this once," she said, then nodded to the door. "You're supposed to be off duty, Lukas. Why don't you get some lunch—or whatever it is you eat at this time of day—and come back later? You still have to pull watch tonight; there's no sense wearing yourself out."

He took a last look at the control board and display screens, then turned his chair around. "Very well. You have the conn, Captain."

Chapter 4

Lukas docked the ship with such consummate skill that Kiley had to watch the monitors to detect the exact moment of coupling. She offered him six hours' leave onstation, expecting the customs inspection and off-loading to take at least that long, but he shook his head.

"If it's all the same to you, I'd just as soon sleep," he said. "Transition seems to have caught up with me."

Kiley gave him a quick look as he rubbed his eyes with his thumb and forefinger, but he showed no sign of illness, only an understandable fatigue. He'd broken his sleep period to be on the bridge the afternoon before. Those lost hours, combined with the body's normal reaction to being turned inside out during transition, were more than enough to account for his weariness.

"You're free to do whatever you want, Lukas," she told him.

He nodded and went down the corridor without a backward glance. Kiley scanned the control board a final time, making certain he'd shut down all but the ship's environmental systems, then left the bridge herself.

Jon Robert met her in the corridor leading to the docking hatch.

"Going onstation?" he asked.

She shook her head. "There's nothing I need, and Zyree doesn't offer much in the way of entertainment. What about you?"

"Same here. Lia and Holly decided to have a look around. They said they'd be back in a few hours."

"What about Reese?"

"Still talking to customs. Better him than me." Jon Robert ran his hand through his hair. "If I had to deal with all those forms and regulations every time we hit port, I'd go crazy. I don't know how he does it.''

''Me either. I suppose we should just be thankful he does.''

''I guess. I was on the way to the galley; you want to join me for breakfast?''

''Sure.''

She walked alongside him, lengthening her stride to keep up. They made breakfast in companionable silence, then carried their plates into the dining room.

''How's Lukas doing?'' Jon Robert asked between bites.

''All right.''

''That's it? All right?''

''That's enough, isn't it?''

He put his fork down and stared at her until she couldn't ignore his scrutiny any longer.

''Are you ready to talk about it yet?'' he asked when he had her attention.

''Talk about what?''

''Whatever's been eating at you the past two days.''

''Nothing's eating at me.''

''Kiley, you might be able to fool the others, but you can't con me. You haven't said two words unless someone else has spoken to you first. Wherever you've been, it hasn't been here with us. Something's bothering you—and I have a strong suspicion Lukas is at the root of the problem.''

''There's no problem. He's doing fine. Just fine.''

''A little too well, maybe?'' he asked with disconcerting perception.

She started to say no and stopped herself. He would know she was lying. ''He's good, Jon Robert,'' she said abruptly. ''No, he's better than good—he's the best pilot I've even seen.''

''So?''

''So I spent years learning to fly this ship. Years. Do you know how long it took him to learn her boards? Fifteen minutes.''

''Kiley, he put in those years, too. He didn't just walk on a ship, sit down at the controls and start piloting her. Not even Greg Lukas is that good.''

''You haven't seen him. I could train the rest of my life and never equal him.''

''Is that what's bothering you? That he's better than you? So what? You're good, Kiley. Much better than this ship deserves.''

''That's not good enough.''

"Since when?" he demanded, then sighed. "Kiley, there's always going to be someone better than you, no matter how skilled you are. Ask Lukas if you don't believe me. I'll bet he'd be the first to tell you there are better pilots than he. You probably wouldn't even have to look far to find them. If he's as good as you say, he'll have left a trail of people behind, all trying to best him. I can just about guarantee some will have succeeded. No matter how good a person is, there's always someone else who's better."

"Sure."

Jon Robert's expression hardened. "You sound suspiciously close to self-pity, Kiley Michaelson. I don't like that. I don't like it at all. So what if you aren't the pilot Lukas is? How you compare to others isn't what counts. What counts is that you do the job at hand to the best of your ability." He took one look at her closed face and sighed again. "You don't believe me, do you? I wish I knew how to convince you, because bitterness and envy are dangerous emotions. Damned dangerous. Give them space to grow, and they'll take over your life."

"What would you know about that?" she demanded fiercely. "You weren't the one who spent ten years of your life trying to qualify for the Academy, only to fail the medical exam. You weren't dumped on a father who didn't even know you existed until after your mother decided she didn't want you anymore. You've always belonged. You've always had a place. What could you possibly know about bitterness or envy?"

"A lot. You aren't the only person who ever faced disappointment, you know. There was a time in my life when I was so full of hate, I wanted to die. Worse, I wanted everyone around me to die too."

"I don't believe you," she said flatly. She had never heard him so much as raise his voice. He couldn't possibly have hated anyone as much as he was suggesting.

"You should. You were the reason."

Kiley stared at him in disbelief, too stunned to reply. How could he have hated her? When? He was the only person in her entire life who'd given her love without reservation. He had comforted her a hundred times after Jon Senior had ridden her from morning to night, criticizing every move, every decision she made, demanding an impossible perfection. He could not have offered that comfort and hated her at the same time. He couldn't have!

Only things hadn't always been that way between them, had they?

Long-forgotten memories surfaced, and she buried her face in her hands. She'd been eight when her mother decided she wanted to take a job on a commercial ship so she could be with the man she'd fallen in love with. The only problem was, the ship didn't allow children. She had been a good mother until then—Kiley had to give her credit for that. Still, she had decided motherhood wasn't for her, not when it meant giving up the rest of her life.

To her credit, she had spent several months trying to trace Kiley's father, Jon Michaelson. She had met him during one of the *Widdon Galaxy*'s layovers. His wife, Enorra, had been pregnant with Jon Robert at the time, and their shaky marriage had been at its coldest point. Enorra hadn't been happy on the ship, she hadn't been happy about having another child, she hadn't been happy with him.

Jon went to a station bar to escape the frigid tension on the ship and found himself sitting next to Kiley's mother. She listened sympathetically while he talked, and when she suggested they go back to her quarters, he offered only a token protest. He had been quite drunk by then, he told Kiley flatly on the only occasion he talked about her conception. He assumed her mother had taken appropriate precautions, if he ever gave the matter any thought at all. Her mother never told him she'd decided she wanted a child, never said she had chosen him to be the father precisely because he would not be around afterward to make demands or interfere.

He was shocked, then, when he received her mother's message saying he had a daughter. She told him he had three months to pick her up; otherwise, she would become a ward of the station. Most likely, she would be placed with a foster family on the nearest planet. She would have had no difficulty finding a home. Epiphany was a newly colonized agricultural world, and the planet's inhabitants were only too eager to find extra pairs of hands to run the agricultural machinery required to manage their gigantic farms.

Kiley could only imagine her father's reaction to that message. Years later, he still refused to talk about it. Still, he had come. Whatever his other faults, Jon Michaelson believed in honoring his responsibilities. If Kiley was his, he would not let her be raised by strangers. He insisted on genetic tests, and when they proved positive, he agreed to take custody of Kiley.

She didn't know anything was happening until her mother took her to the *Widdon Galaxy* and handed her over to Michaelson on the dock.

"This is your father, Jon Michaelson," she said. "You'll be living with him from now on. I'm going with Liam. You can't come." And then, without another word, she walked away.

Only Michaelson's unbreakable grip kept Kiley from running after her. She cried out, she screamed, but her mother ignored her. Other people turned to stare briefly before returning to their own business, but her mother never looked back.

Michaelson lifted her up, ignoring her flailing limbs, and carried her to a cabin on the ship. He locked her in and disappeared for two hours. When he returned, his arms were full of clothes, books, and games—everything a growing child could possibly need. He set the packages on her bunk, then sat down beside her.

"I'm sorry we had to meet this way, Kiley," he said gruffly. "I can't begin to comprehend what you must be feeling, but you must be terribly frightened and angry. I wish I could make your hurt go away, but I'm afraid only time can do that. I want you to know, though, that you'll always have a place on this ship. You're my daughter and I'll take care of you as long as you need me. I don't expect you to like or trust me right away; good relationships take time to develop. All I ask is that you give us—and yourself—that time."

He had been right; she was both frightened and angry, and the emotions took months to subside. It didn't help that Jon was not a patient or gentle man by nature. He believed in strict discipline and he demanded levels of perfection no child could achieve. Years later, she finally understood that discipline and demands were the ways he showed he cared, but by then it was too late to change the way things were between them.

Alone and afraid, she cried herself to sleep every night. Lia, at sixteen, understood the infidelity Kiley's existence represented and resented her with a passion that was all the more terrible for being denied. Even Jon Robert seemed to reject her at first. She'd tried hard to make friends with the tall, awkward boy, but he had rebuffed her every overture. He went even more frigid after Jon Senior discovered her interest in piloting the ship and included her in the daily flight lessons he gave Jon Robert. Then, suddenly, he had changed. When? And why?

She thought back and a forgotten incident fell into place. It had happened after she made her first major mistake on the bridge. Jon had raged at her for fifteen minutes after she touched the wrong control and shut down the ship's recycling system. She stumbled off the bridge, wiping the tears from her eyes. Jon Robert followed her to the corridor. She expected him to gloat, but he just stood there watching her, a funny expression on his face.

"What are you staring at?" she demanded furiously.

"Nothing," he said, then added in a rush, "He won't stay mad long. He never does. Uncle Ty says to ignore him when he yells. He says Dad doesn't know any other way to talk."

"He won't let me go back on the bridge. Not ever."

"Yes, he will. He always let me, even after I shut down the main engines."

"You're kidding!" she said. "You really shut them down? In midflight?"

"Yup."

"What did he do?"

"He yelled at me, the same way he yelled at you. I had to clean the main corridor by myself and do double lessons for a month, but he let me go back. Don't worry. He'll let you, too."

"Maybe."

"He will," Jon Robert said positively. "Ask Uncle Ty."

She shook her head. The big, silent man frightened her. He and Jon were partners, but she wished he wasn't on the ship. He made her uncomfortable. He was either looking right through her as if she didn't exist, or right into her, as if he saw all her most secret thoughts.

"You don't like Ty, do you?" Jon Robert asked, reading her involuntary grimace with uncanny ease.

She shook her head. "He's big. He scares me."

"He doesn't scare me, and he doesn't yell the way Dad does, not even when I do something dumb." Jon Robert paused, then said casually, "I was going to watch a movie in the common room. You want to come along?"

She had gone, and from that time on, they had studied and played together, parting only when he went into the engine room to be with Ty. Not even for Jon Robert would she brave the giant's domain. Jon Senior had continued to give them both flight instruction. Good as they both became, they never managed to attain the level of perfection he demanded, but they did learn to weather his storms.

Kiley became the ship's backup pilot and Jon Robert quietly turned more and more of his attention to the engine room. She stopped fearing Ty after a time, and even came to like him after he spent months patiently teaching her the rudiments of starship propulsion systems. But it was only after his death that she had realized how much Ty had meant to them all. Jon Robert's patience, his soft-spoken words of counsel, his empathy and understanding had all come from Ty. She wondered sometimes what would have become of them without his moderating influence. The thought didn't bear contemplation.

"You really did hate me, didn't you?" Kiley said, lifting her head from her hands. "I took your place with Jon. He was teaching you to pilot the *Widdon Galaxy*, but as soon as he found out I was better, he concentrated on me instead. Oh, you had to study too, but I was the one he cared about. You must have been furious about that."

"For a while, yes."

"I didn't mean to come between you. It's just that I was so afraid of Jon, and of being left again, I'd have done anything to please him. I didn't stop to think what I might be doing to you—and you never told me."

He shrugged. "It didn't hurt long. For the record, I stopped hating you the first time Jon bawled you out. Before you came, I thought I was the only one who couldn't do anything right. Then you showed up and made the same mistakes I did. It was such a relief to find out I wasn't hopelessly stupid, I couldn't help but like you."

"But I did take his attention away from you. He wanted you to pilot the ship before I came—and so did you."

"If I did, it's because it never occurred to me that I could do anything else. Kiley, I never cared about being captain, not the way you do. I was always happier in the engine room with Uncle Ty than I was on the bridge. If you hadn't come along, I might never have figured that out."

"I guess I was good for something, then."

"You were good for a lot more than that," he said. "You still are."

"Sometimes I don't feel that way."

"Well, you should." He paused, then said carefully, "Kiley, I don't understand why Lukas has upset you so, but before you start eating your heart out over not measuring up to him, maybe you ought to consider where all that supposed ability has brought him: right here. If he's so great, what's he doing on the *Widdon Galaxy*? Why did the *Hilea* dump him on Demarker?"

''I don't know. It doesn't make sense to me, not after seeing him work.''

''Me either, but they must have had a reason.'' He shook his head over the puzzle. ''Do you like him?'' he asked abruptly.

''Like him? What does that have to do with anything?''

''Just answer the question. Do you?''

She thought about the pilot's stiff-necked pride, his anger when she had tested him coming out of jump, and about the way his lips had twitched as he tried to hold back a smile moments later.

''You do, don't you?'' he said, watching her face. ''So do I. Holly and Lia, too. Even Reese doesn't object to having him around. Do you know he spends time helping Lia out with the garden every morning after his watch ends? Well, he does. He even pitched in and helped Holly and Reese clean the engine room. They're going to start on the corridors next week. They've all talked to me about him. They want to know if we're going to ask him to stay on after we reach Aumarleen.''

''They want him to?''

''Yes.''

''I don't believe it. We spent all that time worrying about their reaction and they end up liking him? You said we'd have to make sure they didn't push him into corners because he couldn't handle the pressure, and what does he do? He walks in and wraps everyone on this ship around his finger with a smile. How could we have been so wrong about him?''

''Are you sure we were?''

''What do you mean?''

''For a man on a one-way trip, he's tried awfully hard to please everyone. It's almost as if he's deliberately going out of his way to make us like him.''

''Hoping we'll ask him to stay on after Aumarleen?''

''Maybe.''

''Do you really think so?''

Jon Robert thought a moment, then sighed. ''No. Not really. I honestly think he's being helpful because it doesn't occur to him to do anything else. Kiley, maybe we were wrong about him. Maybe he just had a run of bad luck. It can happen. If he's as good as you say, maybe we should ask him if he'd be interested in staying on with us after Aumarleen.''

''We don't have the money to hire his kind of talent,'' she said sharply. ''He could be captaining a corporate ship, and you're going to offer him a backup pilot's job on a worn-out freighter?''

"Maybe he doesn't want a corporate job. Maybe he's looking for something else. Something we *can* offer him."

"What?"

"Peace. Freedom. The right to be himself, without having to conform to some company's standard of behavior. Corporate ships can be hell, Kiley, especially when all the organization cares about is profit. Maybe a family ship is what he's been looking for and he just doesn't know it."

"Sure, and maybe we'll strike it rich on Aumarleen, too."

"Kiley, I'm not trying to convince you to sign him on if that isn't what you want. You're the one who has to work with him. If he doesn't suit you, then he goes. But if he does, why not ask him to sign a longer contract?"

"He'll say no."

"He might not. There's only one way to find out for sure—ask him."

"Jon Robert—"

"No, don't decide now. Think it over. We have a week until we reach Aumarleen. That should give you time to make up your mind what you want to do."

"Very well, I'll think it over. But if I don't want him, he goes—agreed?"

"Yes."

She looked away, then said quietly, "I'm sorry for what happened. Back then, with Jon Senior."

"I'm not. I haven't been sorry since the first time Jon yelled at you. I just wish you'd been around sooner."

They remained at Zyree seven hours, waiting their turn to have the medical equipment they carried unloaded. Reese used the time to good advantage and managed to pick up an unexpected consignment of spices that had missed connections with the freighter originally contracted to carry it to Aumarleen.

The additional cargo lifted the family's spirits noticeably and left Greg Lukas wondering just how close to the edge the Michaelsons were operating. They must be right on the border, he decided, if such a small load was cause for celebration.

Not an easy way to live, he thought as he finished checking the boards for the hundredth time since coming on watch that night. No wonder they often sounded tense and looked strained—they worked harder than any single group of people he had ever met. More importantly, they worked together, despite what appeared to be vast differences in temperaments and tastes.

We had different mothers, Kiley had said, the words so charged
with emotion he would not have touched them for a year's salary,
even if she had given him the opportunity. They were different,
all right, but there was a sameness about them, a core of determination and resolution that spoke eloquently of a common will
to succeed. If any group of people could make an aging freighter
pay for herself, he'd bet they'd be the ones.

He was going to miss them, after Aumarleen.

Lukas sat back in the pilot's seat and closed his eyes. The last
five days had gone by so quickly that he'd hardly noticed them
passing. Only twelve hours to Aumarleen. He should be thinking about packing, about finding another berth, anything but the
Michaelsons. He sighed. No use wishing things had been different, that he could have met them on better terms, somewhere
besides Demarker. Wishing didn't change anything. He could
only go forward and make the best of what came.

No matter how bad it proved to be.

"Sleeping on watch, Lukas?" a cool voice asked from behind
him.

"Just resting my eyes," he said as Kiley slipped into the
copilot's seat.

"Would you like some coffee?" She held out a cup, then
spotted an identical container already sitting on the ledge beneath the control board. "Looks like I'm too late."

"Holly brought some by on her way to bed."

"No need to sound defensive. She's done the same for me
more times than I can count. Jon Robert and Lia, too. They
know how long eight hours can be when you're tied to your
post." She scanned the displays, her eyes going to the chronometer first. Fifteen minutes to transition. "Everything set?"

"Yes. Jon Robert called in from the engine room a few minutes ago to say he's standing by."

"Did you feed an initial course into the computer yet?"

"Yes. I'll call it up if you want to check—"

"Don't bother. I'm sure whatever you worked out is fine."

She turned to him, her direct gaze intensely uncomfortable.
She had a talent for putting him on the defensive. For the life of
him, he couldn't understand how a woman eight years his junior
could make him feel so intensely uncomfortable. He hadn't been
this nervous since he'd reported for duty on his first ship. Just
once, he would like to know what she was thinking. She laughed
when she talked to Jon Robert, and listened intently to Reese's
suggestions about future ports of call, but the moment she turned

to him her expression went utterly smooth, offering no clue to her thoughts or feelings.

"What time are we due to arrive at Aumarleen?" she asked, dragging his attention back to duty.

"About sixteen-fifteen, give or take a few minutes," he said.

"I suppose you'll be looking for another berth once we get there?"

"Yes."

"On another freighter?"

"If that's where the work is," he said noncommittally. He scanned the board, grateful for an excuse to look away from her.

"What if you can't find anything?"

"I'll wait until something turns up. It always does."

"Just like we did. On Demarker."

"That's right."

"You don't ask much of luck, do you?"

That did it. He'd answered her questions out of politeness so far, but he'd had enough.

"With all due respect, Captain," he said, "I fail to see the point of this conversation. I appreciate your concern, but it isn't necessary."

"You never make things easy for the other person, do you, Lukas?" she exploded. "Damn it, I'm not asking questions to make conversation, or because I'm worried about you. Demarker aside, you appear perfectly capable of taking care of yourself. I'm asking because I want to know if you'd consider staying on with us."

"What?" he asked, not believing what he heard.

"I'm offering you a job, Lukas. Backup pilot on the *Widdon Galaxy*. If you want it."

He just stared at her. "You're offering me a job?"

"I know we can't pay you the kind of wages you're used to." She rushed the words, her face flushing. "All we can offer is room and board, and maybe enough money for a night out on the station when we're in port."

"For how long?"

"What?" she asked, the question obviously not what she'd expected to hear.

"How long will the job last?"

"I don't know. As long as we need you. As long as you want to stay with us. We didn't have a set time in mind. I know we can't pay you what you're worth; we'll understand if you want to leave because you have a better offer."

"If I work for you, then it will be for a percentage."

"What?"

"I said I want a percentage of profits, not a salary."

She gave a short, bitter laugh. "There won't be any profits. Not on this ship. Everything we make above operating expenses goes straight into her maintenance fund. She's overdue for a complete refitting."

"Maybe. Then again, maybe you'll stumble across a cargo big enough to pay for two refittings," he said stubbornly. "It's been known to happen. To the right ship, in the right place. I'll work for a percentage or nothing."

"Lukas, if you work for a percentage, you *will* be working for nothing."

"I'll take my chances—just like the rest of you."

She started to say something. Stopped. Looked at him so intently, he wondered if he'd gone too far, revealed too much.

"I don't understand you," she said slowly. He thought she spoke as much to herself as to him. "You're being irrational. Absolutely irrational."

"You have a lot of nerve calling *me* irrational, Kiley Michaelson. Irrational is sinking your whole life and every credit you earn into a ship that's older than you are. Irrational is working eighteen hours a day, just so you can have the privilege of working another eighteen the next. I may be irrational, but you Michaelsons are just plain crazy. Except for Holly, of course. She's the only sensible one among you. Probably because she's not really a Michaelson, except by marriage. At least, not yet."

"Lukas, if that's any example of the way you talked to the *Hilea*'s captain, it's no wonder he dumped you on Demarker."

"That worries you, doesn't it?" he returned. "You just can't stop wondering what I did wrong—or if I'll do it again."

She flushed again, but did not look away. "Of course that bothers me," she said. "How could you expect otherwise?"

"I didn't," he said bitterly. A monstrous wave of anger gushed up, breaking past the barriers he'd set so carefully. Without stopping to consider the consequences, he said harshly, "You want to know what happened on the *Hilea*? Fine. I'll tell you. I didn't get along with the ship's crew. They didn't like me and they didn't trust me. Captain Radaeus decided I was more trouble than I was worth and released me the moment he didn't need me. And now you will too, won't you? After all, if the *Hilea*'s crew couldn't trust me, how can you?"

She wouldn't meet his eyes. She looked down at the control

board, touching the keys, doing anything to avoid looking at him. He'd ruined his chance with her. He knew he had and could have cut his throat. Then she looked up, eyes dark with an emotion he could not read.

"That must have been very difficult to admit," she said quietly. "I'm sorry. I don't deny I was concerned about their reasons for letting you go, but I didn't mean to make you talk about an experience that could only have been extremely painful."

"You didn't force me."

"Didn't I? After that lecture I gave about trust last week, I don't think I left you much choice."

"Maybe. Then again, maybe I thought you had a right to know what you were getting before you signed me on for more than the trip to Aumarleen."

"I know what I'm getting, Lukas," she said with sudden assurance. "You're the best pilot I've ever seen, and the most honest. You may have had problems with the *Hilea*'s crew, but I haven't noticed any with us. We'd like you to stay on. All of us. If you want to, that is."

Did she mean that? After months of going from berth to berth, knowing he was accepted on sufferance only, did he dare believe he had found a place where he was not only needed, but wanted? He searched her face quickly, but found no hint of duplicity or pity. She meant what she said.

"Well, Lukas? Do you want the job or not?" she demanded when he could not find his voice.

He took a deep breath and said, "I do, Captain."

"Kiley," she said with a smile, tension evaporating. "Please, call me Kiley. I've had enough formality this past week to last a lifetime."

"Only if you'll call me Greg," he said. "Everyone else does."

"I think I can manage that—Greg. Now, if you've nothing better to do, how about earning your keep? We're coming up on transition, in case you hadn't noticed."

"I noticed, Kiley. I noticed."

Chapter 5

Return was not possible.

Chirith stared at the star charts displayed on the wall and came close to despair. They showed no barrier, but it was there and it was impassable.

They had landed on the far edge of it on their journey out; otherwise, they would not have survived. But what it was, or how far it extended, they could not say. They had sent several probes out to explore it, but all had failed at the moment of contact.

The ship's engines had been damaged on the way out, and they could no longer match their pre-jump range, prohibiting a return to their starting coordinates. It was possible the barrier did not extend all the way back, but they could not take that chance. They would not survive another encounter with instability.

Already they had strayed too close to the edge. The Quayla had lost control of the ship again and two more had died before they could reverse course. The Quayla had not spoken to them for some time afterward. They now sent reconnaissance instruments ahead, charting the edge of the zone as they went.

Chirith and the ship's elders had gone over and over their options, and each time they had decided the only safe course was to continue traveling along the barrier until they found a way around it. It could not extend forever. Once they found an end, they could make the series of jumps required to take them home.

They searched on and on. The barrier stretched ahead interminably. For all they could tell, it continued into infinity. They sent a message home, but Chirith doubted it would ever arrive. He suspected the barrier repelled messages as well as ships.

They found two habitable planets in the course of their travels. They discovered the remains of the *Itieth* on the second one. It had landed at the edge of the barrier, too, but had suffered more extensive damage than the *Nieti*. The captain's records said that over half the crew had died before momentum carried them into normal space. They barely made it to the planet before the Quayla and the ship failed completely. The survivors started to build an outpost, hoping another ship would be sent to search for them. It was only a matter of time, they told themselves.

Too much time.

They had expected difficulties breathing the planet's air and drinking its water, but they had not anticipated so many hostile microorganisms. They could not develop protective antigens quickly enough. They perished, one by one, until only two were left.

Then one.

Then none.

They never found the body of the last crewman, although they searched. They built a funeral pyre anyway and Chirith said the ritual of death. When the fire burned down, the *Nieti*'s crew returned to their ship, and they redoubled their search for a way home.

A second ship was always sent if the first did not return. If that vessel disappeared, too, the way would be sealed forever.

They were the second ship.

There would not be a third.

Chapter 6

Kiley had a new contract for Lukas drawn up on Aumarleen. She brought a copy back to the ship. He read the document carefully, then stopped when he came to the clause specifying payment as a one-sixth share of the ship's profits.

"I thought we agreed on ten percent," he said.

"You're putting in one-sixth the work. You should receive one-sixth the profits."

"Ten percent is the standard rate," he said stiffly.

"I don't care what's standard. This is the *Widdon Galaxy*; we make our own rules."

He shook his head, stubbornly refusing to give in. That pride again, she thought angrily. She had suspected his request for a percentage of profit in lieu of wages stemmed more from sympathy for their shaky financial balance than greed over potential profits, and now she was certain. Well, the family had their own measure of pride, and she was not about to take what amounted to charity. Jon, his wife Enorra, and Ty had managed to hire additional crewmen before Jon Robert and Lia were old enough to help out. If they could find a way to pay their help, so could she.

"One-sixth, Lukas," she said, "and that's final."

"A tenth. And I told you to call me Greg."

She glared at him. He glared back. He stood with his shoulders squared and knees slightly bent, as if facing an attacker. Only his head didn't fit the pattern; he should have tucked his chin in, but it jutted out instead. He cared more about pride than reason and common sense. He fit in with the family, all right. Sometimes he fit in too well.

"We don't need your charity, Lukas," she said, deliberately emphasizing his last name.

"I'm not offering charity, Captain. There's no reason this ship can't make a profit, and when she does, I intend to have my share. My fair share."

"You realize we're arguing about nothing, don't you? There won't be a profit to split!"

"There could be. If you changed your runs, expanded into newer territory where other ships aren't going yet, you could charge twice the rates this quadrant will bear."

"And run empty half the time. We know these ports, Lukas. Running outside our territory would be asking for trouble."

"I'm not asking you to go into unexplored space."

"Just the fringes. I told you, we don't take chances. We can't afford to."

"You can't afford not to. The freight's out there, Kiley. You just have to know where to find it."

"We don't."

"But I do. I've been there, Kiley. I know what I'm talking about."

"Maybe so, but I don't know the routes and Reese doesn't have contacts at the stations. I'm telling you, we can't afford the risk."

"You can learn the routes and Reese won't have any problem making new contacts. He's a good agent, Kiley. Much better than you give him credit for being."

"I have never doubted Reese's abilities."

"No?"

"No."

"Then you respect his opinions?"

"Yes, of course I do."

"And you'd listen to him if he recommended visiting new ports?"

"Of course."

"Then why don't you? Kiley, I've listened to the two of you talking, and every time he so much as suggests alternate routes, you change the subject. He'd like to branch out, but he won't push the issue because you don't want to leave your nice, safe, familiar runs."

"That's not true. I can take this ship anywhere the family decides to go. Anywhere."

"I never said you couldn't. I'm not the one who's questioning your skills—you do that well enough all by yourself."

"Has Jon Robert been talking to you? What did he say about me? What?"

"Nothing. He didn't say anything—although I appreciate the suggestion he might. Maybe I should have a talk with him. I've worked with a lot of other pilots over the years, Kiley Michaelson, but I never met one as insecure as you, for as little cause. I wish you'd relax. We'd all be a lot more comfortable."

"For a man who hasn't signed a contract yet, you're being remarkably outspoken," she said sharply. "We don't need you telling us where to go or what to do. The ship needs a backup pilot, not another captain."

His eyes narrowed. "Are you suggesting that's what I want? To replace you as captain?"

"I didn't say that."

"No, but I'm beginning to believe you thought it. No wonder you've been so tense around me. Kiley, I've captained enough ships to know the job is all work and responsibility, and precious little reward. I can assure you, I have no further aspirations in that direction. But that doesn't mean I can't make suggestions, and as long as I'm working for a percentage of profits, I intend to do my best to insure there are some."

"By getting us to try new routes?"

"If that's what we need to do."

"Very well, Lukas, make all the suggestions you want. Just don't forget who makes the final decisions."

"You do, Captain," he said easily. "You make the decisions and I collect my ten-percent profit. Agreed?"

He was willing to settle for ten percent? Fine. Let him have his way.

"Agreed, Lukas," she said.

"Good. Let's go to the registry office and make this official. The sooner we get back, the sooner we can start planning which new ports of call to visit first."

Kiley gave him a long look. "Lukas, has anyone ever told you that you're utterly and completely impossible?"

"One or two have tried," he said with a grin, "but I never believed them."

Maybe he brought them luck, or maybe their luck had been due to change. Whatever the reason, they had no problem finding freight during the next month, even at the two new stations Lukas suggested adding to their usual routes.

They had discussed the different runs in a family meeting,

and Reese had endorsed the idea so wholeheartedly that Kiley was forced to believe Lukas had been right about her brother-in-law's desire to branch out. Stung by the suggestion that he had not pursued the idea earlier because she'd be too upset about taking the ship into unknown territory, she plotted the new courses and took them through jump herself, summoning every ounce of cool competence she possessed.

"Dead on target," Lukas said after they came through their second transition into unfamiliar space. "I can't for the life of me see why you worry so much about your ability, Kiley. I've seen fleet commanders who couldn't come closer to target."

She didn't answer. She spent a great deal of time ignoring Greg Lukas. Their schedules insured they generally saw each other only at shift changes, but there were times they both had to be on the bridge. Either of them could have handled jump or docking alone, but the maneuvers were easier with two sets of eyes and hands.

He made her nervous, though. He didn't mean to, but she simply could not relax around him. He seemed to share her discomfort, for he certainly acted differently around her than he did with the rest of the family. He laughed and argued with them as if they'd been friends for years, but when he was alone with her, he adopted the casual, disinterested manner of a near-stranger.

The difference in attitudes had puzzled her at first, then hurt, then reassured. Whatever the reason for his tension, he understood the need to keep their relationship on a firmly professional basis.

With that unspoken understanding between them, they gradually settled into a routine. Eight hours on, four off, four on, eight off. The cycle went round and round, changing only when they stopped in port. Their stays were never long; docking fees added up too fast. They stayed overnight only at the two new ports they visited, both of which charged significantly lower rates than Aumarleen.

Lukas disappeared for several hours at each. She wondered how he spent his time, but did not ask. However curious she was, he came back sober and on time, and that was all she had the right to know.

Lukas was good for them. He freed Jon Robert of bridge duty, and her brother and Holly finally had the time to themselves they so desperately wanted. Lia had changed, too, and he appeared to be the reason. Kiley had worried about his visits to the garden at first, afraid that her sister was attracted to him and that the feeling might be mutual. She said as much to Holly, but the other woman said Lukas spent most of the time listening to Lia talk. She thought he came closer to being a counselor than a suitor.

Reese must have felt the same way, for he showed no sign of resenting Lukas's presence. He, too, was happier than he'd been for some time. He spent their entire time in port talking to other agents and bargaining for cargo. True to Lukas's prediction, he had no difficulty establishing new contracts, and came back from his trips onstation brimming with enthusiasm.

No doubt about it, the *Widdon Galaxy* was a happier ship than she'd been in years, all thanks to Greg Lukas. And if Kiley couldn't seem to share in that sense of renewed energy, then the fault must lie in her. Still, she had the ship and the freedom that went with shipboard life. Every time she looked up at the home world circling the stations where they docked, she told herself she was lucky to be who and what she was instead of some planetbound dweller, forever chained to the same world.

She had been on only one planet in her life, Everest, and had hated every moment. The hot, heavily scented air made her head ache, and the blue sky overhead weighed down oppressively. You could not see the stars from a planet, except on a clear night. There was too much light, or too little. The air was too cold, or too hot. There was no reassuring vibration of smoothly functioning machinery beneath her feet. Everything was too wild, too unpredictable. Perhaps she would have adapted in time, but she never had a chance to find out.

She had gone to Everest to take her final qualifying tests for admission to the Academy. She had studied for ten years to get that far, and if Jon Senior had pushed her toward that goal at first, she had taken up the standard on her own soon enough. How else would she have the chance to become more than a freighter captain? The Academy accepted only the best and graduates never lacked for work, even if they chose to leave the Corps after their six years of mandatory service.

She had wanted to be one of the best, had wanted the challenge. She nearly had been. She had passed every academic, psychological, and physical test they had given her—all but one. That test had ended a lifetime of hopes and dreams.

Lugarian's Maneuver.

The most basic tactic in military strategy. Quick, short jumps made in rapid succession that let a ship disappear from one location and reappear elsewhere, seemingly instantaneously. The only drawback to the maneuver was the necessity of undergoing multiple transitions within the space of minutes—transitions that seemed to turn physical bodies inside out. Most people in normal physical condition could handle two or even three short jumps in rapid succession. A few could even string together four or five, though their reactions and judgment were significantly impaired.

But some people's bodies did not adjust to the stress of transition normally. For them, the effects of multiple transitions accumulated at a geometric rate. They made the first jump as well as anyone, but their performance declined noticeably after the second, and they usually lost consciousness after the third. If they attempted a fourth jump, they risked irreparable physical damage, if not outright death.

There was a name for that inability to tolerate multiple, rapid transitions: Wycker's Syndrome. Most people never knew they had it. Commercial ships had no reason to execute Lugarian's Maneuver, so few people ever had a chance to learn they suffered from the disability.

Kiley Michaelson found out she had Wycker's Syndrome on the frigate *Ascension*. The doctor supervising that final test of Academy candidates had been very kind, but all the kindness in the world could not make up for failing to do what all the other candidates had managed—remaining conscious after the third jump.

The Corps sent her back to the *Widdon Galaxy*. She had dreaded her first meeting with Jon, but he had been unexpectedly consoling.

"You can't help the way you're made, Kiley," he'd said.

If her failure disappointed him, he didn't say so. He just put her back to work piloting the ship. Jon Robert had offered sympathy too, but he never fully realized what losing her chance at the Academy had cost her. Of them all, Lia came the closest.

"I'm sorry, Kiley," she had said. "I know how much you wanted to join the Corps." Something in her eyes said she knew a great deal about lost hopes and dreams. In that moment, Kiley finally understood how unhappy her older sister was. All those years she'd thought Lia didn't like her, but it wasn't her at all. It was everything, the father who didn't know how to love, the ship that offered no escape. Herself. Everything.

"I'm sorry, too," she had said in return, and Lia had understood she wasn't talking only about her own disap-

pointment. They had been closer after that. Not friends.
Kiley did not think they could ever be friends—they were
just too different—but they had reached an understanding.

She had resisted anger and despair, had fought to make the
life she had on the *Widdon Galaxy* enough. Mostly she succeeded, but there were times when she didn't. Jon Robert was
right—envy and bitterness were dangerous emotions. Once
they'd taken root, they didn't ever go away. Not completely. Not
even when you saw that the Academy didn't mean everything
after all, that even graduates didn't always find life good or easy.

Greg Lukas hadn't.

She'd known him for an Academy graduate the moment he
sat in the pilot's seat. A person simply didn't get the training
he'd had anywhere else. She was certain he had spent more than
the mandatory six years in the service, too. He might wear
civilian clothes, but on him they became a uniform.

Reese had picked up on his background as quickly as she had.
He asked Lukas if he had attended the Academy. Lukas had said
yes. Just that, nothing more. She couldn't begin to guess what
had happened to make him leave the service, but something had.
Something he wouldn't talk about. He was very polite, very
frank, and utterly closed. The conversation had died on the spot.

The same thing had happened when Holly asked Lukas if he
had any family still living. "No," he said, again speaking politely, again closing off all possibility of further questions. They
didn't ask him anything else after that. How could they, when
he clearly wanted his privacy?

In the end, they simply let him be. In return, he gave them
good counsel and endless hours of labor. Kiley considered the
trade more than even. For the first time since Jon's death, the
ship was making a profit. They had a future, and it was looking
better by the moment.

And then, on a run to Jeross, their luck changed again.

Reese had signed a contract to transport agricultural machinery to the station. They had been there only once before, and
had no guarantee of finding a cargo for the return trip to Aumarleen, but after a short discussion, they'd decided to accept
the shipment. They had done well lately; they could afford one
run with empty holds.

The trip went routinely until transition. Lukas was in his cabin,
sleeping. He had offered to break his sleep, but Kiley had told
him she could manage; she would need him more later, as they
approached the station and had to deal with Traffic Control.

Holly and Jon Robert were working in the engine room, and Lia had put Reese to work in the garden, writing up pollination records for the flowering forellium she was attempting to hybridize.

"One minute to transition," Kiley announced. She had a green board, and Jon Robert was standing by to shut down the jump engines as they entered normal space. She watched the chronometer, counting the seconds.

The familiar wrenching started precisely on time. Her vision blurred and the bridge wavered, on the verge of dissolving. She tried to breathe and could not. Her skin crawled with electricity and a powerful hand seemed to reach inside her body, grab hold, and try to turn her inside out. She held on to reason, fighting back nausea and an irrational fear the world would never come right again. The fear was a purely physical response, she told herself firmly, nothing more than a normal biological reaction to stresses the human body had never been designed to endure.

And then, just when she thought she could not endure the sensation another moment without screaming, they came through.

And were pulled back into the void again.

The fear that struck then had nothing to do with physiological responses and everything to do with wholly rational panic. This can't be happening, her mind screamed. They had come through transition; they should be back in normal space. But the bridge kept on flickering. The controls before her wavered, dissolved, came back, and dissolved again. She had been reaching for the board, preparing to shut down the jump engines and bring the main engines up to full power. Her fingers continued moving and she made contact with the controls, but nothing happened.

An alarm went off, the sound mixing with the rumbling vibration of jump engines running at maximum capacity. The noise pierced her ears, but she barely registered the pain. All her attention was on the short-range scanners. They were picking up another object, less than a hundred kilometers away. Something big. Something that glowed and wavered, then disappeared as another wave of dissolution struck the ship.

The board went red as the hand reached inside Kiley and tried to pull her stomach out through her throat. She managed to lean over the side of the pilot's chair, and then her stomach did turn inside out.

The bridge swirled around sickeningly and the piercing alarm continued to sound. They had lost the momentum they needed to carry them through transition and into normal space. The jump engines were still running at full capacity, tearing up the space around them, trying to push them *through*. The main engines were grasping for a foothold in normal space, but they couldn't find one.

Kiley's hand went to the controls and increased power to all engines. An entire row of lights went red; she was pushing the ship too hard. The aging vessel couldn't handle the load. But she had to. She had to! Kiley hit the intercom.

"Jon Robert, I need more power!" she said.

". . . engineering panel . . . overload . . ." he answered, his static-distorted voice fading, coming back. ". . . have . . . cut power! Now!"

"No! Shut everything else down, but keep the engines on— all of them!" They could not fall back between. They would never come out again.

She started cutting power to all nonessential systems herself, fingers hitting switches as fast as they could move. The *Widdon Galaxy* lurched, grasped normal space, slipped back, grasped again. The image of a distant star and two planets flashed on the monitors, then dissolved again.

They weren't going to make it. They had come close, but they weren't going to make it.

"Kiley, can't . . . both . . . engines . . . full . . . time!" Jon Robert's frantic voice said. ". . . have to . . . down! Now!"

We can't! she wanted to shout, but she had neither breath nor time for words. The ship shook so wildly, she thought she would break apart the next instant. But death, quick and clean, would be infinitely better than whatever awaited them if they fell back into the hole they had torn in normal space.

"Come on," she begged silently as the ship lurched, grabbing for a piece of normal space, making a final, desperate bid for life. In the same instant, Kiley heard Jon Robert cry out over the open intercom, followed by the sound of Holly's voice. After that, there was silence.

Absolute, complete silence.

Nothingness. No lights. No air. No sound.

Was that death, then? That absence of . . . everything? The utter peace and security of knowing there was nothing to do save let go and float free?

She gasped and air rushed in, tearing her lungs in pieces. She took another breath. This one came easier. Lights started to flicker on the control board as the emergency backup system kicked in. She read the few sensors that functioned, taking in the data with dull eyes. All engines shut down. Life support out. Shields gone. She should be doing something, but it was hard to think, harder to move.

Power. They had to restore power. Had to get the main engines on so they could raise the shields. Without them, they were sitting targets for anything that passed, from cosmic radiation to space debris, or another ship. How much time had passed already? Thirty seconds? Sixty? Too much. She reached for the intercom, but before she could touch the button, Holly's panic-stricken voice spilled into the bridge.

"Kiley, Jon Robert's hurt!"

"Hurt? How? What happened?"

"The main engine control panel overloaded. It was about to fail. Jon Robert tried to shut it down, but it wouldn't respond to signals from the engineering board. He tried to cut the power manually, but the panel shorted when he touched it. Kiley, he's not breathing!"

"Holly—"

"We have to do something!" she shrieked.

"Holly, listen to me. Listen to me!" she shouted, trying to get through. "We'll take care of Jon Robert, but we have to have power. If we don't get the shields up right now, we'll all die!"

"But Jon Robert—" she wailed.

"Forget Jon Robert! You have to get the main engines going again. Rig a bypass through the environmental panel if you have to, but get me power to the shields! Holly, are you listening to me?"

Kiley thought she wouldn't answer, then heard a dull "Yes."

"Can you rig a bypass?"

"Yes."

"Then do it. Now!" She didn't hear anything. Only a breath that might have been a sob. She heard a rustling, something shuffling, then metal banging. She hit the intercom again.

"Reese, Holly needs you in the engine room!"

"He's already on the way, Kiley," Lia answered. Her voice sounded hollow, as if she had faded out during transition and not come completely back.

"Lia, he's going to need the emergency life-support unit. It's in the storeroom. Can you get it to the engine room by yourself?"

"Yes," she said, her voice stronger, more certain. She'd manage. For Jon Robert, she could manage anything.

The overhead lights flickered, then came on at reduced intensity. Holly must have rigged something. The control board lit up, a solid bank of red lights. The shields came up and one light went green. Two others changed to amber, then a third.

"Kiley, you should have shields and emergency life-support systems now," Holly said.

"Is Reese there yet?"

"Yes." Her voice was so flat, it was almost inhuman. "He's giving Jon Robert CPR, but he's still not breathing."

"He'll make it, Holly," Greg Lukas said into the intercom.

Kiley jerked around. She hadn't heard him come in, but he'd been there long enough to take a seat in the copilot's chair and start switching the long-range scanners and air-revitalization systems back on. His feet were bare and he wasn't wearing a shirt, but he was there. He stopped working long enough to give her a reassuring look, but the conviction didn't reach his eyes. They looked as sick and worried as she felt.

She heard a clatter in the engine room, shuffling, then Reese saying, "Clear!" A noise she didn't want to think about followed, then Reese's voice. "Breathe, damn you! Jon Robert, breathe!"

Silence. Then, an eternity later, Reese announced, "I have a pulse! He's breathing on his own." He managed to sound elated and exhausted at the same time.

"How is he?" Kiley asked.

"His hands are burned, but he's going to make it."

She blanked out. One minute she was sitting there, listening to Reese, and the next she was bent forward, her head on her knees.

"Don't sit up yet," Lukas warned as she tried to move. His hand was against her neck and he held her down when she tried to straighten. "Give yourself a minute or two to get over the shock."

She opened her mouth to tell him she didn't need a minute, but before she could speak, she started shaking. The tremors started deep inside her chest and extended out to her arms and legs. Lukas put his arm around her shoulders, holding her until the reaction was over. It did not last long and as soon as it passed, she sat up, pulling away from him. He released her immediately.

"I'm sorry," she said, not looking at him. "I didn't mean to fall apart like that."

"I'd be more concerned if you hadn't."

"Jon Robert—"

"They're taking him to his cabin. He's still unconscious, but Reese says he's stable. He wants to get burn gel on his hands, then he'll go back to the engine room and help Holly finish rigging the bypass."

"She's still there?" Kiley said, reaching for the intercom. "She doesn't have to stay. Not now. If she wants to be with Jon Robert one of us can—"

"Let her be, Kiley." Lukas caught her hand before she could press the button. "She's furious with herself for freezing up. Give her a chance to work off some of that emotion before she sees Jon Robert. So what happened? I thought the ship was going to come apart on us."

"We must have missed our coordinates and landed in an out-bound zone. There was another ship beside us, headed into jump. It looked like space was tearing apart around us. God knows what happened to them, but they won't come out where they planned to. If they come out."

Lukas was shaking his head. "It wasn't your fault," he said. "I checked our coordinates as soon as I got here. We're right where we should be. They were the ones who jumped in the wrong zone."

"Right or wrong, we're both in trouble." She stood up, every muscle in her body protesting. "I need to clean up the mess I made," she said dully. "Will you see if you can get any of the scanners working?"

He nodded and turned back to the control board. Kiley went to the washroom just inside the entrance to the bridge and grabbed a hand towel. She spent the next five minutes scrubbing the deck beside the pilot's chair. She had to give Greg Lukas credit for tact; he kept his attention on the monitors before him and didn't once comment on the fact that she'd thrown up.

"Well?" she said, sliding back into the pilot's chair.

"It's not good. We have shields, short and long-range scanners, and basic life support, but that's about all I can bring up until we have more power. The main engines are on, but Holly's only taken them up to twenty percent. She doesn't want to push them any harder until she can check for damage."

"Greg, I'd like to go down to the engine room for a few minutes. I know you haven't had much sleep, but if you could cover here for another fifteen minutes—"

"Take as long as you need. I'll stay until you get back."

She stood up. "Thank you," she said.

"For what? Staying? I don't mind."

"No, not for that. For coming to the bridge, instead of going to engineering. I . . . I needed you here."

"Kiley, this is my station. This is where I belong—the same as you." He pointed to the corridor with his head. "Go on," he ordered. "I'll call you if anything happens."

She found Holly standing in front of the first row of the six-foot cabinets that housed the ship's circuitry. Two spent fire extinguishers and a jumble of medical equipment from the emergency life-support kit littered the floor. Kiley glanced at the debris, then hastily averted her eyes. She didn't want to think about what must have happened here a short time before.

"How bad?" she asked, looking at the cabinet.

Holly pushed back her hair. She looked like she was one breath away from tears.

"Bad," she said. "We lost every board in the main engineering panels. Not even Ty could repair this kind of damage. We have a few spare boards in the ship's stores, but nowhere near the number we'll have to replace. Kiley, the money—" Her voice quavered and broke off.

"Don't worry about the money, Holly. You'll have whatever you need to make repairs as soon as we reach Jeross."

"It isn't that. Not really. It's just that we had finally started to make a profit, and now this—"

"It can't be helped, Holly. We'd have replaced the boards anyway once we had the money for a refitting. We'll just do it a little sooner than we planned."

Holly nodded, not looking at her. She took a breath, then said in a rush, "Kiley, I'm sorry about the way I froze up. I don't know what happened. I just . . . lost control. I couldn't think. I couldn't move. I thought Jon Robert was dead, and nothing else mattered. Not the ship, not you, or Lia and Reese. Nothing."

"Holly, you don't have to explain. I'd have felt the same way if I'd been here instead of you."

"No, you wouldn't. You'd never have lost control."

"You don't know that, and neither do I. Holly, that wasn't my husband lying there, only my brother. And much as I love Jon Robert, there is a difference."

"I shouldn't have frozen. I should—"

"Holly, stop criticizing yourself! If anyone should apologize, it's me for yelling at you. I just didn't know how else to make you listen. You did what you had to do, and that's all that matters. Without you, we wouldn't have any power at all.''

"Not that we have much," she said, pushing her hair back again. Her mouth tightened as she shut the cabinet door. "I switched the life support and scanning systems over to the environmental board, but that's the most I can transfer without overloading it, too. I don't have sensors to monitor the main engines, and I can't tell if they were damaged. They seem to be running all right at twenty-percent power, but I don't dare push them any harder.''

"Twenty percent will do. It will take a little longer to reach Jeross, but we'll still get there. Once we do, we'll make repairs.''

Holly nodded, but her eyes had started to glaze over and Kiley doubted she had registered a single word.

"You need a break," she said. "Why don't you go see Jon Robert, then get a few hours' sleep? Greg and I can monitor the few systems we have from the bridge. We'll call you if there's any sign of trouble.''

"I should start pulling the damaged boards," she said. "That will save us some time once we reach port.''

"You'll have plenty of time for that after you've rested. Go on. There's nothing here that can't wait.''

"All right, if you're sure. But you promise you'll call me if anything happens?''

"I promise.''

Holly hesitated, then stumbled out of the room. Kiley stood there a moment longer, trying to control her despair. The circuitry could be replaced. Jon Robert would heal. They would recover. They had before and they would this time.

Somehow.

She took one last look at the damaged cabinet, then went back to the bridge and told Lukas what she'd seen.

"You might as well go back to bed," she said when she'd finished. "There's no need for both of us to stay here.''

"If one of us leaves, it ought to be you. You look like hell. If you ask me, you have a classic case of transition shock. If either of us should be in bed, it's you.''

"I'm no worse than anyone else on the ship," she returned sharply. "Besides, I couldn't sleep this time of day if I had to. You can relieve me in three hours, at our regular shift change. Go on, captain's orders.''

He started to argue, then clamped down on whatever he was

going to say and vacated the copilot's chair. ''I'll be back in an hour,'' he said from the hatch, then left before she could respond.

The room was quiet without him. Too quiet. Kiley checked the long-range scanners, then sighed and started running the few systems checks available. She sat for a long time after she had finished, as close to complete despair as she'd come in her life.

Chapter 7

Lukas returned to relieve her an hour later. Kiley didn't bother arguing. Instead, she went to the engine room. Holly was supposed to be resting, but she was there, already at work pulling the damaged circuit boards out of their cabinets. Kiley helped her for several hours, then went back to the bridge to give Lukas a break. When he returned, he insisted on standing both the evening and night watches. By that time, she was past the point of argument and simply nodded.

She had already ordered Holly to bed. Her sister-in-law had checked on Jon Robert first, then had gone to the spare cabin, where she could sleep without disturbing him. Kiley was on her way to bed, too, but first she wanted to check on Jon Robert herself. She met Lia coming out of his room.

"How is he?" she asked.

"Stable. He started complaining about his hands before he was fully conscious, so Reese gave him a shot for the pain. He's been asleep ever since."

"How bad are the burns?"

"Bad enough. He needs a doctor, Kiley."

"We're at least a day and a half from Jeross and I don't dare push the engines any harder. Can he go that long without treatment?"

"It doesn't sound as if he has a choice," she said. She looked years older, her face white and drawn.

"I'd go faster if we could, but the risk—"

Lia waved her hand, cutting her off. "I know—you're doing the best you can. Don't look so worried, Kiley, he won't die. Reese said he'd keep him so doped up, he'll never remember any of this." Lia rubbed her eyes wearily. "I'm going to bed.

83

Reese is already asleep. He's set the alarm and he'll check on Jon Robert in a few hours."

"Lia, are you all right?" Kiley asked, worried about the other woman's drawn appearance.

"No, but I'm no worse than anyone else on the ship. A combination of too much stress on top of a rough transition. All I want is to sleep for a week."

"Then go to bed."

"I am. You should, too. You look terrible."

"I will, as soon as I've seen Jon Robert."

Lia nodded again, then went down the corridor to her cabin. Kiley waited until the door shut behind her, then went in to see her brother.

He lay on his back, hands pillowed on top of the blanket that covered him. Long, transparent sleeves filled with a pink gel encased his arms from his fingers to his elbows. Fluid dripped down an IV tube attached to his left arm. Scraps of his shirt still littered the floor—Reese must have cut it off. Jon Robert's face was white, and dark circles stood out under his eyes. His chest rose and fell slowly and she thought he was sleeping. She started to leave, but he stirred.

"Kiley?" he asked, his voice coming from a long distance away. He blinked, as if he were having trouble focusing.

"Here," she said quietly.

"Think I . . . messed up."

"It wasn't your fault."

"We make it . . . back?"

"Yes."

"Everyone else okay?"

"Yes."

"The ship—"

"Is fine. There's some damage, but nothing that can't be fixed."

His eyes closed and he had to force them open again. "Sleepy," he said. "Can't stay awake."

"Then don't try. You're supposed to be resting."

"Reese gave me . . . something for the pain. Works. Can't even feel . . . my toes."

"They're still there," she said with a smile. His eyes closed again and she touched his shoulder. "Jon Robert, I'm going to leave so you can sleep. Is there anything you need before I go?"

"No."

"I'll leave the intercom on voice-activate. Greg will be on the bridge. If you do want anything, just call out."

He nodded without opening his eyes. She started to leave, then stopped as he struggled to speak again.

"Kiley?"

"Yes?"

"What's wrong?"

"Nothing's wrong, Jon Robert. We're all fine."

"Don't believe you. Something's wrong. Know you . . . too well." He fought unconsciousness. "Kiley . . . if you're in trouble . . . talk to Greg. Can't help myself . . . but he will. I'm sure . . . he will."

"Jon, I swear, there's nothing wrong. I don't want you worrying about anything except getting well. That's an order."

"Hear you . . . Captain," he said with a ghost of a grin, and then, "Kiley, promise you'll talk to Greg if you need help. Please?"

"I promise," she said. Her words seemed to reassure him, for his eyes closed and his head slipped to one side of the pillow. His breathing deepened and steadied. She waited a moment to be certain he was sleeping, then left.

She thought she would fall asleep as soon as her head hit the pillow, but she didn't. Instead, she turned from side to side, trying to find a position in which some part of her body didn't ache. Transition sickness, she told herself. They were all suffering the consequences to one degree or another. Even Lukas had moved more slowly than normal when he slid into the pilot's seat. The effects shouldn't last long; a day or two and they'd all be back to normal.

All except Jon Robert.

She heard Holly shouting, "I think he's dead!" Reese's "Breathe, damn you! Jon Robert, breathe!" followed by the scream of engines trying to claw their way into real space. The ship shuddered, jarring her awake. It took her a terrified instant to realize that it wasn't the ship that shook, but her own body. She was freezing.

She drew the blanket around her and huddled into a miserable ball, trying to sleep again. But every time she closed her eyes, the sounds and voices came back. She lay there until she couldn't stand the torment another instant, then threw back the blanket, rose, dressed, and went out into the corridor. If she couldn't sleep, then maybe she could eat. The thought of food made her stomach turn over, but she quelled the nausea ruthlessly. She hadn't had anything since breakfast; she'd feel better if she ate.

She pulled a leftover meat pie from the refrigerator. It was almost warm. With the power to the freezers and refrigerator off, it wouldn't be long before all but the dehydrated food started to spoil. Another expense they couldn't afford, she thought dully. She shook her head, pushing that worry aside with all the others. She poured a glass of tea from a pitcher in the refrigerator. On impulse she poured a second glass and made her way to the bridge.

"I thought you'd gone to bed," Lukas said when she appeared, sounding more like an accusing parent than her copilot.

"I couldn't sleep. Here, I brought you some tea." She handed the glass to him. He took it, looking her over from head to toe with too-observant eyes. He started to say something, read the warning in her eyes, and took a drink of tea instead.

"Any sign of traffic on the long-range scanners?" she asked, swiveling the copilot's seat around and sitting down.

"Not yet. We won't be in range of Jeross Traffic Control until the day after tomorrow. We probably won't see any other ships before then."

"Keep a close watch anyway, especially on the rear scanners. Another ship could be on us in a matter of minutes. We constitute a hazard traveling at this speed, and we'd be hard-pressed to make a quick maneuver."

"Yes, Captain," he replied, with only the faintest hint of sarcasm.

"I suppose you already thought of that."

"The problem had occurred to me," he said dryly.

"I'm sorry. Sometimes I forget you aren't Jon Robert or Reese."

"Is that supposed to be some kind of backhanded compliment?"

"If you like," she said with a shrug. She finished the meat pie, washed it down with the rest of her tea, then sat there turning the empty glass around and around in her hands.

"Kiley, is anything wrong—aside from Jon Robert and the ship, that is?" Lukas glanced sideways at her.

"Isn't that enough?"

"I'd have thought so, but apparently you don't. Well?"

She looked at the glass. Turned it around again. And again.

"Kiley, I don't want to pry, but if talking will help, I'll be glad to listen," he said quietly.

"It's nothing. Really. It's just—"

"What?"

"Greg, when you were captain of a ship, did you ever have to do something you didn't want to do? Something you hated yourself for?"

He was silent so long, she thought he wouldn't answer, but then he did.

"Yes." That was all, but the haunted look in his eyes gave her the encouragement she was looking for.

She turned the empty glass around again, then closed her eyes. "Jon Robert almost died," she said. "If he had, it would have been my fault."

"Kiley—"

"Don't try to tell me otherwise. I pushed the engines past the point of safety. I wouldn't listen to him when he told me the main panel was overloading. And then when he was hurt, I told Holly to leave him alone. Greg, I ordered her to let him die!"

"No! You ordered her to save the ship and everyone else's life. There's a difference."

"Not that I can see."

"Kiley, you made the most difficult decision a captain ever faces. You risked one life to save everyone else's. No one expects you to feel good about making such a choice, but don't do yourself the injustice of believing you had an alternative. You didn't. Not if we were going to come through alive."

"I couldn't make that decision again. I wouldn't."

"You could and you would. You couldn't help yourself. You're captain of this ship because you have the strength and judgment to make that kind of decision—not because you have pilot's papers. The rest of the family knows that. You didn't hear any criticism from them, did you?"

"No."

"You won't, either. Your responsibility was to act in the best interests of the ship and the family, and you did. You won't hear any complaints from any of them. Believe me."

"Maybe, but it doesn't make *me* feel any better."

"You will. In time."

"Did you?" she demanded. "Well, did you?"

The bleak look was back. "No."

"So why should I be any different?"

"Maybe because you're a better captain than I was."

"Me? You must be joking. You're the one who can walk onto a bridge and be at home in less than fifteen minutes."

"I warned you, Kiley—don't confuse piloting a ship with captaining her. So what if I learned the controls in a few minutes? I trained for years so I could do precisely that."

"At the Academy," she said.

He hesitated. "Yes."

"I suppose Jon Robert told you I wanted to go there. No? Well, I did. I passed all the tests, too. All but one. I have a problem with transition, Lukas. I can't make consecutive jumps."

"You have Wycker's Syndrome?" he asked sharply. "No wonder you were so sick. Kiley, you should be in bed. You have to rest."

"Don't lecture me, Lukas. I get enough of that from Jon Robert. I'll sleep when I'm ready." She turned the glass again. "Funny, isn't it? To have a disability all your life and never know it?"

"No, it's not funny," he said. "It's not funny at all. I don't have to ask how much you wanted to go to the Academy; I know how much work it takes to pass even the initial exams." He paused, then said quickly, "Kiley, I'm sure you must have been disappointed, but even if you'd been admitted, you might have found the Academy wasn't all you expected. Sure, they teach you to pilot a ship. If you're good enough, they'll even make you a captain. In time. But you'll have paid a price for that privilege, one you might have considered too high if you'd known what it would be in advance. The only problem is, no one tells you the price up front; all they show you is the goal. By the time you find out the true cost, it's too late to reconsider. Besides, you've already acquired all the skills and experience the Academy could have given you, right here on the *Widdon Galaxy*."

"I don't believe you."

He sighed, and she had the oddest impression she'd disappointed him—for the first time.

"I'm not surprised," he said heavily. "There was a time when I wouldn't have believed it either. I guess it's just one of those things you have to learn for yourself." He rubbed his eyes with his thumb and forefinger, as if trying to wipe away some inner vision.

"Greg—" she started, but he cut her off.

"Go to bed, Kiley. You need the sleep and I need to concentrate. I can't talk and work at the same time."

He had never given her an order before, and on any other

occasion she'd have refused to obey on principle alone. But the sight of his closed, weary face stopped her.

"All right," she said. "I'll go."

She started for the door and stopped, feeling guilty about their conversation. She had needed to talk, but if she'd known how many unhappy memories she would awaken, she'd never have turned to him for counsel. She could not make the memories go away, but there might be something she could say to mitigate the harm she'd done.

"Greg, I will think about what you said," she said quietly from the doorway, then left before he could respond.

They reached Jeross some twenty-eight hours later. Traffic Control had monitored their slow progress with obvious concern, but Kiley had refused to declare an emergency.

"We don't need to announce the extent of our difficulties to the entire station," she'd told Lukas, "let alone every ship in port that's monitoring the com traffic. Reese has enough trouble finding cargo when the brokers think the ship is in good running order. If there were even a hint we're in trouble, no one would risk shipping freight with us."

"Word will get around as soon as you start buying parts."

"Not if we spread our purchases over several wholesalers. You can tell Traffic Control we have a minor engine malfunction, but that's all."

"Very well, Captain," he said, making no effort to hide his disagreement. Still, he repeated her words smoothly to the controller at Jeross and declined an offer of assistance.

"What about Jon Robert?" he demanded, switching off his headset. "You are going to request an emergency medical team for him, aren't you?"

"No, I'm not. That would raise the very questions I'm trying to avoid. Lia and Reese will rent a cart and take him to the hospital as soon as we've docked. It will only mean an extra fifteen minutes or so."

"He's gone this long? What's an extra fifteen minutes after thirty hours?"

"Precisely."

A burst of static on Kiley's headphones heralded another transmission from the station. Kiley guessed Lukas had more to say, but mercifully, the woman controller began reeling off docking instructions, forcing him to turn his full attention to her.

He managed to wrangle a central berth out of the woman and Kiley maneuvered the ship smoothly into place. Reese rented a motorized cart, and he and Lia took Jon Robert to the station hospital. Holly looked after them with empty eyes, then turned to Kiley.

"Let's get started," she said.

"Holly, if you want to go—"

"You need me more here," the other woman said flatly. Kiley didn't argue. She was right.

They spent the afternoon poring over wholesalers' inventory lists, searching for the boards they needed and comparing prices. They were lucky—everything they required was in stock somewhere on the station. They split their purchases among three dealers. Lukas might think them paranoid, but she had seen what happened to other ships in trouble, had heard the rumors that started circulating before they ever docked and witnessed the averted glances and cool politeness that met their crews. You didn't admit weakness or need unless you had no other choice, not if you wanted to stay in business.

Reese returned from the hospital shortly before the first of their orders was delivered. He stopped long enough to pick up a copy of their manifest, then headed for customs to start clearing the cargo for off-loading. Lia was still at the hospital, waiting for the doctor's report. Kiley and Holly were clearing out the last of the damaged boards in the main panel, which left only Lukas idle. Kiley set him to work inventorying the spoilage in the freezers and throwing the useless food out. He knew the job had to be done, but he clearly thought his time and energy could have been put to better use and said so.

"And I said I want you to take care of the freezer," she snapped back. *You have a problem obeying orders, Mister?* her harsh look demanded.

She knew she'd made a mistake the moment the words were out of her mouth. She'd let frustration get the better of her and she'd taken out her emotions on him. And now it was too late. As ill-advised as her challenge was, she had given it. She couldn't back down.

Lukas stiffened. For a moment, she thought he would walk out on her, then and there. How could she have been so stupid? With Jon Robert unable to work, they needed Lukas more than ever. Only an idiot would have antagonized him for no reason. They faced each other for ten seconds that stretched into infinity; then Lukas broke the impasse.

"As you wish, Captain," he said frigidly and walked off. Kiley could have cried. She was going to pay for that brief display of temper. She just hoped the bill wouldn't come due at the same time as all the others that were mounting up so rapidly.

Jon Robert's hospital charges would run at least two hundred credits. Replacement food stores would cost another two hundred. And the boards—she could have cried again after she and Holly added up the total. One thousand, three hundred and thirty-three credits. All the money they had saved toward the ship's refitting and all their personal savings amounted to just over eighteen hundred credits.

If the hospital bill didn't run too high, if the food didn't cost too much, they would have just enough money left over to pay their port fees. Just. But if they didn't find a cargo on Jeross, they wouldn't be able to pay their docking fees at the next port. If they didn't find a cargo, they were going to lose the ship.

Reese took the news grimly. Kiley hated to put that much pressure on him, but he wasn't the only one to feel the stress. They had no money to hire station technicians to replace the boards—she, Holly, and Lukas would have to do that themselves. With docking fees running forty credits a day, they had a maximum of seventy-two hours to complete the job.

Estimating the hours of labor required to fit the new boards in the control panel and run the exhaustive tests without which they wouldn't dare leave port, she knew another moment's despair. They couldn't do all that in three days. There just wasn't enough time.

But the alternative was losing the *Widdon Galaxy*. If they couldn't pay their docking fees, the station would seize the ship and auction her off. The family would receive any excess funds from the sale, but there wouldn't be enough to start five people on new lives. They had to finish installing the boards in seventy-two hours, even if it meant working around the clock.

So work they did. Lia came back from the hospital early in the evening. The gel had prevented further damage to Jon Robert's hands, but the burns had been severe enough to require several skin grafts. The surgery had gone well, and there was no sign of damage to ligaments or tendons, but he would not be able to return to the ship until late the next day.

Kiley asked Holly if she wanted to go to the hospital, but she shook her head. "There's too much to do. Jon Robert will be sleeping anyway. He'll understand if I don't go."

She was still trying to atone for her earlier lapse. Kiley started to tell her they could do without her help for a few hours, then stopped. The fact was, they couldn't. She nodded instead and the two of them started fitting new boards in the panel, stopping only for a late dinner. Lukas had finished his inventory of the ship's food stores and he joined them after the meal. He stayed as far from Kiley as he could, deliberately avoiding her.

They worked far into the night, quitting only when they started making too many mistakes. Kiley slept three hours and went back to the engine room. She found Lukas already there. Holly arrived a few minutes later, and they kept up a steady pace until lunchtime. Lia had prepared the meal for them and they sat around the table, shoveling the food in mechanically. Jon Robert was back on the ship and doing well. The doctor said he would probably sleep most of the next few days, and his hands would have to stay bandaged for several weeks. He would have to see another doctor as soon as they docked at their next port of call.

"He won't have a problem with jump, will he?" Kiley asked Lia at lunch. Transition was hard enough on healthy tissue, let alone damaged cells.

"The doctor said he should be fine, as long as we don't jump tomorrow. He gave Jon Robert some pills to take a few hours before transition, to make him sleep. Jon Robert didn't want them, but the doctor said he'd realize his mistake a second into transition, and then it would be too late."

"I'll see he takes them," Holly told them in a tone that left no room for doubt.

"What about the food?" Kiley asked. "Have we dumped everything that spoiled?"

"Yes," Lia answered. "We lost everything in the freezers and all the fresh fruit and vegetables. I have Greg's inventory. Can I start replacing what we need?"

"Yes. Just watch the cost. We can spare two hundred credits, but no more."

"We can save on delivery charges if we bring everything back ourselves. I'll need help, though. Reese is still looking for cargo; I haven't seen him all day. If one of you could come with me for even a few hours . . ."

"Greg," Kiley replied without hesitating. Holly couldn't be spared and he was the slowest worker. She saw his clenched jaw and tacked on a hurried, "Please?"

He wasn't happy, but having a choice seemed to mollify him, and he nodded agreement. He and Lia decided to go right after lunch. Kiley followed Holly back to the engine room and they wearily began fitting yet another panel into a cabinet.

Jeross was a city in space. Nearly as large as Aumarleen, the station orbited the fifth planet in the binary system. A staging area during planetary colonization and development, it now served as the way station through which everything destined to go on or off world traveled. Exotic foods, fine cloth, people, technology, ideas—the entire commerce of the human race passed through Jeross going one direction or the other.

Like any crossroads, the station offered myriad possibilities for success or ruin. Lucky people with impeccable timing grasped their opportunities and amassed fortunes. Others, less lucky and talented, grasped and seized ruin. Serenely unaware of the struggle, unaffected by the electrifying energy generated by the thousands of traders endlessly searching for the next, consummate deal, the station circled the planet below, cared for by only the few who made her continued existence their lives' work.

Strangers were the rule onstation, rather than the exception, and Lukas and Lia received little attention as they visited the frozen-food suppliers located in the upper reaches of the station. They stopped at several shops, checking prices and variety, spreading their purchases around. They took the first load back to the ship, then set out for the station's central trading district. They would find no wholesalers there, but the careful buyer could still find a bargain—and infinitely more variety.

Lia kept her mind strictly on food and firmly resisted the impulse to pause before store after store displaying shimmering cloth, glittering jewelry, intricate electronic equipment, and entertainment disks. She looked, though. Her eyes took in everything, starved for color, light, and stimulation. The Michaelsons had done their best with the ship. Lukas had to give them credit for understanding the importance of bold colors, different textures, and light, always light. But even the most comfortable ship could not avoid sterility. When change is possible only through deliberate action, there is no spontaneity or adventure. What remains is dull, boring routine.

"In here," Lia said, turning into a shop on her right. She walked past the rows of packaged food displays, eyeing them critically, then went to the terminals at the side of the store and started checking her list against the inventory. "They have everything we still need," she announced a few minutes later, ''and their prices look reasonable to me.'' She began selecting items, one eye on the list in her hand and the other on the total sale amount, which grew at an alarming rate.

''That's it,'' she said when the total stood at thirty-eight credits.

''You didn't get everything,'' Lukas said. He'd been double-checking her selections against the list she held, knowing how easy it was to mark the wrong item and end up with something like an entire case of synthetic protein that was thoroughly nutritious—and so disgustingly unappetizing none of them would eat it. ''You still have a page to go.''

''But I'm out of money,'' she said firmly. ''If I've learned one thing over the years, it's when Reese and Kiley say two hundred credits, they mean two hundred credits. Don't look so worried. We won't starve.''

''We won't have much variety, either.'' He hesitated, then lifted the pen and started paging through the inventory list, impulsively marking the first items that caught his eye, running the bill up another forty credits.

''Greg, stop!'' Lia said, trying to take the pen away. ''I told you, I don't have the money to pay for anything else.''

''I'll pay,'' he said, still scanning the screen.

''You? No,'' she protested, then louder, ''No!'' when he marked another item.

''I eat, too. I have the money. Why shouldn't I buy my share of the food?''

''Because you work for us. We're supposed to give you money—not take it from you. Stop!''

''All right,'' he said agreeably. He set down the pen and hit the enter key.

''Greg!''

''Lia, don't start an argument. Please? We can use the food and I have the money, so what's the problem?''

''The problem is Kiley and Jon Robert. Not to mention Reese. They won't take your money, Greg. They'd rather starve first.''

''So don't tell them I helped out.''

''But Kiley will ask about the bill—''

''She'll ask how much you spent and you'll tell her the truth: two hundred credits. She won't bother looking at the sales receipts. Not now.''

''She will later. She and Reese go over everything. You know that!''

''So what will they do when they find out? Insist on paying

me back? Fine. Let them, when they have the money." He stood up and pocketed the list. "Come on, let's pay up."

He went up to the counter at the front of the store. Two other customers stood in line before them. The young man working behind the counter dealt with them expeditiously, his deft movements belying his big, gangling frame. He turned to Lia and called up her order.

"That will be seventy-eight credits " he said, holding out his hand for her card.

"Forty go on this one," Lukas said, holding out his own card. The clerk gave him a funny look, then took the two cards and started punching in the numbers. He verified Lia's handprint against her ID, cleared the charge to her card, then had her sign an invoice.

"You next," he said to Lukas.

Lukas placed his hand over the glass on the counter. "Something wrong?" he asked without any real concern when the screen flashed and the clerk didn't move.

"No," the man said, jerking his attention back from wherever it had gone. "Here, you need to sign." He held out the lightpen and Lukas wrote his name. The clerk watched his signature appear on the screen, as if checking it manually, even though the computer would have rejected anything but a positive match.

"Here," the man said, pulling the card out of the slot and shoving it toward Lukas. He took it, suddenly wary. Something was wrong. The clerk's hands were shaking and he refused to look directly at either of them. He knew there was nothing wrong with his card or his credit, so that couldn't be the problem. What, then?

"Do you want to take this with you or have it delivered?" the man asked abruptly.

"We'll take it," Lia said. "How long do you need to get the order ready?"

"Ten minutes. No more than fifteen."

"Fine. We'll get a cart and be right back."

They went out into the street, and didn't have to go far before finding an idle cart. Lukas inserted his card in the charge slot before Lia could get hers out. She started to protest, then subsided into the seat with a sigh. Lukas blessed her for that. Kiley would have argued for half an hour over who was paying before giving in with such ill grace that he'd have wound up wishing he'd let her have her way.

Motorized vehicles used the center of the wide passageway

between shops. There was little traffic and Lukas had no difficulty maneuvering the two-seated cart back to the shop. He had been worried about the limited cargo space in the rear, but had finally decided they could get everything in if they packed carefully.

The clerk looked up when they returned. "Your order's in the stockroom," he said, pointing to a door at the side of the store. "My brothers will help you carry it out."

The young man's brothers were just as big as he, and just as unfriendly. They didn't look directly at him, just asked where to go and started carrying boxes out to the cart. They put them where Lia pointed, then went back for another load. Lukas made the first trip with them, then stayed to help Lia stow the food.

"There's just one more box," the taller of the two brothers said two trips later.

"I'll get it," Lukas told Lia. "No, stay here," he said when she started to follow. He said the words without thinking, not certain why until he was back in the store. The moment he stepped inside the atmosphere struck him, sullen, brooding and heavy, laden with some undercurrent of tension that made the skin across his neck crawl. The clerk still stood at the counter, but his brothers had disappeared. Lukas looked at the young man, scanned the rooms instinctively, saw no one, and started for the stockroom.

The box sat in the center of the floor. He squatted to pick it up, stood, turned, and found the clerk standing in the door. Someone moved in behind Lukas and he swung his head around.

The other two brothers had taken up positions directly behind him, one to his left, the other to his right. Slowly, very slowly, he set the box down. Don't make any sudden moves, he thought. Don't do anything to antagonize them. Whatever you do, don't antagonize them.

"Greg, what—" Lia's voice broke the silence. She had come into the shop to find him. She took one look at the scene in the storeroom and froze.

"Lia, get out of here," Lukas said, not moving a muscle.

"Greg, what's—"

"Get out of here!" The order struck her like a blow. She fell back a step. Looked at the men. Looked at Lukas. And ran.

Afraid, but not panicked. That thought consoled him momentarily. Then he forgot it as the clerk stepped through the door and closed it with an irrevocable thump.

"Are you going to tell me what this is all about," Lukas said to the clerk, trying to sound calm despite the sweat trickling down his back, "or am I supposed to guess?"

"You have to guess?" Sarcasm dripped from the young man's voice, poisonous as venom falling off a snake's fangs. "You of all people shouldn't have to guess—*Captain* Lukas!"

And then he knew, making connections with a burst of intuition that flashed like lightning across his mind before leaving him in darkness.

"Crowther," he said.

"You didn't forget. I didn't think you would. How could you? Then again, Bernie didn't mean anything to you, did he, *Captain*? He wasn't *your* brother, after all. Why should you have cared what happened to him?"

"I cared."

"Oh, sure. Right up to the moment you killed him."

"I didn't kill your brother, Crowther. I did not kill Bernie."

"No, you just stood there and watched while he died. Did you feel anything, Lukas, anything at all? Or did you just laugh?"

"Crowther—"

"Shut up! I don't want to listen to you! I used to pray I'd have a chance to make you pay for what you did to Bernie, but I never thought I would. And then you showed up in the store. At first, I didn't recognize you. The video Dad got of your sentencing wasn't all that clear and you look different without your uniform, but I knew it was you when I saw your name. I'll make you sorry you ever came to Jeross, Lukas. I'll make you sorry you were ever born."

I already am, he wanted to say, but Crowther wouldn't have believed him. You couldn't reason with that kind of hate. You just backed away, circling, trying to find an opening, a way out, because you knew you wouldn't survive the coming collision by meeting it head-on.

"Afraid, aren't you? Maybe even as afraid as Bernie was before he died? I'll bet you don't feel like laughing now, do you, Lukas? No, you saved that for the trial. The trial where they found you guilty—then let you go free!"

"They didn't exactly let me go free, Crowther. If you know about the trial, you know that."

"You're here, aren't you? You're walking around, aren't you? You look free to me. And alive. Most of all, you're still alive, aren't you? You let two of your crew die, but you're still alive. Poor Bernie, always the one with his eyes on the stars.

He should have stayed on Jeross, but how could he know he'd meet people like you out there? How did you ever get to be an officer, Lukas? Didn't anybody see you for the scum you were, or did you wait until later to sell out—when you found out just how great the profits could be?''

Lukas didn't waste his breath replying. Crowther wouldn't listen—he'd been dreaming vengeance too long. Bernie was dead, and he didn't care what had happened, or why. All he cared about was getting even.

"You're going to pay, Lukas," he said. "And this time, it won't be an easy 'rehabilitation.' " He signaled his brothers with a jerk of his head. Lukas took another step back, his eyes never moving from Crowther's face, though all his other senses extended out, trying to locate the other men. They were still behind him, one to either side. He would only have one chance to break away, and the door was his only hope.

He feinted to his left, broke right. He came close. So very close. His hand was on the door, swinging it open, when one of them hit him from behind with a full-body blow that smashed him against the door, slamming it shut again. Fingers grabbed his hair and rammed his head against metal. A light flared in the dim room, then went out. The hand jerked his head back, preparing for another blow.

"Slow down, Hank!" one of the others warned. "You'll knock him out if you hit his head again, and then he won't be able to feel his ribs go, one by one. Or his hands. Or his legs. We don't want him dying, either—just hurt. Hurt so bad, not even the hospital can make him whole again. Hurt so he'll spend the rest of his life wishing he'd died instead of Bernie—right?''

The hand in his hair tightened. Relaxed. "Right," Hank said, and swung Lukas around.

His head spun and his eyes refused to focus, but he knew he had to move. He made himself go limp, then pushed away from Hank with all the strength he had left the moment he felt the other man relax. He had one dizzying instant of freedom before another body rammed him, throwing him to the floor with a force that drove the breath from his body. A knee ground into his back as the weight above him shifted. He tried to roll over, but before he could move, something slammed into his side. Once. Then again. And then again—on the other side.

He cried out as his ribs broke. He would have held the sound back if he'd had time to prepare himself for the pain, but it burst across him so suddenly, and was so much more agonizing than he could possibly have imagined, that the cry was out before he could stop it.

"That's more like it," a voice panted above him. "Get him up, Willis. Get him up!"

Hands caught him under the arms and lifted. The broken bones grated. He did not cry out this time; he did not have the breath. He could hardly see through the pain, but he saw the fist coming. It landed square in his stomach, driving out the last air remaining in his lungs. The fist drew back, punched again. Lukas doubled over, his arms tearing at the shoulders where the other two held him with locked grips.

Another blow. Another. He lost count. The only sounds were Crowther's grunts as he threw all his weight behind each blow and the sickening smash of flesh against flesh. The two men held him up for a time after his legs gave way, and then the one on the right released him abruptly. His arm twisted in the other man's grip, threatening to come out of the socket as he sagged to his knees. Something wide and incredibly rigid caught him full across the back just above his waist, throwing him forward. The man holding his arm let him fall, and he hit the floor with a thud. Instinct screamed at him to curl into a ball, but he could not move. A foot drove into his other side, lifting him off the floor. Another foot caught him on the opposite side. His attackers found a rhythm, hitting shoulders, ribs, and hips, jerking his body with each strike.

Angry voices shouted. He heard them, but couldn't make out the words, and then he stopped trying because he was falling again, far, far down a widening black hole. He tried to hold on to consciousness, but his fingers could find no purchase. With a sound that might have been a strangled sob, he let go and tumbled down, traveling far from pain, far from anger, far from memories. He hit the bottom of the well and found surcease at last in oblivion's embrace.

Chapter 8

The *Nieti* still had not found a way home. They continued to search, but had found no end to the barrier that barred their return. The Quayla had spoken to them for a time, but it had gone silent again. Chirith feared for its sanity. If it failed them, they would all die.

More than a few had given in to despair, believing they would never find a way back. Chirith refused to consider the possibility. They would find a passage. They had to.

The ship's elders had supported his decision to continue the search, but they suggested returning to their starting point and traveling in the opposite direction.

"Perhaps the barrier does not extend so far that way," they argued. He suspected they were more interested in moving the ship closer to the habitable planet in case the Quayla failed, but he did not voice that thought—nor did they. If the Quayla learned of their concern, it would likely misinterpret it as criticism.

He argued that since they had come this far, they should continue on, but his words lacked conviction. In truth, he had cared about nothing since Hinfalla's death. But he had responsibilities and he could not evade them.

In the end, he did as the rest of the elders wished. He turned the ship around and took her back the way they had come.

Chapter 9

The speaker beeped for the second time that afternoon, announcing an incoming call. Kiley bit back an impatient oath and pulled her head out of the circuitry cabinet.

This had better be important, she silently warned the caller. Reese had called once, saying he'd found cargo destined for Aumarleen, but only if they could guarantee departure the next day. She hesitated, then told him to accept the load. What did they have to lose? If they couldn't leave by then, a breach-of-contract suit would be the least of their worries.

He wouldn't bother calling back to confirm the deal, so that meant he'd either missed out on the shipment after all, or someone else was calling. Lia? She glanced at her watch, thinking her sister had been gone longer than expected, then looked again, unable to believe the time. Lia and Lukas should have been back hours ago.

Trouble.

She knew it before she hit the speaker button, and every nerve in her body went on alert.

"*Widdon Galaxy*, Captain Michaelson."

"Captain, this is Philip Boscoe, assistant to Josef Cernak, station administrator. There's been an incident involving one of your crewmembers. The administrator requests your presence in his office immediately."

"Who was involved? What kind of incident?"

"Administrator Cernak didn't give me the details, Captain. He simply asked me to arrange a meeting. Station security is on the way to your ship. They'll escort you here."

"Boscoe—" she said, but he had already rung off. She swung around and found Holly standing behind her, white-faced.

"Kiley, what's going on?"

"I don't know, but Lia and Greg are overdue."

"Jon Robert—if Lia's been gone all this time, then no one's checked on him all afternoon."

"Go see him. I'm sure he'd have called if he needed anything, but you'd better check. Why don't you get yourself some dinner, too? I didn't realize it was this late."

"What about you?"

"I'll eat when I get back." If I still can. "Holly, how much time do we need to complete the repairs?"

"A good ten hours, with both of us working."

"And the system checks?"

"Another eight or ten."

"We have to be out of port by sixteen hundred tomorrow. That doesn't leave much spare time."

"We'll make it."

"Or go down trying," Kiley said with a weary sigh. "I'll be back as soon as I can, but I don't know how long—"

"Don't worry about the repairs. I'll come back as soon as I've checked on Jon Robert and eaten. Go on—the security officer will be waiting for you."

A woman wearing a green jumpsuit with white piping was waiting just outside the tube connecting the ship to the station. She jumped to attention as soon as she saw Kiley and waved her toward a two-seater cart displaying the station's emblem. "This way, Captain."

Kiley got in and the woman took off at full speed, maneuvering sharply across the congested dock area. They cleared security, then took a ramp up to Level Twenty, where the station's executive offices were located. The woman pulled to a stop at the end of a corridor. "Administrator Cernak's office is the second door on the right," she said.

Kiley swung her legs out of the cart, straightened her shoulders resolutely, and started down the corridor. The guard watched her the entire distance, turning away only when she stepped inside the door.

She found herself in an enormous office with white walls and soft, mossy green carpet. Towering plants filled the room, some reaching up to the ceiling, others trailing from hanging planters suspended far overhead. Five desks were scattered amid the plants. Three were empty. A woman sat at the fourth, in the middle of a video conversation. A youngish man sat at the fifth. He wore a camel-colored suit and a yellow shirt of such impeccable fit, they must have been tailored. Kiley took one look at him and decided he had never known a moment of financial worry or personal insecurity in his life. Still, she didn't make the mistake of believing anything but a quick brain hid behind that elegant facade. Not in the administrator's office on a station the size of Jeross.

He stood as she approached his desk. "Captain Michaelson? Philip Boscoe. The administrator is waiting for you. This way, please."

He took her across the room and opened a door on the back wall. "Administrator, Captain Michaelson is here," he said, then stepped back to let her enter.

"Come in, Captain," Joseph Cernak said. "Come in."

He rose from behind his desk and offered his hand. His shake was strong and short, a perfect match to his bold features and brusque manner. He might have been fifty, but he looked younger. A few strands of gray showed in his dark hair, but they only added to the overall impression of maturity and formidable authority. His assured manner said he had nothing to prove; he knew his worth well. His office might give him tremendous power, but Kiley suspected he used his authority sparingly, having long since discovered the merits of more subtle means of persuasion.

"Have a seat, Captain." He gestured to a chair in front of his desk.

She sat. "I understand one of my crewmembers is in trouble," she said, plunging straight in. No need to waste courtesy words with Cernak, not when he was the type to go straight to the point himself.

"That's correct." He glanced down at a paper in front of him. "Greg Lukas. I believe he's your pilot?"

"Backup pilot, yes. Is he in trouble of some sort? What's wrong?"

"Captain, how long have you known Lukas?"

"About a month. Why? What does that have to do with anything?"

"Do you have any idea where he came from, or what his background is?"

"I know he attended the Academy and served in the military, and that he's been piloting commercial ships the past year."

"That's all?"

"Mr. Lukas prefers to keep his private life private. I respect that desire. He does the work he's paid to do and does it well. That's all I needed to know." She shifted impatiently. "Administrator Cernak, I'm running on a very tight schedule. I don't have all day to sit here talking, unless there's some point to these questions?''

"Captain Michaelson, your pilot was involved in a serious incident several hours ago, along with Station Commissioner Jason Crowther's three sons. Apparently the commissioner's fourth son, Bernie Crowther, was killed a year ago while serving under the command of your pilot, Lukas. According to documents Commissioner Crowther has submitted to me, Commander Lukas was court-martialed after the incident. He was accused of taking his ship and an unauthorized civilian into a restricted zone in an apparent attempt to collect and transport out proscribed materials. The court found him guilty.''

"You can't be serious! Greg Lukas a smuggler? He wouldn't steal ten credits, let alone proscribed materials.''

"That's not what the military found. In addition to theft, he was also implicated in the deaths of two crewmen, Bernie Crowther and KenTarn Adrick. They were reportedly killed after learning what Lukas and the civilian were doing. The court found that the civilian, Lyle Gordon, committed the murders, but the Crowther brothers claim Lukas shared the responsibility.''

"I don't believe you," Kiley said flatly.

"I have a copy of the verdict, Captain," Cernak replied. He handed her a sheet of paper.

The words were there, formal and undeniable. They stood out in clumps: do find . . . Commander Gregory Lukas, SN 4173-255-72415, Captain of the Starship *Kelsoe Moran* . . . did unlawfully enter the Belurian Quadrant . . . with the intent of acquiring and selling proscribed materials . . . It is the verdict of this Court that Commander Lukas be summarily discharged and stripped of all benefits and privileges of rank, including but not limited to back pay and pension, and that he be remanded forthwith into the custody of Chief Medical Officer Alec Renard, for the purpose of rehabilitation therapy . . . do further recommend that, after successful completion of therapy, and in light of his previous meritorious service, he be granted a commercial pilot's license, pursuant to the request of Admiral James Sorseli . . .

There was more, but Kiley stopped reading. The paper in her hands shook, but whether the reaction resulted from shock or anger, she could not have said.

"You can begin to see why the Crowthers confronted Lukas when they discovered who he was," Cernak said. "I'm afraid what followed wasn't pleasant. Commissioner Crowther is an able man, but his sons are more inclined to brawn than brains. Bernie was the only one with any intelligence. They knew about the court's verdict and they didn't believe the sentence sufficiently harsh. When they saw their chance at a little homemade justice, they decided to take matters into their own hands.''

"Is he dead?" Kiley asked numbly, forcing herself to say the word, not daring to look at the Administrator's eyes for fear of reading that truth in them.

"No, of course not," Cernak hastened to assure her. "He's probably wishing he was, though. According to security, he took a severe beating, but his life is not in danger."

"My sister—she was with him—"

"She's fine, Captain. Security took her to medical detention, along with Lukas. They've been holding her until they completed their investigation."

"I want to see her."

"You can, but I'm afraid there are a few matters to be settled first." Cernak paused, shuffled a pile of papers together on his desk as if collecting his thoughts, then said, "Captain, this incident poses a major problem for me. On one hand, I can't let a blatant attack go unpunished, but on the other, I don't think a jury on this station would find the Crowther brothers guilty if your man decided to press charges. Jason Crowther is universally respected and well liked. As appalling as he finds his sons' behavior, he's not about to stand by and see them go to jail for trying to avenge their brother's death. I've spent the last hour trying to calm him down. He's agreed to reimburse Lukas for any medical expenses he incurred, in exchange for a promise not to press charges."

"How very generous of him."

"More generous than you know. I wasn't joking about his popularity—or his influence. There are more than a few people on this station who'd be happy to complete what his sons set out to do in hopes of winning his favor. I don't like violence, Captain, and I won't stand by while murder is committed on my station. I've already accepted Commissioner Crowther's offer on Lukas's behalf. In exchange, I've agreed that Lukas will be declared persona non grata on Jeross. He is not to return, ever. You and your ship will be welcome here, but not while he's onboard. If you try to dock while he is, you'll be turned away. Is that clear?"

"Yes."

"I've arranged for security to escort Lukas back to your ship as soon as the doctor releases him. A guard will be stationed outside to insure that he stays there until you leave, and to prevent any unauthorized personnel from boarding. That's for your protection, Captain. So far, we've been able to keep this incident quiet; there was a crowd outside the store, but security cordoned the area off before they transferred the Crowthers and Lukas to detention. I've told the commissioner his sons won't be released until your ship leaves port, but I expect the story will still get around. One of the guards will say something, the commissioner will let a comment drop—it doesn't matter how it happens, the story will get out. It always does. The guard will be there to stop anyone who tries to board without your permission."

"Is that all?"

"That's all, Captain. Boscoe is arranging for an escort to take you to detention. I don't anticipate any further problems, but if you do run into difficulties, please advise him. He has my full authority to expedite matters for you in any way he can." Cernak pressed the intercom on his desk. "Philip, is the captain's escort here yet?"

"Yes, sir," the young man replied.

"She's on her way out," Cernak said. He rose and went to the door, opening it for her. "Captain, I want you to know how deeply I regret what happened. Jeross is an orderly station. Our problems run more to efficient waste recycling and the occasional fraud than assault. If I thought Lukas could file charges and receive a fair hearing, I wouldn't hesitate to encourage him to do so. But he wouldn't. If you value his safety, you'll get him off Jeross as quickly and quietly as you can."

"We plan to leave tomorrow, Administrator—assuming he's fit to travel."

"If he isn't, let me know." Cernak smiled, his eyes going a warm, sparkling brown. "I wish we'd met under more favorable circumstances, Captain. It's been a pleasure talking to someone who didn't waste the first fifteen minutes shouting accusations and the last fifteen making excuses. You are, in fact, the only reasonable person I've spoken with all day. If you happen to come back this way again, please let me know. I'd like to take you out to dinner."

"Well that's a first," Boscoe said after Cernak closed his door. "I do believe the administrator is interested in you. Josef hasn't asked a woman out since his wife divorced him five years ago. It's about time he started looking at someone else."

"I hardly think he was interested in me personally, Mr. Bos-coe."

"No? I wouldn't be so sure. I'll bet he logs a standing order to be notified if your ship docks again. You'd better come prepared for a sustained assault if you return, Captain. Josef Cernak can be a very persuasive man when he chooses. Very persuasive."

"I'm sure he can, but I doubt I'll be back." She glanced around the room and saw only Boscoe. "I thought someone was supposed to take me to detention."

"The guard's waiting outside, Captain."

She expected another cart, but the security officer, a man this time, led her to an elevator. They went straight down for sixteen floors; then the guard walked her through a maze of corridors so convoluted she doubted an escaping prisoner could have found his way out. He stopped in front of a door labeled INFIRMARY.

"In here, Captain," he said, opening the door for her.

She walked in and found herself in a brightly lit reception area. Chairs lined the walls behind her and to her sides. A counter ran the length of the room, separating the waiting area from another corridor along the back wall, which was broken by a series of doors, all closed. Lia sat in a chair on Kiley's right, her head buried in her hands.

"Lia?" Kiley asked quickly, going to her, afraid she'd been hurt despite the administrator's assurances.

"Oh, Kiley! I'm so glad you're here," she said, jumping up. "They said they'd called you, but it took so long . . ."

Her face was red and blotchy from crying. Her hands shook and she clasped them together quickly, trying valiantly to regain her composure, but not quite succeeding.

"Lia, did they hurt you?"

"No," she said immediately.

"What about Greg?"

"I don't know. They took him in there," she said, pointing to one of the doors. "The nurse came out an hour ago and said they were still working on him, but that's all they've told me. Kiley, those men kept shouting at Greg, saying he'd killed their brother, that he'd been court-martialed, and the court hadn't done anything to him. One of them got away from the guard and tried to attack him again, daring him to deny what he'd done, and he didn't. Kiley, how could he have done that? How!"

"I don't know, Lia. He's the only one who can answer that."

"Well, he isn't getting the chance. I don't ever want to talk to him again. Ever!"

"Lia, calm down! You're nearly hysterical."

"You would be too! All we did was go in the store to buy food, Kiley. That's all. Greg was helping them carry it out. When he didn't come back, I went in to see what was keeping him. He was back in the stockroom and those men were standing around him. He was afraid and told me to leave. I couldn't think of anything to do except call security, so I ran to the store next door. They took forever to come. When they finally did, I thought Greg was dead. He was lying on the floor and those men were kicking him. He didn't move. He never even made a sound. Kiley—" She started crying again and Kiley put an arm across her shoulders.

"Don't cry, Lia. You did the best you could," she said, knowing even as she spoke the words were useless. Some people had to cry their fear and anger away; others bundled it up inside and held it like a barrier between them and the world.

"Lia, you don't have to stay here any longer," she said when her sister's sobs died down to sniffles again. "Why don't you go back to the ship? There's a security officer outside. He'll have someone take you back." No need to mention he wouldn't let her go otherwise.

"Are you sure? I'll stay if you want . . ."

"Go ahead. I'll wait until Greg's ready to come and—"

"Kiley, you're not bringing him back! No! I don't want you to. Reese won't either, when he hears what he did. We can get another pilot. Leave him here, Kiley. Please, leave him here!"

"I can't do that, Lia. He has to come with us—station administrator's orders." And all the friendly dinners in the universe wouldn't have talked him out of that decision.

"He says we have to take him with us? He can't do that. No one has the right to order us to take him if we don't want to. He can get a job on another ship."

"Not on Jeross, he can't. Like it or not, he's coming with us as far as Aumarleen. Aside from the fact those are Administrator Cernak's orders, we need him now that Jon Robert can't work."

"We can hire someone else," she said stubbornly.

"With twenty credits? Because we'll be lucky to have that much by the time we get out of here."

"We'll find a way. Besides, I don't think he's going to be much help. He looked worse than Jon Robert. And if you expect me to nurse him too, you can think again," she added defiantly.

"Lia, can we leave this discussion for later? Please? We'll talk when you've had time to calm down."

Lia started to say something, read Kiley's expression, and reconsidered. "Are you sure you don't mind if I go back?" she asked, eyes averted.

"Positive."

"Then I will." She hesitated, then said, "You know the really awful part of all this? They didn't know who Greg was until he used his credit card. He was only trying to help. I didn't have enough money for everything so he bought the rest of the food himself and gave them his card to pay."

"And you let him? Lia!"

"He said you could pay him back later when you had the money. I don't think the clerk recognized him, though; only his name. Why did he have to be so nice, Kiley? Why?" she demanded as she went out the door.

Why indeed.

Alone, she felt anger returning full force.

Damn Greg Lukas! Damn him for appearing so honest and open, all the while hiding the truth about his past. Damn him for frightening Lia and putting her in danger. Damn him for getting hurt just when she couldn't do without him. Damn him most of all for worming his way into their lives, making them like him, making them *depend* on him! Jon Robert had been right about him from the very first—he was trouble. Only now it was too late to turn their backs and walk away, as they should have done on Demarker.

"Captain Michaelson?" a woman asked. Kiley turned around and found a nurse behind her. "The Administrator's Office notified us you were on the way down. Dr. Ferrill said to tell you he'd be out in a few minutes."

"I want to see Lukas."

"The doctor would like to talk to you first."

"Is he with Lukas?"

"Yes."

"Fine. I can see both of them at the same time." She went to the door Lia had pointed out. The nurse protested, of course, but Kiley was in no mood to listen. Every extra minute she had to wait jeopardized their chance of leaving the next day. She wondered what Josef Cernak would say if he discovered they couldn't leave Jeross because they couldn't pay their docking fees. Maybe he'd waive them to get Lukas off-station.

Angrily, she turned the knob on the door and threw it open.

Lukas was sitting on an examining table in the center of the room, his side toward her, a heavy white bandage wrapped tightly around his chest.

He took a severe beating, Cernak had said. She'd heard the words, but their meaning didn't register until she saw the massive bruises, swollen into ridges, that covered virtually every inch of his arms, sides and back. How could anyone do that to a man, she wondered dully, sickened by the sight.

The doctor was standing behind Lukas, trying to ease his left arm into his shirt sleeve. "Easy now. That's right," he was saying as Kiley barged in. He looked up, startled, and Kiley saw Lukas bite back a sharp, involuntary cry as the fabric caught on his elbow and jerked his arm.

"Sorry," the doctor apologized. He finished helping Lukas into his shirt, then spoke to Kiley. "Captain Michaelson, I presume? I'm Dr. Ferrill. I'll be with you shortly. If you'll just wait outside?"

Kiley barely heard the words. All her attention was on Lukas. He had turned his head toward her. She had expected pain and shock-pale skin, but she was not prepared for the huge bruise covering the left side of his forehead. Bad as it was, though, the bruise wasn't what captured her attention—it was his eyes. She looked into them and saw the man on Demarker, the one pushed so far beyond hope and the end of his resources that he no longer cared what happened to him.

"Oh no," she said under her breath, the words slipping out as involuntarily as his cry had moments before.

"Captain, if you'll wait outside?" the doctor prompted again.

She nodded, not trusting herself to speak, and went out, closing the door behind her. She sat on the seat Lia had occupied, her own head buried in her hands, and did not look up until she heard the door open.

"Come with me please, Captain," Ferrill said. He led the way to his office, a small cubicle with barely enough space for his overflowing desk. He was about the same age as Cernak, but he looked older. His hair was completely gray and his lived-in face testified to years of living life to the maximum, good times and bad. Shrewd blue eyes observed her from beneath shaggy brows. She returned his gaze stiffly, aware that he had her on the defensive, not liking the position one bit.

The doctor motioned her to a chair, then sat behind the desk with a heavy sigh. "I'm getting too old for this job," he said, the bright gleam in his eyes belying the words. "I'm sorry to keep you, Captain. I'm sure you must have many demands on your time; however, I did want to speak with you about Mr. Lukas's condition before you took him back to your ship. I take it Administrator Cernak told you what happened?"

"Yes."

"He's a lucky man, Captain. If the Crowther brothers had had time to finish what they started, he'd be dead. As it is, he has six fractured ribs, a concussion, extensive bruising from his knees up, and a severe strain to his left shoulder. He had minor internal bleeding in his spleen and kidneys, which we were able to control with microsurgery. His urine may show traces of blood for the next day or so. You don't need to be concerned about that unless the bleeding seems excessive or continues beyond the second day."

He paused, as if reviewing mental notes. "He'll probably have the most discomfort from the fractured ribs. I've bound them, but he needs to remain as quiet as possible for the next three to four days. That may not be as easy as it sounds; between the ribs and bruises, he's going to have a difficult time finding a position that's comfortable. I gave him something for the pain when he regained consciousness; the injection should last most of the evening. I'll give you some pills he can take once the shot wears off. The prescription says one every four hours, but he can have one every two to three hours for the first day, if necessary."

"He is going to be all right, though?"

"I won't deny I'd like to keep him under observation for twenty-four hours, but as long as you call me if his condition starts deteriorating, I don't think he'll be in danger. Someone should check on him every few hours throughout the night, though, just in case the concussion proves more serious than the scanners indicate, or the internal bleeding starts up again."

"We'll do that. What about taking him through jump? Doctor, we're due to leave tomorrow for Aumarleen. It will be seven days before we're back in port."

Ferrill frowned. "It would be better to wait a few days, Captain."

"We can't. If we don't leave tomorrow, we'll lose our contract."

Ferrill considered. "He's basically strong and healthy. He should be able to manage, but jump could set him back several days. The greatest danger is that he'll move during transition; if he does, the fractured bones could shift position and puncture a lung. I'll give you a sedative to make him sleep. Have him take it an hour before you jump."

"Is there anything else we need to do? Any special diet or restrictions?"

"He shouldn't have anything to eat but liquids and soft foods for a few days. I don't think you'll find that a problem—the real difficulty will be getting him to eat at all. He should have something, but don't try to make him eat an entire meal until he's ready. Other than that, the quieter he stays, the faster he'll heal. Oh, and keep the bindings on his ribs—don't let him take them off, no matter how uncomfortable he says they are. They may be, but he'll be in a great deal more pain if he takes them off. He should see another doctor as soon as you reach Aumarleen for a follow-up examination."

"Anything else?"

"As far as his physical condition is concerned, no. There is one other matter, however. Captain, is Lukas normally as withdrawn as he was when you saw him a few minutes ago?"

Kiley looked away. "He's a private person, Doctor. He keeps to himself more often than not. But no, he's not normally that withdrawn."

"Have you seen him like that before?"

"Once."

"Was he also under stress then?"

"I . . . I believe so."

"Captain, were you aware he underwent rehabilitation therapy?"

"Not until today."

"Do you know anything about the process? Anything at all?"

"Only that it's used in lieu of a prison sentence in cases where the court feels a criminal's attitudes can be modified sufficiently to insure his safe return to society."

"That's all? You don't know anything about the techniques used during therapy?"

"No."

Ferrill riffled the papers on his desk, buying time. "Captain, the practice of rehabilitation therapy is based on the theory that most criminals don't believe themselves guilty of the crimes they commit—or more precisely, they believe they had justifiable reasons for committing those crimes. They lack a sense of guilt. The therapist's goal, therefore, is to induce that sense of guilt, at a sufficiently strong level to deter further criminal acts.

"I won't go into the precise techniques used, but therapists generally rely on drugs that flatten the subject's resistance to suggestion, followed by extensive hypnotherapy sessions. In the hands of a good therapist, the process can approach an art; with a less qualified practitioner, however, the sessions can become a marathon, with the subject desperately trying to cling to his values and beliefs, and the therapist putting forth equal effort to tear them away. I've seen a few men who underwent therapy at the hands of unskilled practitioners. They accepted their guilt, but usually at the cost of their personality. They had their freedom and they continued to function, but to anyone who knew them, they appeared to be little more than shells of their former selves.''

''And you're saying that's what happened to Greg?''

Ferrill shifted uncomfortably. ''I can't be certain, Captain, but I'm suspicious. Highly suspicious. It would account for his withdrawal—and for the fact that he made no effort whatsoever to defend himself. Did you see his hands? There isn't a mark on them. The only damage the Crowthers incurred was self-inflicted. That isn't normal behavior, Captain. I don't know a man who'd stand there and take the beating Lukas did without putting up a fight, however ineffective.''

''Maybe he didn't have a chance. If one of them hit him first and stunned him, he might have been too dazed to fight back.''

''Possibly, but I think it more likely that someone stripped him of the belief that he had a right to defend himself. His therapist's goal would have been to convince him he had committed a great wrong, then to prevent him from justifying that wrong to himself. That inability to defend his acts verbally may have translated into an inability to defend himself physically, as well. I hasten to say that I can't be certain that's the case. His lack of response could have resulted from some other cause entirely. But I am suspicious. If I'm right, I'd like to know who treated him, because that man or woman should never be permitted to engage in therapy again.''

''Doctor, are you sure you aren't overreacting? You said yourself he has a mild concussion, and he must be in a considerable amount of pain. On top of that, whatever drug you gave him for pain is bound to have dulled his senses—it wouldn't have worked otherwise.''

''You saw him, Captain. Do you honestly believe I'm overreacting?''

Kiley rubbed her forehead. ''No. But I have seen him withdraw before, when he was sick. He seemed perfectly normal once he recovered.''

"Perhaps I'm wrong, then.''

"What if you aren't?'' Kiley asked. "Is there anything that could be done for him if his therapy was badly handled?''

The doctor sighed. "Maybe, but intervention could result in even greater damage. The therapist who worked with him will have set up incredibly strong blocks in his mind to prevent any attempt at altering the belief set he created—and quite rightly. Otherwise, there'd be nothing to stop Lukas from deciding what he'd done wasn't so bad after all.'' Ferrill sighed again. "On the whole, he's probably better off as he is. If he recovered from his previous withdrawal, there's every reason to believe he'll recover from this one—provided he receives the same positive reinforcement.''

"That may be a little difficult,'' Kiley said. "Doctor, we didn't know much about him before. It was enough he did his job. But to keep him on, knowing he was involved in the death of two of his men—I'm not certain we can do that.''

"I understand, Captain. I do. But I will offer one piece of advice—whoever Greg Lukas was before therapy, he's not the same man now. I'd most earnestly suggest you base your response on the man you know him to be today, not the man he was.''

Kiley rubbed her forehead again, suddenly too tired to cope with anything, not Lukas, not Jon Robert, not the ship, not even Josef Cernak's interest in her.

"Captain, are *you* all right?'' the doctor asked, sounding concerned.

"Yes. Yes, of course I am. It's just been a difficult day. Doctor, is Greg ready to leave now? I have to get back to the ship. I've been away longer than I can afford as it is.''

"He's ready. My nurse should have filled the prescription for Emanecet. I'll have her give you the sedative, then you can go.''

The doctor rose and she followed suit.

"It might be better for you to wait here while security helps Lukas out, Captain,'' he said. "No matter how careful they are, they're bound to hurt him. You may not want to be around.''

"If he can take it, so can I,'' she returned.

But she nearly couldn't.

The two guards were surprisingly competent and gentle. They helped Lukas stand, then sit again in a wheelchair, then stand and sit again once he reached the cart waiting in the corridor.

But all the painkillers and care in the world did not help when every movement, every touch was agony. He clenched his jaw and managed to hold back all sound, but his skin lost what little color it had regained by the time he was seated in the cart, and the doctor was concerned enough to run another scanner check before releasing him.

The trip onboard the ship was a repetition of the walk down the corridor. Much as Kiley hated the idea of having station security on her ship, she could never have managed Lukas alone. The men helped him undress, settled him in his bunk, then nodded politely to her and left.

"Greg, I have to go," she said, "but I'll leave the intercom on voice-activate. If you need anything, call me."

She was positive he heard, but he didn't respond. She hesitated, knowing she should say something, unable to find the heart to offer either the words of support and comfort the doctor had suggested, or the angry renunciation Lia had wanted. She rubbed her forehead again, then gave up on finding any words at all and went back to the engine room.

She found Holly there, leaning against one of the closed cabinets, her eyes closed. She lifted her head when she heard Kiley come in. Kiley took one look at her distressed face and knew she didn't have to ask if Lia had talked to her yet.

"How's Greg?" she asked.

"He'll survive. Just don't ask me if that's good news or not, because I honestly don't know. I take it Lia made it back?"

"Yes. She told Reese and me what happened. Kiley, is what she said about Greg true? Was he really court-martialed?"

"Yes."

"I can't believe it. I just can't believe it."

"I saw the documents, Holly. It's true."

"But he wouldn't do anything wrong. I know he wouldn't!"

"Maybe not now, but he did then."

"Kiley, what are we going to do about him? Lia's all for throwing him off the ship right now. She tried to convince Reese to tell you we have to leave him behind."

"What did he say?"

"That he wanted to talk to you before he made any decisions."

"Well, that's something. Maybe he can calm her down. She was almost hysterical when I saw her."

"I'm not surprised. She's spent a lot of time talking to Greg, Kiley. He's a good listener, and I think she may have told him things she hasn't even told Reese. I thought the talks were help-ing her. She's been happier and more relaxed the last month than any time since I've known her. She trusted him, Kiley, and now she's acting like he betrayed her.''

''I'm afraid that's something she'll have to work out for her-self. We have to take him with us; we don't have a choice. The station administrator has a security guard posted outside the ship to make certain he doesn't leave.''

''And after we reach Aumarleen? What then?''

''We need him—at least until Jon Robert can work again. The four of us simply can't manage the ship alone, and we don't have any money to hire a crew. He may not be much help for a while, but he's better than nothing. Once Jon Robert can use his hands again, we'll talk about letting him go. Until then, we simply don't have a choice.''

''We may need him longer than that,'' Holly said. She hesi-tated, then said bluntly, ''I'm pregnant.''

''Oh, no!'' Kiley said without thinking, and could have killed herself.

''I know,'' Holly told her, sounding as miserable as she felt. ''The whole first year we were married, we tried so hard and nothing happened. I guess we started thinking nothing would.''

''How far along are you?''

''Just over two months. Kiley, I can work quite a while, but there'll be a few months when I won't be able to do much. I'm sorry, but—''

''Oh, Holly, don't be. I'm happy for you. Really. You just caught me by surprise. We'll work something out, I promise.'' She couldn't believe Jon Robert hadn't said anything. She didn't see how he could have kept the news a secret for even a day.

''I haven't told Jon Robert yet,'' Holly said, as if reading her thoughts. ''I know this is going to sound crazy, but I'm afraid to.''

''Afraid? But why? He'll be ecstatic.''

''Until he remembers what happened to his mother.''

Enorra had suffered a miscarriage during transition, hemor-rhaged, and bled to death. She could have called out for help, but she had chosen to die instead. Lia had gone into her parents' cabin looking for her and found her lying in a pool of blood, and the memory of her death had tainted the ship for years.

''He's going to tell me I can't stay on the ship,'' Holly said. ''I know he is. Kiley, I refuse to let him force me to spend the next seven months on some horrid station, even if we could afford the expense. The *Widdon Galaxy* is my home. I don't want to leave. Promise me you'll make him let me stay. Please!''

"I'll do my best, but I can't make promises. Not about that. I think he'll come around, though, if you give him time. But you have to tell him, Holly, right away.''

"I will, once we're away from here.''

"Then we'd better get back to work, because we aren't going anywhere until those boards are installed. Holly, are you sure you feel up to this? You've already put in a long day, and—''

"I knew it—as soon as people find out you're pregnant, they start treating you like an invalid. I'm fine, I swear.''

Kiley took her at her word, but that didn't stop her from sending Holly to bed three hours later. The other woman had agreed to go, but only after eliciting a promise that Kiley would follow soon after. Kiley gave the promise freely—and broke it just as easily.

She did take a short break a few hours later to check up on Lukas. He hadn't moved. She wasn't sure he could. He was still groggy, and swallowed the pill she gave him without question. She asked if there was anything else she could do. He shook his head and continued to stare dully at the wall. She hesitated, searching for the right words, and again she could not find them. Maybe later, when they were away from port, she'd be able to think of the right thing to say. She left him in the dimly lit room, with nothing save his pain and memories to keep him company during the long night that followed.

Chapter 10

Kiley and Holly began the system checks early the next morning while Reese supervised the cargo loaders. He joined them at midmorning and they completed the tests shortly after noon.

"All sensors read green," Holly announced from the engineering control board, "including main engines."

"You're sure there's no sign of damage to them?" Kiley asked, voicing the nagging fear that had plagued them all since transition.

"As sure as I can be without taking them up to full power, and we can't do that until we're well away from the station."

Kiley looked at her watch, blinking to clear her eyes as they blurred with fatigue. "Any reason we can't leave immediately?" she asked Holly. The other woman shook her head. "Reese?" She turned to her brother-in-law.

"The cargo's loaded and I have the customs declarations. Security delivered the supplies Lia and Lukas purchased from the Crowthers last night. I put them away. I don't see why we can't go as soon as you clear our departure."

"I'll call Traffic Control, then. Why don't you two get something to eat? I'll join you as soon as I set up a departure time."

"Sounds good to me," Reese said.

"Me too," Holly agreed. "I'll just check on Jon Robert first. What about Greg? Do you want me to stop by and see how he's doing, too?"

"It might be better if Reese did—if you'd be willing, that is," she added quickly, turning to him. "He hurt too much last night to care who was bringing the bedpan, but he refused to use one this morning, even though he still couldn't get up. I don't think he'd mind so much if you . . ."

"Say no more," Reese told her, holding up his hand. "I'm no nurse, but I'll do what I can."

"He can have another pain pill if he wants one. They're in the bottle on his desk. He should try to eat something, too. You might see if he'll drink one of those milkshake mixes Jon Robert likes. I know, they taste terrible to me, too," she said when Reese made a face, "but he probably isn't going to think anything tastes good, so maybe he won't notice how bad they are."

Reese looked skeptical, but he shrugged. "I'll take a glass to him, but don't blame me if he won't drink the stuff."

"I won't. And Reese, thank you."

Traffic Control proved surprisingly cooperative and Kiley had no difficulty setting up their departure for 1400 hours. She discovered the reason for that cooperation at the end of the conversation.

"We're supposed to pass on a message to you, Captain," the controller said after reeling off their approved course and speed. "It's from Administrator Cernak. He said to tell you he eats dinner at eight o'clock. He said you'd understand what he meant." The controller obviously didn't and just as obviously would have liked to.

"Message understood, Traffic." She cut off the transmission, thinking wryly, that should be worth an hour's gossip.

She stayed on the bridge long enough to switch on the banks of monitors and sensors and see row after row of beautifully green lights. She ran another series of systems checks anyway, and couldn't find anything wrong. They'd done good work, despite Jon Robert's absence.

She stood up and went down to the galley. Lunch first, then they could leave. She had just finished making a sandwich when Reese walked in.

"How's Greg?" she asked.

"Fine, for a man one step this side of death's door. Can you believe it? That damned fool wanted me to help him get out of bed! It was all he could do to lift his head without passing out, but he wanted me to help him get up so he could go to the bathroom!"

"You didn't—"

"Of course not. He wasn't happy, but what could he do?" Reese's mouth lifted in a complacent smile. "I'm beginning to see why nurses have such a terrible reputation for being tyrants. There's a certain amount of satisfaction to be had in telling people they're going to do what you say, like it or not. But I don't have to tell you that, do I? I'll bet that's the real reason you wanted to be a captain. Come on, admit it.''

''What, and lose all the mystique associated with my position? No way.''

Reese laughed. It was the first time she'd heard that sound in days, and she'd forgotten how very good it could be.

''Luck's changing, Kiley,'' he said.

''Maybe,'' she said, more cautious than he. ''Maybe.''

''Well, we're due for a spell of good luck if anyone is. All of us—Lukas included.''

She nodded, not trusting herself to speak. She started to leave, but he put his hand on her arm, stopping her.

''Kiley, what are you taking?'' he said, all the laughter gone. ''What?''

''You heard me. You haven't slept for two days. You're taking something or you wouldn't still be on your feet. I want to know what.''

''Why? What difference does it make? I know what I'm doing.''

''What you're doing is endangering us all.''

''No! I wouldn't do that, Reese. I wouldn't! I know my limitations and I don't plan to exceed them. I'll sleep as soon as we've jumped. Seven hours, Reese. That's all I need.''

''I still want to know what you're taking. Come on, Kiley. You're not going anywhere until you tell me.''

He meant what he said. She held his gaze as long as she could, then shrugged and pulled the bottle out of her pocket.

''Here,'' she said, tossing it to him. ''Satisfied?''

He read the label, then tipped the bottle to see how many pills were left. ''You really don't intend to take any more of these once we've jumped?'' he asked.

''No.''

''Then you won't mind if I keep them,'' he said, pocketing the bottle before she could take it back.

''You don't have to do that,'' she said angrily. ''I told you I wasn't going to take any more.''

''And I believe you. Let's just say I'm removing all possibility of temptation. I didn't say anything sooner because I do trust you. But with all due respect, you've pushed yourself about as far as you can without seriously impairing your judgment. I don't want you making a decision you'll regret later—assuming there's a later to regret it. And don't act so insulted—you wouldn't have hesitated to say the same to me if our positions were reversed, would you? Well, would you?''

''No.''

''I didn't think so. Now we have that settled, how about lunch? I'm starved.''

They left Jeross, pulling out at full speed with Traffic Control's blessing. Five hours later they reached their jump coordinates. Holly called out a green board from engineering. Reese sat in the copilot's seat, solid and steady. Lia was watching Jon Robert. Reese had given him and Lukas their respective sedatives an hour earlier and both men lay in deep, motionless sleep.

Time, then.

She gave the order. The jump engines came on, and the ship seemed to pause for one timeless moment, gathering all her power into herself. Then she leaped forward, racing toward another kind of oblivion, that timeless moment of—

Between—

Twisted, body and mind turning inside out, screaming *Impossible!* No breath, no life, only an infinite, intolerable chaos of distorted senses, and then—

Through.

Falling, tumbling, engines powering down, row after row of data scrolling up the monitors, smooth, orderly symbols without a single amber highlight. Green lights on the boards. All green.

''She made it,'' Reese said from the copilot's seat. He started breathing again and his hands relaxed their grip on the arms of the chair. ''Not that I doubted her for a moment,'' he hastened to add.

''Not for a moment,'' Kiley agreed, her fingers resting against the control board an infinitesimal moment longer than necessary.

Reese leaned forward, shutting off the monitors and long-range scanners. ''Time, Kiley,'' he said when he finished, pointing to the corridor.

''I'm going.'' She had not lied when she said she knew her limits. She stopped to check on Lukas and Jon Robert. They had both come through unfazed, their breathing deep and regular. One more worry off her mind. She went to her cabin, stripped, and fell into bed with a single, continuous motion. One breath, then she, too, slept.

* * *

She woke knowing what she had to do. She called the bridge first, checking in. Reese had gone to bed, leaving Lia to monitor the controls. No matter; her sister could read a warning light as well as the rest of them and call for help. She told Kiley to take her time coming; she'd only been there an hour and would be glad to stay a full four.

Kiley showered, standing under the hot spray far longer than necessary and luxuriating in the feel of soap and water. More than anything else, she had missed the unlimited supply of water, which they'd had to ration until the repairs had been completed and the ship's recycling system was fully operational again. She washed her skin and hair twice before she finally felt clean. She ran cool water and let the chill wake her fully, then turned the stream off. Jets of warm, drying air came on. Her hair would take forever to dry, so she plaited the damp strands into a braid, then coiled it and fastened it at the back of her head.

She dressed, made up the bunk, and tossed her dirty laundry into the washer built into the bathroom, which would clean, then dry the load. Finally, unable to delay any longer, she gathered up her resolve and went to see Lukas.

He was awake.

He lay on his back, hands clenched at his sides. He glanced at the door when she came in and went even stiffer. He kept his eyes on the ceiling, refusing to look at her. She let him ignore her while she ran the scanner down his chest and legs. The bruises had taken on color in the last day, standing out blue-black against the white bandage around his ribs. They covered his chest, shoulders, arms and sides, stomach, hips, and thighs. The sight of them made her cringe, but she hid her response. The bioscanner readings were not normal, but they were within acceptable tolerances in all categories, and there was no cause for serious alarm.

"Have you had a pill since you woke up?" she asked when she'd finished.

He shook his head. She filled the glass beside his bed with water, then went to the desk, shook a pill out of the bottle, and brought it back to him.

"Here," she said.

He looked, then shook his head again. "I don't want it."

"Greg, don't be a fool. You hurt. The pill will help. They aren't addictive, if that's what you're worried about."

"No."

"Then what's the problem?"

He said something, the words too low to be understood.

"What?" she asked.

"They make me dream," he repeated, only marginally more intelligibly.

"Nightmares, you mean?"

He muttered something that might have been *yes*.

"I didn't hear that," she said, and then when he did not reply, added sharply, "Greg, answer me!"

"Yes, nightmares!" He spoke clearly and angrily that time. "I don't want any more."

"Very well," she said equitably. "I'll see if I can find something else in the medicine chest. What do you want for breakfast?"

"I'm not hungry."

"Hungry or not, you're still going to eat. What do you want? Eggs? Soup? A milkshake?"

"I don't want anything," he insisted stubbornly.

Anger wasn't going to help, she told herself. She took a deep breath, then put the pill back in the bottle and went down to the supply room. Jon Robert kept the medicine chest fully stocked with drugs for every conceivable emergency. She searched among the analgesics, reading labels until she found one whose warnings didn't sound too dire. She took the bottle to the galley, hesitated in front of the packets of dry mixes, thinking it would serve him right to get another one of the milkshakes, then took pity on him and chose a clear soup instead. She mixed the contents with water, heated the soup to lukewarm, covered the cup, and went back to his cabin.

"Here," she said, offering him the pill first.

He looked at it suspiciously. "What is it?"

"Prodacaine."

He looked at the tablet, but made no move to take it.

"Greg, if you want to get up today, you're going to have to take the pill. I'm not going to have you passing out on me the moment you stand up."

His jaw clenched. Then he grabbed the pill and swallowed it.

"You can wash it down with this," she said, holding out the soup. "Come on. You don't have to drink it all. Half will do for now."

He drank exactly half. "I want to get up."

"Very well," she agreed. "I'm afraid you'll have to make do with my help, though. Reese just went to bed and he won't be awake for hours. You still want to try?"

Reese was right—issuing ultimatums was surprisingly easy once you got the hang of being a tyrant. She thought Lukas might strangle on the anger he bit back.

"Yes," he said when he finally had himself under control again.

"You'll have to tell me what you want me to do," she said, afraid for all her bravado. She didn't see how he was going to stand alone, and if she touched him, she couldn't help but hurt him. Some of her apprehension must have come through, because he gave her an angry look.

"I don't know why you're so worried," he said. "It's going to hurt me a lot more than you."

It did, but not as much more as he thought. She helped him sit up and move his legs to the side of the bunk. Standing was the worst. His ribs prevented her from putting her arm around his side, nor could he take her hands and pull himself up on his own. She ended up with one of her arms around his waist and his arm around her shoulders. He fell back the first time he tried to stand, then gave the second effort everything he had. He made it to his feet, but had to lean against her for a full minute before he could breathe again.

"Greg—"

"I can make it," he said furiously, mouth set in a stubborn line. She flinched, then relaxed as she realized his anger was directed toward himself this time. He let her help him as far as the bathroom, then told her to leave.

"Go on!" he told her fiercely, supporting himself against the wall. "I can manage."

She left him that much pride. He called her back a few minutes later and they made the return trip. Getting back down was no less painful than getting up, but it went faster. He was perspiring heavily by then, and his breath came in shallow, wheezing gasps. She wondered if she'd been wrong to help him move, but after a moment's rest the gasps slowed down and the wheezing quieted.

"Are you going to survive?" she asked.

"Possibly," he said between breaths. "Just . . . possibly." And then, stiffly, "Kiley, I'm sorry—"

She cut him off immediately. "Let's skip the apologies, shall we, Greg? I think I've heard them all before."

"Yes, you have, haven't you?" He turned his head to the wall, the bleak look back on his face. "I'll leave as soon as we get to Aumarleen," he said. "I wouldn't have come back to the ship at all, only they didn't give me a choice. But I will go. I promise.''

"That's what you want? To leave?''

"Yes.''

"Just like that? No regrets, no sense of obligation—you'll just walk off?''

"Kiley? I don't understand . . .''

"We gave you a berth when you couldn't find one,'' she said. "We took care of you when you were sick. We even offered you a contract. And now you're talking about walking out when we need you most? Well, you'd better think again, Greg Lukas. You may have run out on your other commitments, but this is one you're going to honor.''

"What about Jeross? The Crowthers? They told security about me. I heard them. And security told you, didn't they?''

"About the court-martial, you mean? Yes, they told me. So?''

"So you don't want me on your ship. Nobody would. That's all right. I understand. I'll leave as soon as we get to port.''

"You leave and we lose the ship, Lukas? Do you hear me, Lukas? Without your help, we're going to lose the *Widdon Galaxy*. It's that simple. But then, maybe that's what you want. You lost everything of value yourself; maybe you'd like the same thing to happen to us?''

"No! Of course not!''

"Then stop talking about running out on us. Want you or not, we need you. In a few months, we'll be back on our feet and maybe, just maybe, have enough money to hire someone else on. But until we can, you're not going anywhere. Is that clear?''

"No, it isn't clear at all.''

He was afraid. Afraid to look at her for fear of what he'd see, afraid to believe they wouldn't ostracize him even though they demanded he remain onboard. His fear undid her. Withdrawal she could cope with. Anger, and even hate, she could ignore. But not fear. It did not come naturally to him, and the sight of it left a bitter taste in her mouth.

"Greg—Greg, look at me.''

He did. Afraid or not, he found the courage to do that.

"Yes, we know about your court-martial. We also know you were sentenced to rehabilitation therapy. I may be wrong, but it's my understanding that that changes a man. Whatever he was before, he is not the same after. I don't believe you would harm us in any way. Not deliberately. I'm willing to take a chance on that. We aren't going to force you to leave the ship, Greg. Not here, and not on Aumarleen. You don't have to leave unless you want to."

She waited for her words to sink in, but he just kept looking at her, disbelieving. She sighed. "Think about it, all right? If you really want to leave when we reach Aumarleen, we can't stop you. Your contract has no definite term; you can break it whenever you want. But if you want to stay, you can. It's up to you. When you've decided what you want to do, let us know."

She started to go.

"You don't even want to know what happened?" he asked in a strangled voice.

She turned around with deliberate slowness. "Yes, of course I do. Who wouldn't? But I'm not going to ask. I don't know if you can understand this, but if you tell me what happened, I want it to be because you chose to—not because you thought you had to."

He stared at her. If she'd hit him, he couldn't have looked more stunned. She sighed. "Greg, you're tired. Why don't you get some sleep? I expect things will be clearer once you're feeling better. I'll be on the bridge, if you need anything."

Kiley ate breakfast, then went forward to relieve Lia. Her sister looked better today, her fair skin no longer red and swollen from crying, her shoulders no longer slumping in fatigue. She brightened as soon as Kiley appeared. Lia had never liked the bridge—too much to go wrong, even during jump. Still, she sat her shift when she was needed without complaint.

"You didn't have to come so soon," she said. "I could have stayed longer."

Kiley shrugged. "There wasn't anything else I needed to do. I could use a break in a few hours, though, if you don't mind coming back."

She shook her head. "Give me a call when you're ready. I'll be in the garden."

She rose, offering Kiley the pilot's chair, then stood there awkwardly after Kiley sat down.

"How's Greg?" she finally asked, sounding defiant.

"Better," Kiley said. She finished scanning the board, then turned around, wondering what Lia was really asking. "He managed to get up this morning. He'll probably be able to leave his cabin tomorrow."

"You're going to let him stay, aren't you?"

"Lia—" She stopped, trying to find the right words, but they didn't come any more easily for her than they had for

Lukas. "Yes," she said at last, deciding the simplest words were the best. "I am."

"How can you? Kiley, he was responsible for the deaths of his men. They trusted him and look what happened to them. Who's to say he won't do the same to us?"

"Me. I say he won't. Nothing he's done so far has given me cause to doubt his judgment or intentions toward us. We need his help, Lia, and I'm willing to give him the benefit of the doubt unless and until he gives me cause to decide otherwise."

"You don't think a court-martial constitutes sufficient cause for doubt?"

"I think that court-martial happened a long time ago, to a different man," she said, choosing her words carefully. "Lia, try to forget what happened on Jeross for just one minute and think about the Greg Lukas we know. Can you honestly say he's given you reason to believe he'd do anything at all to harm any one of us?"

"Not deliberately, no. But he still hurt us. All of us. People know who he is now, Kiley. They know he's on our ship. It may take months before the stories start floating around, but they will. You can count on that. Who's going to trust us with him onboard? Who?"

"The same people who have trusted us all along. So what if word gets around? All the shipping agents and brokers care about is how well we meet our schedules and how low our rates are. They may not be happy we have Lukas on the crew, but they aren't going to stop doing business with us just because we do."

"Some will, and you know it."

"Maybe a few. But not the majority."

"Those few can make or break us. You don't have to tell me how precarious our situation is; I've seen how Reese worries. You're making a mistake, Kiley, and that mistake is going to cost us all."

"Well, if it does, you'll get what you always wanted, won't you? A nice stable home on some station. No more traveling, no more worrying this jump will be the one that goes wrong, no more twelve-hour shifts. I don't see why you're so upset. If we lose the ship you'll have everything you ever wanted."

"Will I? What if I was wrong about what I wanted? What if it wasn't a station after all? Reese would be miserable there, and I couldn't have my garden. It would take too much space and there isn't much space on a station, is there?"

Kiley stared at her, aghast. "Lia, am I hearing you right?

After all these years of hating the ship, you've suddenly decided she's not so bad after all? Why? What happened?''

She lifted her chin. "Who says anything happened? Maybe I changed. Then again, maybe I just figured out what I really wanted. Do I have to have a reason?''

"No, but I don't understand what made you change your mind so suddenly, unless Greg—'' She stopped abruptly.

"Unless Greg somehow convinced me to? Is that what you were going to say? As if I owe him something? Well, I don't. Oh, he listened to me talk, I have to admit that. No one else has for years, so I guess I owe him for that. But he didn't make me change my mind, and whatever I owe him, I don't think the debt extends to supporting him when he deliberately hid his past from us.''

"Nobody's asking you to support him.''

"No, but you're going to expect me to get along with him, aren't you? Like him or not, want him or not, you're going to ask that, right?''

"Yes.''

"All right. I'll try. But don't ask me to treat him like family, or even a friend, because I won't.''

"Polite is all I ask, Lia. The rest is up to you.''

Kiley turned back to the control board, thinking the conversation was over, but she was wrong.

"You're in love with him, aren't you?'' Lia asked.

Kiley's hands stopped moving. She made herself finish entering the data request, then turned around.

"Just what makes you say that?'' she said with all the cool composure she could summon.

"You wouldn't be half so eager to defend him if you didn't care about him, and it doesn't take much talent for observation to see the way you look at him when he isn't watching—or the way you freeze up when he is. And he acts the same way. Honestly, having the two of you in the same room is enough to drive a normal person crazy.''

"You're mistaken, Lia.''

"Am I? If you're so sure about that, why don't you ask Jon Robert what he thinks? Or Holly? They'll tell you the same thing. Even Reese notices the tension when the two of you are together. You care about Greg. You're just afraid to admit it.''

"No.''

" 'No' what? You don't care, or you aren't afraid to admit it? Which is it, Kiley?''

"I'm not saying I don't care about him. I do—the same as I care about everyone on this ship. We're family, Lia. All of us, including Lukas. He worked hard to earn a place on this ship. I didn't make that place for him, he made it for himself."

"But you could make it permanent—if you married him."

"Me? Marry him? Lia, the question doesn't even come up. It won't. He won't stay with us forever. He's too good to be content piloting a ship this size for long."

"Who else is going to give him a job? Especially now? He's really lucky you fell for him, isn't he? If you hadn't, he'd be leaving the ship at Aumarleen."

"That's not true."

"Isn't it? Well, you should know. But I'm warning you, Kiley, if you let love get in the way of your better judgment, you aren't the only one who's going to be hurt—we all are. Think about that the next time you start defending Greg Lukas."

She whirled around and left. Kiley made herself face the control board again and start scanning the displays. Lia might be right about some things, but she was wrong about Lukas. He didn't care about her, not the way Lia meant. He couldn't. He had lost more than rank and honor a year ago—he had lost all belief in himself as well. Empty inside, he had nothing to offer. All the love and support in the universe would not begin to fill the void in him. Nothing would, until he found a way to believe in himself again.

Jon Robert showed up on the bridge late that afternoon, his long-sleeved shirt slit at the wrists so he could pull it on over the heavy bandages covering his hands. Some of the color had returned to his face, but he looked years older. Still, he managed to produce a lopsided grin that somehow made everything right again.

"I thought the ship could use a real pilot," he said as he twisted the copilot's chair around with his elbow and sat down, "so I came along to take charge."

"With those hands?" she answered with a laugh. "You couldn't even punch the intercom to call for help."

"You're wrong there. I've found that elbows are great substitutes for fingers. Of course, you sometimes hit more than one button at a time, but what the heck—you can't have everything. No, the real problem is feeding myself, and unfortunately, I don't see any way around that one. Do you have any idea how embarrassing it is to have someone else spoon food into your mouth, even if it is your wife?"

"No, and I don't think I want to. Jon Robert, how are you feeling? Really?"

"Aside from the constant pain and frustration? Not bad. Not bad at all. Better than our friend Lukas, if even half of what I've been hearing about him is true. Sounds like you've had your share of problems while I was out of commission."

"You might say that."

"I've heard one story from Lia and another from Holly and Reese. I might as well hear yours, too. What happened, Kiley?"

She told him.

"If you're thinking you have to keep him on because of Holly and me, we can work something else out," he said when she finished. "Reese can always fill in for me in the engine room and I can help you here on the bridge. He can stand in for Holly too, when the time comes."

"She told you, then?"

"Yes."

"And?"

"And I'm the happiest person on this ship," he said with a goofy grin that told her all she needed to know.

"You're going to let her stay on the ship, aren't you? She was afraid you wouldn't."

"Yes. She convinced me that forcing her to stay on a station wouldn't be fair to her or the rest of you. But that's only if a doctor says there's no danger to her or the baby."

"She'll be fine. You're going to have to buy a tutorial on childbirth, though. Someone will have to deliver the baby if we can't get to port in time."

"You don't suppose Lia—no, I didn't think so. Well, I'll do my best, but that's one job I'm not looking forward to. Kiley, you still haven't answered my question about Lukas. You aren't keeping him on just because of us, are you?"

"No." She hesitated, not sure she dared tell even Jon Robert her true reasons. But if she couldn't trust *him* to be open and fair, who could she trust? "I'm afraid for him," she said at last. "Afraid of what will happen to him if we tell him we don't want him, either. I'm not sure he has the resources to recover from another rejection. You saw how he was after the *Hilea*'s captain left him behind; that's nothing compared to the way he'll feel if we turn on him, too."

"You're talking as if we have an obligation toward him. We don't, Kiley."

"We have one to ourselves, though. He's given us everything

he had to offer. He's worked as hard as any of us, for as little reward. I don't think I can look at myself in the mirror if we repay him by turning our backs when he needs help."

"And he does need help, doesn't he?"

"Yes."

"Kiley, we may not be the best people to offer assistance. Have you considered that?"

"If we don't, who will?"

He didn't have an answer. He looked down at his useless hands, then back at her. "You've already asked him to stay, haven't you?" he asked, his voice going flat, as if the exertion of walking to the bridge and carrying on a fifteen-minute conversation had suddenly caught up with him.

"Yes."

"Without a vote?"

"Holly and Reese both agreed with my decision. I wasn't acting unilaterally, no matter what Lia said."

"What Lia said is best left unrepeated. No offense to her, but she's about as impartial on the subject of Greg Lukas as you are. Kiley, are you sure about this? You're asking us to take a tremendous chance, gambling on him. Are you absolutely convinced he's worth the risk?"

That was what he said, but his real question was something else again: Are you prepared to take the responsibility for what happens, not just to him or the ship, but to all of us?

"Yes," she said. The word was little more than a whisper, but her voice did not waver.

"Then you have my support. I'll back you both, all the way. What do you want me to do?"

"Talk to him, Jon Robert. Just . . . talk to him. See if you can't convince him we aren't going to condemn him out of hand. I tried, but I don't think he believed me. Maybe he'll listen to you."

"You're the most persuasive person I know, Kiley Michaelson. If you couldn't convince Greg Lukas we want him, then I don't see how I possibly can. But I'll try. I will try."

Kiley stopped off to see Lukas that evening. Reese had already brought him dinner. He had told Kiley the pilot hadn't been interested in food, but had managed nearly a full meal after Reese promised to cover his bandages and let him take a shower, provided he ate first. He had worried the entire time Lukas was in the shower, but he had come through with no apparent ill-effects. His legs had started to give out toward the end, and he'd needed help getting back to bed, but Reese thought he would be up and walking around on his own by the next day.

She stopped just inside the door to his cabin, not turning on the light in case he was asleep. He lay on his back in the dimness, so quiet she started to leave. She stopped as his eyes opened and he struggled to sit up.

"Kiley?" he asked.

"Yes. I thought I'd see if you needed anything. A pill? Something to drink?"

"No. Reese already took care of all that."

"Fine. I'll see you in the morning. Good night, Greg."

"Kiley, wait."

"Yes?"

"You said you wanted to know what happened. I—I want you to know I'd tell you if I could, but I can't. The truth is, I don't remember most of it."

"You don't remember?" she said incredulously.

His mouth tightened. "The doctor who did my therapy said it was better that way. He said it was enough that I knew what I'd done, without recalling the specific details. He let me read the transcripts of the trial, but that was all."

"Greg, I don't understand. Why would he have wanted you to forget?"

He clenched his hands. "He said I reacted very strongly to my crewmen's deaths. He said he was afraid I would dwell on my guilt obsessively, and that would be just as bad as another man justifying what he'd done." He shifted restlessly, then burst out, "I wish he hadn't done that. The transcripts were just words, a story that happened to someone else, not me. I don't care what I did, I'd rather remember! If I could stand by while my men died, then I can live with the memory. I tried to tell him that, but he wouldn't listen. He said he knew what he was doing, that I had to trust him. So I did. But sometimes . . . sometimes I wish I hadn't. Kiley, was I wrong?" he asked in a rush, his voice raw with torment.

"To trust him? No, of course not," she said, not certain at all. "He must have had a reason for what he did. He must have."

"I wish I could believe that. I try to, but sometimes it's hard. It shouldn't be. I know I'm supposed to let go of the past, but I just can't seem to."

"Greg, you must," she said, certain of that if of nothing else. "You can't go on like this, doubting yourself, withdrawing from others. It isn't healthy. Whatever you did, however wrong you were, you don't have to keep on paying for the rest of your life.''

"Don't I?"

"No," she said firmly.

He looked as if he wanted to believe her, but didn't dare.

"Greg, I told you earlier we wanted you to stay on the ship because we needed you. That was true, but it wasn't the whole truth. We want you because we value you. You've done more than your share of the work since you've come onboard and you're a better pilot than I'll ever be. You won't make much money with us; we're farther from a profit than ever. But if you're willing to stay, there's a place for you here."

"Even knowing what I did?"

"Even then," she replied. "All we care about is who you are now. That may be hard to believe, but will you try? Will you at least try?"

She thought he was going to refuse, but then he closed his eyes and nodded.

"And you'll stay here, on the *Widdon Galaxy*, on the same terms as before?" she added. "We do want you, Greg. Maybe the other ships you served on didn't, but we do. Will you stay?"

A pause. Another nod.

That was the only time Lukas spoke of his past. Kiley had hoped he would relax and open up after that beginning, but he did not. If anything, he shut himself off more tightly than ever, as if their conversation had been a momentary lapse he deeply regretted. Oh, he made a determined effort to appear friendly and cooperative, but it was an effort, and the strain showed.

So did the effects of his sleepless nights. His nightmares were apparently continuing, even though he'd stopped taking the pain medication, and black smudges marred the skin under his eyes.

He had insisted on returning to work two days after their conversation. Kiley knew his pride well enough by then to let him stay an hour. She didn't have to urge him to leave when she returned to the bridge; by then it was all he could do to stand. He lasted longer the next day, and longer still the day after that, but the sleepless nights took their toll, and his recovery took longer than any of them had expected.

They completed the trip to Aumarleen, then looped out to Larabee and worked their way back to Aumarleen again, arriving two weeks later. They cleared customs, unloaded the cargo holds, and collected their fees. Reese already had a line on a shipment of manufacturing equipment destined for Siddorn, one of the new ports they had started visiting, and he called back after an hour in port to confirm the contract.

An hour after that, Kiley received a call from the dockmaster's office, requesting her immediate appearance.

PART TWO

Alien Touch

Chapter 11

Kiley Michaelson wasn't what he expected.

That was Daniel Keenan's first thought as Dockmaster Simon Tyrell ushered her into the private conference room he had agreed to let Keenan use. Her file held one picture, taken when she applied for admission to the Academy, but eight years had passed since then and she had changed considerably.

Her dark hair had grown longer, and she wore it in a neatly braided coil at the back of her head instead of loose upon her shoulders. She had lost weight, and her face no longer had the rounded fullness of youth. Her eyes held a wariness that had been absent eight years before, suggesting that the intervening period had not been entirely kind. Dark shadows under her eyes hinted at long-standing fatigue, and he wondered just how bad conditions in the *Widdon Galaxy* were. They hadn't been able to learn much about the family, except that Jon Michaelson had died two months earlier and his children were struggling to retain possession of the ship. Judging by her appearance, the battle had not been easy.

"Captain Michaelson, this is Daniel Keenan," Tyrell said. "As I told you, he asked me to arrange this meeting. I'll leave the two of you to discuss your business." He stepped back into the corridor and the door closed with quiet finality.

Keenan stood and rounded the conference table.

"Come in, Captain Michaelson," he said warmly. "Have a seat." He pulled out a chair at the table for her, but she remained where she was, looking him over warily.

He waited while she took in his dark, curly hair, blue eyes, freckled nose, and the stocky frame that required frequent exercise to remain within acceptable weight bounds. He found himself wondering what she made of him, and his estimation of her went up a notch. Omanu had been right. She would require careful handling.

"I want to know who you are and what this is all about," she said, making no effort to conceal her hostility.

"Of course," he replied easily. He took out his identification card and handed it to her.

She didn't miss the significance of the silver color. Her eyes widened momentarily, then her expression went utterly blank as she read the words engraved on the card: *Keenan, Daniel J., Captain, Consolidated Alliance of Planets Space Corps. SN 6417-112-41238.*

"You aren't in uniform, Captain," she said, looking at his casual blue sweater and pants. "Is this supposed to be some sort of unofficial visit?"

"Not exactly."

"Then what *exactly* is it?" She handed his card back.

He hadn't expected the meeting to go entirely his way, but her hostility surprised him. What now? Try to talk his way around her ill-humor, or hit her hard and fast with as many facts as he was able to reveal? He took one look at those direct eyes and gave a mental sigh. All the charm he possessed wasn't going to sway her; either he gave her the facts, or he could forget about winning her cooperation.

"I'm here about Greg Lukas," he said, and watched her stiffen. "I understand he's been working aboard your ship the last few months. Is that correct?"

"Yes."

"Did you know he'd been in the service, Captain?"

"Yes."

"Do you know why he left?"

"I take it you're referring to his court-martial?" she asked coolly.

"Yes." Keenan hesitated. "Captain, Greg and I were friends at the Academy. Good friends. I can understand your reluctance to talk about him with a stranger, but I assure you, I mean him no harm. On the contrary, I believe I may be able to help him."

"Help him? How?"

"I'll tell you, but won't you please sit down first? What I have to say may take some time; we might as well be comfortable."

She held still so long he thought he'd lost her, but then she moved abruptly, sitting in the chair he had pulled out earlier without once taking her eyes off him.

He sat down across from her, his hands on the table where

she could see them, open and relaxed. One hurdle jumped. He studied her a moment, decided once again she'd balk if he offered anything but complete honesty, and plunged in.

"Captain, I'm here because a few questions have arisen concerning Greg's court-martial. The exact nature and source of those questions is classified, but they were sufficiently disturbing to warrant an investigation. My superiors were naturally concerned that he'd be reluctant to discuss events he's spent the past year trying to forget, so they asked me to see him. They thought he'd be more comfortable talking to an old friend than an officer he'd never met."

"I don't see what I have to do with all this. You should be talking to Greg, not me."

"I asked the dockmaster to arrange a meeting with you because I don't believe he *will* talk to me—not until I'm able to convince him a new inquiry is in his best interests. That may not be easy. I'm hoping you can help me."

"And how am I supposed to do that—short of tying him to a chair and forcing him to listen, that is?"

"You're his commanding officer. Presumably you have some influence over him. I was hoping he'd cooperate if you asked him to."

"You mean, if I order him to," Kiley corrected.

"If that's what it takes, yes."

"Captain, I wouldn't agree to do that, and even if I would, it wouldn't help. Greg doesn't remember anything about the trip or his court-martial. You can ask all the questions you want, but you aren't going to get answers."

"Is that what he told you? That he doesn't remember?" He must have sounded incredulous, for her eyes flashed, bright with anger.

"Are you insinuating he's lying?" she asked, a dangerous stillness to her voice.

"Captain, a man doesn't forget a court-martial. He may want to, but I can assure you, he doesn't."

"And I'm telling you he did."

Keenan almost stood then and walked out of the room, ready to tell Omanu just what he could do with this assignment. Lukas remembered, all right—he just didn't want to admit it. But something in her expression stopped him. She honestly believed what she'd said, and she didn't look gullible. The Greg Lukas he'd known at the Academy could never have lied convincingly enough to take her in—he just didn't have the practice. Lukas might have refused to answer questions—he'd done that frequently when their conversations ran to topics he could not, or would not, discuss. But lie? He'd no more have done that than disobey orders.

And yet he had. He had taken his ship into a restricted zone. Or had he?

Wasn't that why he was there—because someone, somewhere had started to ask those same questions?

"Captain, are you certain he truly has no memory of the court-martial?" Keenan asked. "That he isn't just trying to avoid talking about it?"

"Yes." She replied with such conviction that he found himself believing her. "Greg says he doesn't remember anything about the trip. All he knows is what he read in the trial transcripts." She stopped, then said diffidently, "The therapist who did his rehabilitation said that was best."

"His therapist said *what*?" Keenan demanded, so shocked he forgot himself momentarily.

"Greg said the doctor told him he had reacted very strongly to what he'd done and that carrying around that much guilt would be as bad as feeling too little." She hesitated, on the brink of saying something more, but held back, almost as if she was afraid of putting her thought into words. Then uneasiness won out. "That isn't right, is it?" she asked suddenly, appealing to him. "It didn't sound right to me. And Greg . . . Greg doesn't understand his reasons either. But how can he doubt what he was told? The doctor had to know what he was doing, didn't he?"

Keenan's breath caught in his chest. Didn't he, indeed?

"Captain, a therapist would undoubtedly attempt to alter Greg's perception of the past," he said, very carefully. "But he would not do anything to block his memory. That would defeat the entire purpose of rehabilitation therapy."

"Well, Greg doesn't remember. I know you think he's lying, but he isn't. I'd swear he isn't."

"I believe you," he said, and to his amazement, he did. She started to say something more and paused. "Captain?" he prompted.

He saw reticence battling with disquiet in Kiley's face. Disquiet won. "If his doctor had done something . . . wrong, would that have been enough to make Greg lose confidence in himself, or be unable to respond to a physical threat, or have repeated nightmares?"

The moment froze. He had had similar experiences before, when the universe itself seemed to stop, then start again, though somehow different, slightly skewed. You adjusted to the shift—indeed, forgot it had happened—but everything around you had changed subtly nonetheless.

He reached inside himself for all the emotional calm of his profession. "I take it these aren't hypothetical questions?"

Again the battle, then the reply. "No."

"Captain, I don't know why Greg's doctor told him he should forget what happened, but you're correct—that wasn't right. And yes, it could result in the kinds of problems you've described." A deep breath. Calm. "You're worried about him, aren't you?"

She hesitated. Nodded.

"If what you're telling me is true, you should be. He needs help. Professional help."

"He won't see a doctor. Both my brother and I have tried to talk him into going to one, but he wouldn't even consider the idea. I think he's afraid a doctor will tell him there really is something wrong with him. That doesn't make sense, does it? That he thinks something's wrong, but he's afraid to find out he's right?"

"Oh, it makes sense," Keenan said. He paused, wondering if he was about to make a mistake, then decided to take the chance. "Captain, if I told you I've had psychiatric training, that I might be able to help Greg, would you be willing to arrange that meeting with him? On your ship, in familiar surroundings where he'd be comfortable? If I can talk to him, I think I can persuade him to accept the help he needs."

"From you?"

"Yes."

"Why? So you can ask him questions about his court-martial?"

"In part. But that's not the only reason. He was my friend, Captain. If he's in trouble, I want to help him."

"If you were such friends, where have you been the past year?" she demanded bitterly. "Or did you think he was guilty, like everyone else?"

"I didn't know about his trial until two weeks ago," Keenan returned evenly. "If I had, I'd have made an effort to see him, guilty or not."

"Would you?"

"Yes, I would," he said firmly. "I admit, there are questions I want to ask him, but I'm concerned about him, too. I wouldn't be much credit to my profession if I weren't.'' He hesitated, then went for broke. ''We aren't just talking about Greg's good name now, are we, Captain? We're talking about his life. That's what really has you worried, isn't it? Not that he has nightmares, or seems frightened or indecisive, but that he may actually reach the point where he finds life unendurable?''

Another gamble, but not as great as the last one. It was the most logical explanation for the depth of her apprehension and the way she was trying to hide that fear from both of them.

She closed her eyes. He waited patiently and was rewarded when she said, ''Do you really think you can help him?''

''Yes.''

''When do you want to see him?''

''This afternoon. Say thirteen hundred hours?''

''You'll come to the ship?'' she asked.

''Yes.''

''We'll be there.''

Keenan remained seated after she left. The door opened again.

''That's one worried captain,'' his superior officer said. He came into the room and sat in the chair Kiley had just vacated. On the short side, Hal Omanu had a round, cherubic face and the single-minded determination of a marathon runner. He looked out of place in civilian clothes, but he'd been the one who'd insisted on them. No sense calling attention to themselves unnecessarily, he had said. You never knew who might be watching. Or when. His black eyes searched Keenan's, seeking his reaction to the woman he'd just interviewed.

''Worried is a mild description,'' Keenan said.

''Sounds to me like she has cause for concern. Lukas must be walking a fine line between sanity and total personality disintegration if her tension is anything to go by.''

''I wouldn't go so far as to say that.''

''No, you wouldn't—but I'll bet you agree. No wonder Renard's nursing assistant filed a request to have the case reviewed after he left Zerron Base. Whatever Renard did during those treatment sessions apparently didn't have much to do with rehabilitation. Could he really have made Lukas forget the trip to Gynos Three?''

''Given his assistant's report on the quantity of drugs he used and the excessive length of the treatment sessions, it's possible. Extremely difficult, and decidedly dangerous, but possible.

Omanu, if he did that, he must have been told to. He wouldn't have had a reason to otherwise.''

"Lukas kept insisting that Admiral Sorseli ordered him to take Lyle Gordon to Gynos, but no one believed him. The admiral ordered him to take a civilian into a restricted zone? And verbal orders at that, with no one to witness them? A five-year-old could have come up with a better story. Maybe that's what made me wonder about Lukas's guilt in the first place. He didn't lack intelligence or perception. He had to know that no one would believe such a story, but he kept repeating it, over and over. He was so convincing, his counsel actually started to think he might be telling the truth, but there wasn't much he could do. It was the admiral's word against Lukas's. Still, he might have raised some difficult questions if Lukas hadn't behaved so erratically.''

"But he did."

"Yes."

Keenan sighed. "Something happened to Greg on Gynos—that much is certain. But even if we assume he was telling the truth about being ordered there, I still don't see why Sorseli wanted him to make the trip. What could possibly have been so valuable on that planet that Sorseli would risk his entire career—maybe even his life—to obtain it?''

"He may not have thought the risk was all that great," Omanu countered. "Sorseli was the quadrant commander, after all. He probably thought he could keep the trip a secret. And if he couldn't—well, it would have been Sorseli's word that he didn't order the *Kelsoe Moran* to Gynos against Lukas's claim that he did. Given the admiral's spotless reputation, and the fact Lukas's credit card showed a recent substantial deposit, there wasn't much doubt who a court would believe.''

"That still doesn't explain what Sorseli was after.''

"Whatever it was probably had something to do with the reason Gynos was declared a restricted zone in the first place. I've been trying to find out what lay behind the ban, but I've run into clearance problems. Even Admiral Quiller is having trouble getting answers. I have no doubt he'll succeed, but it may take time.''

"There's one person who knows what was on Gynos," Keenan pointed out.

"Greg Lukas?''

"Yes. He and the two crewmen who accompanied Gordon to

the planet may have discovered what Gordon was after and become alarmed.''

"That could account for the confrontation during which Gordon and the crewmen were killed," Omanu agreed. "Stuart McLaren, Lukas's first officer, came up with a similar theory after he landed on the planet and found the three dead men. The only difference was, he assumed it was the two crewmen who realized Lukas and Gordon were engaged in an illegal act. He said Lukas must have conspired with Gordon; otherwise, Lukas never would have agreed to take his ship into a restricted zone. McLaren must have hated Lukas to jump to that conclusion so readily.''

"It's no secret the two didn't get along," Keenan said. "I'm not surprised. From what I saw in his records, McLaren was one spoiled brat. He should never have been admitted to the Academy, let alone advanced to first officer's rank. Greg tried to work with him, but McLaren refused to believe his attitude or performance had room for improvement. He was furious when Lukas gave him a negative fitness review and told him he couldn't possibly recommend him for promotion.''

"Lukas's second officer, Lieutenant Sharon Gyles, said the men were barely on speaking terms after that," Omanu said. "McLaren requested an immediate transfer, and Lukas approved the request, but the reassignment hadn't come through when the *Kelsoe Moran* left for Gynos. McLaren may have seized the opportunity to discredit Lukas when he found him outside the shuttle on Gynos, so dazed nothing he said made sense. Lukas didn't help matters by throwing himself in front of the shore party when they tried to board his shuttle. They had to forcibly restrain him before they could enter.''

"They thought they understood the reason for his behavior after they found the three bodies inside.''

"Yes. McLaren said it was clear Lukas had suffered some sort of breakdown. He claimed the only possible causes were guilt over his men's deaths, or fear of being arrested and tried once the ship returned to base and Sorseli found out about the illegal trip. With Lukas behaving so irrationally, the shore party was quick to buy McLaren's hypothesis. They spread it to the rest of the crew as soon as they returned to the ship.''

"Gyles was the only person who consistently refused to believe Lukas was guilty," Keenan said.

"Yes, but there wasn't much she could do. McLaren was the ranking officer and he wouldn't let her speak to Lukas. He wouldn't even let the ship's medic examine him, despite the fact he was clearly not well. Sorseli couldn't have been luckier.''

"It may not have been luck—not if he knew about the negative fitness report and the tension between the two men. He may even have blocked McLaren's transfer. If you had to send a ship out on a dubious mission, what better choice could you make than one whose captain and first officer were barely on speaking terms? Even if Lukas had questioned Sorseli's orders, he would never have shared his doubts with McLaren.''

"Which left Sorseli with only one real risk—that Lukas would claim he was innocent and demand a drug-assisted interrogation to prove he was telling the truth.''

"He did, too,'' Keenan said. "Unfortunately for him, he panicked when they started to give him the drug. They tried to continue anyway and he went completely berserk. They had to call off the interrogation. If anyone had any doubts about his guilt before, they didn't then. Even his own counsel decided he must be lying.''

"Sorseli may have set Lukas up, but he convicted himself,'' Omanu agreed. "The admiral was quick to pick up on McLaren's theory that Lukas had suffered a breakdown, but he said it resulted from an inability to handle the stress of command. Sorseli said pressure must have been building on Lukas for some time, but gone undetected. He took personal responsibility for failing to notice what was happening. He must have been laughing the entire time he testified at Lukas's sentencing, acting the part of the concerned commanding officer and recommending the court show leniency by ordering rehabilitation therapy—all the while knowing his own man would act as therapist. Still, he was taking a terrible risk. I can't believe he was willing to let Lukas go free afterwards.''

"What did he have to fear? No one believed Greg in court. With his memory blocked, he was no threat to Sorseli at all.''

"He will be if—no, when—he recalls what happened,'' Omanu said. His gaze sharpened. "Quite the concerned physician, weren't you, Daniel, talking about helping your friend? I hate to act like the heavy-handed superior, but you sounded suspiciously close to forgetting the mission in favor of the man for a minute there. In case you need reminding, you're here as a Section Two's senior interrogator, not Greg Lukas's personal psychiatrist.''

"The two aren't mutually exclusive roles, Omanu. You won't learn anything from Greg unless I can repair the damage Renard apparently did. That may not be easy. Renard had all the time and drugs he needed to break down his resistance. Once he did, he undoubtedly tied his blocks to Greg's most irrational fears and painful memories. Breaking past those blocks will be extremely difficult and the process will jeopardize whatever mental and emotional stability Greg has left.''

''But you can do it.''

''Only if Greg gives me his complete trust. Even then, he'll fight me—Renard will have done his best to make sure of that. If Captain Michaelson's assessment is correct, Greg's already unstable. If I push him too far, too fast, he could lose his sanity.''

''We need his testimony. If we're right—if Sorseli did order him to Gynos—the case must be reopened. Admiral Quiller says Sorseli has all but one of the votes he needs to be named director of the Corps when Vladic retires next year. He's apparently been working hard at convincing the Board of Governors he's the best choice—new blood, new ideas, and all that.

''Quiller didn't think he was anything to worry about at first. He was certain the rest of the Board would see Sorseli was more interested in furthering his own career than the Corps, but Sorseli's campaign seems to have reached almost everyone, including several of the other admirals. He has strong support from several civilian Board members whose governments have been strongly hinting it's time for the Consolidated Alliance of Planets to start meaning just that. They've been talking about setting up an interplanetary government, and they want their own worlds to play substantial roles in running the resulting bureaucracy. They think they've found the Corps supporter they need in Sorseli.

''That's bad news. He's always been more interested in military action than exploration and reconnaissance. He's on record as saying the Corps should take a more positive role in regulating affairs on repressive or anarchic planets. The only problem is, who decides what's repressive or anarchic? Sorseli? The new bureaucracy the civilians would like to set up? Admiral Quiller doesn't like the direction Sorseli and his supporters would take us, and neither do I. I don't think that's the Corps you signed on for, either.''

''No. No, it isn't,'' said Keenan glumly.

''Admiral Quiller thinks the Corps could remain neutral with any of the other admirals as director. Unfortunately, he's in a difficult position. He can't oppose Sorseli directly. He insists the head of Section Two has to remain above Board politics, even if that means standing by while Sorseli is named director. Right now, it looks like the only person who can stop Sorseli is Greg Lukas. If he knows anything, anything at all, that might discredit the admiral, let alone implicate him in a criminal matter, we have to find out. I don't care what you have to do to remove those blocks, Daniel. I want them down.''

"I'll do my best, Omanu, but I'll need time.''

"How much? A week?''

"At least. Maybe more.''

"That means we'll have to hold him here.''

"No! We won't win his cooperation if we start by locking him up,'' Keenan objected.

"Then where?''

"I'd prefer to work with him on the *Widdon Galaxy*. He'll be more relaxed and receptive to treatment if he's in familiar surroundings.''

"The Michaelsons aren't going to like sitting in port a week,'' Omanu pointed out.

"That wasn't quite what I had in mind. I doubt they can afford to be tied up here even that short a time, not if what we've learned about their financial status is true. No, I was thinking more about accompanying them to their next destination.''

Omanu shook his head. "Captain Michaelson will never agree to that, particularly once she realizes what you'll need to do to Lukas. He won't be able to work while you have him pumped full of drugs; she won't take kindly to that. Then too, there's the risk he'll become violent, no matter how carefully you handle him. In fact, violence is a distinct possibility if you're right about the blocks Renard set up. She'd be crazy to endanger her ship or crew. You're deceiving yourself if you think she will.''

"No, I'm not. She cares about Lukas, Omanu. Maybe you missed that, but she cares deeply. I think I can convince her to let me go with them. As for losing Lukas's services, they'll do that anyway, whether he's here or on the ship. And if we do try to hold him here against his will, I'd be willing to wager she'll raise hell with the station administrator. If she does, you'll get the publicity you're so intent on avoiding. It's in all our best interests for me to work on the *Widdon Galaxy*. Besides, if there's the least chance Greg is in danger, a moving target will be harder to hit than a sitting one.''

"So you are worried about the admiral.''

"No more than you—or was your insistence on civilian clothes and secret meetings a sudden descent into paranoia?"

"I was merely being cautious."

"Then stay that way. Leave Lukas on his ship. I can handle Kiley Michaelson. She won't be a problem."

"Very well, go with them—if you can. Let me know their itinerary and I'll meet you at their next port of call." Omanu stood and went to the door. He paused. "I'm trusting you on this, Daniel. You've earned that trust in the past, so I'll stand by your recommendations about Lukas as long as you're making progress with him. If that progress stops, though, I'll have to step in and order you to do things my way. Oh, and Daniel, one last piece of advice: Don't get so involved with Lukas you forget to watch your own back. It's a fair bet someone else may be."

Kiley Michaelson was waiting for Keenan on the dock in front of the *Widdon Galaxy*. He was prepared to hear her say she'd had second thoughts about arranging the meeting, but she remained resolute.

And tense. And worried.

Keenan glanced at her as they walked through the access tube leading to the ship, more than a little concerned. Either Lukas was in worse shape than he suspected, or the captain had other, equally pressing problems. He wondered how long she'd been under such strain—and how much longer she could go on coping before she started suffering psychological problems of her own.

"This way, Captain Keenan," she said, taking him down the ship's main corridor. "Greg's in the common room with my brother, Jon Robert. You said you wanted to see him someplace where he felt comfortable, and that seemed as good a place as any."

She stopped in front of a door on the left side of the corridor, glanced at him, took a breath, and opened the door. Lukas was sitting on the edge of a chair, his back to them. A tall, broad-shouldered blond man sat on the couch in front of him. His hands lay on his legs, wrapped in bandages. A plate of food rested on Lukas's lap, and he was holding a glass to the other man's mouth, helping him drink. He poured too fast and some of the water spilled on the man's shirt. They both began to laugh—so quickly and freely that Keenan guessed this wasn't the first miscalculation of the meal.

As the door opened, the blond man looked up and saw Kiley and Keenan, and his laughter died. Lukas swung around. Keenan had anticipated a negative reaction, but not complete shock. Lukas's smile vanished, and what remained on his face came close to terror. He put the glass down on the table beside him, but he forgot the plate of food. It slid to the floor as he stood, landing upside down.

"Kiley, what—" he began. Then the moment of shock passed and was replaced by a flash of anger that brought all the color back to his face and more. "What are you doing here?" he demanded of Keenan.

"I came to see you, Greg. I'd like to talk to you."

"Well, I don't want to talk to you. What's more, I don't have to. I'm not in the Corps now." He started for the door, but they were in his way. He stopped, trapped.

"Greg, Captain Keenan only wants to talk," Kiley said reasonably, taking a step into the room. She placed herself between the two men, whether by instinct or design Keenan couldn't be certain. He could be certain of the change in her voice, though. She spoke quietly and reassuringly, but her words carried a note of command as well.

"Is that what he told you? That he just wants to talk? He lied. Kiley, he works for Section Two. He's an interrogator—the person they call in to make a man talk when he won't say anything voluntarily. It doesn't matter if the man being questioned is a member of the Corps or a raider. If someone wants to know something from him, they call in Section Two."

"Greg, he isn't going to force you to say or do anything you don't want to. You have my word on that."

"You're right, he isn't going to—because I'm not giving him the chance. I don't know what you want, Keenan, but I'm not cooperating and you can't force me to."

"Before you go jumping to conclusions about what I want, you might at least hear me out," Keenan said, deciding the time had come to show a little determination of his own. "Section Two works *for* men as well as against them. I'm here because some questions have arisen about your court-martial, questions that could mean reopening the case."

"I don't care what you've heard, or what you think you've heard, the matter's closed. I don't want anything to do with you or the Corps. Not ever again!"

"If it's over for you, why are you still having nightmares?" Keenan asked quietly.

"Who told you—" Lukas stopped and stared at Kiley. Keenan had seen men comprehending betrayal before, but never with such staggering pain. "You told him that?" he said to her, the force of his reaction hitting her like a physical blow. "What else did you tell him? What!"

"Nothing," she said, her face white as Lukas's.

"I hope not, because anything you said, he'll use against me. Or he would, if he had the chance. But he isn't going to. Do you hear me, Keenan—I'm not giving you the chance!"

"The only person you aren't giving a chance is yourself," Keenan said sharply. "Greg, you were the best friend I had at the Academy. Do you honestly believe I'd ever do anything to hurt you?"

"People change."

"They don't change that much."

"No? Some would say I did."

"Would they be right?" Keenan countered.

"I won't answer that. I know all about your tricks to get a man talking, Keenan. I won't play along. I don't have to talk to you, and I won't."

"Greg, do you really want me to leave you alone? Go away and forget everything?"

"Yes!"

"Okay, I will. But before I do, I want to ask you two questions. Only two. If you still want me to leave afterwards, I will. I'll even give you my word that no one else will come back in my place. Just answer the questions first."

"And if I don't agree? What happens then?"

"I'll have you detained. I'll still ask my questions, Greg, but in a time and place of my choosing—not yours."

"You can't do that," Jon Robert said. He had remained silent until then, but now he rose and went to stand beside Lukas. "You can't detain a civilian. You don't have the authority."

"I do. What's more, the station administrator will back me up. You can hire every lawyer on Aumarleen, but if I claim he's being held for reasons of military security they won't be able to order his release for a minimum of forty-eight hours. That should be more than enough time to ask all the questions I want."

"You can say that and call yourself his friend?" Jon Robert demanded heatedly. "I don't know what code of honor you live by, Keenan, but it must be pretty twisted."

"You're wasting your breath," Lukas told him, not taking his eyes off Keenan. "There's no sense arguing with the military— I learned that a long time ago. You have two questions? Fine.

Go ahead and ask them. But I will only answer two. After that, you're leaving.''

"Greg, if you still want me to go by then, I will. You have my word.''

"For what it's worth. Go on, Keenan, what's the first question?''

"What did the court find you guilty of doing? The specific acts?''

Lukas flushed. "Why do you want to know that?'' he demanded. "You've obviously seen my records. You know the answer.''

"I want to hear the verdict in your own words. Come on, Greg, what did the court find you guilty of doing?''

Lukas clenched his jaw. He looked at Jon Robert and Kiley, as if appealing for help. When it did not come, he turned back to Keenan and said in clipped, precise words, "I took an unauthorized civilian on a military ship into a restricted zone, in return for fifty thousand credits. I accompanied that civilian to Gynos Three with the intention of removing proscribed materials. I stood by while that civilian killed two crewmen who accompanied us to the planet. Is that close enough?''

"Yes. Now, for my other question: Did you do it?''

"Of course I did,'' Lukas returned heatedly. "They found me guilty, didn't they?''

"I'm not asking what the court decided—I want to know what *you* say. Did you accept money from that civilian? Did you take him to Gynos Three? Did you stand by while he killed your crewmen? Answer me, Greg. And this time, tell me what you believe inside yourself, not what the court said. Come on, Greg. Did you do those things or not?''

"I—'' He started to say "did'' and stopped. Tried again, and still could not. Looking from Kiley to Jon Robert for help, he received none. They were watching him as intently as Keenan. Waiting for him to answer.

Keenan was saying something, but he didn't hear the words. Before he knew what was happening, the officer had crossed the room with swift strides and taken him by the shoulders, as if about to shake a response out of him.

"Greg, answer me!'' he said. "You shouldn't need this long to give me an answer. Yes or no—did you take your ship into a restricted zone against orders? Did you stand by while your men were killed? Did you?''

Yes! his mind shouted. *Yes!* But he could not say the words.

He tried, but they wouldn't come. He wanted to tear himself away from Keenan, but he couldn't seem to make his feet move. He thought he was going to be sick or pass out—he wasn't sure which. His knees started to give way, and Keenan grabbed him, wrapping an arm around his chest.

"No!" Jon Robert shouted from behind them, but it was too late.

Keenan's arm closed around his side, hard, and Lukas cried out involuntarily. Keenan let go immediately and then Lukas did fall. His knees hit the floor, then his hands. He stayed there, not moving, trying to breathe past the pain, trying not to throw up.

"What the . . ." Keenan recovered from his momentary shock and dropped down beside Lukas. He pulled his shirt open, saw the bandages and fading bruises, started to swear, then cut himself off. He knelt there silently, hands on Lukas's shoulders, supporting him. His grip was warm and strong, and well remembered. Keenan had held him the same way one other time, when Lukas had taken an unintentional blow during unarmed combat training.

Funny how much better Keenan had been at those lessons, Lukas thought. It was the sole class in which his performance had exceeded Lukas's. Practice, he'd said. His mother had taught martial arts and he'd been taking lessons since his fifth birthday. Keenan had never intended to hurt him, never would have, only Lukas kept trying to take him by surprise, to make the unexpected move, to best him. He'd made an unexpected move all right, and had wound up planting himself right in front of a kick Keenan hadn't had time to pull.

"What happened to him?" he heard Keenan demanding of Kiley. He didn't know about Jeross, then. Maybe she really hadn't told him everything. She was talking now, though, answering all his questions. She was upset. He had learned her voice well; the cool precision didn't deceive him. There was anger there, anger over what the Crowthers had done to him and anger directed toward herself, as if his pain were somehow her fault. He couldn't understand that. The only fault was his. She had nothing to blame herself for. Nothing.

He tried to push himself up. He couldn't stay here on the floor. He had to sit up and let them know he wasn't hurt. But when he moved, Keenan's grip tightened, holding him in place.

"Let me talk to him," the officer said to Kiley and Jon Robert. "Alone."

They looked at each other. Lukas could see their indecision, their desire to protect him. They would not desert him. Not if he needed them. Their stand was both unexpected and frightening. He had done nothing to deserve that show of loyalty, yet they offered it.

"Only if that's what Greg wants," Kiley said.

"Will you ask them to leave, Greg?" Keenan asked, his voice pitched low, for Lukas's ears alone. "I don't think you want them to hear what I have to say. Please?"

He didn't want to, but in the end that seemed easier than an argument.

"Go on," he told Kiley.

She hesitated, obviously reluctant. She and Jon Robert finally left, but not without unhappy, backward glances. Keenan waited until the door closed behind them, then helped Lukas sit back and gave him a long, searching look.

He'd forgotten how blue his friend's eyes were, and how much compassion, kindliness, and concern they could express.

"Greg, I don't want you to say anything," Keenan told him. "Just listen. I didn't ask those questions to embarrass you in front of your friends, or to make you remember something you'd prefer to forget. I asked them because I had to know if you really believed yourself guilty. And you don't. You don't because you weren't! Do you hear me? Whatever the court said, whatever Renard told you, *you were not guilty!* Part of you may believe you were, because that's what Renard wanted you to think, but another, equally strong part doesn't. That conflict is tearing you apart. You're hurting, Greg. You're confused and afraid. You can't go on like this. You can't!"

"There's nothing wrong with me."

"Denying the problem will only make it worse. No matter how much you want to put the unpleasantness behind you, it won't go away—not until you remember what happened. I won't lie to you, Greg. Bringing your memories back won't be easy, but we have to try. It's important, and not just to you. If you're innocent, then someone else must be guilty. That someone must be caught and punished. I know I'm asking a lot of you, Greg, but I promise, once we're done, all the pain, all the conflict will end."

"It won't end if I did what they say. It will be worse."

"What could be worse than the hell you're living in now? Greg, you were a fine officer and a better friend. I wasn't sure about your innocence at first; I admit that. But I am now, and I want you to be certain, too. Please, let me help you."

Lukas wanted to say no, but the word wouldn't come. He was tired. Tired of fighting, tired of trying to go on when all he wanted was to let go and sleep forever.

But when he slept, the nightmares came.

There was no way out, none.

Except for Keenan.

Keenan, who had been his best friend, who knew all there was to know about him, good and bad, and still believed in him. Keenan, who was offering him a chance to believe in himself again. He had to take the chance. If he didn't, what would be the point of going on?

"Greg, will you trust me? Will you let me help you?" Keenan asked, judging the moment right.

"Yes," he whispered.

Chapter 12

While Kiley and Jon Robert waited in the corridor outside the common room, she told him about her meeting with Keenan earlier that morning. Kiley expected him to be angry that she had acted without consulting the family, but he didn't protest. She decided he was too worried about what was going on behind the closed door to question her decision.

The minutes stretched out . . . one, two, five. She didn't like waiting and found herself pacing up and down, trying to release pent-up tension with action. Jon Robert just stood there, eyes on the door. She glanced at him once or twice, but his apprehension offered no reassurance.

The door opened.

She had a brief glimpse of Greg, sitting in one of the chairs, his head in his hands; then Keenan blocked her view of the room. He came into the corridor and the door shut behind him. Jon Robert started to go to Lukas, but Keenan held up his hand, stopping him.

"Don't go in," he said. "Not yet. I think Greg would like a few minutes alone first."

"What did you say to him, Keenan? What did you do?" Jon Robert demanded.

"We talked," the other man replied calmly. "That's all. Just talked." He turned to Kiley. "Captain, I told you this morning that doubts had been raised about Greg's guilt. I can't say more than that, but I can tell you that I'm convinced a further investigation is warranted after talking to him."

"Which means?"

"There are questions I have to ask him. That will be the next step."

"But he doesn't remember what happened."

"Because his memory has been blocked. With a little assistance, however, he may be able to recall what happened."

"Just what kind of 'assistance' are we talking about, Keenan?" Jon Robert demanded. "The kind an interrogator would use? Drugs? Hypnosis? That kind?"

"If I deem them necessary, yes. Those methods aren't just used by interrogators, Mr. Michaelson—they're standard treatment methods used by every practicing psychiatrist I know. If someone has tampered with Greg's mind or memory, they may be the only way to break past the blocks that have been erected."

"Does he know what you'll be doing?" Kiley asked, only a shade less suspicious than Jon Robert.

"No. Not yet. But only because he wasn't ready to listen. Captain, he admitted he needs help. That's a tremendous step, and it didn't come easily. He needs time to recover from that strain before I tell him what I'll be doing. I assure you, though, I will tell him. I'll have to, if only because I'd be risking irreparable damage to his mind if I didn't have his complete cooperation."

"You can say that and ask us to trust you in the same breath?"

"Captain, I'm trying to be honest with you. I'm not going to tell you this will be easy or pleasant, because it won't. Greg is in trouble—serious trouble. The incident on Jeross may have precipitated a crisis, or he may have been building up to it for some time, but either way, he's on the verge of a complete breakdown. You sensed that yourself, or you wouldn't have told me as much as you did. You've done your best for him, but you aren't professionals and you can't get him through this on your own."

"While you, on the other hand, can?" Jon Robert demanded.

"I can try."

"What, no promises?"

"No, Mr. Michaelson. No promises. I'll give him all the support I can, but I can't guarantee he'll come through intact. Too much depends on him, on his ability to trust me, even when it seems I'm causing him unendurable pain. And I do mean pain. It may not be physical, but it will be no less real to him. It's possible it will become so great, he won't be able to deal with it."

"You're going to take a man who's already under intense stress and turn up the pressure another notch—is that what you're saying? If you push him hard, Keenan, he'll explode."

"No he won't, not the way he's internalizing. He thinks he's to blame for everything that's gone wrong. The only person he's a danger to is himself. He wouldn't hurt anyone else, not intentionally."

"I think he's right, Jon Robert," Kiley said. "You said yourself Greg's different this time. Quieter, not so angry."

"This time? What do you mean, this time?" Keenan demanded. Kiley looked at Jon Robert. *Tell him or not?* she questioned. He hesitated, then shrugged, the movement so imperceptible no one else would have caught it.

"Captain?" Keenan prompted.

"Greg was sick when we first took him on. Nothing serious, just a fever. But we were worried about him at the time. He seemed to be under a great deal of stress then, too. He acted . . . frightened. We were afraid he'd blow up if we pushed him too hard, but when he recovered from the fever, he was fine." She looked to Jon Robert for confirmation, and he nodded. "In fact, we thought we'd imagined everything."

"But at the time, you believed he was frightened?"

"Terrified," Jon Robert answered. "His ship had left him on a station in the middle of nowhere, with no hope of another berth for at least a month. He was sick and he had nowhere to go, no one to turn to. He wasn't going to come with us at first. Kiley wasn't exactly offering top wages, and he was too damned proud to admit he couldn't find anything better."

"But he did come. Why?"

Jon Robert looked at Kiley and shrugged. "I'm not sure," he said. "At the time, we thought he'd decided no amount of pride was worth being stuck on Demarker. Then again, maybe he took one look at us and saw a couple of suckers."

"I doubt that," Keenan said with a smile so warm that the heat went all the way through Kiley. "More likely, he saw two people he thought he could trust. And that's saying something, believe me. The last thing Renard would have wanted was for him to trust anyone."

"Well, he does trust us," Kiley said. "There is that. You too, apparently." And he had. She'd detected no fear of Daniel Keenan in him. Of the military, perhaps, but not of Keenan. She glanced at Jon Robert. *Do we cooperate with him or not?* she asked silently. He weighed the matter, clearly unhappy with the alternatives, then nodded.

"If he's willing to let you treat him, then I guess we'll have to go along," she said. "The only problem is, our cargo is being loaded tonight and we're scheduled for departure at four hundred hours tomorrow morning. I—I just don't feel right about leaving Greg behind.'' Jon Robert nodded in agreement, and a surge of relief washed through her. He was still with her. Whatever happened, she could count on him.

''No matter how much he trusts you,'' she continued, ''I'm afraid he's going to feel like we're deserting him. The ship means something to him, Captain. She's as close to security and a home as he's had for a long time. I don't want to take that away from him.''

''I'm glad you feel that way,'' Keenan said, ''because I was hoping you might agree to let me work with him onboard the _Widdon Galaxy_.''

''You mean come along with us?''

''If you'll let me. Greg will be much more relaxed here, surrounded by people he trusts. I can't overemphasize the value of that sense of security. It might make all the difference for him.''

''I'd have thought you'd prefer to work in a medical facility,'' Jon Robert said.

''Why? Because they have a staff trained to deal with emergencies? Because they could call in security if a patient turned violent?''

Jon Robert flushed at the officer's sharp tone, but stood his ground. ''Both,'' he said. ''I'm a certified medic, Keenan. Someone has to be, on a ship that's usually days away from a port. I've learned enough to know you're creating a potentially dangerous situation, no matter what you say. Greg may be internalizing now, but that could change, particularly if you start pressuring him. You're either very confident or very naive if you believe you can handle anything that might come up alone.''

''But I won't be alone, Mr. Michaelson, will I? You and your family will be here every minute. And, unless I miss my guess, you'll all be watching every move I make. Isn't that so?''

''You said that, Keenan. Not me.''

''You didn't have to. The message came through loud and clear. Let me give you an equally clear response: You are welcome to watch me as critically as you like—as long as you don't interfere. If you have questions, if you think I'm pushing Greg too hard, too fast, tell me. I'll listen. If I can, I'll even explain what I'm doing and why—on the sole condition that what I say goes no farther than you and you alone. I believe I'll be able to convince you I'm acting reasonably and prudently. What I will not do, however—under any circumstances—is let you come between Greg and me once I've started working with him, because that would be disastrous. If you know as much about this as you say you do, you must know such interference could cause as much damage as anything I might be doing, if not more."

"Provided you know what you're doing."

"I do. I have a degree in psychiatric medicine, Mr. Michaelson. Most Corps interrogators do. I'll be more than happy to show you my credentials and license to practice if you'd like to examine them."

"That won't be necessary," Jon Robert said stiffly. He turned to Kiley. "Are you willing to go along with him, Kiley?" he asked. "Because if you aren't, we can find another doctor for Greg. He's not the only psychiatrist on Aumarleen."

"No, but he's the only one Greg trusts. I think we have to let him try, Jon Robert. I don't see any alternative."

"All right," her brother said. "You can have your chance, Keenan—on your terms. I just hope you can deliver, for all our sakes."

He walked away, missing Keenan's unspoken reply. Kiley saw it, though.

So do I, the psychiatrist's worried eyes said. *So do I.*

Kiley assigned the psychiatrist the first cabin after the common room when he returned to the ship later that day. "You can use the room next door, too, if you need it," she told him. *For your sessions with Greg,* she meant, but couldn't bring herself to say the words.

Keenan had left the ship immediately after his meeting with them and returned several hours later, carrying two bulky cases in his hands. A bulging duffel bag large enough to hold all his clothing and a complete personal kit hung from one shoulder. Kiley was surprised by the amount of baggage; he looked as if he'd come to stay for weeks instead of days. Still, he settled in with a minimum of fuss and joined the family a short time later for dinner.

They did not have a chance to eat together often, and Lia had taken the opportunity to cook a meal more aptly described as a feast. Conversation flowed easily around the table, and they all laughed more than once at Jon Robert's expense. His bandages would come off in a few more days, but until then he had to suffer the humiliation of being fed by the closest pair of hands. Fortunately for him, they proved to be Holly's that evening.

"I can't resist the opportunity to practice," she said to Keenan, which led to a discussion of her pregnancy. She turned the conversation back on him a moment later, asking him about himself, his family—he had parents and an older sister, but no wife or children—and soon she, Lia, Reese, and Keenan were talking away, too involved to notice Kiley and Jon Robert's lack of participation or Lukas's silent withdrawal.

Lukas hadn't wanted to come to dinner, but had given in because coming was easier than finding excuses for staying away. He pushed the food around on his plate with a fork, forcing down one or two bites, pretending an interest he didn't feel.

Keenan wanted to see him that evening.

"I need to run a few routine tests before we proceed," he had said earlier. "Just a quick physical and a Reidiger Profile. You've answered the questions for the profile before, so you know there's nothing difficult about it."

Lukas had nodded, but he'd have given every credit in his account to avoid the physical, the profile, and the ordeal they presaged.

Keenan rose almost as soon as they finished eating and beckoned to Lukas. He stood up, avoiding the looks the Michaelsons gave him: Holly's warm and reassuring smile, Reese's casual nod, Lia's somewhat less warm but no longer hostile glance. Kiley and Jon Robert made no gesture at all. They just sat there looking worried. Their concern had comforted him earlier, but now it weighed upon him heavily. He had to go on, if only to justify their faith in him. He couldn't back out, however much he wanted to.

Keenan took him to the spare cabin and told him to strip, then proceeded to give him the most thorough physical he'd had since leaving the service. The psychiatrist didn't comment on his bruises, but he did pause over his ribs for some time with the scanner. "The fractures are knitting together nicely," he said, studying the image on the screen before him, "but you'd better keep the binding around your chest for another week. I know it's uncomfortable, but it provides support and protection, and you still need both."

He put the scanner away and brought out a portable computer.

He set it on the desk in the corner of the room and told Lukas to sit down and answer the questions on the screen. "I'll leave you alone for this," he said. "Call me when you're done, or if you have any questions."

The queries on the profile were not the same ones that had appeared on his Academy admissions test, but they ran along similar lines. His worst problem was deciding whether to answer them honestly or give the answers he thought he should make. In the end, he settled for honesty. The test designers had built in a number of validity checks. He might succeed in hiding his true personality, but the resulting profile would be skewed. Keenan would have no difficulty determining that he'd been evasive, and would likely use his replies to look for patterns to that evasion. Lukas would probably end up telling the psychiatrist more by lying than by being honest.

The profile took over an hour to complete. He called Keenan when he finished, and the officer sat in front of the computer and punched a few keys. He studied the resulting display a moment, his face giving nothing away, then turned to Lukas.

"Why don't you sit down, make yourself comfortable," he suggested, nodding to the bunk. Lukas sat, but he didn't relax. Keenan carried the desk chair across the room and sat in front of him. He smiled warmly, but Lukas refused to respond.

"Greg, I think you already have some idea of what I intend to do," he said, "and I'd have to be blind not to see you're worried sick. I won't tell you to put your fears aside; that's asking too much. I will ask you to trust me, however. I know that won't be easy, so to help you out, I'm going to tell you exactly what I plan to do. Are you listening?"

"Yes."

"Good. We'll start by talking. That's all, just talking. Once you've relaxed, I'll hypnotize you so I can explore the extent and depth of any blocks Renard constructed. At some point, I'll undoubtedly wish to use drugs to lower your resistance to me so I can begin tearing those blocks down. If there were a way to avoid them, I would, but I don't believe there will be. No matter how much you consciously desire to cooperate, you'll fight me. That would be a natural response under any circumstances, but Renard will have reinforced the instinct to prevent anyone else from interfering with his work.

"I'll warn you in advance, you'll be very uncomfortable during that stage, possibly even hostile. If you do find yourself responding to a person or situation with irrational anger, I want you to try to remember that I said it might happen, and control yourself as best you can. Will you try to do that?''

Lukas nodded, not trusting himself to speak.

"You aren't going to feel normal once I start using drugs, so don't be surprised or alarmed. At best, you'll feel dull and unusually sleepy; at worst, you'll actually feel ill after a session—so sick you want me to stop. But I won't, no matter how bad you say you feel, physically or emotionally. I can't, or I'll leave you in worse shape than you're in now. Having said that, I'm going to give you one more chance to back out. If you have any doubts about my intentions toward you or my ability to treat you, this is the time to say so. There won't be any turning back once we start.''

Lukas's hands clenched. He forced them to relax. "I don't," he said.

"You're sure?" Keenan pressed.

"Yes."

The psychiatrist studied his face, as if trying to decide whether to believe him. Lukas tried to return the look without flinching. He must have been convincing, for Keenan suddenly smiled, the light reaching all the way into his eyes.

"You'll do fine, Greg. Just fine. We'll start tomorrow morning. I'm going to give you something to help you relax and sleep tonight. It's a sedative, and a strong one at that. You won't be able to stay awake more than fifteen or twenty minutes after you take it, even if you try. Don't worry about that; it's normal. If you have any other reaction, though, tell me immediately. The same goes for any other drug I give you: if you suddenly start feeling strange—hot, cold, dizzy, breathless, whatever—you call me, no matter what time of the day or night it is. Understood?''

"Yes."

Keenan stood up, went to the bathroom, and came back with a glass of water and a tiny pink pill. The tablet didn't look powerful, but Lukas still hesitated before picking it up. He put it on the tip of his tongue, then swallowed it quickly before he could change his mind. "Anything else?" he asked, anxious to leave.

"That's all for tonight," Keenan said. "I'll see you in the morning."

Keenan hadn't exaggerated the effects of the sedative. Lukas was already dopey by the time he reached his cabin, and was staggering before he finished showering. He fell into bed and slept so deeply that he didn't even wake when they went through transition.

Keenan had another pill for him the next morning, a white one twice the size of the tablet he'd taken the night before.

"You'll like this one," he said with a grin when Lukas complained about the other pill's strength. "It will help you relax, too, but you probably won't notice anything except a general sense of well-being. Go on, take it."

He did. Reluctantly. He waited for something to happen, but nothing did, and he finally eased his watch on himself. Keenan just talked during that first session, asking Lukas what had happened to him in the years that had passed since the Academy, and volunteering stories of his own about medical school and his work at the fleet hospital before he'd been assigned to Section Two. After a time, Lukas forgot he was talking to anyone but an old acquaintance.

Keenan told him he could leave after two hours. The sense of anticlimax was almost as nerve-racking as his tension before they'd started talking. He wanted to report for his usual watch, but Keenan told him flatly that he could not work on the bridge or in the engine room while he was taking the drugs. In the next breath, he insisted Lukas stay busy.

"You need something to keep you occupied, not to mention an outlet for tension," he said. "Why don't you ask Jon Robert if he has a job you can do that doesn't involve working with vital machinery?"

"The corridors outside the cargo holds could use cleaning," Jon Robert said when he asked. "The scrubbers don't require any exertion, just monitoring, so you shouldn't have any trouble running them. Why don't you start on that? If you finish there, Lia could use a hand updating her pollination records—she's behind on them."

He spent the rest of the day dutifully cleaning the cargo corridors and didn't see Keenan until bedtime, when the doctor showed up at his cabin with another of the pink pills. He tried to refuse the sedative, but Keenan didn't give him a choice.

"Doctor's orders," the psychiatrist said, his expression brooking no argument.

Lukas swallowed the pill and spent another night in oblivion. He woke the next morning with great difficulty. His eyes didn't want to open, and when they did, they felt swollen and heavy.

He complained about the sedative again, but all Keenan did was hand him another one of the white pills.

"Take it and sit down," he said.

He started that morning's session by asking Lukas what he'd done the previous day, then asked how he liked working on a family ship and what he thought of the Michaelsons. They talked for a while and Keenan told him he could leave.

"That's all?" Lukas asked incredulously. "I've only been here a few minutes. I know you want me to relax before you really start working, and I'm trying, but you aren't going to accomplish anything at this rate."

"Is that how long you think you've been here? A few minutes?"

Keenan's tone alerted him. The officer watched him stiffen, then said softly, "Check your watch, Greg. It's lunchtime."

He looked at the dial and a wave of panic swept over him. He could account for only fifteen minutes of the last four hours. Keenan let the realization sink in, then spoke in that same quiet voice. "You don't need to be so worried, Greg. Nothing happened. We just—"

"Talked," Lukas said, biting off the word.

"That's right."

"You hypnotized me."

"Yes."

"What did I say?" he demanded, his voice rising. "What?"

"You know I can't tell you that," Keenan said. "I will say you're a remarkably good subject, though. You were very cooperative and we made good progress."

"I won't be so cooperative the next time," he replied angrily.

"No? Well, we'll talk about that later. You need a break; why don't you eat lunch and take a short nap, then come back here at fifteen hundred hours."

There were times Lukas regretted the way the ship's doors slid closed. He would have liked slamming Keenan's in his face. He wasn't going to go back, but he somehow found himself in the spare cabin at 1459, and four more hours disappeared. When he came to again, his throat was dry and sore, and he was so tired that he couldn't even summon the energy to wonder what he'd said.

He ate dinner and went to his room. Keenan showed up a short time later with another of the pink pills. Lukas took it without protest and was unconscious within minutes.

The next day passed in a blur. Gripped by a thick, heavy

fatigue, he could barely move. His throat ached from talking too much and, despite the pill, he hadn't slept well the night before. The nightmares had been worse than ever, and Keenan's sedative only made it harder to wake from the black terror that pursued him. He went so far as to ask if Keenan could give him another, more powerful sleeping pill, but the psychiatrist shook his head.

"I'm sorry, Greg, but the one you're taking is as strong as they come," he said. "The dreams will go away soon, but until then, you'll just have to put up with them."

He didn't argue. He was too exhausted. The weight of the fatigue pressing down on him had become almost intolerable. It took an act of will just to get out of bed and shower the next morning. He turned the water to cold, hoping the shock would clear his head, but it barely registered. He turned off the water and, as he did, saw the needle mark on the inside of his left elbow. He thought he was going to be sick for an instant, but the panic only lasted a moment before it dulled and fatigue took over again. He dressed, made his way to Keenan's cabin, and lost another day.

There were more needle marks the next morning, but by then he no longer cared. It was all he could do to drag himself out of bed, shower, and dress. He had to stop to rest before going to the galley to get breakfast. He pulled out the first package he touched in the freezer. He didn't want food, but he had to eat. The only problem was, he couldn't open the wrapper. He was still fumbling with it, trying to figure out how to pull it off, when Jon Robert and Holly came in to make their breakfasts.

"Is something wrong, Greg?" Jon Robert asked, giving him a funny look.

"I can't open this," he said dully.

"Let me help," Holly said, reaching for the package.

"No!" he said wildly. It was his! She wasn't going to take it away from him!

She came at him and he swung out, striking her arm with enough force to send the package in his hand flying. It hit the counter and split open. Tiny, frozen green balls spilled out on the floor, rolling in all directions. He could have cried. It would take forever to pick them up. He would never get to Keenan's cabin on time. Keenan was going to be angry with him. It wouldn't matter that he had tried to cooperate. That wasn't enough for the psychiatrist—nothing was enough.

He squeezed his eyes shut so the tears that suddenly filled

them couldn't fall. A sob started at the back of his throat and he clenched his jaw so it couldn't escape. It broke free anyway. Another one came up behind it, and then another.

"Call Daniel!" he heard Jon Robert say urgently. A moment later, an enormous arm closed around him. The engineer may have intended to offer only comfort, but all Lukas felt was the sudden restraint. He twisted around, trying to break free.

"No!" he shouted. "No!"

Jon Robert's arms closed tight around him, and this time there was no doubting their intent. The other man's hands might be bandaged, he might have to struggle awkwardly to hold him, but he was not going to let him go. Lukas made another attempt to break free, only to freeze as Keenan burst into the room.

The psychiatrist must have been in the shower. His hair was dripping and he'd stopped only to pull on a pair of pants. He held a pressurized injector in his right hand. He stopped inside the door, making a lightning assessment of the situation, then came straight for Lukas.

This time the "NO!" was a scream, but it didn't ease Jon Robert's grip or slow Keenan's advance. The psychiatrist shoved the injector against his arm and pressed the trigger. The drug stung going in, sending a wave of heat coursing up the length of his arm. Lukas twisted wildly and this time managed to break free of Jon Robert's grip, only to have Keenan grab him instead. That was worse, much worse, because the psychiatrist could use his hands. And he did. He held him without mercy as the drug spread through his body, across his chest, down to his feet, and up to his head, where it exploded. Flames engulfed him, burning him from the inside out, consuming him. He heard himself cry out one final time and then there was nothing.

He did not remember anything at all for a long time after that. Then slowly, very slowly, patches of gray began to show in the darkness. A thought would form, rise up like a bubble, then break before it reached the surface of his mind. Eventually, one of the bubbles finally reached the surface and he had a moment's awareness.

He was talking to Keenan. He thought he had been talking to him for a long time, but it could have been only an hour. He couldn't tell. He didn't know what he was saying and he didn't care. He thought Keenan cared because the other man kept prompting him if he stopped talking, but he himself didn't. Words didn't matter. He didn't matter. The ship didn't matter.

Nothing mattered. Not then, not for many days.

Or was it years? Or only hours?

He didn't know.

That should have bothered him, but it didn't. Nothing did.

Until Kiley talked to him.

Another bubble reached the surface. He blinked and found himself in the dining room. A plate sat on the table in front of him, a slice of meat on one side, mashed potatoes, peas, and some yellow fruit on the other. A fork lay on the plate, within reach of his hand, but he made no effort to lift it. The fading echo of voices still rang in his ears; other people must have been in the room, eating and talking, but they had gone and only Kiley remained.

She was standing beside him, her hand on his shoulder. She had never touched him before. Not like that. He looked up, surprised. She was tired, he thought dully. The dark circles were back under her eyes and she looked thinner. A part of him said he was to blame for that. He'd done something wrong, failed her somehow. He felt a moment of shame, but that passed. At least she wasn't angry with him, he thought gratefully. Sick with worry, maybe, but not angry.

"Greg, you have to eat," she was saying.

He shook his head. "I'm not hungry."

"Greg—" she started, then took a look at his expression and broke off. "I'm sorry. I don't mean to nag. It's just that I'm worried about you. We all are."

"I'll be all right."

"Of course you will," she said, straightening. "I have to get back to the bridge, but if there's anything you want, anything you need . . ."

"I'll let you know," he finished, proud that he managed a smile. She wasn't deceived, though. She gave him a last, unhappy look, then left.

He pushed his plate aside and put his head down on his arms. Something was wrong with him, very wrong, but he didn't know what, let alone how to make it right. *Daniel will know,* a voice said inside him. *You have to talk to Daniel. Now!*

Urgency gripped him without warning and he pushed himself up abruptly. He swayed, light-headed from the sudden movement, then started for the door. At Keenan's cabin he pressed the button beside the door. The psychiatrist had not set the lock, and the door opened with a soft swish. Keenan was inside, sitting at the desk, reading something on the portable computer's screen. He looked up, startled.

"Greg? What are you doing here? You're supposed to be eating dinner. What's wrong?" he demanded, his voice sharpening.

"Now, Daniel. Do it now," he said. *Do what?* his mind screamed in panic. *Do what?*

But if Lukas didn't know, Keenan did. He crossed the room in three steps, looked closely at him, then nodded.

"Next door," he said, putting a hand on Lukas's arm. He gave him the gentlest of nudges when he didn't move, guiding him into the other room, over to the bunk.

"Lie down, Greg," he directed. He waited until he had, then crossed to the desk, opened a drawer, and took out a disposable syringe and a vial containing a colorless fluid. He filled the syringe, one eye on Lukas and the other on the hypodermic. When he finished, he came back to the bunk, and rubbed the inside of Lukas's arm with something cold and wet. Lukas didn't look down. He kept his eyes on the psychiatrist's face, clamping down on the panic that threatened to overwhelm him as the needle slid in. What's happening? What? his mind demanded. And then it was too late to ask, for the drug was already flowing into his vein. Keenan slid the needle back out, reached across him to put it on the shelf alongside the bed, and sat down beside him. One hand gripped the fist he had made and the other settled on his shoulder.

"The nialgin will take effect almost immediately, Greg." His grip was strong and comforting. He let go briefly to touch Lukas's face, then his neck, and then his hand settled back in place.

"Don't be afraid," he said quietly. "You're safe here. I won't let anything hurt you. I promise."

Lukas was afraid, but it was too late to run now. Much too late. He gasped for breath as he started to go under, and Keenan's fingers tightened against his shoulder. The next thing he knew, he was coming up, rising way too fast. It felt like an aborted jump, a transition that went on and on until his stomach turned inside out and he was violently sick.

"Don't fight it," Keenan was saying urgently, but he didn't listen. How could he help but fight? Keenan pressed an injector against his arm as his stomach spasmed again. This time, though, there was no pain, no vision of flames. Instead a soothing, all-enveloping warmth engulfed him. He thinned out and his body turned into a soft, white cloud that dissipated with the first puff of a gentle summer breeze.

He dreamed the old, hideously terrifying nightmares he could never remember afterward. He fought desperately to wake, to free himself from them, but each time he came close to the surface something shoved him back under again. He resisted, terrified of what lay at the bottom of the well of darkness, but down he went, despite his best efforts, and the dreams started all over again.

He came up at last. He lay on the bunk in the cabin next to Keenan's, a blanket pulled tight around his shoulders. His muscles ached, as if he'd held himself rigid all night. His eyes felt puffy, the lashes sticky and wet. He must have cried in his sleep. Again.

"Greg, are you awake?" Keenan was saying.

He stirred. Nodded.

"Can you turn over?"

Obediently, he rolled over on his back. Keenan had a scanner in his hand. He pulled back the blanket, ran the wand over him, read the results, then set the instrument aside and gave him a warm smile.

"Just checking," he said. He pulled the blanket back up and sat down on the edge of the bunk. "You had a rough night. Do you remember anything about it? Anything at all?"

"Being sick. I remember that. And dreaming."

"Are you feeling sick now?"

"No."

"Would you like something to eat?"

Lukas considered, then shook his head.

"We're in port at Siddorn," Keenan told him. "We'll be here until this evening. I have to leave you for a few hours; I'd rather not—this isn't a good time—but I must. I want you to stay here and rest until I come back. Will you do that for me?"

"Yes."

Keenan smiled and pressed his shoulder. "You're a good patient, Greg," he said, "the best I've ever had. You're going to start feeling better soon. Very soon. We still have some work to do, but the worst is over. In fact, your memory will start coming back over the next few days. It won't all return at the same time. I've set a few blocks of my own so everything won't hit you all at once. Don't let that upset you; the blocks are very flimsy and you could work your way around them with no difficulty. Please don't try, though. Just let the memories come as they will. If you find them too upsetting, or if they start coming too fast for comfort, let me know. I can help.''

Keenan paused, searching his face. "Did you follow all that?" he asked.

"Yes."

"Good. I want you to go to sleep now, and don't wake up until I say you can."

His eyes closed obediently and he slept. This time, there were no dreams.

Chapter 13

Omanu had set their meeting for 0930. The room Keenan's superior officer had taken on a lower level of the station contained only a bed, a table, and a straight-backed, armless chair sitting in the far corner. The bed had not been slept in, and the alcove that served as a closet was empty. Omanu either had another room, or was staying on the ship that had brought him to Siddorn.

He stood aside to let Keenan enter, then shut the door and set the security lock. He took one look at Keenan's face and motioned him to sit on the bed. "What's wrong?" he said flatly, as if he suspected a disaster had occurred and was simply waiting for confirmation.

"Do I look that bad?" Keenan asked with a rueful smile. "Sorry, but it's been a difficult week. Productive, but difficult."

"Lukas is all right, then? For a minute, I thought . . ."

"He will be, but he's going to need more time, Hal. I want at least five more days with him. A full week would be better. I've been able to clear the blocks Renard set, and I've found out what you wanted to know, but I had to set blocks of my own to prevent him from consciously recalling anything yet. He's going to be extremely upset when he realizes what's happened to him, and there are . . . a few other problems."

"Anything to prevent him from testifying?"

"There shouldn't be—as long as he isn't pushed too fast."

"I get the message, but I don't like it—and not just because Admiral Quiller is on my back. We've had a few reports out of Zerron base suggesting that Sorseli's unusually tense and worried. They may not mean anything, but we can't afford to take the chance he's somehow learned about the investigation. There's no telling how far he might go to stop Lukas from testifying

171

against him. You could be in danger, both of you. The sooner we have Lukas in protective custody, the better I'll feel.''

"You might, but he won't. He's suppressed a tremendous amount of fear and anger, Omanu, not just toward Sorseli, but the Corps as well. If you detain him now, he's just as likely to direct that hostility toward us as the admiral. If I can keep him on the *Widdon Galaxy*, in a neutral environment, I believe I can keep his anger focused on Sorseli, where it belongs—but I can't guarantee that if you have him detained.''

"Where are the Michaelsons going next? Do they have another cargo lined up?''

"Yes. They're ferrying two shuttlecraft to Cardos.''

"Cardos! That station's little more than an outpost. What's more, it's inside Zerron Base jurisdiction. Can't they find another shipment?''

Keenan shook his head. "That's all Reese could come up with.''

"We could arrange something—''

"They signed the contract a half hour ago. The cargo is being loaded right now.''

Omanu swore. "When are they planning to leave?''

"This afternoon. They should reach Cardos in seven days, ship's time.''

"Can you guarantee that Lukas will be ready to go to Everest with us by then and testify?''

"He should be, Hal, but I can't make any promises.''

"I'm not happy about this, Daniel. Not happy at all.''

"I don't see any alternative," Keenan said. He hesitated, then added, "Hal, I'm not exaggerating Greg's instability. He's been through a great deal, and he's walking a fine line between sanity and madness. If anything upsets him, anything at all, he may fall off on the wrong side. I think I can bring him through intact, but only if you leave him on the *Widdon Galaxy* and give me the time I need.''

"All right, I get the picture. You can have your extra week— but that's the limit.''

"Thank you.''

"Thank yourself. It isn't the first time you've persuaded me to do something against my better judgment." Omanu stood up, as if he needed physical activity to release his tension. He walked two paces to the door and turned around.

"Daniel, Admiral Quiller finally persuaded Vladic to let him see the original documents ordering Gynos restricted. We know what Sorseli was after now. There was a starship on that planet. An alien starship. It had apparently crashed. It hadn't been there long when the exploration and reconnaissance team surveying Gynos found it. They saw no sign of life, but Admiralty took one look at their report and shut down operations in that sector so fast, rumors were flying for months.

"All the centuries looking for another civilization and finding nothing, then suddenly they had evidence that real, live aliens were out there. Worse, those aliens had a technology so advanced, our people couldn't even guess how their ship was powered, let alone how they controlled it. There wasn't an object on that ship that remotely resembled an instrument board. They couldn't even positively identify the bridge. They took one look and panicked. Whoever those beings were, wherever they came from, we don't begin to match their capabilities. The Admiralty and Board decided the only prudent course was to isolate the sector completely. With luck, the ship was far from home, and maybe off course. Others might not come looking for it, but if they did, there was no sense advertising our presence."

"So we've just been sitting around, watching the sector to see if anyone else shows up? That's all?"

"Yes."

"That doesn't sound like the Corps to me."

"I told you, Daniel, they panicked. I think they've had second thoughts since then, but no one wants the responsibility for authorizing an outreach expedition—not while there's the slightest chance it might end in hostilities with beings who appear to have a superior technology."

"How did Sorseli learn about the ship?"

"He was captain of the deep-space exploration ship that found it. He knew about it from the very beginning. In fact, his quick action in sealing off leaks about the ship's existence went a long way toward winning him his promotion to rear admiral and a seat on the Board. He must have talked to someone, though, sometime. He has friends in the private sector, Daniel. Powerful friends. Admiral Quiller's guess is that he told one of them about the ship, and that person jumped at the chance of studying any alien artifacts Sorseli could obtain."

"In return for what? What could anyone have offered Sorseli that would have made the risk of entering a restricted zone worthwhile?"

"Admiral Quiller thinks he may have been promised a vote—

the deciding vote he needs to become the next director of the Corps.''

Keenan sat back, taking that in. Omanu gave him time.

"I still think he was taking a tremendous risk," Keenan said at last. Sooner or later, someone on the *Kelsoe Moran* would have said something about the trip. The story would have made its way back to the Admiralty. You know it would have."

"Would it? Perhaps not, if Sorseli really wanted to cover his tracks. Ships have been known to have accidents, to disappear during jump. He could have arranged for the *Kelsoe Moran* to have an accident. Or disappear."

"You're saying he'd deliberately sabotage one of his own ships—kill every man and woman on board?"

"I'm saying that might have been a contingency plan if his original scheme didn't work out."

"And the original scheme?"

"I think he planned to implicate someone else for entering the restricted zone from the beginning. He'd have his artifacts and someone to be prosecuted for retrieving them. Artifacts that, I might add, seem to have made their way to a very influential defense contractor for detailed analysis. Sorseli appears to have maneuvered the decision to examine them and the choice of contractor most adroitly."

"And Greg Lukas took the blame for everything. That's going to cost Sorseli, Omanu. He made a disastrous mistake, turning Greg over to Renard. Next to that, sending the *Kelsoe Moran* into the restricted zone is going to look like a minor violation."

"Entering or sending a man into a restricted zone is grounds for a sentence of death in a court-martial. How could ordering therapy for Lukas be worse than that? Even if Renard deliberately tortured him, physically or mentally, I don't see how the Admiralty would consider that more serious than the intrusion."

"What Renard did came close to torture. Damned close! But that's not why the Admiralty will be so upset. What's going to infuriate them is the part of Lukas's story no one ever heard, thanks to Lieutenant Stuart McLaren and Admiral James Sorseli."

"What are you talking about, Daniel?" Omanu demanded, his eyes narrowing.

Keenan stood and pulled two disks out of his pocket. He handed them to Omanu. "I started recording our sessions to be used as evidence against Renard when he was prosecuted for criminal misconduct—and he will be if I have anything to say about it. I kept on recording after Greg started talking about what happened on Gynos.''

"The sessions were that bad?" Omanu asked absently, turning the disks over in his hands as if by doing so he could see their contents.

"They were brutal. Renard didn't have an easy time overcoming Greg's resistance, and somewhere along the way the battle became personal. He hated Greg before they were through. The feeling was mutual. Unfortunately, Renard had all the weapons. Greg didn't stand a chance. Renard went after him day and night, deliberately trying to break him. Once he did, his work was easy.

"He knew Greg nearly drowned when he was a child—the incident is part of his service record because his parents died in the accident. They were sailing enthusiasts. Their boat was caught in a sudden storm and it capsized. Greg was rescued by another boat, but his parents were never found. He's been terrified of water ever since. He had some idiotic idea that he needed to overcome his fear when he was at the Academy, so he signed up for a swimming class. The only problem was, he found out his anxiety was so irrational, determination alone might not be sufficient to conquer it.''

"But he tried."

"He did. In fact, he impressed his instructor so much, Abbot started giving Greg individual lessons. Greg should have been able to pass the proficiency exam at the end of the class with no difficulty, but the moment he got in the water, he froze up. He would never discuss what happened later, but I think he suddenly realized just how much was riding on the exam. If you fail any course at the Academy, even swimming, you're out. No exceptions.''

"You don't have to remind me," Omanu said. "I remember the pressure vividly. It didn't matter how bright or fit a person was, he was still afraid of washing out. They wanted you to feel that, of course. If a person was going to break under stress, they wanted it to happen at the Academy, under controlled circumstances, not in the field. It was hard to understand at the time, though.''

"So you can understand how devastated Lukas was. I've never seen anyone so sick in my life as he was when he came back to our room. He wouldn't say anything. He just started packing. He was almost done when Abbot came in. He told Greg he'd had no choice but to report the incident to his commanding officer, but he had asked that Greg be given a second chance at the final, in view of his history. He said he'd argued that letting Greg prove he could rise above his fear would be a better test of his fitness and character than any exam the Academy could devise. He must have been very persuasive, because his commanding officer said Greg could have one more chance at the final, provided he took it the next day.

"Greg didn't sleep at all that night. His entire future was on the line, and he knew it. I'm not sure who went to the pool the next day, but I don't think it was the Greg Lukas I knew. He'd shut his mind and emotions down so tightly, he was little more than an automaton. He passed the test, but he never went back to the pool again, and he wasn't himself for days afterwards."

"But he did recover. He went on to graduate third in his class."

"Yes, but unfortunately for him, the incident became part of his service record. For most commanding officers it would have been a positive indicator—a sign Greg had faced adversity and overcome it. Renard, however, saw it as evidence Greg had experienced profound psychological and emotional stress. Whatever Greg had become since those experiences, the memories were a still a part of him. Renard searched for them. He made Greg relive the boating accident, his parents' deaths, even the swimming test, then he manipulated the emotions associated with those memories, twisting and reinforcing them until they became an emotional wall of monumental proportions. When the wall was insurmountable, he tied his memory blocks to it.

"Hal, there was no way Greg could have recalled what happened to him on his own. To do so, he'd have been forced to face his deepest terrors magnified a hundred times. If he so much as started to recall anything, he would have found himself suffering from such acute anxiety that he'd be forced to back off instantly."

"I'm surprised Lukas didn't seek professional help to deal with that fear. He must have known it was abnormal," Omanu said.

"Renard did his best to make it virtually impossible for Greg to relate to other human beings in any capacity whatsoever, let alone ask for help. He left scars so deep, years of therapy couldn't remove them completely. Worse, he left them deliberately, with full knowledge of what he was doing to the man. When he comes to trial over this, I want to be there to testify against him.

I guarantee he won't ever practice medicine again. If I have my way, he'll receive some rehabilitation therapy of his own."

"That may not be possible."

"Not possible? Why not? There's more than enough evidence to—"

"We can't find him, Daniel," Omanu interrupted. "He hasn't been seen since Sorseli granted him his discharge. It's beginning to look like he may not be alive. He was all that stood between Sorseli's testimony being absolutely airtight should the case ever be reopened. Sorseli may have decided he posed an unacceptable risk." Omanu gave Keenan a penetrating look. "Are you still sure you don't want Lukas in protective custody?"

A shaft of sudden, very personal fear shot through Keenan. Then he pushed it aside and said resolutely, "Greg isn't ready to leave the *Widdon Galaxy*. I'd give my pension if he were, but he isn't."

"Very well, you're the interrogator. What you say goes. But I won't pretend I'm happy. Without Lukas, we don't have a case."

"You have the tapes," Keenan said, nodding to the disks Omanu held. "I think you'll find they contain more than enough evidence to convict Sorseli."

"Tapes won't stand up in a trial, Daniel. Not when they can be so easily edited."

"These will. I was careful when I made them. A chronometer is visible at all times, so no one can claim they've been edited. I specified the names and dosages of the drugs I was using, and I administered them with the recorder running. The tapes show all my questions and all Greg's replies. I don't think there will be any doubt about the fact that Sorseli ordered him to Gynos, or that what happened to him there is an authentic experience."

His tone alerted Omanu. "What are you talking about? What happened? What experience?"

"Watch the tapes. I'd rather you heard the full story from Greg himself, in his own words, his own voice."

"I'll look at them right away," Omanu said.

"Don't plan to sleep after you do. I couldn't."

"That's obvious. You look terrible. Are you sure you don't want some support? An assistant to back you up? I know how emotionally draining an investigation like this can be, even if you aren't dealing with a friend. If you—"

"I don't want any help, Omanu. I started this; I want to be the one to finish it."

"All right, but once Lukas is safely on Everest and has given a deposition, you're going on a month's vacation. That's an order, Daniel. I'll put it in writing if I have to."

"You won't. Right now, even a month sounds too short."

"Maybe it is," Omanu said, looking at him with a sudden, assessing frown. "I've been pushing you pretty hard the past year, perhaps too hard. I don't want to lose you, Daniel. You're the best interrogator Section Two has. If you need more time, I'll be glad to approve a leave of absence."

"What if I want more than that, Hal? What if I want . . . out?" He hadn't planned to ask that question—had not even considered it consciously—but it burst forth with a force that surprised both of them.

Omanu searched his face. "Do you?" he asked at last.

"I don't know," Keenan replied, then said in a rush, "I'm tired, Hal. Tired of lies, tired of seeing men's lives broken and knowing I'm responsible. Maybe I want to stop being an interrogator and go back to being what I was—a healer."

"Daniel, for every life you may have broken, another has been made whole—or kept whole in the first place. I know you wanted to continue working as a staff psychiatrist at the fleet hospital, but you're much too fine an interrogator for Admiral Quiller to let you go without an argument. There are plenty of staff psychiatrists, but there are damned few investigators who have your unique combination of objectivity and empathy. By all means, take a leave if you need one, but please, don't make any rash decisions until you've had time to sort things out. I'm sure you'll feel differently once you've had time to relax and reevaluate."

"And if I don't?"

"If you don't, we'll talk about a transfer."

"I have your word on that, Omanu?"

"Do you really need it?"

Keenan sighed. "No."

"I should hope not. But if it helps, you have it. If you really want to be reassigned, I'll see that you are."

"Thank you, Omanu. And it does help—knowing I have an out."

"I know," the other man said with a wicked grin. "That's why I gave you one."

Chapter 14

An alien ship was orbiting the habitable planet.

A smaller craft was on the planet's surface, near the ruins of the *Itieth*. Chirith approached the scene warily. His people were traders of goods and information, always searching for the unknown and exotic. A new species meant new opportunities, but it could also mean new threats. The Miquiri had no need for new worlds, no desire to dominate, but not all species were equally nonaggressive. Prudence dictated a cautious approach.

The alien ship was primitive; the Miquiri had abandoned such wholly mechanical constructs a millennium ago. Still, Chirith did not make the mistake of underestimating the vessel's capabilities, or her crew's willingness to engage in battle. Any race capable of travel through space was not without resources.

He and the ship's elders debated contacting the aliens at all, but there was never any real question they would do so, not when these people might know a way around or through the barrier. The only real question was the extent to which they should expose themselves. They could approach openly, signaling the larger of the two vessels and asking for talks, or they could take a more cautious approach, disabling the larger vessel temporarily, then descending to the planet's surface and contacting the smaller group of aliens. If the aliens did prove threatening, the smaller group would be easier to deal with.

They opted for caution. They approached the vessel on the planet hopefully, but the scene they found when they landed was so repugnant that they nearly abandoned their plan. The vessel contained four aliens. Three were dead. The fourth stood over them, a weapon in its hand. It had obviously killed the others, but why? Had they turned on it first? Had they been infected by some local contaminant that drove them insane? Had the living one killed them because they were in agony? Or had it murdered them?

Under any other circumstances, Chirith would have retreated home then and there and reported contact with a violent and potentially hostile race. But he could not go home. Nor could he simply leave, much as he wanted to. They could not ignore the possibility that the aliens knew of a passage through the barrier.

Despite their revulsion, they decided to proceed with the contact. There had been one reassuring sign: the creature had not fired on them. In fact, it had dropped its weapon as soon as it saw them. His crew had disabled it anyway. They did not dare take the chance it carried other weapons, less obviously threatening.

The ship's medical staff wanted to examine the alien to be certain it had not been infected by a planetary contaminant, and to assess any bacteria or viruses it carried to be certain they were not harmful to the Miquiri. They also asked for permission to run physiological and neurological tests in the hope of discovering vital clues to the creature's innate characteristics and biologically programmed responses.

Chirith looked from his advisers to the monitor showing a picture of the unconscious alien. The creature was intelligent. It deserved the respect and honor they would accord an equal, but the circumstances in which they had encountered it demanded they treat it as a laboratory specimen. He hesitated, then told the medical staff to make their examination.

What they found was highly disturbing.

"The alien being presents no biological threat to our species," Chirith was told, "but its physical reactions are faster than its mental ones. Its sensory system is overdeveloped and its mind does not have complete control over its body's responses. It is intelligent, but it tends to lose rationality when subjected to stress. It would likely attack if threatened."

"Or if it perceived a threat?"

"Yes."

He had seen and heard enough. He could not risk contact. They were alone, without support of their own kind. He could not endanger his ship and he did not wish the aliens to learn any more about them than they already had—not when he was unable to warn his own people about aliens first. No one argued the wisdom of that decision.

No one, that is, except the Quayla.

It had not communicated with them directly for some time but it came to life now, writing its message across the wall in huge, red letters.

"I do not believe the alien is a threat," the Quayla wrote. "I believe I can communicate with it. If I can reach it, I will be able to determine its true nature. Please, let me try!"

Chirith distrusted the Quayla's motives. He suspected it was more interested in exploring the alien's highly developed sensory system than establishing communication. Still, he agreed, if only because he was not certain what the Quayla would do if he didn't. They did not know how extensively it had been damaged by their passage through the barrier, but there was no doubt it had suffered. They did not dare risk upsetting it further, not when their lives rested in its hands.

They let the Quayla have its way, but the moment it touched the alien, the creature collapsed. It could not stand the contact any more than Chirith or the rest of his crew could.

"Is it damaged?" Chirith demanded of the medical officer who hurried to examine the unconscious alien.

"It does not appear to be" was the cautious reply.

He turned to Tirie. "Have you gathered all the data you can from their ships?"

"Yes," she replied. "There is much to analyze, though. It may take a long time to decipher their language and interpret their records. Chirith, are you sure we should leave without making any attempt to contact them? This one made no attempt to harm us. The others might prove friendly if approached cautiously."

"We can't take the risk," he said brusquely, adding more gently, "It's not just ourselves we endanger, it's all Miquiri."

"But they may know a way around the barrier!"

"If they do, we will soon discover it. We have their records."

"What if we can't read them? What if they do not mention the barrier? What then, Chirith? Will you have us run from them forever?"

"We can always contact them later, if that becomes advisable. For now, it is not." He turned to Rietier, his watch commander. "Put the alien outside the ship, then prepare to leave the planet at full speed," he ordered. "We must be gone before its fellow creatures arrive."

Chapter 15

Lukas's memories began to return over the course of the next two days. Some came back during his sessions with Keenan. Others returned without warning, of their own volition. The first time that happened, he was in the galley. He'd gone in to fix something to eat and found Lia already there, making dinner for herself and Reese. She gave him a cautious look, as if she were trying to assess his mental or emotional condition. It was the same look Jon Robert had given him earlier that day when they passed in the corridor.

Except for the incident with Jon Robert and Holly, and the few words Kiley had spoken to him in the dining room, he was aware of almost nothing that had happened in the past week. But if he didn't know what he'd said or done, everyone else clearly did—and regarded him warily in consequence. Getting back on a normal footing with the Michaelsons was not going to be easy.

He forced a smile, hoping that would reassure Lia. "I thought I'd fix something to eat, but I can see I'd be in your way. I'll come back later, after you've finished."

"You don't have to go, Greg," she said quickly. Too quickly. She must have realized that, because she added more naturally, "You can eat with us if you want. There's plenty. As usual, I seem to have made enough for five."

"I don't want to be in your way—"

"You won't be," she said firmly. "In fact, I could use your help. You can slice the melon on the counter while I finish cooking the vegetables."

He took the knife she offered and started to work. One moment he was slicing the ripe, orange fruit, and the next he was in the courtroom on Zerron Base, looking at the orange, yellow, and white base emblem on the judge's dais. The judge was reading the court's verdict.

". . . do find . . . guilty . . ."

He had said more, but that was all he'd heard.

Guilty.

Lukas's counsel, Lewis Fornay, had tried to warn him that his story wouldn't be believed unless he could come up with substantiating evidence, but the verdict still came as a shock. Right up to that minute, he'd hoped something would happen to make them doubt Sorseli's testimony. But it hadn't. It was over. All of it. He was—

"Greg, is something wrong?"

He came back to the present with a thud and found himself leaning against the counter, almost doubled over. Lia started toward him, then stopped as he straightened, still clutching the knife he'd used to slice the melons.

"What's wrong?" she whispered.

"Nothing." He put the knife down quickly. "It's nothing. I—I don't think I'm very hungry after all. If you'll excuse me, I'll—"

"Greg, wait!" Lia said sharply as he started to go. "Daniel warned us you might have momentary lapses as your memory returned," she went on when he stopped. "That's what happened just now, isn't it? Some sort of . . . lapse? He said they might be disturbing, but they'd be far more frightening for you than us. I think maybe he was right. You don't look at all well. Do you want me to call him?"

"No," he said quickly. "Please, don't."

"But—"

"I'm fine now, Lia. Really."

"You're sure?"

"Yes."

"Then you'll stay for dinner?"

"I don't—"

"No arguments. You've missed too many meals already. Come on. You can carry the plates into the dining room and I'll call Reese."

That moment passed, but there were others. A few happened when he was alone, but most occurred during his sessions with Keenan. The psychiatrist discontinued the drugs he had been using; instead, he simply asked question after question, taking Lukas from his first days at Zerron Base to the trip to Gynos, drawing the events out of him, one by one.

It did not take Lukas long to appreciate the extent of his friend's skills—or his influence over him. Keenan gave him a few moments to rage over Sorseli's perfidy, McLaren's sulking insubordination, and Gordon's cold refusal to offer explanations, then told him to let go of his anger. And he did, every time. One moment he would be so furious he could have killed Sorseli if he'd been in the same room, and the next, he was completely detached.

He worried about Keenan retaining such a frightening degree of control over him, despite the fact that the psychiatrist no longer gave him drugs. If he had trusted him one iota less . . . but he did trust him completely, and that blind faith frightened him as much as his sudden shifts from rage to calm. He wouldn't have trusted anyone so well under normal circumstances, not even his best friend—which meant Keenan must have done something to him, something that would insure his continuing cooperation. But when he turned on the psychiatrist, accusing him of just that, Keenan only smiled.

"Of course I did," he said easily. "I set a number of very deep, very strong suggestions that you trust me while you were in a highly receptive state. I find that expedient for the time being. Before you work yourself into a frenzy over the idea, though, let me also tell you those suggestions have very definite bounds. They work because you want to cooperate with me— no matter what your conscious mind says to the contrary. The moment you truly don't want to, you won't have any difficulty resisting a direct order, let alone a suggestion."

"I don't believe you."

"Have I given you any cause to doubt me yet?"

"No," he admitted grudgingly.

"I won't, either. I will never knowingly say or do anything to hurt you, Greg. You have my word on that. Now, I want you to take a deep breath and relax. When you're ready, I want you to go back to Gynos and tell me what happened after you landed on the planet."

He went back. He was in the shuttle with his two crewmen and Lyle Gordon. Gordon was saying Lukas and his men should stay in the shuttle while he went outside. Lukas hadn't liked those orders, hadn't liked Gordon. But Sorseli's instructions had been explicit: Follow Gordon's instructions when they reached Gynos, no matter what he said to do. So he had. He let Gordon leave the shuttle, taking a sizable collection box with him. The civilian was gone some three hours—long enough for Lukas and his two crewmen, Crowther and Adrick, to grow thoroughly uneasy.

There was nothing about Gynos itself to engender such tension. Though they had set down in the planet's temperate zone, the outside temperature and humidity were high. But instead of jungle, the terrain consisted mostly of tall grasses, broken by clumps of taller vegetation that more closely resembled shrubs than trees. Gordon headed for one of those clumps. They lost sight of him in the grass, but he stirred up several flocks of birdlike creatures as he neared the bushes. They flew high into the air, then returned to their original perches as he continued on. The only other signs of life they saw were the insects that occasionally flew past the shuttle.

No, the planet wasn't responsible for their uneasiness. It was Gordon, his secretiveness, his insistence that they stay on the shuttle. Crowther and Adrick had looked to him after Gordon disappeared from view, eyebrows raised.

Do we stay here, or follow him? they asked silently. He hesitated, sorely tempted to see what the civilian was up to. Nevertheless, he motioned them to close the hatch. The planet hadn't been declared a restricted area without cause, and he had no desire to find out the reason. It was bad enough being there in the first place.

They waited, the minutes stretching out into hours. Lukas made his prearranged call to the *Kelsoe Moran* every half hour, and watched the sun climb high in the sky, then start to descend. Crowther and Adrick talked quietly in the back of the shuttle, glancing his way occasionally, uneasy and speculative as all the crew had been since leaving base. Sealed orders bred suspicion. But these were good men and they'd served under him long enough to follow his instructions without question, even if they had their doubts about the assignment at hand. He wouldn't have chosen them to accompany him otherwise.

Gordon returned in the late afternoon, his collection box floating ahead of him on a cushion of air as he guided it with the remote control in his right hand. At the same moment he entered the clearing, McLaren called Lukas from *Kelsoe Moran*.

"Captain, we have a bogey," McLaren reported, his voice raised. "Range one thousand kems. No, make that five hundred. Mr. Wilczk, check your board! That can't be right—nothing could travel that fast in real space!"

"McLaren, what's going on up there?" Lukas demanded,

one hand on the com button, the other going out to start the shuttle's engines.

Silence. Then, "Sorry, Captain. We had a reading, but then it vanished. Wilczk's checking his board. It must be malfunctioning. Sensors show noth—"

Static.

"McLaren, I didn't copy that. Please repeat."

More static. Garbled noise. ". . . losing power . . . shipwide malfunc—"

Then nothing. He attempted to contact the ship once more, then whipped around and checked on Gordon's progress. He was less than twenty feet away, walking slowly. Adrick and Crowther were on their feet, as alarmed as he was.

"Adrick, Crowther, hurry Gordon up. Help him get that thing inside."

They started moving before he finished speaking, opening the cargo hatch and jumping lithely to the ground below. They ran to Gordon, spoke urgently. He glanced at the shuttle, then sent the box ahead at full speed and came at a run, Adrick and Crowther close behind.

He slowed the box just before it rammed into the shuttle, aligned it carefully, then sent it on in and lowered it to the floor. Adrick swung himself up into the shuttle, then gave Gordon a hand. Crowther followed a second later, securing the hatch behind him.

"Strap in," Lukas ordered them, preparing to start the shuttle's engines.

"Captain, what's going on? I demand an answer!" Gordon said.

"The *Kelsoe Moran*'s having problems, Gordon. We have to leave. Sit down and strap in."

"Adrick said something about a bogey. It that true?"

Lukas would not have believed anything could divert his attention from the *Kelsoe Moran*, but a peculiar note of strain in Gordon's voice did. The civilian was white with fear. No, not fear—horror.

"They thought they did," he said, looking at the civilian intently. "But it may have been a malfunction. McLaren reported they were losing power, then we lost contact with them."

Gordon went whiter still. For a moment, Lukas thought he might pass out. "Gordon, what are you so upset about?" he demanded, his internal warning systems going on full alert. "If

I didn't know better, I'd say you know something about all this. Something I don't.''

Gordon pulled a disrupter.

Adrick and Crowther had started to strap in. Now they shucked off the straps and lunged to their feet in unison, reaching for their own weapons, but they were too slow. Gordon whirled around, positioning himself so he could cover all three of them.

"Tell your men to sit down, Captain, or I'll fire on them. Tell them!" he ordered.

Lukas went rigid, weighing their odds of reaching their weapons before Gordon could fire. They didn't have a chance.

"Sit down," he told them. "Do as he says."

They hesitated, then subsided reluctantly.

"What's going on, Gordon?" Lukas demanded. "What are you so worried about?"

"Nothing. I'm sure it's nothing."

"What are you sure is nothing? Come on, Gordon. You know something. I can see it in your eyes. Tell me!"

"I'm sure whatever's wrong with your ship has nothing to do with my mission. Since you're so worried about her, however, I suggest we return immediately."

Lukas did not move. Gordon wanted to return to the ship, did he? He wasn't so sure he wanted to accommodate him.

"That was an order, Captain," Gordon said. He pointed the disrupter straight at Lukas's chest. "Sit down and prepare to take off."

The uneasiness that had dogged Lukas the past eight days, from his meeting with Sorseli to the present moment, coalesced in that instant. Something was very wrong with this mission. Sorseli had told him the Admiralty had ordered the mission to Gynos, but he suddenly found himself wondering if that was really true. Wondering and doubting.

"What's in that box, Gordon?" he asked, his eyes going to the container that filled most of the empty space at the rear of the shuttle. The gray box looked harmless enough, but appearances could be deceiving.

"Nothing to concern you, Captain. I'm ordering you to sit down and take us back to your ship." Gordon moved his hand just enough to remind them that he held a weapon.

"Not before I know what's in that box."

"Captain, Admiral Sorseli ordered you to obey me. If you value your career at all, you will do just that, because if you don't, you'll find yourself demoted to ensign, and this time there won't be any accelerated promotions. Sit down!''

"No," Lukas said. He stepped to his right, drawing Gordon's eyes and the disrupter away from his men. "I don't know what's going on here, but you are going to put that weapon down. Until you do, this shuttle isn't going anywhere.''

"I can fly the shuttle, Captain. I don't need you. In fact, you're becoming a decided hindrance. Either you sit down and lift off, or I start firing. Your men will die first, Captain, but you'll be next in line. You have my word on that.''

"Gordon, if you kill us, you'll have to deal with the entire crew of the *Kelsoe Moran*.''

"Admiral Sorseli gave me a set of orders handing over command of the *Kelsoe Moran* to your first officer in case you became a problem, Lukas. I don't believe he'll hesitate to obey them—whether you're alive or dead. Now sit down and lift off!''

"Very well, Gordon. We'll leave," he said. He glanced at his men, then turned, as if taking his seat.

What happened next could not have taken more than ten seconds, but at the time, it seemed to go on forever. Lukas swung around, pulling his own weapon, even as Adrick and Crowther lunged to their feet and rushed the civilian, moving between him and Lukas. Gordon opened fire on them, his disrupter catching both of them in one burst of lethal fire. After the beam struck Adrick, then Crowther, it swung toward Lukas. Lukas fired his own weapon, but Gordon was already falling to the floor, rolling. Lukas dropped as well, landing behind the pilot's chair.

Where was Gordon?

He held his breath, listening, not daring to move. He guessed the other man could see his legs so he kept them still. If he didn't move, Gordon might believe he'd been hit.

Gordon rolled across the floor and came to a stop behind the rear shuttle seats. Lukas forced himself to remain limp. Gordon gave him thirty seconds, then stood and took a cautious step forward. He thought he had hit Lukas, and was coming to investigate. Lukas had a chance—one final chance.

Gordon took a second step, then a third. He was halfway down the aisle now. One more step and he'd be able to see over the pilot's chair and look down on Lukas. One more step and he'd be able to raise his weapon and fire. Lukas moved his right hand imperceptibly, changing the setting on his weapon from stun to full power. On stun, the disrupter would fire a single, one-second burst, then cut off automatically. That was enough if you already had your target centered in, but if you didn't, the time required to lift your finger from the firing button and press it again could mean the difference between life and death. He wouldn't have time to aim; he would have to start firing the moment he moved and keep on firing, hoping to catch Gordon with the sweeping beam.

Gordon took the final step and Lukas exploded, throwing himself over on his back and bringing his arm into firing position in the same motion. He opened fire the moment he started moving, the beam from the disrupter swinging up toward the ceiling in a wide arc and catching Gordon just as he fired. His beam went wide, missing Lukas by several inches. Their eyes met for a timeless instant; then the light in Gordon's dimmed and went out. His legs buckled and he fell to the floor.

Lukas took an unsteady breath. Another. And found himself sitting in the common room on the *Widdon Galaxy*, hands wrapped around his stomach, head nearly touching his knees. Keenan was at his side, saying something. He wasn't sure what, only that some of the anguish faded and his guilt reached a level that could be borne.

He had killed Gordon. Worse, he had killed Crowther and Adrick as surely as if he'd fired on them himself. They'd moved on his orders. *Bad orders!* He should have done as Gordon said, should have taken the man and his cargo back to the ship. His men would be alive and nothing that had happened afterward would have come to pass. He'd been wrong. Wrong!

"Greg, listen to me," Keenan was saying. "Listen to me! Gordon was prepared to kill all three of you from the moment you left the *Kelsoe Moran*. Yes, you ordered your men to attack him, but what else could you have done? Take him back to your ship with God knows what in that box? You'd have been risking the safety of your entire crew and ship if you'd listened to him."

"If I had listened to him, Crowther and Adrick would still be alive."

"Would they? Greg, if you hadn't stopped Gordon then, if you'd taken him back to Zerron Base, they might still have died. Sorseli couldn't afford to have anyone talk about that mission. Not ever. If you'd returned to base, there's a strong possibility you'd have been ordered back out on patrol before your crew could go on leave. Your ship might have met with an accident on that patrol. A fatal accident. Crowther and Adrick wouldn't have been the only ones who died if that had happened. Your entire crew would have.''

''What are you talking about?'' Lukas demanded, looking up. ''Sorseli had no reason to hurt us. My crew knew we were on a secret mission. They knew better than to talk about where we'd been and what we'd done. None of them would have said a word.''

''Sorseli couldn't be sure of that. He couldn't take the chance that even one of them might forget himself and mention your ship had gone into a restricted zone. Because he sent you there on his own authority, Greg! If his superiors found out he'd done that, he'd have been the one facing a court-martial, not you. Your order to attack Gordon may have resulted in the deaths of two of your crew, but you may have saved all the others!''

''I don't believe that. You're wrong. Wrong!''

''We'll never know, will we? I believe Sorseli would have gone to extreme lengths to protect himself, but you're right: I can't be sure. Neither can you—one way or the other. What I am sure of, however, is that you made the best decision you could at the time. You were an exemplary officer, Greg. I don't believe you'd have reacted to the situation on that planet as you did without good cause. I think you saw something dangerous in Gordon, something too dangerous to be allowed back on the *Kelsoe Moran*. I think you acted in the best interests of your ship and crew. I don't think you took lives, Greg. I think you saved them.''

Lukas shook his head, not willing to believe Keenan. The psychiatrist sighed.

''Greg, I know you feel guilty about your men's deaths, but you can't go on punishing yourself forever. You made a decision—a command decision. You acted on the facts available to you at the time. You're trying to second-guess yourself in hindsight, and that isn't fair. I want you to consider the facts honestly and carefully, and decide if you really should have acted any differently, knowing only what you did at the time.''

Keenan left him alone for the rest of the day so he could do just that, but try as he did, he never found an answer that pleased both of them.

That was not the only difficult moment in the days that followed. He had trouble recalling what had happened immediately after his men died, and not even Keenan's calm reassurance that he shouldn't worry about the blurred fragments eased his fretting. The gaps in his memory covered all the time until his return to Zerron Base and his court-martial. He remembered that well enough—his stubborn refusal to enter a plea of guilty, his furious anger when Sorseli denied he had given him the orders to enter the restricted zone, his bitterness when the court announced the verdict that had become a foregone conclusion.

The sole surprise had been his sentence. He'd expected to serve time, and the order for rehabilitation therapy had come as a complete, horrifying shock. The thought of anyone attempting to alter his mind and memories upset him so much that he pleaded with his counsel, Lewis Fornay, to refuse the sentence and insist he be given penal time instead. Fornay would not listen.

"Naturally, you're concerned about the treatment methods used in rehabilitation therapy, Commander, but I assure you, there's no cause for alarm. You're an excellent candidate for rehabilitation, and it will give you a chance for a normal life. Penal time won't. You'd be crazy to throw away twenty years of your life. You may think you're bitter now, but what you're feeling is nothing compared to the anger you would have after years in prison. Believe me, rehabilitation therapy is the best thing that could happen to you."

He hadn't believed Fornay, but that hadn't mattered. They'd taken him to the base's medical facility as soon as court was dismissed. He spent the next day undergoing one test after another. He would not answer the doctors' questions, but he had to submit to their physical and neurological examinations—a security guard saw to that.

By evening, he was so upset and exhausted that he actually felt relieved when they locked him in the cubicle that was to be his room for the duration of his stay. A nurse brought him dinner, but he didn't eat. She took his untouched tray away an hour later, without comment. The door locked behind her and he relaxed for the first time, thinking they had left him alone for the night. He was wrong. A half hour later, Renard made his first appearance.

"Mr. Lukas, Dr. Alec Renard," he said by way of greeting. "I will be your therapist. I was afraid you'd be worried about what will be happening to you during the next few weeks, so I stopped by to see if you had any questions you'd like to ask?"

Lukas said nothing.

"Not one?" Renard asked, lifting his brows when Lukas remained silent. "Surely you must have a few—the nature of your treatment, the duration of your stay?"

Lukas did not respond. He had questions, all right, but they would only reveal the nature of his fears—weaknesses he was convinced Renard would use against him later.

"Still determined not to cooperate, are you?" Renard said. "My staff told me you'd done your best to be difficult all day. I'm sorry to hear that, truly sorry. You're only making matters worse for yourself. Still, a certain degree of apprehension is understandable, if counterproductive. I believe I'll have the nurse give you a sedative tonight. It's important for you to feel relaxed and rested when we start work tomorrow. She'll have orders to see you take the pill, so please don't refuse it. Get a good night's sleep. I'll see you in the morning."

Renard left and the nurse came in a moment later. Lukas had intended to refuse the pill, despite the doctor's warning, but he changed his mind when he saw the security guard who followed her into the room. The burly man gave the impression he'd like nothing better than a struggle—one which could result in only one outcome. Lukas took the tablet and swallowed, his eyes on the guard all the while. He was asleep within fifteen minutes.

The next thing he knew, someone was coming into his room. He forced his eyes open and caught a bleary glimpse of a male nurse standing beside his bed. He tried to lift his head, but his body refused to respond. His limbs felt heavy and lifeless. He didn't think he could have moved if the bed had been on fire.

The nurse pulled the blanket away from his arm, swabbed the inside of his elbow with antiseptic, and slid in a needle before he realized what was happening. He did react then, but it was too late. Whatever the man had injected was already coursing through his body, making him horribly dizzy and sick to his stomach. The nausea passed within minutes, but what replaced it was infinitely worse. He lost all sensation. He was awake and knew he lay on the bed, but he could feel nothing. Panic hit him, blind and utterly irrational, but even that didn't last. His eyes closed and he started drifting away, coming back only when someone spoke to him.

"Good morning, Greg," a man said. "How are you feeling?"

"Renard—" It took all his strength and concentration to say that single word. The sight of the therapist sent fear coursing through his bloodstream, and the lethargy that gripped him eased momentarily. He fought to hold on to his apprehension. Fear could give you strength if you knew how to use it. The Academy had taught him that.

"Now, Greg. There's no reason to be so obstinate," Renard said as Lukas tensed. "I'm here to help you, not hurt you." His voice was warm and reassuring, but Lukas didn't believe him, not then and not in all the hours that followed.

He had no real recollection of what passed after that, only a vague sense that Renard's tolerance quickly changed to anger, then outright hostility as Lukas fought him. And he did fight, resisting every suggestion, every instruction as long as he could, as if his very life depended on that struggle.

But despite his determination, he found himself failing. He started losing time, and whenever he regained a semblance of alertness a nurse would appear and give him another injection. Sometimes it was the man, sometimes the woman. They were always accompanied by a security guard. He fought them, too, but the guard held him down with no difficulty.

The stretches of darkness overtook him. With them came an overwhelming sense of despair, a depression that sucked away all life, all energy. He felt his mind and body collapsing in upon themselves and knew he had lost the battle. He tried to gather his strength, to make one last stand, but he could not. He lost his grip and fell into oblivion.

He woke hours or days later—he didn't know which—and found himself sitting in Renard's office, aware that something had happened to him, but neither knowing nor caring exactly what. Caring took too much effort. He needed all his energy just to listen to Renard's questions and give his listless responses.

He spent days in that office, learning about his guilt, going over his faults in detail. Endless, dispiriting days.

"That's all you recall about the sessions with Renard, Greg?" Keenan asked quietly, bringing him back to the present with a jerk.

"Yes," he said. He thought there was more, but depression lay so heavily upon him that he could barely summon the energy to give Keenan a reply, let alone search his memory again.

"It's probably just as well," the psychiatrist said quietly. He came over to Lukas and put his hand on his shoulder, then squatted down so he could see his face.

"Are you all right?" he asked.

"No," Lukas whispered. The reaction caught him then. He started shaking and could not stop. He thought he was going to be sick. He thought he might start screaming and never stop—

for what Sorseli had done, for what Renard had done, for all he had lost and would never have again.

"Daniel, help me," he said desperately, terrified he was going to lose control and start slamming himself against the walls like a caged animal trying to batter its way free.

But Keenan failed him for the first time. "What do you want me to do, Greg?" the other man said. "Make it all go away? Make it not be true? I can't do that. It is true. It happened, and nothing I can say, nothing I can do, can change that."

Lukas was angry. So angry he could have killed. If Sorseli or Renard had walked into the room at that moment, he would have murdered them without a moment's hesitation. He said as much to Keenan, expecting the psychiatrist to tell him he'd find himself incapable of such an act, but the other man surprised him again.

"I expect you could," he said calmly. "There have been times when I felt like killing them myself."

"You? You couldn't hurt anyone," Lukas said incredulously. "Why do you think they decided to send you to medical school instead of letting you finish your senior year at the Academy? They knew you could never hurt anyone. If you'd been any less brilliant they'd have washed you out, but you were too good to lose. So they found another use for you instead, the same as they found a use for me. They're good at that, aren't they, Daniel? Finding uses for people."

"Yes. Yes, they are. But the people get something in return, too. The system wouldn't work if they didn't."

"What do you get, Daniel? You tear people's lives apart for them. What do they give you in return?"

"I see that justice is done. I help the people I can, when and where I can."

"How, by ruining two lives instead of one? You may convict Sorseli, but that isn't going to help me, is it?"

"Help you? I don't understand, Greg. What do you mean?"

"Even if they find him guilty and clear me, I can't go back to the service, can I?" Lukas said, voicing the ugly, black certainty that had been growing inside him for several days. "I can't go back because they won't have me, will they?"

The psychiatrist hesitated. For an instant Lukas thought he might actually lie, but honesty won out. "No," he said quietly. "No, they won't. Do you know why?"

Lukas stood up, unable to remain still. "Renard did something to me, didn't he? Something you can't fix. I know he did. I can feel it. I can't—''

"Can't what, Greg?"

"I can't command again. Whatever it takes—the certainty, the assurance—it's gone. And it isn't ever coming back, is it? I remember how I felt before, but I can't make the feelings come back. The profile you did yesterday told you that, didn't it? Only you weren't going to tell me."

"Not yet. I wanted to give you a little more time."

"Time for what? To realize I'll never be the man I was again?"

"No!" Keenan said sharply: "To realize the man you *are*. Not what you were, not what you might have been—what you are."

"A second-rate pilot fit only for commercial freighters."

"Is that what you think?"

"That's what your test said, isn't it?"

"You may be many things, Greg Lukas, but second-rate is not one of them. You may not be able to serve in the Corps any longer, but you're still a better pilot than ninety-nine percent of the men on commercial ships."

"But not good enough to captain a ship again, not even a company ship. They have the same tests you do. They'd never hire me for anything but a pilot's job."

"Perhaps not, but that isn't the real issue, is it? The real issue is whether you honestly want to be a captain again. And you don't, do you, Greg? No matter how much you think you ought to, you do not want to captain another ship, do you?"

Lukas was silent a long time, but Keenan waited for his reply, not letting him off the hook.

"No," he said at last.

"Greg, only an idiot would be upset over not having something he didn't want in the first place."

"But I *should* want it."

"Maybe the Greg Lukas who went to the Academy should have, but not you. Like it or not, you have changed. And like it or not, you're going to have to live with those changes."

"Along with everything else you keep telling me I have to live with."

"Yes."

"You're asking a lot of me."

"No more than you can give."

"Don't be too sure about that."

"I am. I know you, Greg—the man you were, and the man

you are now. You have much more to offer than you're willing
to believe at the moment.''

He didn't argue. What was the point? He knew the truth. Greg
Lukas had died in Alec Renard's office; the man who left Zerron
Base was a mere echo of the person he had been. Keenan could
offer all the understanding and compassion in the universe, but
it would not be enough to ease his anguish over all he had lost
and could never regain.

Chapter 16

Kiley turned around as soon as she heard his footsteps. "Good evening, Greg," she said. "I understand you're ready to start standing watch again."

"Yes." He stopped just inside the door, as he had his first day on duty, waiting for permission to proceed further.

"I'm glad," she told him with a smile. "It's good to have you back." She stood up and offered him the pilot's chair.

He hesitated a moment longer, then walked forward and took his place.

"I want Greg to start working again," Keenan had said that afternoon. "Just a few hours a day. His system is clear of drugs, so you don't have to worry about that, but we still have some work to do, and I'd rather he didn't pull a full shift until we're finished. Four hours should be enough to keep him from sitting around brooding, without causing an unnecessary strain."

"Standing watch during jump won't prove much strain," she'd returned dryly. "There isn't much to do except monitor the boards."

"I think he'll find that's enough at first."

She had searched Keenan's face, wondering what he wasn't saying, as she always did when he spoke. It wasn't that he lied. She had no doubt that what he did say was the absolute truth as best he knew it. The problem was all that he didn't say, and she suspected that was a lot. She found herself constantly on the defensive around him, a state she heartily disliked.

It didn't help that she seemed to be the only one who felt that way about him. He had fit in with the rest of the family as easily as Lukas had; even Jon Robert's initial hostility had quickly softened. It didn't take a trained observer to notice that the daily sessions took nearly as heavy a toll on him as on Lukas, or that he was giving his friend an almost frightening degree of attention and concern.

Moreover, he had kept his promise to talk to Jon Robert if her brother had any questions about his treatment methods, and they had had several discussions. Kiley didn't know what they talked about—neither Keenan nor Jon Robert would discuss the conversations. Whatever the psychiatrist said, he had clearly calmed her brother's apprehensions, and he took the psychiatrist's side every time she questioned what he was doing.

She wished someone had taken the trouble to ease her concern. There had been times in the past week when it had been all she could do not to interfere, Jon Robert's trust in Keenan notwithstanding. Even now, glancing sideways at Lukas, she wondered if she hadn't made a serious mistake ever listening to the psychiatrist.

He was not the same.

It wasn't just that he'd lost weight, or that his eyes had new, haunted depths. It was everything about him, from the military stiffness that had returned to his posture to the sharpened intensity with which he observed his surroundings. He watched her and the rest of the family as if he were meeting them for the first time, and while he met their overtures with politeness and respect, nothing they said or did seemed to touch him. She had understood his withdrawal while Keenan was drugging him to the point of oblivion, but he wasn't drugged now and he continued to hold himself apart. Except from Keenan, of course. There were no barriers between them, and their closeness hurt her in a way she wasn't prepared to acknowledge.

She didn't know what had transpired behind the closed doors of the passenger cabin, but whatever had gone on had changed Greg Lukas irrevocably. She had guessed he was about Lia's age when they first met, but he acted much older now, widening the gap between them to a chasm. The deference that she had once attributed to uncertainty was now a matter of politeness, and there was no uncertainty in him that she could see. Shadows, yes, and great unhappiness, but the vulnerability that had once given her the courage to approach him had vanished. She saw no sign that it would ever return.

And yet there was a moment, as he settled himself in the pilot's chair and looked at the boards, during which she caught a glimpse of that other man.

"It looks . . . different," he said, almost as if talking to himself. "Like a part of me knows it and a part doesn't." And then

the moment was gone and he was turning to her, fully in control
again.

"You don't have to stay unless you want to," he told her,
leaving no doubt that he would prefer to be alone.

"Very well. You're on for four," she said. "I'll be back at
twenty hundred to relieve you."

He nodded without looking at her. She hesitated, still
uncertain about leaving him alone, but he had already gone
to work and was scrolling the most recent status report up
the display screen, studying the numbers with all his usual
concentration.

He glanced up and she colored as his cool, clear gray eyes
met hers. "I can handle the bridge, Kiley," he said. "I wouldn't
be here if I couldn't."

"Of course not. She's all yours, Greg," she forced herself to
say lightly, then made a hurried exit.

She wasn't hungry, but she went to the galley and fixed dinner
anyway. It would be a long night on the bridge, and she'd better
eat now, while she could. She took her plate into the dining
room, expecting to find it deserted, but Keenan was there, fin-
ishing a late meal of his own.

"Hello, Kiley," he said with his warmest, friendliest smile,
the one she trusted the least. "Come on in and join me. I was
hoping I'd see you."

"Really?" she replied coolly, taking a seat as far away as she
judged she could without distancing herself too obviously.

"Greg made it to the bridge?"

"Yes."

"Did he have any problem orienting himself?"

She paused, her fork halfway to her mouth. "No, of course
not. Why should he?"

Keenan shrugged. "No particular reason, but he's gone
through a great deal the last week and a half, not the least of
which were heavy doses of drugs designed to influence perception and memory."

"He seemed fine to me," she said, bending her head over her
plate.

"Kiley, is something wrong?" he asked quietly. "I don't want
to interfere where I'm not wanted, but if there's any way I can
help—"

"Nothing's wrong, Keenan," she said firmly.

"Jon Robert's says you're pushing yourself too hard," he
told her, his blue eyes intent. "He and Reese say they've both

offered to work longer shifts on the bridge, but you won't let them.''

"Jon Robert should talk—he was back to work in the engine room before the bandages came off his hands.''

"Kiley, he's worried about you. They all are.''

"They don't need to be.''

"Don't they? I'm not sure I agree. When I see a person driving herself as hard as you are, I have to wonder just what she's trying to prove—or what she's running away from.''

Kiley put her fork down carefully, looked straight at him, and said, "You may be Greg Lukas's psychiatrist, but you are not mine. Is that clear, Keenan? I don't need or want your concern. I have a job and I'm doing it, the best way I know. I won't let Jon Robert on the bridge because he's putting in a full day in engineering, despite the fact he isn't completely well yet. Reese is already on an eight-hour shift and, quite frankly, that's as long as he can stand watch and remain alert. He does his best, but he's a shipping agent, not a pilot.''

"Kiley, you can't keep up this pace. Even you must be able to see that. If you don't wear yourself out physically, then you'll certainly burn yourself out mentally and emotionally. You don't want to end up hating the ship and everything about her, do you?''

"That's not likely to happen, Keenan.''

"Daniel. I told you to call me Daniel. And it doesn't take professional training to see you're well on the way to doing just that.''

"I'm not," Kiley objected. "Besides, I'll catch up on my sleep once Greg comes back to work. I know you want a few more days with him, and that's fine. But after that, there's no reason he can't stand watch again, is there? Well, is there?'' she demanded when he didn't reply immediately.

"There's no medical reason," he said with something suspiciously close to pity in his eyes. "But I'm afraid he's going to have to leave the ship once we reach Cardos. He and I will be going to the Admiralty's headquarters on Everest on the first available transport. I'm sorry. I know how much you depend on him, but right now he's more important to the Corps.''

"He hasn't said anything about this.''

"Only because he's been too preoccupied with his own problems to think about the effect his leaving will have on you. But that won't stop him. He has to come, Kiley. There are people who want—and need—to talk to him. What he has to tell them is important. More important than staying on this ship.''

''To you maybe, but to him? Why should he have to go to Everest? Why can't you just take a sworn statement?''

''That won't be good enough. Not in this case. But he won't have to stay forever, and I'm pretty sure he'll want to return to the *Widdon Galaxy* once the Admiralty is finished with him.''

''If he leaves, he won't come back,'' she said flatly. ''Why would he? Once he's been proven innocent, he'll be able to return to the service, won't he? And he will. Of course he will.''

''I don't think you have to worry about him returning to active service.''

''Why not?'' she demanded. ''If he's innocent of the charges against him, what's to stop him?''

The professional wall Keenan raised against the world went up; then just as abruptly, for no reason she could see, it fell.

''Kiley, even if he wanted to return to duty, which he doesn't, he can't. He's no longer fit for command.''

''No longer fit—what are you talking about, Keenan? Of course he's fit.''

''Is he? Has he ever, even once, shown the least ambition to be anything but the pilot of this ship? Well, has he?''

''No,'' she admitted grudgingly.

''That's bothered you, hasn't it? You knew he had the skill and training to be captain, but you couldn't understand why he didn't have the ambition. You still don't, do you? Because you can't imagine anything else yourself. If captaining a ship is all you've ever wanted, how can he want anything less either?''

He was right about that much—she never had understood how Lukas could be content to remain a mere pilot. A part of her had not entirely trusted him for that very reason. But if Keenan said Lukas had no desire left to command, then it must be true.

''What happened to him, Keenan? What could possibly have changed a man that much?''

''That's for Greg to tell you, if he chooses. All I can say is that he will never be a threat to you—not when it comes to commanding this ship.''

''I never thought he was.''

''No? I think you did. In fact, I think a part of you never completely trusted him because you didn't understand why he didn't want to captain this ship. *You* did—he should have, too. What's more, there was a time when you'd have been right. Would you like to know something interesting? If I were to put your Academy admission profile and Greg's alongside each other, I'd have a difficult time telling the difference. You'd have gone a long way in the service, Kiley Michaelson. As far as you had the will and ambition to take yourself.''

''And those words are supposed to be some sort of comfort, Keenan? Because if they are, I don't need them.''

''What do you need, then? The ship? Your family? Or are they just a way to prove you aren't a failure, despite the fact that you didn't qualify for the Academy? Is that why you're so bent on trying to run the ship single-handedly? To prove you can? To prove you're fit to command?''

''I don't have to prove anything, Keenan. Not to you, not to anyone.''

''No? Then why do you keep trying to?''

''I don't.''

''Don't you? You ought to stop and take a look at yourself sometime, Kiley Michaelson. A long, close look. You might be surprised at what you see.''

Kiley took a deep breath, controlling fury. ''I don't know which is worse, Keenan: reconstituted dinners or unsolicited advice passing as professional concern.''

The psychiatrist's eyes flashed and she thought he was going to respond angrily, but then he laughed. ''And to think I told my commanding officer I could handle you with no problem. He wouldn't call me his best interrogator if he could see us now. He thinks I can make anyone open up and reveal their innermost secrets, but I can't even get you talking. I'd like to, Kiley,'' he said, suddenly earnest. ''I'd like to be your friend.''

''You might stand a chance if you'd stop being a psychiatrist first. I told you, I don't need your help and I don't want it.''

''How about my friendship? Would you be willing to accept that?''

''If that's what you're truly offering.''

''It is. All right, Kiley, I'll quit playing the psychiatrist on one condition: that you call me Daniel. Everyone else does. Do you think you could manage?''

''I don't see why not—Daniel.''

''And if you do want to talk to me sometime—as a friend— I'd be glad to listen.''

She had started to pick up her fork, and her hand froze in

midair. "If I didn't know better, Keenan, I'd say you'd just tried to break our agreement."

"Kiley—"

"I meant what I said! I don't need or want your help—not in any capacity."

"Then I'll let you be," he said, and to her surprise, he did.

Lukas spent the next morning with Keenan, then worked all afternoon in the garden with Lia before reporting to the bridge for the evening shift. Kiley almost didn't let him stay. He moved with unnatural slowness and barely gave the boards a cursory glance as he settled in place.

"Are you sure you're up to working a full shift?" she asked, hoping he would take the question for the concern it represented and not implied criticism. "You look worn out."

"I'm fine. Daniel just kept me longer than usual this morning. Go on, take your break."

"All right, but if you do find you're too tired—"

"I'll call you—I promise. Now go."

She gave him a last, skeptical look, then left. She didn't believe he would actually keep his word, but two hours later, he called her cabin.

"Kiley, this is Greg. Can you come to the bridge?"

His voice sounded strong and steady over the intercom, but there was an edge to the words that had her on her feet before he finished speaking.

"On my way, Greg."

She reached the bridge in less than a minute. Lukas was still in the pilot's chair, but he was bent forward, hands wrapped around his stomach as if he was ill.

"What's wrong?" she asked, alarmed.

"I don't feel very good," he said.

"Have you called Daniel?"

He shook his head and wrapped his hands tighter around himself. They were shaking. No, he was shaking, deep shudders that racked his entire body.

She reached for the intercom and pressed the button for Keenan's cabin. "Daniel, are you there?"

"Yes," he answered immediately.

"Greg's sick. I need you on the bridge."

"I'll be right there."

He arrived almost as quickly as she had. She had been standing in the narrow space between the pilot's and copilot's chairs, and she moved as soon as he appeared, making way for him. He didn't even look at her; all his attention was on Lukas.

"Greg, what's wrong?" he asked. She saw the worry that flashed across his face, but all that came through in his voice was concern, underlaid with something remarkably close to gentleness.

"Feel sick," Lukas said.

Keenan put a hand on his forehead, then tipped his chin back so he could see his face.

"When did you eat last?" he asked.

"Lunch."

"Nothing since then, not even to drink?"

"I had some water. That's all."

"Greg, have you been having memory flashes this afternoon?"

"I don't know. Maybe one or two. Nothing that made any sense." He stopped, squeezing his eyes shut. "It's starting again," he said desperately. "Daniel, make it stop. I don't think I can stand this. Please, make it stop!"

"Greg, I want you to take a deep breath and relax. Can you hear me? Take a deep breath. That's right. Now take another. And another." He said something else, but his voice was pitched for Lukas's ears alone and Kiley couldn't make out the words. Whatever they were, Lukas responded immediately. His breathing slowed and his arms loosened their grip around his stomach.

"That's better," Keenan said warmly a moment later. "Just keep taking slow, deep breaths." He gave him a minute, then said, "Are you feeling steady enough to walk? I think we should go to my cabin."

"Yes," Lukas answered from some distance away.

"Get up, then."

Keenan put his hand out and Lukas rose. He moved slowly, unsteadily, but was walking on his own.

"Daniel—" Kiley started, but Keenan cut her off with a warning shake of his head.

"Later," he said.

The two men were halfway across the bridge when Lukas swayed. He grabbed the chair in front of the backup engineering board, clutching it as if his life depended on his grip. His breath was coming too fast again.

"It didn't stop when I killed Gordon, did it?" he said abruptly.

"I thought it did, but I was wrong. I must have been wrong. Why else would I have been so terrified when McLaren found me? I hadn't done anything to be afraid of. You kept skipping over that part, almost as if you didn't want me to remember it. Why not? And the time—they didn't restore power on the *Kelsoe Moran* for six hours. Six hours! I was on Gynos all that time and I don't remember anything about it. One minute I was looking down at Gordon, and the next I was outside the ship and McLaren was shaking me, asking questions. What happened? Why was I outside the ship? Why was I unconscious? Why was I so frightened? I killed him in self-defense. There was no reason to be so frightened. I don't—"

"Greg, we need to talk," Keenan interrupted, "but this isn't the place. We're in Kiley's way. Let's go to my cabin . . . Please," he urged when Lukas did not respond.

But the pilot didn't hear. He was breathing faster than ever, his eyes focused on some inner vision. "Something happened after I killed Gordon, didn't it? I remember . . ." He trailed off, then said in a rush, "The shuttle lost power, then there was a noise, like something banging against the hatch. There was something outside the shuttle. Not just the hatch, but the whole shuttle! The hatch started opening. I hadn't touched the control, but it was opening. Someone was out there. No, not someone— something!"

His voice rose, thick with terror. He swung around, his eyes wide open, focused far beyond Keenan. "There were people, only they weren't human! They made me go with them. They did things to me. Things that hurt." His voice had been rising the entire time he talked, but his next words ended in a near scream. "Daniel, they're hurting me! *Make them stop! Please! Make them stop!*"

Keenan caught him. "Greg, listen to me! I know you were frightened and in pain on Gynos, but you're not there now. You're on the *Widdon Galaxy* and you're safe. What happened on Gynos is over. All over!"

But Lukas wasn't listening. His breath came in great gulps, hard and fast. Kiley saw his scream coming, felt it building inside herself. The instant before it broke free, his body convulsed, his muscles going so rigid that she thought his bones would break under the strain. But it wasn't his body that gave way, it was his mind. His eyes rolled back and he sagged against Keenan, unconscious.

"Kiley, help me," the psychiatrist said, catching Lukas and holding his limp weight against his body.

She swung the chair around and helped Keenan lower Lukas into the seat. For a time, the silence on the bridge was broken only by the sound of their breathing.

She was cold. Her hands hurt, they were so cold. Shock, she told herself. It's just shock. It will pass. She understood why Lukas had been sitting with his hands wrapped around his stomach a few minutes before. She wanted to hold herself the same way.

Keenan must have sensed her reaction. "Are you all right?" he asked, giving her a worried look.

She nodded and took a deep, steadying breath. "Daniel, what happened to him?" she asked, some of Lukas's horror finding its way into her voice.

"I can't—" he started, then broke off as Lukas stirred and opened his eyes.

The pilot appeared puzzled. He started to ask Keenan how he'd come to be sitting there, then broke off abruptly as remembrance cascaded down. His chest began rising and falling as he gasped for air again.

Keenan gripped his shoulders, holding on as if his grasp were all that was keeping Lukas with them. "Greg, you're not on Gynos now," he said. "No one's going to hurt you. You're safe. I know they hurt you, but it's over now. All over."

He kept on talking, voice low and soothing. Lukas didn't respond at first, but then his eyes came back into focus. They found Keenan and latched on to him.

"I can't stop it from coming," he said raggedly, "and it hurts. It hurts so much!"

"Greg, we've talked about these memories before, remember? I know they're painful, but you can handle them. You've buried them so long, they've assumed terrifying proportions, but there's nothing in them you can't accept, I promise."

"I can't . . ." he started, then trailed off, his eyes pleading with Keenan, as if he wanted to believe him, but didn't dare.

"You can," the psychiatrist replied with absolute conviction. "Trust me, Greg. The worst is over. Do you remember what I told you to do when the memories started to come back? To relax and take deep, slow breaths? Do it, Greg. Let yourself go. There's nothing to be frightened of. In fact, it's getting harder and harder to understand just why you were so upset, isn't it?"

"Yes," Lukas whispered. His breathing slowed again. His eyes closed, then opened. "I want . . ."

"Yes, Greg? What do you want?"

"I want to talk. You said we'd talk . . ."

"And we will, but first we need to get off the bridge. We're interfering with operations. Why don't we go to my cabin? I think you can stand up now. Why don't you try?" He helped Lukas rise, steadying him when he swayed. He glanced past the pilot, at Kiley.

"Later," he told her, the words both an order and a promise. She let him take Lukas away. What else could she do? That didn't stop her from worrying, though. She sat watch, diligently monitoring the boards, but it was Lukas's face she saw, twisted in agony, and his voice she heard, pleading with unknown captors, begging them over and over to stop the torture.

Kiley thought Keenan would conveniently forget the explanation he had promised, but he came back to the bridge an hour before her watch ended. He swiveled the copilot's seat around, sat down, leaned back, and closed his eyes with a sigh.

His face sagged with weariness and his clothes looked like he'd slept in them. She doubted his commanding officer would approve of him at the moment. Then again, maybe he would; perhaps results sometimes outweighed appearances, even in the Corps.

Keenan didn't say anything immediately, and Kiley turned back to the boards, giving him time to relax. She had almost forgotten him when he spoke a few minutes later.

"You like piloting a ship, don't you?" he asked with idle curiosity. He was still leaning back, but his eyes were open, watching her work.

"Yes," she said simply.

"I never did. Not the way you and Greg do. It was always the unknown that interested me—new planets, unexplored space. The service was the only way a man could reach the frontier, so I went to the Academy. It took me three years to admit I'd made a mistake and would never be command material, no matter how I tried to conform to their mold. If I hadn't been too smart for my own good, they'd never have let me in. I knew the answers they were looking for on the psychiatric profiles they ran, so I gave them. The academic work wasn't a problem either, but I didn't have the least desire to lead others and it got harder and harder to hide that.

"I was never so relieved in my life as the day I decided to go to my adviser and tell him I wanted to leave the Academy. Unfortunately, the relief didn't last. I spent the next two days taking their tests all over again—with honest answers this time. The second day, they kept me going for fourteen hours on a series of tests I couldn't begin to decipher. I didn't know what I was saying by the time I finished, but it must have been something right because after they evaluated the results, they offered to put me through medical school."

He paused, staring blindly ahead. "I'd never even considered the idea before. I wasn't sure I wanted to be a doctor, even if their tests said I had the aptitude. But it was a way to stay in the service and maybe even do some of the exploring I'd always hoped to do. Ships need physicians, after all. So I went. I knew I could handle the academic work—no modesty about that—but I didn't expect to love it. The more I learned, the more I wanted to know. I had my plans all set. I'd finish school, then apply for a post on a deep-space exploration ship. I didn't have any doubt I'd get the assignment I wanted—first in the class almost always does."

"But you didn't," she said.

"Not exactly. I was all set to spend the rest of my life in deep space when they sent us out in the real world to work on the wards at the naval hospital. I found out medicine was about more than books and ideas. It was about people, too. People who hurt. People too sick to care if they lived or died. People so sick, all they wanted to do was die. My last rotation was on a psychiatric ward. By the time I'd been there two weeks, I knew I wasn't ever going exploring. It's funny how agonizing the knowledge seemed at the time—and how quickly I forgot I'd ever wanted anything else. I'd have been a lousy commander, and a mediocre scientist, but I'm a great psychiatrist."

"As good as that, are you?" Kiley asked with a smile.

"Well, almost. I guess you noticed a lack of ego isn't one of my weaknesses."

"I did. Maybe I should let you give me a few pointers after all."

"I'd be glad to," he replied, a shade too readily for comfort.

"I'll bet you would," she said dryly. "On second thought, I think I'll settle for being what I am. Good or bad, at least it's a known quantity. I probably wouldn't recognize myself after a few sessions with you."

"You might be wise at that, considering the way I handled Greg today," he said, sobering. "I should have realized how close he was to breaking past the last of my blocks. But he's so damned stubborn, he refuses to admit he's in trouble, even to himself. For what it's worth, I gave him a lecture about responsibility to his ship he won't ever forget. If he didn't realize how much influence I still have over him before that, he does now."

"He must hate that."

"Yes, he does." Keenan grinned. "He always was insufferably proud; it will do him good to realize he isn't invulnerable."

"I don't think he believes that, Daniel," she said, unable to maintain a pretense of calmness any longer. "Not after the past week."

"No," he said heavily, the grin vanishing. "No, he doesn't."

"Daniel, what did he see? *Who* did he see? He said they weren't human. Is that true? That he saw—aliens?"

"Kiley, I can't talk to you about that. I really can't. Whatever my oath as a physician doesn't cover, my oath to the Corps does. If you know what's good for you, you'll forget everything you heard tonight."

He was so chillingly serious, she knew she was right. Greg Lukas had seen aliens on Gynos Three.

How many times had humans joked about what they'd do if and when they discovered other intelligent life in the universe? How many times had they wished they could find someone—anyone—capable of reason, of exchanging ideas? They had speculated on the possibility of other intelligent life-forms for centuries, and in the end they had yet to find one. Mankind had been lonely all those years, but it had also been safe.

Suddenly the universe wasn't so lonely anymore. Or so safe.

"Daniel, who were they?" she asked, so caught up in the idea of another race that she ignored his advice. "Where did they come from? And why did they hurt Greg? I know they did—he was in agony just remembering what they did. Why did they hurt him?"

"Kiley—"

"Don't try to put me off. I want answers. Greg is a member of my crew. If he or any of the rest of us are in danger, I want to know. Now!"

"There's no danger—at least, not here, not to you. I don't believe those people hurt Greg deliberately. They were probably

just doing what any group of scientists would—studying a new
life-form.''

"By torturing it?''

"No, of course not. At least, not intentionally. He didn't have
a pleasant time, but there was only one test that actually resulted
in pain.''

"What test? Come on, Daniel, you've told me this much. You
might as well tell me the rest.''

She didn't think he would reply, but a part of him must have
wanted to talk, regardless of oaths, because he said abruptly,
"You understand, I can't be certain about any of this. I can
guess, but that's all I'm doing—guessing. Still, from what Greg's
said, it sounds very much as if they were running some sort of
deep scan designed to measure his sensitivity to stimuli and map
his neurological system. The test started with sensations that
were almost imperceptible. The only problem is that it didn't
stop there—they kept heightening the intensity of the stimulus
until the pain was so unbearable, he passed out. He thought the
test took hours, but I don't think it could have lasted more than
ten or fifteen minutes from start to finish.''

"Fifteen minutes or fifteen hours—what's the difference? They
had to have known they were hurting him. He was screaming,
wasn't he? Why didn't they stop?''

"Because they're heartless scientists? Because they wanted to
know exactly how much he could endure? Because they didn't
understand what his screams meant? I don't know, Kiley. I don't
have the answers. All I know is that, with the exception of the
final test, one of them stayed beside him the entire time. It kept
stroking his arm, as if trying to offer reassurance or comfort. It
couldn't know its touch was as bad as, or worse than, any of the
tests. But it did try to ease his fear, and even went so far as to
stop the proceedings several times when he became unduly agitated.''

"But not during that last test.''

"No, not then.''

"What happened after that?''

"They released him. He was semiconscious when his crew
found him, but he was still dazed. If the ship's medical officer
had been present, he would undoubtedly have diagnosed a case
of acute shock, given him proper treatment, and the true story
would have come out. But he wasn't there, and Greg's first officer had reasons of his own for wanting to discredit him. He
claimed Lukas had taken the *Kelsoe Moran* into the restricted

zone illegally, and accused him of being responsible for his men's deaths. He said Lukas had obviously suffered a breakdown, either from guilt, fear over being found out and tried, or both.''

"Why didn't Greg tell his crew what really happened?''

"He tried, but he was still too disoriented to offer any rational explanations for his crewmen's deaths or his own behavior. Afterwards, he was under arrest and his first officer, McLaren, refused to let anyone see him, including the ship's medic. By the time they returned to port, it was too late for Greg. He had always buried his memories of the aliens. It was either that, or lose his sanity. Still, hiding the memories didn't mean they weren't still there. They were, and they kept coming back to haunt him. Night after night they came back.''

"The nightmares he had? That's what they were about?''

"That and his trial. Kiley, he made the service his life, and all he received in return was disillusionment and dishonor. Some hurts go too deep for apologies. Even if he could return to the Corps, he wouldn't.''

"But that was his life.''

"Once, maybe. It isn't now.''

"Then he really might be willing to come back to the *Widdon Galaxy* after he's testified?''

"He might. He's been happy on this ship—as happy as a man with his problems could be. He might come back if you want him to.''

"If *we* want him to? You must be joking! Of course we do! We need him, and not just as a pilot. He's been good for us. He has sound ideas and he's given us good advice. He listens to everyone, without siding with anyone. He fills a place that's been empty since Jon died. He balances us. We all want him to stay, even Lia.''

"Then tell him so. I think he might stay if *you* ask him to.'' Had he emphasized the "you"? Kiley looked at him sharply, but he was yawning. "I should have known better than to talk to you when I was so tired. I've said more than enough to earn a court-martial of my own if anyone finds out what I've told you. See that they don't, Kiley, or we'll both be in trouble.'' The words were light enough, but the warning in his eyes was real. He stood up. "I'm going to bed,'' he said. "Good night.''

"Daniel, wait!'' she called out, but he had already gone. She half rose, as if to follow him, then sank back into her chair. Whether he had talked to her by accident or calculated choice, it was clear he'd said as much as he intended to. She could question him from now until Cardos, but she doubted he'd say another word on the subject of Greg Lukas and the aliens.

Reluctantly, she turned her attention back to the control board and started catching up on status reports. Daniel Keenan wasn't the only one who'd overlooked duty that evening: she'd been so intent on their conversation, she had completely forgotten she was supposed to be standing watch. It was a good thing Jon Senior wasn't around—he'd have banished her from the bridge for a month for such a complete lapse of concentration.

Chapter 17

He dreamed he was back in the shuttle on Gynos.

His crewmen lay dead near the rear hatch, and Gordon was a lifeless lump behind the pilot's seat. His thoughts were not on the dead men, however. The shuttle's power had died—the same way the *Kelsoe Moran*'s had. It was very dark and very still. There were noises outside the hull.

The hatch started to open.

He took a step back, as if a few inches of space could save him from whatever lay outside. He was trapped, with no place to run, no idea what lay ahead. But he was about to find out. He waited, his breath coming in shallow gasps.

The hatch opened. Faint light spilled in, just enough to outline the figures that stood on the other side, and beyond them the faintly glowing walls of a passageway. There was not enough light to make out details, but it did not take much illumination to tell him what he was seeing was not human.

The Corps had a procedure for everything, including first contact with an alien race. It had been written over three hundred years ago and had never been changed. The standing orders read: *Do nothing. Hold your ground and observe all you can, but do nothing that could possibly be construed as a threat. Above all, do not fire upon them—not even to save your own life, or the lives of your crew. Report back if you can, leave an oral or written record of your contact if you can, but consider your life expendable.*

"No sense giving them a demonstration of our weapons," one of the instructors at the Academy had amplified. "Our technology may be inferior. We won't be able to do much about that, but we can retain one advantage: the element of surprise. If they are hostile and we return force with submission, they will underestimate our will. If they fire and we do not, they will not be able to determine our weapons' capabilities. Your orders are to learn as much as you can about the aliens—their intentions, their physical characteristics and abilities, their technology. You will do everything in your power to preserve and transmit this information to your commanding officer, short of an act of force.''

Cadets had listened to those orders for three centuries and wondered if anyone would obey them if aliens actually appeared. Orders that told soldiers to lay down their weapons and let themselves be killed didn't go over well with enlisted men and women—much less officers. The more cynical cadets said the orders were simply the Corps's way of having someone to blame if the first contact went sour.

Lukas had never expected he'd be asked to follow those regulations. None of them had. His hand tightened around his disrupter and then—with what he thought would likely prove the most regrettable act of his life—he disarmed his weapon, laid it in the pilot's seat, and let his hands fall to his sides, empty.

An instant later, some kind of beam caught him across the chest. There was no pain, no sensation at all, but his limbs lost all strength and sensation. He fell heavily. One of the aliens boarded the shuttle and crossed over to him. It must have used its weapon a second time, because after that, he was aware of nothing for a time.

He returned to consciousness in a chill, dark place. No, not dark—his eyes had been covered. Hands were fumbling with his clothing, undoing the fastenings, pulling the garments free of his arms and legs. He would have fought then, orders or no orders, but his body refused to respond. And then it was too late. His clothes were off and he was being pushed down and back until he lay on a long, hard, cold surface. They restrained him, fastening straps around his chest, arms, and legs. Sensation was returning to his body and strength followed moments later, but by then he was tightly secured. He twisted against the bindings, trying to break them, but they held firm—then and in all the horrifying hours that followed.

The aliens started exploring him, hands alternately cutting and scraping, poking and prodding, going over every inch of his skin, from head to toe. When they finished that, they systematically began violating every orifice of his body.

His mouth came first. They inserted a rigid object between his teeth that held his jaws wide open, then pushed a long, soft-sided tube down his throat. The tube wormed its way along, feeling like a living mass alternately compressing and expanding its body. He gagged and his throat muscles spasmed, fighting the intrusion.

The tube continued moving, down toward his stomach and out into his lungs. He couldn't breathe. He gasped, lungs frantic for oxygen, but all that entered his mouth was more of the tube. He panicked then, struggling so fiercely that one of the aliens began stroking his arm, as if by doing so it could calm him. It could not know the feel of its long, thickly padded fingers, alternately stroking and pressing against his skin in some disjointed pattern, was nearly as bad as the horror of having a living, writhing object crawl its way into his body.

He started to black out from lack of oxygen. He felt himself going and he could not stop the slide. There was a period of darkness; then he came to again. The tube was gone and he could breathe freely—until they started inserting a smaller tube into another orifice. His body convulsed repeatedly during the two explorations that followed. The soft-sided tubes did no physical damage, but the feeling of living objects worming their way into his body pushed him to the point of madness. He wanted to lose consciousness again—he prayed to—but his mind would not oblige.

They left him alone briefly after they withdrew the last tube. To let him recover? To decide what to do next? Both? They were not gone for long, however, and when they returned, they began covering him with something that felt like finely meshed netting. They stretched it from his head to his feet, tucking it under his shoulders, back, and legs so that it touched him everywhere. He envisioned himself wrapped inside a giant web, helpless prey for whatever spider lay in wait.

The aliens withdrew. A moment later, the threads started vibrating.

At first, the sensation was not unpleasant. Intermittent, barely perceptible, it felt like a warm breeze gently caressing his skin. In another time and place, he might have enjoyed the stimulus. But this was now, and the soothing breeze rapidly became a maddening itch he could not scratch. He writhed, trying to escape the net, but he could not dislodge it. If anything, he drew it into closer contact.

And then, just when he thought he could not stand the itch another moment, it disappeared. A breath later, something reached deep inside him and . . . stroked. He caught his breath as a wave of exquisite pleasure shot through his body. Once. Again. And yet again. The sensation built until it became a different kind of torture. His body arched as the hand stroked him again. And again. An hour before, he would not have believed anything could have been worse than the pulsing tubes in his body, but he discovered he was wrong as the hand reached inside him one last time and he lost control of himself in a different, infinitely more humiliating way.

The threads stopped vibrating. He thought it was all over, but the net came back to life almost immediately. Only this time, the fine strands felt like acid-dipped wires that burned their way through skin and muscles wherever they touched—and they touched everywhere: face, chest, back, arms, and legs. Even the bottoms of his feet did not escape the contact.

The wires sank deep into his body, eating their way down to his very bones. He screamed and felt no shame about that. None. Human beings were not made to endure such agony. Their bodies should fail long before pain reached such unbearable levels. He cried out, pleading with his captors to stop the torture, to let him die, but the pain just increased.

His voice gave out first, then his mind, then finally, an infinity too late, his body.

He woke to darkness. He did not know where he was at first, but then awareness returned in a rush. The net no longer covered him, but a residue of the agony it had caused lingered on. Pain flickered sporadically along one nerve, then another, jolting him like a shorted electrical wire.

It took him some time to realize he was not alone, that hands were touching his body again. This time, though, they were washing him, cleansing him of the stench of fear and pain with long, slow sweeps of a warm, moist cloth.

He jerked reflexively and hands pushed against his arms and legs, holding him down. The pressure was light, intended only to quiet him. He could have overcome it with a struggle, but he made no attempt to do so; he no longer had the will to fight. Instead, he lay where he was, quiescent, letting the hands do what they would. He might even have slept for a time, because the next thing he knew, he was being lifted and supported as the hands pulled his clothing back on.

When he was dressed, the hands guided him to his feet. Two of them helped him stand, then guided him across the room, where the one on his left took his left hand and placed it against a solid barrier. For an instant he felt only the chill smoothness of metal; then electricity shot through his hand and up his arm. He thought he was being tortured again. The alien who had placed his hand against the wall grabbed his arm, as if to tear it away, but it acted too slowly. A blast of incomprehensible emotion swept through him. Guilt. Terror. Pain. The emotions were so overpowering that he felt himself starting to scream yet again. Another wave of sensations and images came at him and his mind recoiled. He thought he screamed again, but he was never sure, because after that there was only darkness.

The echo of that final scream woke Lukas. He was drenched with sweat and his heart pounded in his chest. He had been dreaming. Again. He looked at the chronometer. He had slept for two hours and twenty minutes—longer than the night before, but not long enough. Not nearly enough. He should roll over and try to go back to sleep again. He should call Keenan and ask for a sedative. But he did neither. He could not face another repetition of the nightmare that was no dream. Not twice in one night.

Keenan said Lukas was ready to stand watch again. He assured Kiley that the pilot was really fit for duty this time, and she didn't question his assessment until Lukas reported to the bridge. He looked as if he hadn't slept more than a few hours since she'd seen him last. She was about to order him back to bed, but he spoke first.

"I owe you an apology for the other night," he said stiffly. "I should have realized I wasn't up to standing watch. I endangered us all. I'd like to have another chance, but if you don't trust me any longer, I'll understand."

"If I don't— Greg, the only reason I wouldn't want you on the bridge of this ship is if you didn't want to be here. Besides, you weren't the only one who failed to give their full attention to duty the other night; I did a pretty good job of that myself."

"That doesn't excuse my behavior."

"Greg—"

"No, let me finish—this is difficult enough to say without you trying to make things easy for me. I've learned a lot about myself the past few days. Most of it hasn't been pleasant. I want you to know I lost command of my ship because I did the one thing a captain must never do: I panicked. I failed my responsibility to the Corps and I failed myself. What I did once, I could do again. To you. To this ship."

"Greg, I don't know what happened on Gynos, but I do know you. If you panicked, then anyone else would have, too."

"I wasn't anyone else. I was the captain of the *Kelsoe Moran*. It was my duty to remain in control of myself and my ship. I didn't, and I deserve everything that happened afterwards."

"How can you say that?" she demanded, appalled by his words. She wondered if Keenan had any idea that he was harboring those feelings. "I don't know where you got the idea a ship's captain is supposed to be somehow better, stronger, or more capable than everyone else, but you're wrong! You may have been captain of the *Kelsoe Moran*, but you were a human being first, with a full set of human weaknesses. The only thing abnormal about you, Greg Lukas, is the way you're condemning yourself for failing to meet some standard of behavior no human could possibly achieve."

Her criticism struck like a lash. "You're a fine one to be talking about impossible standards," he shot back. "At least I admit I failed mine. You're still trying to prove you can do twice as much as anyone else, twice as well—all because you failed some Academy admissions test. You'd better take a good, close look at yourself before you start lecturing me about impossible standards, Kiley Michaelson."

She stared at him in shock. She could not believe he had really said those words. But he had, and with realization came blind, irrational anger. She flung herself out of her chair and slammed off the bridge. She didn't know where she was going, only that she had to keep moving before she said or did something she'd regret the rest of her life.

She ended up on the cargo deck. She didn't remember getting there, but once she was in the long corridor, she started pacing the length of the deck, walking from one end to the other as fast as her legs would take her. It didn't take a psychiatric degree to realize Lukas had been taking his frustration out on her—or that he would undoubtedly hate himself later for having done so.

The problem was, he'd spoken the truth: He wasn't the only one with unrealistic standards. She had spent the last eight years of her life pushing herself harder and harder, never stopping, just to prove she wasn't a failure. It hadn't mattered that the family never thought less of her because she hadn't made the Academy. It didn't even matter that the fault was beyond her control, a quirk of genes, not a weakness of mind or character. All that mattered was that she had failed to achieve the only goal she had ever cared about in her life. She could not forgive herself for that, not ever.

Because the only measure of worth was success.

Unless you attained your goals, you were worthless. That wasn't what she'd been raised to believe, but somehow, somewhere along the way, that feeling had attached itself to her with sealing glue. The only problem was, sometimes the means of achieving success lay out of your hands. As much as you wanted to prove yourself, you couldn't, because you didn't control all the factors—like the genes with which you were born.

But if you tried your hardest, did your best, and still failed, did that mean you were a failure as a person? Did that mean your whole life was over? Or did it only mean you had to go out and find a different set of goals, like becoming pilot of whatever ship was available, even if she was only an aging freighter. Wasn't it a success of sorts to run that ship safely and at a profit, however marginal it might be?

Couldn't you still succeed, even if you failed to achieve your heart's first desire?

Jon Robert wasn't a failure. Daniel Keenan wasn't. They had both started out to be one thing and found themselves becoming something else along the way, but no one could call either one of them failures. If they could make alternate choices and be happier with them than their original ones, couldn't she do the same?

But she still felt like a failure inside. And that was wrong. Wrong! What counted was that you did your best. If you failed, you picked yourself up and tried again, or you went on to something else. Either way, you had to keep on going, keep on finding reasons to live. Because if you didn't, one day you would wake up and realize that you might as well have died, for all that your heart continued to beat.

Her feet slowed, then stopped in front of the elevator. She had been wrong to punish herself for a failure over which she had no control. She'd been wrong to think being captain of the *Widdon Galaxy* wasn't a high enough measure of success. She had to change, had to find new goals and standards. If she didn't, she would never have a moment's peace or happiness in her life. Jon Robert had tried to tell her that. So had Daniel Keenan. Maybe she should start listening to them.

First, though, there was something else she had to do.

She went back to the bridge. Lukas was still there, his head bent over one of the displays. He stiffened when he heard her footsteps, but he did not look around.

"I'm sorry, Greg," she said. "I shouldn't have told you how you ought to feel and I shouldn't have walked out on you. I was just so angry, I had to leave. You were right. I have been setting impossible standards for myself, then compounding the sin by hating myself for failing to meet them. I'm the last person to be criticizing you, even by implication. Maybe you did fail. I don't think so, but maybe you did. Maybe you'll fail in the future. You could. So could I. I guess that's the chance we have to take— all of us. What I do know is that I want you here on the *Widdon Galaxy* as long as you want to stay. Failure or not, you're still the best pilot this ship has ever had, myself included."

He turned around. For a moment she thought he would lash out again; then he put his hands to his eyes and rubbed them. When he looked at her, his expression was bleak.

"The only person who owes an apology is me. What I said was unforgivable. I didn't mean to hurt you, but the words just came out. I couldn't stop them. Daniel would say I was letting my frustration do my talking. He says I need to practice a little more acceptance and self-forgiveness. He's probably right, but it isn't easy, forgiving yourself for failing to be all you wanted or expected."

"No, it isn't," she said quietly.

"I guess you have to try, though."

"It would appear so. If you ever want to be happy, that is."

He swallowed. "Kiley, I have to go to Everest. There are people at the Admiralty I have to talk to—I have to tell them what happened on Gynos. I don't want to, but I have an obligation to them, to the Corps. I'm not sure how long I'll have to stay. It could be a week; it could be months. I know you'll have to hire on another pilot while I'm gone—you can't get by without the help. I don't expect you to hold my place, but if you're between pilots when I'm free, then I'd like to come back. If you'll have me, that is."

"Greg, you don't even have to ask. Of course we'll have you. You're welcome on the *Widdon Galaxy* for as long as you choose to stay."

She thought everything would be all right after that.

Until they came out of jump a day later, straight into an ambush. One moment they were making a routine entry into normal space, and the next, warning sirens were clanging at full volume.

Not again was Kiley's first, panicked thought. They could not be meeting another outbound jump in the wrong corridor of space. That couldn't happen twice in a lifetime. When they completed transition normally, her racing pulse settled a beat or two.

She scanned the short-range sensors and saw nothing. If there was another ship out there, she had to be some distance away. Jon Senior had set the warning alarm to go off if their scanners detected another ship within any range, no matter what its distance. He had never quite trusted her or Jon Robert when they were alone on the bridge. She should have reset the sensor parameters to more normal tolerances, and she wouldn't have had to undergo such a scare.

"We have traffic," Lukas said from the copilot's seat. His voice was calm, but the alarms must have rattled his nerves, too, for the hand that reached to adjust the image on the long-range scanner shook. "One ship, stationary, bearing 030.02.293, distance eight-fifty kems," he announced.

Kiley cut the warning alarms with an impatient sweep of her hand, and the bridge fell silent once more. "Who—" she started to ask, then broke off because Lukas's fingers at the controls were already moving. The profile of a ship appeared on the monitor between them. "She's a long-range cruiser," he said. "Delta class. I wonder what she's doing out here? Cruisers don't usually patrol shipping lanes." His words were casual, but his voice held a thread of tension that hadn't been there a moment before.

Her hand was poised over the main board. She had been preparing to reduce speed, but unaccountably she held back.

"What's going on?" Keenan demanded, coming through the hatch at a near run.

At the same moment Jon Robert's voice sounded over the intercom. "Kiley, what's wrong? I show all systems green here."

"All green here, too," she said, then broadcast the rest of her reply shipwide. "We have company. The ship's a little close for our warning system's comfort, but she's still some distance away. There's no danger."

"Kiley, she's started moving," Lukas said. "She's headed our way." He studied the image on his monitor, keyed in a request for more data, then said tightly, "Navigation plots an intercept course."

"How long before she overtakes us?" Keenan asked before Kiley could voice the same question.

Lukas's fingers moved over the control board. "Four minutes, eighteen seconds. Daniel, she must be operating out of Zerron Base. There's no other military installation within range."

"Has she signaled to us yet?"

"No."

"Not at all? Not on any frequency?"

"Negative."

"Any chance she's on a routine patrol?"

"Possibly, but the base would be more likely to assign a frigate to patrol shipping lanes."

"I don't like this," Keenan said. "I don't like it at all." He turned to Kiley. "Can we can outrun her?"

"Are you joking? A freighter outrun a Corps cruiser? We couldn't possibly. Besides, why should we? We have nothing to hide."

"Kiley, I don't want to alarm you unnecessarily, but if that ship is from Zerron Base, it may be no coincidence she's here. She may have been waiting for us. If Admiral Sorseli has learned that Greg's case is being reopened, he may have decided to act."

"Act? You mean to try to stop Greg? I don't believe that, but even if it were true, how could he possibly have known he'd be on this ship, let alone that we'd be in this quadrant at this particular moment? She can't be after us."

"It isn't that hard to track someone down if you want to. Every time Greg signed onto a new ship, he left a paper trail behind. I had no difficulty following that record. Sorseli wouldn't have either. Don't make the mistake of underestimating him, Kiley. His very life may be on the line. He isn't the type to sit by idly while everything falls apart around him."

"I still don't see how he could know where we'd be. We didn't know ourselves until we found the shuttle cargo on Siddorn."

"He'd know if he was the one who arranged to have the shuttles shipped."

"If he— Daniel, are you suggesting he arranged for us to get that cargo? That he set us up? That's ridiculous!"

"Kiley, the cruiser is hailing us," Lukas said, cutting in. "Do you want to reply, or shall I?"

"I will." She reached for her headset, but Keenan caught her wrist.

"Please be careful," he said urgently. "Don't volunteer anything."

She started to make a sharp retort about her ability to handle communications on her own, but Keenan's anxiety stopped her short. Did he know more than he was saying? He was not an alarmist. If he was this worried, maybe she should be, too. The cruiser was probably on a routine patrol; they didn't often stop cargo ships, but it wasn't unknown. Still, a little caution now might save a lot of grief later. She donned the headset and switched on the microphone.

"This is Captain Michaelson of the freighter *Widdon Galaxy*," she said to the blip on the screen. "Please identify yourself. Repeat, please identify yourself."

Her earphones crackled; then a man's voice said, "This is Captain Rubaric Tichner, commanding officer of the Consolidated Alliance of Planets Space Corps ship *Railion*. We have been informed that a vessel carrying contraband weapons will attempt to enter this quadrant sometime in the next three days. We have orders to stop and search all incoming ships. Cut all power to your engines and stand by to be boarded."

Lukas had sworn as Tichner identified himself.

"You know him, Greg?" Keenan asked when the transmission was finished.

"We've met."

"You didn't like him?"

"No."

"Why not?"

"Nothing specific. Really. It's just that he's strictly a by-the-book officer. He was always more worried about justifying his decisions than making the right one." He hesitated, then said flatly, "He was one of Sorseli's chosen few, Daniel. If there was a special mission, if there were prizes to be given out, Tichner was first in line."

The two men exchanged glances. Kiley didn't like the look that passed between them.

"Kiley, we have to get a message to my superior, Hal Omanu," Keenan said abruptly. "He's waiting for us on Cardos. We have to let him know we're in trouble."

Lukas glanced as his displays. "They're jamming long-range transmissions," he said. "We can't send a message. Besides, I don't see what good it would do. Omanu's too far away to help."

"Captain Michaelson, did you receive my transmission?" Tichner's voice demanded harshly in her earphones. "You are under orders to cut all power to your engines."

She didn't like the sound of that order, any more than she'd liked the looks Keenan and Lukas had given each other a moment before. Running before a Corps ship was unthinkable, but she was rapidly coming to the conclusion that cutting power and letting Tichner board might prove even less wise.

"Greg, we can't outrun them, but is there any chance we could outmaneuver them?" she asked. "If we made a short jump, they wouldn't be able to find us right away, would they? We still have enough speed to do that. They'll follow, but we'd have enough time to send Daniel's boss a message and let him know we're in trouble."

Lukas was shaking his head angrily before she finished speaking. "Kiley, we can't. You might be able to handle a short jump, but not another long one—and that's precisely what we'd have to do. If we run, Tichner will be certain to follow, and he'll come at us shooting. We'll have to jump again, or there won't be enough left of any of us to look for."

"You're saying we should let him board?" she replied. "What if Daniel's right? If Sorseli did send Tichner to find us, you aren't the only one who's in trouble—or do you honestly believe they'll let the rest of us go, knowing we'll tell everyone who will listen what happened as soon as we reached Cardos? Daniel's right—we don't dare let him board. I want you to plot a jump. I don't care where—just get us out of here and buy us enough time for Daniel to send his message."

She turned to the psychiatrist. "Do you know how to use a transmitter?" she asked.

"Yes."

"Then sit down and get your message ready."

He didn't waste time replying. Moving to the backup communications board, he strapped in and started punching keys with a rapidity that said he did indeed know what he was doing.

Kiley took a deep breath, then switched on her microphone. "We're a commercial freighter on legitimate business, Captain Tichner. We have a deadline to meet. I have full documentation for the ship and cargo. I'm transmitting a copy of our registration and manifest to you now."

She turned to tell Lukas to call up the information, but he was already calling it to his screen. He hit the transmit key at her nod. He might not be happy, but he was still with her.

"That isn't going to hold them for long," he warned.

"I know." Kiley hit the shipwide intercom. "It looks like we may have trouble after all," she announced. "Jon Robert, shut down nonessential systems and channel all available power to the main engines. Prepare to start the jump engines."

"Restart the— Kiley, what's going on up there? We can't jump again. Not this soon! *You* can't!"

"Jon Robert, I don't have time to explain. Give me full power to the main engines and stand by to jump. The rest of you, find a secure place and brace yourselves. This may be a rough transition."

"I have a second ship on the long-range sensors," Lukas said. "Bearing 630.03.129, distance one thousand kems. She's closing in on the starboard side; intercept in . . . six minutes." He turned to face her. "Kiley, you're making a mistake. We may be able to evade them for a few hours, but that's all. Even if we can make a second, longer jump, we won't lose them. They'll be within range by the time we can rebuild speed. They'll follow us wherever we go."

"Maybe, but we have to try. Greg, we don't have time to waste arguing. Lay in a course." He didn't move. "Do it!" she ordered sharply.

Her earphones crackled and Tichner's voice sounded in her ears again. "Captain Michaelson, your papers may be quite legitimate, but we must still insist on examining your holds. If you do not stop all engines and stand by to be boarded immediately, I'll be forced to fire a warning shot. Is that understood? You're jeopardizing your ship and crew, Captain! Cut all power to your engines!"

Her hands gripped the arms of her seat. If Keenan was wrong about Tichner, if the cruiser was on a legitimate mission, then running was wrong. On the other hand, if Tichner was after Lukas, running was their only chance.

She reached for the microphone and switched it on, summoning all the self-righteous indignation she could muster. "You have the wrong ship, Captain, and this delay may well cost us our profit for the trip. However, since you've given us no alternative, we'll switch all engines off. Please adjust your course and speed. You're closing on us too fast for safety."

She cut off the microphone and earphones and turned to Lukas. "Do you have the coordinates locked in?"

His jaw clenched. "Yes."

"I want you to give Keenan time to transmit his message after we jump, then take us to the safest place you can find. I'll leave the coordinates up to you; you know this sector and I don't." She hesitated, then spoke again in a voice stripped of all emotion. "I may not be in any condition to pilot the ship after jump, so you'll have the conn. Whatever happens, I want you to remember the ship comes first. Not me, the ship. Is that clear?"

He would not meet her eyes. For a moment, she did not think he would agree. He nodded.

She hit the intercom. "Jon Robert, start the jump engines." She heard static in her headset even as the comfortingly familiar rumble shook the ship. It was too late to reconsider, too late to wonder if she was risking their lives over a hastily drawn conclusion. There was time only to reach for the main board and—

Jump.

Body twisting outside in. Breath ripped from lungs. Heart laboring to beat . . . just . . . one . . . more . . . time. Events running in slow motion and fast speed at the same time. Disjointed memories flashing: the green hillsides of Everest, Jon Senior slumped on the floor, victim of a massive stroke, a baby crying—where had that memory come from? A recent port visit? A recollection dredged up from childhood? It came and went too quickly to be identified. They all came and went too quickly. Or too slowly. There was no telling which.

A moment of quiescence, a single breath, the merciful thought that it was over, it must be over—and then she turned outside in. And went through the whole thing all over again.

She knew she survived, because she thought she had died. Still, she was slow to return to consciousness. She registered the sound of Lukas's and Keenan's voices long before she understood their words. Their calm told her all she needed to know, though. They had come through safely.

For the moment.

Kiley forced her eyes open. They went to the boards first. Green lights, all the way. They were one minute and twenty-three seconds out of jump. She had been unconscious long enough to lose the ship a hundred times over if there had been trouble.

"Kiley, what's going on!" Jon Robert was demanding over the intercom, fear taking on the sound of anger. Terrible to be so far from the bridge, isolated from the decisions, knowing nothing, worried about everything. Terrible to be forced to trust, without facts, when all your judgment screamed out *wait, let's talk this over!*

"Kiley, answer me!" His voice was rising.

She beat Lukas to the intercom. "Sorry, Jon Robert," she answered. "A Corps cruiser was waiting for us when we came out of jump. She ordered us to stop and be boarded. She accused us of carrying contraband.''

"But that's—"

"Ridiculous. I know. Keenan thinks Sorseli may have set us up. He thinks the admiral knew Greg was on the ship, that he was going to try to stop him from going to Everest. Whether that was true or not is irrelevant now. We've already broken one law by attempting to evade them, and they aren't going to be in the mood to listen to explanations when they find us again. We'll be jumping again as soon as we can build sufficient speed.''

"Kiley, you can't—"

"I can. I may not feel very good for a few days, but I'll make it. Greg may have to take the conn. If he does, I want you to obey any and all orders he gives. Our lives may depend on it. Is that clear?''

Silence. A bitten-off "Yes."

"Thank you. Continue to build speed. Shut down all but essential life-support systems and divert as much power to the main engines as you can.''

Another pause, not quite so long. "Affirmative," he said. A moment later the lights on the bridge dimmed and a bank of sensors on the control boards went yellow.

"Any traffic?" Kiley asked, turning to Lukas at last.

"Not yet.''

"Where are we?''

"About five thousand kems from our last location. Coordinates 030.02.596. We're building speed as fast as we can; it looks like Jon Robert is pushing the engines well into the red zone.''

"Did Keenan get his message off?''

"Yes.''

"How long do we have before they find us?''

"I don't know. I'd say at least an hour, but probably no more than three or four. Tichner knows our pre-jump course and speed; he won't have any difficulty calculating our maximum range. After that, it's a simple matter of laying down a grid and searching. He has at least one other ship to help him, maybe more if he's decided to call in reinforcements. He can now, without much concern. We ran. That makes us criminals, no matter what else we have or haven't done.''

"Any chance your boss can help us out, Keenan?" Kiley asked, swinging around to look at him.

He shook his head, his face grim. "My message will take

time to reach him. I'm sure he'll act as soon as he receives it, but Tichner will reach us long before he does. We have to get out of this quadrant, Kiley. None of Sorseli's ships is going to give us time for explanations. Our best hope is to head for Kamrick Base—it's under Admiral Jordan's jurisdiction, and she's no friend of Sorseli's. We'll have to surrender to her, but she won't turn us over to one of Sorseli's ships until she's checked out our side of the story thoroughly.''

''Very well, Kamrick Base it is. We'd better hope we can get there before Sorseli's ships find us, though,'' Kiley said. ''Our shields are strong enough to protect us against space debris and high radiation levels, but they were never designed to withstand fire from a curillian beam. They might hold thirty seconds, but we'd have to divert all ship's power to them to gain that much time.''

They were still building speed for the jump two hours later, when the *Railion* appeared on the long-range scanners. She emerged directly ahead of them. A moment later, she was joined by a second ship, then a third.

''Tichner must have called out every ship in the quadrant,'' Lukas said, his tone somewhere between bitterness and despair.

Kiley was too busy to reply. She brought the *Widdon Galaxy* around a full one hundred and eighty degrees, cursing the loss of speed the maneuver cost them. They could not jump directly into the path of the incoming ships; they would either be pulled back, or lose speed as they pulled the other ships in with them. Either scenario represented disaster.

''They're trying to drive us out toward the fringes!'' she said as the ships fanned out. ''Greg, our charts don't cover the territory ahead. They're trying to force us into a blind jump!''

''I know,'' he said. He was bent over the navigation board, running course after course, his whole body tense, as if he could force the computer to run faster by an act of will. ''I remember a few coordinates from my time out here, but none of them are in range.''

''Then pick a set that are. I don't care which direction, just get us as far from here as we can go!''

''It won't do us any good to evade Tichner if we exit jump too close to a planet to pull away in time, or land next to a piece of space debris too large for the shields to ward off,'' Lukas objected.

''If we don't jump soon, it won't matter where we land,'' she said sharply. ''Lay in a course, Greg. Do it!''

He turned back to his screen and punched in another variation. Then a second.

"There has to be another way," he muttered desperately. "There has to be!"

"Closest ship is four hundred thirty kems," Kiley said, eyes moving from one monitor to the next. Her heart sank. All the displays told the same story: The *Widdon Galaxy* was running beyond her capacity. There was still enough space between them and the approaching ships to jump without being pulled back, or pulling one of the others in along with them, but that wouldn't last long. If they didn't jump now, they wouldn't be able to. The closest ship was approaching firing range; it could start shooting at any moment. It would start—

"Greg!" she said urgently, then reached for the keyboard herself. If he couldn't choose a set of coordinates, she would.

"Course laid in," he replied, shoving her hand away before she could touch the controls.

She didn't hesitate. "Jon Robert, jump engines on," she said.

The low rumble started immediately. Whatever her brother might be thinking, he didn't waste time arguing.

"Two ships, three-ninety kems and closing," Lukas said. "Kiley, they're within firing range!"

She gave the blips on her monitor one last look, then took a deep breath to fill lungs that still ached from the last transition and reached for the main board. She gave the order. "Jump!"

Chapter 18

Waking was a foretaste of old age.

This was how she would feel seventy-five years from now, when the weight of five thousand jumps had weakened flesh and muscles, twisted bones and tendons. Kiley's body ached with a fierceness that could not be eased, no matter how she shifted positions. Her mind functioned only marginally, thoughts forming slowly and sticking together, refusing to flow in smooth sequence. When she finally pried her eyes open, the room swirled around crazily, ceiling and walls coming together at steep angles that wavered and tilted.

"Kiley, can you hear me?" Keenan was asking.

He was sitting on a chair set beside her bunk, watching her. His body slumped with weariness, or transition sickness, or perhaps a bit of both, but he straightened and managed a smile when he saw her eyes focus on him. She nodded, then wished she hadn't.

"How are you feeling?" he asked.

"Rotten," she replied, her tongue as thick as her thoughts. She forced it to work anyway. "What happened? Where are we? How are the others?"

She tried to sit up, but only succeeded in lifting her head two inches before the room turned inside out and her stomach tried to crawl out of her mouth. She rolled over on her side and retched uncontrollably.

Keenan reached for her and put an arm around her shoulders, supporting her, then reached into his medical bag with his other hand. He pulled out a pressurized injector and swab.

"No!" she protested, trying to pull away. She couldn't afford to be drugged, not when they were in so much trouble. She had to get to the bridge, had to make certain the others were all right, had to—

A hiss of air, a sting, and then it was too late.

"Take it easy, Kiley," Keenan said, setting the injector aside. "I've given you something to ease your nausea and help you sleep. Just lie back and relax." He set her back against the pillow, and she couldn't stop him—she was that weak.

"Can't," she muttered. "Have to get back to the bridge. Have to—"

"The only thing you have to do is rest," Keenan said. "The ship is safe and everyone but you is mobile, if not a hundred percent fit. There's nothing to worry about. Go to sleep. You'll feel much better when you wake up."

"I don't want—" she started, but her voice slurred and she lost the thought before she could finish voicing it. The dizziness was receding, but in its place came a wave of lassitude so great it overwhelmed her before she could gather the will to resist. Her eyes closed and she slept.

The terrible, aching fatigue was gone when she woke the second time. She came up slowly, evenly, with none of the nausea she had experienced upon her first return to consciousness. Whatever Keenan had given her had done its job well. She glanced at the chronometer and looked again in shock. Perhaps too well—she'd been out nearly thirty-six hours!

She pushed back the covers, got to her feet, and had to grab the chair beside the bed as she nearly blacked out. She held on until the darkness receded, then forced herself to let go. There was nothing wrong, she told herself firmly. She'd just stood too fast, that was all. The dizziness was probably caused as much by hunger as by transition sickness.

She took a cautious step away from the chair, then slowly made her way to the bathroom. She had planned to shower, then go to the bridge, but the short walk nearly exhausted her. She managed a quick wash, pulled on a robe, and headed back to her bunk, deciding she would sit down for a minute or two before she tried to dress.

The door swished open just as she seated herself and Keenan came in.

"Awake, are you?" He spoke lightly, but his smile didn't go all the way to his eyes. "How are you feeling?"

"Much better," she said. That was true as far as it went. She did feel much better. The only problem was, she still didn't feel good. Better not tell him that, though, or he'd order her back to bed for the rest of the day. She searched his face, wondering what was wrong. Something was.

"Daniel, how are the others? Lia and Holly, are they all right? The baby—?"

"They're fine," he said, walking over to the chair and turning it so he could sit facing her. "All of them. Lia was sick after we jumped and she still has a headache, but everyone else is almost back to normal. Holly and the baby fared better than the rest of us; I've run every scan and test I can think of and there's no indication either of them suffered any damage whatsoever."

Kiley released a pent-up breath. "Who's on the bridge? Greg?"

"Yes."

"I have to talk to him."

"Later. I mean that, Kiley," he added when she reached for the intercom anyway. "You can talk to Greg after I've checked you over."

"That isn't necessary. I'm fine."

"If you are, you've made the most miraculous recovery from transition sickness I've ever seen. I owe you an apology. I knew you suffered from Wycker's Syndrome. I knew what multiple jumps would do to you, but I just didn't see a choice. I've had more than one occasion to regret that advice the past few days. You came as close to dying as I ever want to see one of my patients, and it was my fault."

"No, it wasn't. I made the decision, Keenan. Not you."

"Because I urged you to. I should have listened to Omanu. He wanted to take Greg off the *Widdon Galaxy* on Siddorn, but I wouldn't let him. If I had, we'd all be safe."

"What's done is done, Daniel. Besides, I'm all right. Really."

"Are you? I think I'd better be the judge of that. Lie down. I want to run the scanner over you."

"I don't—"

"If you're really as fit as you say you are, I'll pack up my bag and leave," he said. "I promise. Come on; this won't take long."

She gave him a stubborn look. He returned it with a determined one of his own that said he was going to have his way, whether she liked it or not. She sighed and lay down again. He took an exorbitant amount of time scanning her. He paused several times, frowning over the readings, then finally returned the instrument to its case.

"If circumstances were any different, I'd sedate you another twelve hours," he told her. "Your body is still sloughing off cells that died during transition. You need rest, and lots of it. Unfortunately, that may not be easy to come by. We have problems, Kiley. Serious problems."

"What's wrong?" she demanded, sitting up.

He hesitated, as if still uncertain whether he should tell her, then said abruptly, "It's Greg. He hasn't been off the bridge more than four hours since we jumped. What's more, he won't tell us where we're going."

"What!"

"He erased the jump coordinates from the navigation computer. Jon Robert was furious when he found out. For a moment I thought he and Greg were going to have a fight, right there on the bridge. Greg won't discuss our destination with anyone, me included."

"What's wrong with him? He knows we don't have complete charts for the fringe areas! Without knowing the direction and distance of our jump, it could take hours to calculate our position! We'd be running blind!"

"I know, Kiley," Keenan said miserably. "I told him the same thing myself."

"And?"

"And he said he'd talk to you when you woke up, but no one else."

"Not even you?"

"No."

"That's a change. I thought he told you everything."

"Not anymore."

"What else is wrong, Daniel? There must be something more, or you wouldn't look so worried. What is it?"

"I can't be certain, but I think he may be taking us into the restricted zone. It's the only explanation for his behavior that makes sense."

He was so obviously miserable, and she so appalled, that they just sat there for a moment, at a complete loss for words. "Daniel, why?" she asked when she could speak again.

The psychiatrist shook his head. "I don't know. I'd like to give him the benefit of the doubt and say he must not have seen any other choice, but I just don't know. I was hoping he'd tell you. You're captain—he'll respect that. He might give you the explanations he won't give the rest of us. I realize I'm not being fair to you. You need rest, not more stress, but you're the only person he's likely to talk to now that he's shut me out."

He hesitated. "Kiley, I'm not certain he's completely stable yet. I'm positive he'd never harm any of us intentionally, but he came perilously close to a complete breakdown. I thought he was recovering, but events may have pushed him back onto the edge again. He may not be capable of making rational decisions, and if he isn't, then he's endangering all of us every minute he's in command."

"I'll talk to him, Daniel. Just let me get dressed."

Keenan waited in the corridor while she pulled on a shirt and pants, then walked with her to the bridge but stopped short at the entrance.

"Greg's more likely to be receptive if you talk to him alone," he said. "I'll be in my cabin. Call me as soon as you can, will you?"

"I will," she assured him. He gave the doorway one last, unhappy glance, then nodded to her and went down the corridor. She waited until he was out of sight, then walked onto the dimly lit bridge.

Lukas was in the pilot's seat, slouched so far down that all she could see of him was an elbow jutting out to one side of the chair.

"Good morning, Greg," she said, as if this were any of the hundred other shift changes they had made.

He swung around and jumped up, his surprise almost comical. But his appearance was anything but funny: the dark beginnings of a beard roughened his jaw and his eyes were red from monitoring the boards too long. Fatigue had eaten deep furrows into the skin around his nose and mouth, and his facial muscles sagged as she watched, as if the effort of maintaining any expression, even surprise, was beyond them.

"Kiley! I didn't expect to see you this soon. Daniel said you'd sleep at least twelve more hours. Does he know you're here? Maybe I'd better call him and—"

"He cleared me for duty, Greg. Not a moment too soon, either, from the look of you. How much sleep have you had since we jumped?"

"A few hours," he said, a hint of defensiveness creeping into his tone, replacing what had been genuine welcome and concern. "It was enough."

"Was it?" she asked, looking him over skeptically.

He flushed. "Kiley, I don't know what Daniel said to you, but—"

"He said he's worried about you. He said you've shut yourself up on the bridge and refused to tell anyone where we're going. When Jon Robert demanded an answer, you nearly had a fight—on the bridge! He said you're operating under extreme stress, that you're exhausted, and may not be capable of making command decisions. That's what Keenan said. I'm more interested in what you have to say. If you have an explanation for your behavior, I want to hear it—beginning with where we're going and when we'll get there."

"Kiley—" he started, broke off, then made a hopeless gesture with his hand. "Do you mind if I sit down?"

"Not at all," she said, then added more gently, "I'm not exactly up to standing myself, if the truth be told." She sank into the pilot's chair with a grateful sigh.

"You should be back in bed," he said, concern breaking though his defensiveness momentarily.

"Yes. But then, so should you. Now that we've ascertained that, suppose we move on to more important matters—like where we're going."

He closed his eyes and spoke so quietly she could hardly hear him. "Gynos."

"Gynos," she repeated, then said forcefully, "Why, Greg? Why?"

"They were the only coordinates I could remember that were within range." He looked across at her, his face anguished. "The Corps's ships were closing in from all sides. It was either go there or make a blind jump. I couldn't use random coordinates, Kiley, I just couldn't. Not when I knew a safe place."

"You call Gynos safe? After what happened to you there? Knowing what the Admiralty could do to us for entering a restricted zone?"

"It was safer than waiting for Tichner to open fire. He did, too. The beam caught us as we entered transition. It had traveled some distance and didn't do any detectable damage, but the ship automatically diverted power to the shields. I don't think the power loss lasted long enough to affect our speed, but we may not land exactly on target."

"Will that be a problem?"

"I don't think so. There's a fair amount of open space around our exit point."

"What about Tichner? Will he follow us?"

"I don't know. Probably. But he won't enter the restricted zone without getting clearance from Sorseli first. That will take several hours. That should give us enough time to get out of sensor range before he arrives."

"Only to run into company of a different sort? What are we going to do if the aliens are still out there, Greg? Have you thought about that at all?"

"Yes," he said, almost inaudibly.

"And?"

"I think we'd better make ourselves as inconspicuous as possible and leave as soon as Daniel clears you to make another jump."

Thirty-six hours later, they were doing their best to do just that.

Kiley had made it through transition without losing consciousness, but her vision grayed out, and she was slow to regain full awareness. Keenan stayed at her side on the bridge until she did, scanner in hand, mouth tight with disapproval.

"You need a minimum of two days before we jump again," he said. "You hear that, Greg? Two days, and that's only if she wants to survive. Three or four would be better."

"We'll leave if and when we have to," she said shortly and turned to Lukas. "If you see any sign of another ship, any ship at all, standing orders are to build speed as rapidly as possible and jump, is that clear?"

Lukas looked from her to Keenan, not committing himself to either side. She took that as a victory. He had been captain of his own ship; he knew the *Widdon Galaxy*'s safety came first. No matter how difficult he found the decision, she was certain he would act first to save the ship and worry about the consequences to her later.

After a brief conference, they decided to head for the sixth planet in the Gynos system, a giant, red and orange world with four moons.

"We can't hide here long," Lukas had warned as they circled in behind one of the moons. "It's the first place Tichner would think to look."

"Sometimes the obvious choice is the best one, precisely because it is so blatant," she had countered. "Besides, we're less likely to attract attention if we're stationary."

She had yet to test that theory. Their sensors had not picked up any incoming ships, Corps or alien. Had Tichner refused to enter the restricted zone? Had Sorseli thought twice about ordering him in? Or had Omanu received their message and found a way to stop Tichner's pursuit? Most unthinkable of all, was Tichner out there, waiting for them to move and give themselves away? The questions were unanswerable and her tension mounted with each uneventful hour that passed.

She wasn't alone in her anxiety; the rest of the family were showing signs of short tempers and frayed nerves, too. Not for the first time, she wondered if she had been right to let Lukas tell them about his trip to Gynos Three and the aliens he had encountered. Keenan had been adamantly opposed to the idea, but she suspected that had had more to do with an obligation to protect military secrets than any concern about the family's reaction.

Kiley had called the meeting in the ship's common room a few hours before, leaving Keenan to watch the bridge. He couldn't pilot the ship himself, but he could call out a warning.

Lukas did most of the talking at the meeting. He did not go into great detail about his experiences, and his distress over having to discuss the events at all was so obvious that none of them had the heart to ask additional questions.

"I should have told you where we were going," he said, turning to Jon Robert at the end of his recitation, "but I was hoping that if you didn't know, no one but me could be blamed for taking the ship into the restricted zone. Assuming we were allowed to surrender, that is. I'm sorry for that, and for everything else, too. I never meant for you to be dragged into my problems."

"Apology accepted," Jon Robert said. "And for the record, none of us holds you responsible for any of this. It's not your fault Sorseli sent you to Gynos in the first place, and you certainly can't be blamed for the court-martial or for what Renard did to you afterward."

The meeting broke up on that note. They all went away hoping their luck would continue to hold, but ten hours later it ran out.

"Kiley, I have a contact on the long-range scanners," Lukas said over the intercom just as she was sitting down to eat dinner. She dropped her fork and was on the bridge within thirty seconds.

"It's gone," the pilot said tersely when she arrived. "One minute it was there, and the next it was gone."

"What was? Where was it?" she demanded, eyes intent on

the scanners. Lukas pointed to a long-range scanner displaying the system's eighth planet.

"It was there. Just a single blip. It wasn't on my screen long enough to identify."

"You didn't notice it until it reached that point?" she asked incredulously.

He nodded confirmation and she shook her head. If what he had seen was another ship, then it was either traveling at speeds beyond comprehension or it had blinked out of jump and gone right back in again an instant later. Kiley could not imagine any ship exiting jump so close to a planet, but neither could she conceive of a vessel daring to travel at such tremendous speeds in the same location. Lukas must have been mistaken, or the scanner malfunctioning. A ship simply couldn't have been where he said he saw one.

She hit the intercom button for the engine room. "Jon Robert, we may be having problems with the number three scanner. Would you run a systems check on it, please?"

"Will do," he replied. She stood beside the intercom, eyes still on the screen, searching for any anomaly, however small. She found nothing.

"Kiley, I can't find anything wrong with the scanner," Jon Robert reported a minute later. "I ran the full diagnostics program and everything checks out okay."

"Affirmative," she said, then turned to Lukas. "When your ship picked up the unknown target, they were able to track it long enough to tell it was moving at a high speed, weren't they?"

"Yes."

"How good were her scanners?"

"The best," he said, without hesitation.

"Good enough to track an object that might appear as a single blip on ours?"

He considered, shook his head. "I don't think so. They might have been able to pick up a smaller object, farther away, and identify it sooner, but that's about all. What I saw was well within range of your equipment. I don't see how it could have traveled that close without the sensors picking it up sooner."

"Unless it was coming out of jump."

"Yes, but if it did, it went right back in again—so fast it may not even have had time to scan the area, let alone register our presence."

"Well, that's something. Most likely, it was a temporary malfunction, no matter what Jon Robert says. The ship is old; her equipment is bound to start failing eventually.''

He wasn't happy with that conclusion, and neither was she, so they both stayed on the bridge for the rest of the evening, watching the scanners display the same scene hour after boring hour. Nothing moved. They should have relaxed, but waiting for something that didn't happen just increased their edginess.

''This is ridiculous,'' Kiley said at last. She took one last look at the screen and hit the engineering-room button on the intercom. ''Jon Robert, are you there?'' she asked.

''He's gone to bed, Kiley,'' Holly answered.

''When's he due back on watch?''

''Not for another six hours. Reese is spelling me in four.''

''Why don't you call Reese now and have him relieve you early? I want both you and Jon Robert to get some rest. I've had enough of this waiting. We're leaving first thing in the morning.''

''But Daniel said—''

''I don't care what he said. We're not going to sit around here any longer.''

''Kiley, it isn't worth the risk!''

''Neither is waiting around for who knows what to show up. We're leaving at oh-six hundred, Holly. Tell Jon Robert.'' Kiley cut off the intercom and turned to Lukas. ''I want you to get some sleep, too. I'll stand watch the rest of the night.''

''If either of us need rest, it's you. I'll stay and—''

''Greg, I'm not going to play games with you. You may have to cover the bridge alone for some time after transition. I want you rested and alert.''

She expected him to argue, but he gave her a funny look instead. ''As you wish, Captain,'' he said, and left without another word.

If Lukas and the rest of the family were willing to go along with her orders, Keenan was another matter. He was furious when he found out about the early departure and came straight to the bridge.

''Kiley, you may be able to convince the others you're back to normal, but the bioscanner doesn't lie. You may not die if we jump this soon, but you could damage your body irreparably. I won't permit it.''

''The decision has already been made, Keenan.''

''Then unmake it. Kiley, I don't want to go over your head, but I'll appeal to the rest of the family if you force me to.''

''Go ahead, try. I think you'll find they'll stand with me if it comes to a confrontation.''

''I wouldn't be so sure about that.''

''Well, I would. I'm captain of this ship, Keenan. That means something to them, even if it doesn't to you.'' Her confidence shook him. She caught his falter and shifted tactics swiftly. ''Daniel, I won't die. We'll make the longest jump we can. I'll have plenty of time to recuperate between transitions.''

He gave in, as she had known he would, though his acquiescence was graceless. He was as worried as the rest of them. He had expected Tichner to follow them immediately, and the continuing absence of pursuit ships was an acid worry that ate at him constantly. He may have been concerned about her, but she guessed he was as relieved to be leaving as the rest of them. He set only one condition: that she let him stay on the bridge when they jumped.

''If you do have difficulty, I want to be there,'' he said. ''A few seconds might make all the difference.''

She didn't argue that issue—no one would have sided with her.

They moved out of position at 0600, seeing no other ships on the short- or long-range scanners. They needed four hours to build sufficient speed for a long jump, six hours if they wanted to use the coordinates Lukas had chosen as their primary destination. Just six hours, and they would be able to jump out of Zerron Base jurisdiction. But during every minute of every one of those hours they would be running in the open, a highly visible target for anyone who happened to be watching.

Five hours to jump.

Three.

One.

''Fifteen minutes to jump,'' Kiley announced. ''Lia, are you and Reese in your cabin?''

''Affirmative, Kiley,'' Reese said calmly, as if this were a routine run to Aumarleen.

''Holly, Jon Robert, all set in the engine room?''

''Standing by to start jump engines on your signal, Kiley,'' Holly answered.

Kiley's eyes swept the bridge. Keenan was strapped into the backup engineering seat, intent on the monitors before him. Lukas was dividing his attention between the navigation board and the long-range scanners.

He looked up, as if sensing her gaze on him, and smiled.

"Soon," he said. *Soon we'll be safe. Soon this will be all over. Soon.*

They were down to minutes. Ten. Then five. Then one.

It was time.

She reached for the control board.

Chapter 19

"Chirith, the ship is leaving!"

The summons pulled him from a restless sleep. Chirith stumbled along the nearly deserted corridor, fatigue and depression weighing heavy upon him.

Despite intensive searching, they had not found a way around the barrier. They had been about to try another direction when the instruments they had left near the habitable planet signaled an incoming ship.

Chirith was puzzled. He had expected other ships to come long ago, and he had been surprised when none arrived. Hadn't the alien they'd examined told its people about them? If it had, hadn't they believed it? Or were the aliens as wary of contact as Chirith himself? He had decided they would never know the answer to that question. Then a signal came.

They returned to the planet, moving swiftly and cautiously. The aliens had indeed sent a ship, but only one. Had it come seeking a meeting? If so, perhaps it was time to talk. They had had little success deciphering the aliens' records—their data was well coded. The only way to find out if the aliens knew a way around the barrier would be to ask directly. The appearance of a single ship, rather than a fleet, seemed to be a good sign.

Or it would have been, if the aliens had made any attempt to contact them. They hadn't. On the contrary, the vessel appeared to be hiding. But from whom? The *Nieti*? Others of its own kind? He could not tell, and the aliens' abnormal behavior made him hesitate. He had decided to watch to see what developed.

Nothing had, and now it appeared that the ship was leaving. Chirith did not understand what was happening, and that left him feeling profoundly uneasy.

"They continue to build speed," Rietier said as he reached the bridge. "They will be out of sensor range soon."

"They still haven't sent a signal?"

"None we have observed." He hesitated. "Their idea of a signal might not be the same as ours, Chirith. Perhaps we missed the message. Perhaps they did not see us arrive and did not signal in consequence."

"Perhaps. Then again, perhaps they are here on a reconnaissance mission—or as bait in a trap."

"What should we do?"

Chirith watched the ship pull away. Friend or foe? One would be a blessing, the other a disaster. Did this alien vessel offer hope? Did he dare reveal himself on the chance the ship would not only be friendly, but willing and able to help them find a way back home?

They could always run if she proved hostile, he told himself. The *Nieti* was much faster than the alien vessel. If he made contact and discovered they were hostile, he could flee. But if they were friendly . . .

He turned to Rietier. "We will wait until she is at the edge of sensor range. If there are still no other vessels in sight, we will follow her." He stayed on the bridge, watching the ship pull away. Was she friend or foe? Salvation, or bait in a trap, an expendable morsel offered to lure them out of hiding?

"Chirith, we're about to lose contact with the ship," Rietier said as she approached the edge of sensor range. "There is still no sign of other vessels. Shall we follow or not?"

Chirith studied the screen. A single dot blinked, vanished, blinked again, then disappeared for good. The ship was out of range. If they didn't follow now, they would lose her forever.

He closed his eyes, weighing the alternatives, then made his decision. "Follow her, but stay well back. Keep a close watch on the monitors. If you see anything out of the ordinary, anything at all, call out at once."

He had not yet committed himself fully, but he would have to make a decision soon.

Very soon.

Chapter 20

Thirty seconds.

Twenty.

Ten.

"Jump engines on," Kiley ordered.

A deep rumble surrounded them. Her fingers went to the intercom to announce transition, but before she could, every warning alarm on the bridge went off.

"Unidentified ship, five hundred kems and closing fast!" Lukas called out.

"What? How—" She wasted one valuable second giving Lukas a disbelieving look, then she hit the intercom.

"Jon Robert, full power to the jump engines!"

The other ship was too close, but they had already passed the point of no return. She couldn't do anything except divert all power to the jump engines and pray that they would be able to counteract the other ship's pull. If they couldn't—

The lights on the bridge dimmed, and the vibration shaking the *Widdon Galaxy* threatened to tear her apart. Jon Robert hadn't even taken time to answer. He was pushing the ship past the point of safety, calling forth every ounce of power he could summon from her aging engines.

The bridge started to flicker and Kiley's stomach turned upside down. They were entering transition. They were going to make it. They were going to make it!

The lights went off.

Chapter 21

The darkness on the bridge was absolute. Kiley's eyes hurt from trying to see through it.

"Lukas? Keenan? Are you all right?" she asked, her voice rising sharply with an emotion too close to panic for comfort.

What had happened? Where were they? They had started into transition, but they had not completed jump. She was certain of that.

"Here, Kiley," Keenan's disembodied voice sounded behind her.

"Greg?" she asked when Lukas did not answer. She reached across the gap that separated them. She found his arm, then his back. He was bent over, arms wrapped around his stomach. His breath came in shallow gasps and he did not respond to her touch.

"Greg, what's wrong?" she asked sharply.

He still didn't answer. She heard a click as Keenan released his seat restraints. A moment later, he was beside Lukas, hands groping to find him in the darkness.

A long silence during which she could not tell what was going on; then Keenan said softly, "Greg, it's all right to be afraid. I am. So is Kiley. But you can't let your fear control you. Do you hear me, Greg? We need you! You can control fear. It can be used to your advantage. Do you remember them teaching us that at the Academy? Do you remember the first step to control? Take a deep breath. That's right, only this time, hold it. Good. Let it go and take another."

The clenched muscles beneath Kiley's hand loosened, and a moment later Lukas straightened.

"Sorry," he said shakily. "For a minute I thought I was back on Gynos and they were coming." He took another breath, steadying himself. "No power?" he asked, making an effort to assess their situation.

"None," Kiley said.

"Did we jump?"

"I don't *feel* like we did."

"If we had, you would," Keenan said.

"Then we must still be in normal space," Lukas said.

"I hope so," she said fervently. "The alternative doesn't bear contemplation. But if we are, what pulled us back? Tichner?"

"I don't know of a Corps ship that could do that, not when we were already in transition," Lukas said, his voice sounding stronger. "Besides, the ship on the monitor was moving too fast to be one of ours."

A significant silence met those words.

"You're saying the ship on our sensors was alien?" Kiley finally asked.

"I don't know any human ship that could appear from nowhere, overtake us, and completely shut down our power, all in less than ten seconds," Lukas said. "It must have been."

Keenan started to reply, then flinched as a bank of dim lights came on above the main board and a cluster of status indicators flickered to life.

"What—?" he exclaimed.

"Emergency life-support systems," Kiley said absently. "Jon Robert must have found a way to switch them on."

"Kiley, what happened? Where are we?" her brother's voice demanded over the intercom. He was broadcasting shipwide, letting Lia and Reese hear the conversation. She did the same.

"I wish I knew," she said. "Jon Robert, I only have one or two displays working on the status boards and they're all life-support indicators. Can you get an external monitor or scanner working so we can take a look outside?"

"I'll try. Kiley, the engines shut down just before the lights went off—all of them. I was pushing them hard, but there was no reason for an emergency shutdown. They did one, though. We'll have to do a cold start. It will be several hours before they're up to speed. What's going on?"

"I don't know, but a look outside might go a long way toward answering our questions."

Silence, then, "You think there's something out there?"

"There might be."

"Something—not human?"

"Possibly. Can you get me that monitor?"

"I'll do what I can," he said, and the intercom went dead. A moment later, the few functioning readouts on the control board flickered off and a single external monitor came on.

Another ship was floating off their starboard side, so close to them that it filled the entire screen.

An alien ship.

Keenan and Lukas stopped breathing. So did Kiley.

The vessel was half again as large as the *Widdon Galaxy*. She was round, and her smooth hull was a continuous circle, unbroken by external structures.

She glowed.

More than glowed, she pulsed. Swirling colors ebbed and flowed across her hull, ranging in shade from bright reddish-orange to peach to yellow. The colors changed with each pulse, forming swirling patterns. The effect was as hypnotic as firelight, or ocean waves breaking along a straight, empty stretch of beach.

"What the . . ." Keenan breathed. He glanced at Kiley and Lucas, then looked back at the ship. "Greg, is that the ship you saw on Gynos?"

"I don't know. All I saw was an access tube. I—" Lukas broke off, his breath coming raggedly. "Daniel, I don't want to be here. I don't want to see them again. I can't—"

Keenan put a hand on his shoulder and squeezed, the gesture so automatic and absent-minded that he might have made it a hundred times before.

"None of us do, Greg," he said, but his eyes were on the ship and there was a note in his voice that said precisely the opposite. Kiley and Lukas might be afraid, but Keenan was utterly fascinated. He had told Kiley he'd wanted to go on deep-space exploration missions once, and she now saw why. His mind was so full of curiosity and wonder, there was no room left for fear.

"She almost looks . . . alive," he said, breathing the words. "I wonder—"

He broke off abruptly as the ship moved, spinning inward, toward them. Kiley cried out involuntarily as the other ship bumped the *Widdon Galaxy* hard enough to knock her sideways. The monitor screen went blank, and the internal sensors flickered to life again.

"Kiley, what hit us?" Jon Robert demanded.

She fumbled for the intercom, her eyes going from Keenan to

Lukas. "There's another ship out there. I think—I think she just docked. Jon Robert, she isn't human."

"You're sure about that?"

She laughed, the sound too close to hysteria for comfort. "I've never been more sure of anything in my life," she said. "I lost the external monitor when she hit. Can you get it working again?"

"I'll see what I can—" His voice broke off.

"Jon Robert?" she asked. He did not answer.

"What's wrong?" she demanded. "Can you hear me?"

A blue light is coming through the hull overhead," he said breathlessly. "It's—moving around the room. It looks like it's examining the equipment and control panels. It's coming toward us. Holly, get back. Get back!"

Kiley was on her feet, wanting to run to the engine room, held back by the training that said her place was on the bridge. Training won out.

"Jon Robert, what's happening?" she asked frantically.

The intercom crackled with static. It was open, but all she heard was silence. Keenan was already at the hatch. She nodded to him, urging him to go, but before he could leave, Jon Robert answered.

"Kiley, the light just passed over us. I was afraid it might hurt us, but there was no sensation to it at all. It's moving forward now. Toward the bridge."

"It's at midship, Kiley," Reese cut in. "I was on my way to the engine room and it just passed me. It's like a searchlight, only blue. I thought it would be cold, or tingle somehow, but Jon Robert's right, there was no sensation at all. It's still headed forward."

A moment later the light moved onto the bridge. Reese had followed it forward, Lia a few steps behind him.

The light stopped just inside the entrance to the bridge, a transparent blue shaft. Kiley could see why Reese had thought it might be cold. She watched it warily as it started moving again, circling the room in a measured, clockwise motion.

It made one complete circuit of the control boards, looking for all the world as if it was examining them; then it moved inward a few feet and started another circular sweep of the room. Kiley was the first one in its path. She tensed as the light neared and held her breath as it touched her. Her skin turned bluish-yellow, but the others had been right—there was no sensation at all. The beam poised over her for a good ten seconds, then continued on.

"It's okay," she said to Lukas, who was standing next in line. "I didn't feel anything."

He didn't wait to find out. He was backing away from the beam, trying to stay out of range. Keenan moved, putting himself between Lukas and the light, either by design or instinct. The beam found him, paused ten seconds, then slowly moved on again. Toward Lukas. He had retreated as far as he could go and stood with his back to the control board. He watched the approaching light as if it were his most horrible nightmare come to life.

The blue shaft moved over him and he flinched. He stood rigidly, waiting for it to continue on. It did not. Ten seconds passed, twenty, thirty, and still the beam centered on him. And then, just when she thought he was going to break and run, the light started moving again, slowly sweeping the rest of the bridge before coming to a halt at the center of the room. It paused there, then just—disappeared. One instant it was there and the next it was gone.

Kiley blinked, eyes adjusting to the absence of light. Keenan had gone to Lukas and was talking to him, his voice low and urgent. Lukas was not answering. Reese and Lia had come the rest of the way onto the bridge, their faces filled with equal measures of horror and fascination.

"Kiley, what *was* that?" Lia asked.

"I'm not sure, but if I had to guess, I'd say it was a scanner of some kind." She spoke to Lia, but her eyes were on Keenan and Lukas. The psychiatrist had stopped talking, but his hand was still on Lukas's arm. He did not remove it until the pilot moved away a few moments later of his own accord.

"Kiley, are you all right?" Jon Robert asked over the intercom.

"Yes," she said. "The light was here, but it's gone now. Jon Robert, can you get that external monitor back on?"

"I'm still working on it. Give me a few more minutes."

Kiley shut off the intercom and gave the boards a quick scan. There wasn't much to see. They had heat and air circulation, but that was all.

No hot showers tonight, she thought, and had to fight down another surge of hysteria. She was turning away from the board when a red light flashed on.

"Kiley, the main hatch is open!" Lukas cried out.

"Possible malfunction?" she asked immediately.

"I don't think so," he said, his voice now a near-whisper.

She took a breath. "I suppose somebody should go investigate."

No one moved.

She didn't want to go herself, but someone had to. She put one foot forward, then another. Keenan started moving, too. They reached the door at the same time.

"Do you want me to go first?" he asked.

"I will," she said, hoping she sounded more certain than she felt. She was captain—she was supposed to lead. She just wished she felt more like a commander than a coward.

The corridor outside the bridge was empty. There were emergency lights on in the engine room, but the long passageway between them was dark. She turned to the left, toward the main hatch.

It was open. Faint, pinkish light spilled out of the access tube beyond, revealing three figures standing between them and the tube.

The figures moved.

They took one step. Another. Then another. They advanced slowly, deliberately, their steady progress neither threatening nor reassuring.

The light was to their backs and Kiley could make out little about them, except that the tallest was a good three inches shorter than she was. They had two arms and two legs, but that was as much of their physical structure as she could determine, for they wore bulky, protective suits. Their movements appeared clumsy, but that might have been a result of their suits rather than a physical characteristic. Visored helmets covered their heads, and Kiley could not see their faces.

Two of the aliens were carrying palm-sized, oblong objects. They held them pointed toward her and Keenan. The third carried a larger object, narrow at the base and fan-shaped at the end. This one held the object out before it, moving it from side to side, as if scanning the corridor. It turned the object on Kiley, then Keenan. She flinched, but there were no discernible effects.

The alien closest to them raised its right hand and . . . pushed. It made no attempt to touch them, but they fell back a step in reflex. The alien took another step forward. Repeated the gesture.

"I think they want us to back up," Keenan said.

"I believe you're right. I suggest we comply."

They backed up. One step, then a second. The alien continued to make the pushing gesture, and they fell back until they stood at the entrance to the bridge. Either they continued moving down the corridor, or they went back in. Kiley chose the bridge. Better to be there, with the few systems that still functioned at her command, than be a prisoner in one of the cabins.

She half expected the aliens to follow, but they stopped at the door. The one who had made the pushing motion looked inside, then gestured to one of the others, who took up position in the corridor, blocking the exit. The other two started walking down the passage toward the engine room.

Kiley took a cautious step toward the pilot's chair. The alien in the doorway did not stop her. She continued to move, one eye on the alien, until she reached the control board and the intercom.

"Jon Robert, you have company coming your way," she said quietly, her eyes still on the dark-suited figure in the hatch. "Two of them. One is still here, making sure the rest of us stay on the bridge. Don't take any chances with them. If they seem to want you to do something, do it. I don't want any misunderstandings."

"I hear you, Kiley," he answered. "Holly's watching the door. She'll let me know when they're here."

"Can you get the external monitor working again?"

"I'm still trying."

"Do the best you can, but don't jeopardize yourself. Understood?"

He gave a shaky laugh. "Understood," he said.

Kiley released the intercom and surveyed the others. Reese, Lia, and Keenan were watching the alien with varying degrees of horror and fascination. Lukas was watching it, too, from as far into the corner as he could press himself, his hands clamped to the control board behind him. She wasn't sure if he needed the support to stand upright, or if his physical grip was an extension of the mental one he was exerting over himself.

A visual monitor clicked to life above his head, showing a black sky filled with stars. They both jumped. Kiley gave the alien in the passageway a quick glance, but it either had not noticed the display coming on, or it did not care. It was looking at Lia, who had edged closer to Reese.

"Lia, be careful," Kiley warned softly. "Don't make any sudden moves. In fact, don't move at all if you can help it."

"It keeps watching me," her sister said. If she had spoken full-voice, her tone would have been a wail.

"It's watching you because you're moving. Stand still."

"Kiley, they're here," Jon Robert said over the intercom. "I think they want us to go out in the corridor."

"Then do it."

The aliens brought Jon Robert and Holly to the bridge a few minutes later, herding the couple before them with the same pushing gestures they had used on Kiley and Keenan.

"Looks like they want us all together," Kiley said uneasily.

"Easier to watch us that way," Keenan replied, his voice terse.

The alien with the scanner left the other two posted at the door and went down the corridor toward the outside hatch. A few minutes later, three other aliens appeared.

They were not wearing protective suits, and they most definitely were not human—nor any other species of animal, reptile, or insect Kiley had ever seen.

They smelled. Not a bad smell, but a spicy one, like cinnamon, or kistath from Aumarleen. They stood a little shorter than humans and were somewhat narrower. They had two arms and two legs, though the proportions did not seem quite right: their legs were shorter than a human's and their arms longer in relation to their bodies. Their hands had four digits—two shorter appendages like thumbs on the outside, and two longer fingers in the middle. A deep division between the two fingers gave them an independence of movement human hands could not achieve. The fingers ended in thick pads, from which heavy growths that could have been either nails or claws extended a quarter of an inch.

They had rounded heads, slightly elongated in the back. Their faces were smooth, with no protruding cheekbones or brow, and their ears were almost invisible openings on the sides of their heads. Wide, flat nostrils flared slightly as they breathed, as if they were sniffing the air. Their lips lay tight against their teeth, less full and mobile than a human's. For all that, they were not unattractive. Indeed, the clean, smooth lines of their heads, shoulders, and limbs reminded Kiley of sleek sea mammals whose bodies were designed to flow through water with a minimum of resistance. But if they had once lived in water, they had clearly left it far behind.

They did not wear clothes, but thick, short hair covered their bodies. They ranged in color from black to gray to reddish-brown. She could see no obvious sexual characteristics, despite their lack of clothing, and the only difference she could see between them was the variation in hair color. Two carried pouches made of a leatherlike material slung over their heads and shoulders. The pouches were undecorated and appeared well worn.

The three aliens came to a halt just inside the bridge, returning the humans' scrutiny. Then the gray one lifted its hands and gestured, a complicated twisting of arms, hands and fingers. Was it signaling? If so, was it trying to talk to them, or its companions?

Kiley glanced at Keenan, uncertain. *What do we do?* she pleaded silently. He shrugged, for once as much at a loss as she.

Someone had to act. Since she was captain, the responsibility appeared to be hers. Without giving herself time to consider the consequences, she stepped forward and said, "Hello."

Lia burst into hysterical laughter. Reese silenced her with a hand over her mouth. The aliens' eyes went from Kiley to Lia, then back, and the gray one stepped forward. It was an inch shorter than the others. Liquid black eyes that shone like polished obsidian looked into Kiley's. The gaze sent an electric shock racing through her—not because it was so alien, but because it was so unexpectedly familiar. She had seen the same quick intelligence and bright curiosity in Keenan's eyes as he watched the ship pulsing on the monitor.

The alien moved its fingers again in a complicated twisting motion human hands could never duplicate. She tried anyway, lifting her hands and making a clumsy gesture in return. She was rewarded by a high-pitched, piping whistle from one of the aliens in the doorway. Her hands went to her ears in reflex and she fell back a step in alarm.

Was the sound a warning? The alien did not move or make a threatening gesture. Perhaps the noise had been laughter, for the alien in front of Kiley was repeating a portion of its gesture, this time moving its hands with exaggerated slowness, as if to let her see what it did more clearly.

It touched its chest with its left hand, then straightened its arm. It made the same gesture with its right hand, then placed its left hand over its right, palm up, fingers cupped.

It paused, waiting. For what? For her to respond? Kiley hesitated, then moved her arms and hands, copying the motions. There was no sharp whistle this time, just intense curiosity.

The alien made another gesture, this time twisting its fingers.

Kiley watched, then copied it as best she could. It was not easy; human fingers were never designed to shape themselves so, and she fumbled the last part. She just did not have the same dexterity, and her extra finger kept getting in the way. She tried a second time and failed again. The gray alien gestured, a quick motion, forefinger and thumb pressing together and separating. It put out one hand, holding it palm up in front of her, then held out the other in the same way. Kiley hesitated, then followed suit.

The alien touched her hand.

She didn't move.

She didn't breathe.

She just stood there, frozen. Someone shifted uneasily behind her, then stopped moving abruptly as one of the aliens by the door stiffened.

The gray alien pressed her little finger and thumb gently, moving them together to form a circle. It moved her fourth finger so it lay over the two that formed a circle, then lifted the finger and moved it inside the circle, pressing until it touched the palm of her hand. It watched her closely the entire time. Was it afraid she might respond wildly to its touch? She wanted to. The feel of its thickly padded fingers was not unpleasant, but it was intensely disturbing. She didn't relax until the alien stepped away and repeated the gesture it had just guided her through, its own movements quick and fluid.

It waited for her, so she made the sign a third time. She was still clumsy, but she had the sign down now. The gray one made a quick gesture in response, then turned to its companions, whistling something.

Kiley took her first real breath in what seemed like hours. The alien would not be showing her how to form symbols unless it wanted to communicate. Perhaps they meant them no harm after all. Perhaps they just wanted to meet. To talk. There might be hope for them yet.

She no sooner had that thought than everything fell apart.

Afterward she was able to reconstruct what had happened, but at the time it seemed like everyone on the bridge, alien and human, had gone crazy at the same instant.

A light flashed across the external monitor and a ship burst out of jump. She emerged less than five hundred kems away and momentum carried her straight toward them at an alarming speed. High, ear-piercing cries filled the room, as alarming as the ship's warning system would have been had it been working.

A rank scent filled the air, foul enough to make Kiley gag. The aliens near the doorway raised their hands, pointing them toward the humans. The gray alien beside her was pulling an object out of the pouch it carried, but it was not a weapon, for when the alien pressed the face of the black oblong, nothing happened except that another round of piercing notes split the air.

"Kiley, incoming ship!" Jon Robert shouted, just as Lukas called out, "Delta-class cruiser inbound!"

Lia screamed.

Reese and Jon Robert lunged forward, toward the aliens who were pointing objects that looked like weapons at Kiley, Lukas, and Keenan. The ship on the monitors lurched, wobbled, and started to drift off course.

One of the aliens in the doorway swung its hand toward Reese and Jon Robert, pointing the object it carried at them.

Holly cried out a warning, and another round of piercing notes split the air.

"STOP!" Kiley shouted to Jon Robert and Reese, throwing every ounce of authority she possessed into that single command.

The two men faltered, caught themselves, looked her way.

"Don't move!" she ordered. Before she could say anything else, a fissure of light appeared on the wall of the control board, just behind Lukas.

For a moment she thought a seam had opened along the hull and sunlight was pouring in. She opened her mouth to cry out a warning, for death was less than a heartbeat away—then she was glad no sound had emerged as she realized the light came from inside the ship, not without. It moved down the wall, streamed across the control board between the blank monitors, and continued on, headed straight toward Lukas.

"Greg, behind you!" she called out.

He swung around to see what had alarmed her and lost his balance. His hand went out against the control board, grabbing hold less than six inches away from the light. It had pooled at the edge of the board, a mass of glowing pink, yellow, and orange, all swirling together. The color darkened, then brightened again. Lukas froze, staring at the light as if mesmerized. The edge of the pool broke and a streamer spilled out, flowing straight toward his hand.

"Greg, watch out!" Keenan cried. He was a good five feet away from the pilot, but he threw himself toward him as if to propel Lukas away from the light before it could reach him. The aliens in the doorway reacted instantly. Two of them pointed the small objects they held at Keenan. Kiley did not see a flash, a beam, or any other sign the weapons had fired, but Keenan went limp in midair and fell to the floor with a thud, limbs sprawling every which way.

Lukas never moved. All his attention was on the light, which was about to touch his hand. He heard someone scream. Who? Lia? Holly? He had just enough time to wonder, then the room burst apart as the light spilled over his hand and he was engulfed by a maelstrom of thought and emotion that ripped through his mind at hurricane velocity.

Grief. Paralyzing, horror-stricken, agonizing grief crushed him. He had killed. His duty was to protect life, and instead, he had taken it. Worse, he had killed the one he most needed and cherished, the one who had spoken to him, the one who had shared mind, body, and heart with him.

Something had been terribly wrong with the space through which they had traveled. Something had twisted him inside out, so disrupting his ability to function that he had lost control of the ship, had sealed off compartments and taken the air from them, had stopped the recycling systems and internal heating. It did not matter that the failure had been unintentional. He had killed.

Remorse was an icy sword ripping his insides apart, always present, never easing. He could never right the wrong he had done. He clung to sanity, trying to protect those still living, but even there he failed. They could not go home because of him. He could not pass through the barrier. It had no effect on the others, but it tore his mind apart. He was—

Not the one who hurt!

Lukas grasped that small corner of reason and held on to it, fighting to separate his own mind and emotions from the feelings threatening to engulf him. He had experienced this overwhelming rush of emotion once before, on the alien ship. The distress was not his! It belonged to another.

That time he had collapsed before the onslaught. But he had been in a state of shock then, and he was not now. Moreover, he had learned a great deal about guilt and shame in the year since. The emotions were no longer alien to him. They were as much a part of his life as satisfaction, love, or joy.

Failure was inevitable. All men made mistakes; that was the price of being human. Keenan had tried to tell him that. He had also tried to teach him that no man was a true failure unless he refused to admit his mistakes and learn from them. He had not believed the psychiatrist at the time, protesting that some mistakes were too great to be overcome or forgiven—like causing the deaths of men who trusted you. But now, faced by a guilt even greater than his own, he found himself repeating the psychiatrist's words as if they could ease the monumental grief that surrounded him.

For a moment the emotions buffeting him quieted, as if the other was listening to what he was saying. As if it was considering.

And a voice spoke, deep inside his own mind.

"Hu . . . man? What is . . . human?"

Chapter 22

Trap!

Chirith saw the incoming ship appear in a flash of light and tore his transmitter out of the bag he carried over his shoulder. Rietier's urgent warning cry spilled out into the room.

"Chirith, a second ship just appeared! It came in right on top of us! The Quayla may not have time—" He broke off, and came back a moment later, calmer. "The Quayla has disabled the ship, Chirith. I wasn't sure it would have time, but it managed. What do you wish me to do?"

Chirith did not answer because two of the aliens on the side of the room were attacking. His crew raised their weapons, but before they could open fire the creature in front of him cried out. The single, sharp burst of sound froze everyone in the room, his own crew included. The creature made more sounds and the others of its kind stopped moving. Chirith was about to order his own crew to lower their weapons when a light appeared on the wall before him.

The Quayla.

It had to have come across the access tube that joined their vessels. But why? It seemed to be moving toward the alien who stood closest to the controls—the one they had examined on the planet's surface. They had been surprised to find it on the ship. When their instruments had identified it as the same being, hope had surged. It had to have come back to find them. The vessel carried no weapons they could detect; perhaps the aliens truly had come seeking a meeting.

The Quayla was less than a hand's distance away from the alien. What was it doing? Why was it so interested in this particular one? Did it still believe it could touch the alien's mind?

It had failed the first time—why did it think it could succeed now?

One of the other aliens called out to the one the Quayla was approaching, then leaped forward, toward the pool of light.

"No!" Chirith cried out. His warning did not stop the alien, but his crew fired on it. They caught it in midleap and it fell to the floor, unconscious. The other aliens started forward, headed for their fallen companion, but then stopped abruptly, as if remembering the weapons aimed at them. All of them, that is, but the one closest to the Quayla. It was oblivious to all that surrounded it. The Quayla had to be reaching it on some level; otherwise, it would have noticed its companion's collapse.

The Quayla touched the alien's hand. A moment later it changed color, turning deep rose and pulsing wildly. Chirith stared at it in shock. It wasn't just making contact with the alien—it was entering the first stage of joining! Realization struck Chirith's crew at the same moment and startled, agitated cries filled the room. The Quayla join with an alien? It could not! It must not! They lifted their weapons, then let them fall. If it was joining, they would endanger both the Quayla and the alien if they interfered.

Chirith had not believed the Quayla when it had said it could reach the alien's mind. He had thought it was only saying what it wanted to believe. He had been wrong. He had never believed a Quayla would turn to a non-Miquiri for a companion, either, and that had been another mistake. He had known the depth of its need. He should have anticipated that it would do just this, given the opportunity.

Given one who was receptive.

Horror gripped Chirith. If the Quayla merged with an alien, who would it serve? A Quayla would never betray its companion—to do so would be to betray itself. He raised his weapon again, thinking whatever damage he did to the Quayla could not be as great as the threat this joining posed. But before he could fire, the alien cried out.

The being in front of Chirith started forward in response to that cry. Chirith caught its arm, holding it back. One of the other aliens moved, too, flinging itself toward the Quayla. His crew fired on it and it fell. The shorter one that had been standing at its side dropped to the floor with a cry and gathered it up. The alien in Chirith's grasp struggled, calling out to the one who knelt. It struggled to free itself again, angry and frightened. It did not like being restrained.

"I can't let you go," he said sadly. "Much as I would like to stop them, it is too late."

The creature did not understand. He stroked its arm, absently offering reassurance. It did not like that, either. He let it go. It took a step away. He caught it again and held its arm long enough to show it he would not permit it to move, then released it a second time. The alien looked at him with dangerous eyes, but did not attempt to move again. Chirith turned his attention back to the Quayla.

It had changed color, going from rose to a deep, pure red. It was pulsing so fast that its light appeared steady. Normally translucent, it had thickened until he could no longer see through it. He had waited too long. Both the Quayla's and alien's minds were fully open. If he had fired on the alien, he would have damaged both it and the Quayla irreparably. They would never have found a way home.

They still might not. There was no doubt that the alien was receptive, but that did not mean it would be able to withstand the impact of full contact. The Quayla would not have proceeded unless it believed that the alien could, but it was not infallible. Despite its best judgment, some minds proved too inflexible to accept the meshing that was necessary if two were to function as one. He had seen a joining fail once, when a Quayla was transferring itself to a newly built ship. He never wished to witness such horror again.

What is human?

For the second time in the past five minutes, Lukas nearly lost his sanity.

The emotions that filled him, the thoughts that echoed in his mind, were not his. They were not even human. They were—

Alien. More alien by far than the beings who walked on two legs. The light had no body, but it was alive. It thought, it hurt, it communicated. It was alive!

He had had just enough time to think that when a whirlwind hit his mind. He tried to erect hasty barriers, but the storm tossed them aside effortlessly. Otherness poured into him, filling his mind to the point of bursting, packing itself inside his head in tighter and tighter folds.

The pressure shifted abruptly, a physical thing turning around in the space between his skull and brain. It squeezed in, as if trying to force its way into the brain tissue. He could not fight it. There were no weapons to battle such an enemy.

A crevasse opened in his brain and the pressure poured into the breach, flooding his mind like a storm-swollen river overflowing its banks. It swirled through him, washing through every thought, every memory. No part of him was left inviolate.

With the little piece of consciousness that remained, he thought the worst was over. He was wrong. An instant later, images started pouring into his mind in wave after incomprehensible wave. They came too rapidly and were too alien to be grasped, let alone understood. They jostled for position, forcing his own bruised thoughts aside, burying themselves like barbed hooks deep inside the soft matter of his brain. He could not stop them from sinking in, could not even deflect them. Faster and faster they came, a kaleidoscope of swirling lights. Light flared, so intensely bright as to be incandescent. He felt the coming explosion, but there was nothing he could do to stop it. He could only stand and watch as the lights in his brain coalesced into one gigantic sun that went supernova an instant later, vaporizing all that remained of his mind.

Darkness.
Silence.
Total nonbeing.
He was floating in space, free of pressure, free of thought. For a moment, he thought he was free of the thing that had invaded him, but it was still there. It was watching him from deep inside his mind, waiting for him to recognize it. It was him—and not him at the same time.

What are you? he screamed at it.

The reply came from the center of his own mind.

The Miquiri call me Quayla.

Miquiri. Quayla. The words were liquid, lilting sounds, clear and sweet. They flowed joyously, like water tumbling in a rocky brook, now flashing in the sunlight, now running deep through the hushed silence of a forest glade.

I am . . . shipmind, the voice said.

Shipmind? I don't understand, he replied, and was answered with a flood of images and sensations: mathematical calculations, data on the ship's course and speed, the position of objects within and without the ship, the temperature of each compartment, the food stores left in the hold. The mind that touched his controlled the alien's ship, and in return it received a home and passage to places it could not go alone. And companionship. Most of all, it received companionship.

Or it had, until the one who had shared with it had died. Until it had killed its companion and the meaning had gone out of existence.

Desolation swept through him. Never, in all his life, had he known such complete anguish and abandonment, not even when his parents had died. Without its companion, the Quayla had lost all touch with the physical world. Isolated, deprived of sensory input, it had nearly lost its reason. Had its imperative to protect the ship and her crew not been so strong, it would have ceased functioning and dissipated itself long ago, choosing nonexistence over such devastating hurt.

But it could not abandon its responsibilities, no matter how much it wished to. It had never believed it would find someone to share with again, but unexpectedly, it had. It had found him.

Joy as overwhelming as the grief he had experienced moments ago swept through Lukas. Uncontrollable joy, happiness gone wild. He battled for control, terrified of losing himself in the surging emotions. The joy turned into pressure, resisting him because he resisted it. It held on to his mind like a vise. It was crushing him.

Stop! he shouted to it. *Stop! You're hurting me!* He gathered what little remained of himself and sent what he hoped was a terrifying image of himself being killed by the Quayla, just as its previous companion had been killed. The pressure ceased so abruptly that he nearly fell to his knees. For a moment he thought the Quayla had withdrawn completely, but it was still there, buried so deep inside his mind he did not think it could ever be dislodged.

Please. Forgive, it said, the thought feeling unexpectedly contrite. *I did not mean to harm you. Your withdrawal frightened me. I responded without thought. I was afraid you would reject me and I would be alone again. I could not bear that. Please, do not make me live alone again.*

A year ago, he might have been able to resist that desperate appeal—but that had been before his trial, before Renard, before endless dark and frightened hours of his own.

I won't leave you, he said. He could not have, even if he had wanted to. To do so would have been to reject a part of himself.

Joy surged and was quickly dampened. The Quayla was trying to accommodate him.

Better? it asked, seeking reassurance.

Much, he replied. And it was. The pressure and the sense of otherness were still there, but he could think past them now. He could see.

Awareness of his surroundings returned with an abruptness that left him dizzy and disoriented. He looked around the room slowly and found the faces of friends and aliens. The aliens were huge, oversized creatures with hair that grew only out of their heads, and then in such wild profusion as to be a deformity. They were decided curiosities. They were—

Not alien! They were his kind. His!

Lukas reeled with shock. Aliens, friends—he could not tell which was which. They were all the same to him. His breath came in a gasp that sounded like a cry and Kiley started toward him, only to be restrained by Chirith.

He knew them, all of them, human and Miquiri. Memories inundated him. He saw Kiley sitting beside him on the bridge, head bent over a monitor, concentrating on the readout, not aware that he was watching her, trying to understand her. Why had she helped him? Why? Anyone else would have let him sink into the oblivion he had nearly found on Demarker.

Instead, she had taken him on, supported him, encouraged him. She had believed in him when he had not believed in himself. He needed to thank her for that, but every time he tried, something got in the way, something that said "thank you" wasn't quite what she wanted to hear, or what he wanted to say. He started to go to her, to say the words he should have said before, and stopped. Because beside her was Chirith, the person he had cherished above all others except Tirie, his mate.

He saw himself with Chirith on the night he had received word that his mate, Ailii, had died. She had been mate only, not *akia*; she had no love for ships or travel and had lived a planetbound life. They had lived together during their initial, frenzied year of mating, but after that Chirith had seen her only on his infrequent visits home. Still, she had been his mate, and he grieved for her.

He had sat beside Chirith the night the news had arrived, stroking his arm, offering what consolation he could. He doubted his *akia* heard the words he spoke, but he knew that what the mind did not hear, the heart would.

Chirith. Kiley.

He started toward them. They watched him approach with equal degrees of wariness. They had meant more to him than anyone else in his life. Both of them. And now they viewed him as alien.

Both of them.

Chirith released Kiley's arm as he approached, but neither of them moved. No one on the bridge moved. They were all watching him, human and Miquiri alike. He reached Kiley and Chirith and stopped, looking from one to the other. Friend and alien. Both.

He lifted his hands. *Akia,* he said to Chirith in the silent language.

He turned to Kiley, and said the words he had not been able to say before.

"I love you," he whispered.

Did she hear? If so, she made no response. Her body was rigid with fear as she looked from him to Chirith.

"They won't hurt us," he said, his eyes locked on hers. "You don't have to be afraid of them."

He wanted to say more, but there wasn't time. His legs were starting to shake. They weren't going to hold him up any longer, he realized in sudden amazement. He was going to fall.

Two sets of hands caught him an instant before he hit the floor, one human, one Miquiri. They were still holding him a moment later, when he lost consciousness completely.

Both of them.

Chapter 23

So many people, human and alien, had come and gone from Lukas's cabin that Kiley didn't see how he could sleep. But he did—hour after hour.

They had not undressed him, partly because Keenan hadn't expected him to remain unconscious for long, and partly because removing his clothes would have been exposing him to the aliens more literally than any of them cared to do.

"I wish we knew what happened to him," Kiley said.

"Whatever it was, it had something to do with *that*," Keenan replied. He stopped scanning Lukas long enough to give the light on the wall a malignant look, then resumed his examination.

The light had followed them to Lukas's cabin, streaming along the floor, then running up the wall. It had lost intensity, its deep red color fading to rose and its wild throbbing settling down to a slow, steady pulse. The aliens glanced at it periodically, but they did not appear concerned about it.

They had made no further attempts to communicate, although the gray alien who had shown Kiley hand signals had come to Lukas's cabin, and several others had, too. They had stayed for a time, then wandered off, leaving the gray alien and a dark brown one to stand watch over the pilot.

The brown alien also examined Lukas, using instruments of its own. Keenan stiffened when it motioned him away, but he retreated. He watched the inspection closely, prepared to intervene if the alien hurt Lukas, but it only ran its instruments above his body, making no attempt to touch him. Afterward, it went back to the corner of the room where the gray one waited. They exchanged signals, then settled back to wait for Lukas to wake.

Keenan gave them a wary glance, then took the chair from

Lukas's desk and sat down next to the pilot. Kiley wasn't surprised that he wanted to sit; he had awakened only moments after Lukas passed out, weak and disoriented. He still looked pale an hour later—but then, Kiley thought, she probably did, too.

Worry did that to a person.

They were apparently free to move about the ship now, but they could not go anywhere without being observed by one or more of the aliens, who were busily examining every fixture and object on the ship.

Lia's plants had drawn the largest crowd and the most prolonged attention. The first ones into the room had emitted the high-pitched, ear-piercing whistle that seemed to indicate either surprise or intense excitement. The blooming plants proved the most fascinating, particularly the red and orange varieties. So many aliens had toured the room that Lia thought some must be on their second trip, though she couldn't positively identify any of them. Reese stayed with her the entire time, but she didn't appear to need the support. Her garden was a source of great pride to her, and she would bask in the praise of anyone who offered it, alien or not.

Holly and Jon Robert had gone back to the engine room, to keep a watch on the aliens coming and going there. Jon Robert had awakened soon after Keenan, displaying the same weakness and disorientation. He, too, insisted he was fine. Keenan scanned him anyway, then said a shade too cheerfully, "No damage I can see, but you'd better take it easy the next few hours."

Kiley suspected his recommendation would have been more forceful if he hadn't been suffering the same aftereffects himself—and hadn't wanted to be held to his own orders.

He did get some rest sitting in the chair next to Lukas's bunk, but he stood every fifteen minutes or so and ran the bioscanner over the pilot. The alien also checked on Lukas periodically, but its examination was cursory.

Lukas woke some four hours after he had passed out. Keenan rose as soon as he noticed the pilot stirring and started running a scanner over him. Lukas came to with a jerk. He stiffened, made a choked sound, then opened his eyes and looked around the room blankly, as if unable to place himself.

"How are you feeling, Greg?" Keenan asked.

"Okay," he said. He blinked, then pushed himself upright.

He put his right hand over his eyes and rubbed, as if they were bothering him.

"Do you hurt anywhere?" Keenan asked.

"No."

"Kiley says you collapsed after you touched the light. Do you remember what happened?"

Lukas's hand went still.

"Greg, do you remember?" Keenan persisted.

Lukas hesitated, then let his hand fall. "The light—it talked to me."

"It what?"

"It talked to me." He looked at Keenan for the first time. "Daniel, I know this is going to be difficult to believe, but—"

He broke off as the gray alien left the corner of the room and came over to him. It stopped beside his bed, then started signaling with its hands and arms. Lukas's eyes opened wide in . . . what? Surprise? The alien paused and Lukas made a hesitant gesture of his own, his hands moving awkwardly, his eyes slightly unfocused. He looked as though he was feeling his way through the gesture even as he made it. The gray one seemed to understand his reply, though. It gestured again, then touched his upper arm. Its fingers pressed, released, then pressed a second time, the movements so deliberate that they might have been a code.

Kiley expected Lukas to flinch at the alien's touch, but he didn't. He gave the alien a startled look, but his expression softened almost immediately. She could detect no fear in him. On the contrary, the alien might have been as old and trusted a friend as Keenan. Lukas signed something else. The alien responded, touched his arm again briefly, then went back to the corner of the room, where it began gesturing to the brown one.

"Greg, what's going on?" Keenan asked, his gaze going from the aliens to Lukas.

"He—Chirith—asked if I was all right, then asked if he could talk to me as soon as I felt up to a conversation."

"You understood what he was saying?"

"Yes."

"How?"

"The Quayla told me."

"The Quayla?"

"The light."

"The light told you what the alien was saying?"

"Daniel, I know I sound crazy, but I'm not. I swear. The

Quayla runs the Miquiri ship. Its name means *shipmind* in their language. It handles everything, from environmental systems to engineering to navigation. It's like a very advanced computer in some ways, but it's more than a machine, much more. It can think and feel, Daniel. In every sense that counts, it's alive.''

"And it can communicate with you?"

"Yes."

"That's how you understood what the aliens were saying? Through the Quayla?"

"Yes. It isn't easy, though. The Quayla can only see their gestures through my eyes, and my perceptions are different from its last companion's. It has to translate what I see into signs it recognizes, then try to translate the signs into words I understand. We're learning from each other all the time, but communication is still difficult.''

"And tiring?"

"A little."

"For both of you?"

"Well, me mostly," Lukas admitted. "The Quayla doesn't really feel any physical sensations, except through me, but what I feel, it feels. Does that make sense?"

"Of a sort," Keenan said dryly.

"Greg, why did the Quayla join with you?" Kiley asked. "To help us communicate with the Miquiri?"

He hesitated. "Partly."

"And the other part?"

"It was lonely. It needed a companion."

"And it chose you?"

"Yes."

"Why you? Why not one of the Miquiri?"

Lukas blinked, as if the question had not occurred to him before. His eyes lost focus, and then he said slowly, "I was . . . receptive. Not many are. At least, not many Miquiri. It doesn't know about humans. It hasn't tried to reach anyone but me."

"But it could?" Keenan asked sharply.

Lukas was shaking his head almost before the question was out of Keenan's mouth. "I don't know, but it doesn't matter if it can. It only chooses one companion at a time. It might try to touch someone else's mind, but they would have to be very receptive and the contact would be shallow. It would not join with them."

"Just what does that mean, Greg? To join?"

"I—" For the first time Lukas faltered, his eyes going from

Keenan to Kiley, as if uncertain what, or how much, to say. As if uncertain that he could trust them.

"I—" He stopped again, then said, "I told you, it's inside me. It's part of me."

"A literal part?" Kiley asked.

"Yes."

"You mean you can't separate yourself from it? Not at all?"

Lukas looked upset for the first time. "I don't see how," he said. "The joining is for life—or the life of the companion, anyway. It would only choose someone else if I died. It would have to, then. Without a companion, it has no sensory input. It is isolated, starved."

"You realize you're describing a parasite, don't you?" Keenan demanded harshly.

"No!" Lukas said. "It is not a parasite! It shares. The relationship is symbiotic, not parasitic."

"You're saying you gain, too? How?" Keenan demanded.

Lukas's breath was coming faster, as if the psychiatrist's question had upset him. He started to answer, then stopped, his eyes turning inward. His breathing slowed abruptly and his face relaxed.

"I share, too," he said simply. "Daniel, I know you'll need time to accept all this, but you don't have to be afraid, not of the Quayla, not of me. It won't hurt me. It can't. Whatever happens to me happens to it. Besides, there are benefits to the relationship. I know whatever it does, about the Miquiri, about their ship, about the Corps cruiser. She's still out there," he said abruptly, as if just remembering the ship. "We'll have to do something about her soon. We can't risk her firing on us, but she can't run on emergency power forever. Neither can we," he said, as if the thought had just occurred to him. He closed his eyes momentarily, then turned to Kiley. "Tell Jon Robert he can start the engines now. The Quayla won't shut them down this time."

"That's what happened before?" Kiley asked. "The Quayla shut them down?"

"Yes."

"How?"

"It absorbs energy," Lukas said. He hesitated, as if seeking a more complete answer. "It needs a certain amount in order to continue functioning. What it requires is negligible; it takes what it needs from the Miquiri ship and they never notice the loss. But it can absorb much more if it chooses—from another ship, from a sun. It doesn't matter what the source is. If it draws from a ship heavily enough, suddenly enough, the engines overload and shut down automatically. You can start them again, but all the Quayla has to do is draw again, and they do another emergency shutdown. Shields are useless. They were designed to deter sudden energy influxes, not rapid depletions.''

Kiley gave Lukas a long look, then went to the intercom. The aliens were watching, but made no attempt to interfere.

''Jon Robert, can you hear me?'' she asked.

''Affirmative, Kiley,'' he answered immediately. His voice was as calm and certain as ever, the only comforting sound she had heard since Lukas had woken up.

''Greg says we can start the main engines,'' she told him. ''Will you try, and let me know what happens?''

''Hold on.''

The intercom was silent a moment, then Jon Robert spoke again. ''The controls are responding, Kiley. Holly is starting the engines now, but it will be several hours before we have full power.''

''I don't think there's any rush. The Miquiri didn't try to stop you, did they?''

''The Miquiri? You mean the aliens? No, they watched what I was doing, but that's all.''

''Let me know if they give you any trouble,'' Kiley told him.

''They won't,'' Lukas said behind her.

She turned around. ''You sound pretty certain about that.''

''I am. Even if they wanted to hurt us, they couldn't. The Quayla wouldn't let them. I told you, Kiley. It controls their ship. It won't let them harm us, not while I'm its companion.''

''The Miquiri knew that and they didn't stop it from joining with you?'' she asked.

''They didn't have a choice,'' Lukas replied, sounding almost sad. He had turned inward again. He was still talking to them, but his thoughts were somewhere else entirely. ''It would have chosen one of the Miquiri, but the few it could reach on even a limited basis died in the same accident as Hinfalla. It never occurred to them it would join with a human. By the time they realized what was happening, it was too late.''

''They had an accident?'' Keenan asked, his eyes going to the two in the corner of the room.

The aliens were watching them intently. Do they understand any of this? Kiley wondered. Is the Quayla telling them what

Lukas is saying, or are they simply watching, hoping to pick up some clue to what the humans are discussing?

Lukas nodded. "They came out of jump into an unstable region in space, or a barrier of some kind. They still don't know exactly what it was; their instruments don't work when they're near it. The Quayla lost control of the ship. Some—no, many—of the crew died." He was speaking faster, his eyes closed, as if he were describing pictures he saw in his mind. "The ship was damaged and the Quayla came close to . . . I don't know what, there aren't words. Insanity, I guess. It could not interpret the data the ship's sensors were collecting. Nothing made sense. It was like transition, only worse. It was a kind of malignant chaos, one that reached out to tear the Quayla apart. Jump momentum carried them out of danger, but the Quayla and the ship were damaged. The Quayla thinks it has recovered, but it can't be certain. It's difficult to evaluate yourself accurately when the only tools you have are your own senses, and they may be damaged.

"The Miquiri can't go home," Lukas went on, his eyes opening suddenly and moving from Keenan to Kiley. "They've been looking for a way around the barrier for months, but they haven't found one. We have to help them," he said, his voice gaining urgency. "Our ships might be able to find a way where they could not. They might even be able to pass through the region undamaged. They are inanimate; the instability might not affect our instruments the way it did the Quayla."

"Is that what that thing is telling you to say? That we have to help them?" Keenan demanded.

"It's not telling me to say anything!" Lukas shot back. "It wouldn't! Ask the Miquiri if you don't trust me."

"That may be a little difficult, seeing as you're the only one who's been able to communicate with them so far," Keenan replied dryly.

"That is a problem," Lukas answered, his mind racing ahead again. "We have to do something about that, too. Maybe we could write a translation program for the main computer. They have a written language. Some of their concepts, though—there aren't equivalent words. Even with the Quayla's help, it may be difficult. But I think I could rig something. I'll get started right away. We have to tell the Miquiri we'll help them find a way around the barrier. We have to make them understand . . ."

"Understand what, Greg?" Kiley prompted when he did not go on immediately.

"That we're no threat to them. The Quayla is afraid the Miquiri will think it has betrayed them because it chose a human for a companion. We have to assure them it hasn't. They depend on it. It has a responsibility toward them. *I* have a responsibility."

"Even before your responsibility to us?" she asked.

Lukas looked confused. "No, of course not. But I'm not asking us to do anything dangerous."

"You honestly believe you're capable of determining that?" Keenan demanded.

"Of course I am."

"With the Quayla's help?"

"On my own."

"Except, according to what you've been telling us, you aren't on your own, are you?" Keenan drove the point home remorselessly. "You said yourself, that thing is inside your mind. It could easily be controlling you."

"No! That's not true!" Lukas's face had gone absolutely white.

"Isn't it?"

"No."

"Greg, it is." Keenan's voice was soft and utterly implacable.

"No! It may be a part of me, but it is not controlling me, not in any way whatsoever."

"You're sure about that?"

"Positive."

"Then how do you explain the fact that it's drained you to the point of collapse again—after less than twenty minutes of consciousness?"

"I'm not—"

But he was. His arms were shaking and he had to brace his hands against the bed to remain upright. His eyes widened momentarily in surprise; then he said, as much to himself as them, "It didn't realize . . . It didn't mean . . . Daniel—"

He broke off because Keenan was moving. Only the psychiatrist was not going to Lukas to support him. He had pulled a pressurized injector out of his pocket and was putting it against Lukas's neck.

"No!" Lukas cried, throwing his arm out. He deflected Keenan's hand, but the psychiatrist was stronger and faster. He had the injector back in place an instant later, only to have one of the aliens grab his arm—the one who had been holding the scanner.

Kiley had started forward, too. She stopped as the other alien emitted a high, piercing cry. The second alien—Chirith, Lukas had called him—was pointing a weapon at Keenan, the same sort of weapon one of the Miquiri had used on him earlier. The psychiatrist took one look at it and froze. Either he had acquired a healthy respect for the weapon's effects, or he thought it might be capable of more deadly results. He offered no resistance when the alien holding his arm took the injector away, and he did not move when it searched his pockets, then the rest of his body in search of other potentially dangerous objects.

Lukas was struggling to rise. The wall behind him throbbed furiously, a dark, reddish-orange color shot through with violent yellows. The colors subsided as Lukas stood and took a shaky breath, but the Quayla continued to pulse quickly, the light so bright that it hurt Kiley's eyes.

"Daniel, why?" Lukas demanded, his voice shaking with emotion. He put his hands on the psychiatrist's shoulders and pulled the other man around to face him when he did not respond.

"Why?" he asked again.

Keenan just looked at him. Kiley had never seen an expression quite like his before. It seemed to be equal parts fear, defiance, shame, and grief. "Your brain waves have changed," he said bluntly. "They don't match your last reading. They don't match anything human. You were showing abnormally intense activity, even while you were sleeping."

"And that made you think I was dangerous? That's why you were so ready to believe the Quayla had taken control of my mind?"

Keenan didn't answer.

Lukas tightened his grip on Keenan's shoulders, as if he wanted to shake sense into him. "Daniel, the Quayla doesn't sleep. I do, but it doesn't. I know you're afraid of it—so was I at first—but it hasn't taken over my mind or body. It is not a parasite and it does not want to hurt us. Not me, not you, not the Miquiri. Not any of us."

"You may believe that. I don't."

"And there's nothing I can say or do to convince you otherwise?"

"No."

Lukas searched Keenan's face, as if seeking the man he had called his friend. If that man was there, he was buried far inside the Corps officer. Keenan faced Lukas as if he were the enemy, and his expression said he would die rather than break.

Lukas released him abruptly and went to the dark brown alien. He signed something, hands and fingers moving awkwardly. The alien hesitated, then looked to Chirith for guidance. Kiley did not catch the gray one's response, but it must have made one, for the alien handed Lukas the pressurized injector it had taken from Keenan.

. Lukas closed his eyes briefly, as if composing himself, then turned back to the psychiatrist. "Daniel, two weeks ago you asked me to trust you—with my mind, maybe even my life. I did. I still do. I *know* the Quayla is not controlling me. I *know* neither it nor the Miquiri are a threat to us, but I can see believing that would be difficult for you. I forgot you have responsibilities, too, and not just to me. I want you to take this." He held out the injector. "If you really believe I'm that dangerous, go ahead and use it. I won't stop you, and neither will the Miquiri."

Keenan stared at him. He stood rigidly, torn between many conflicting emotions, incapable of action. Lukas waited a moment. When the psychiatrist did not move, he put the injector in his hand and closed his fingers over it.

Keenan looked down at the injector, then up at Lukas. Their eyes locked and held for what seemed like an eternity. Then Keenan's hand opened and the injector fell to the floor. Lukas put his hands on Keenan's shoulders and leaned close, saying something to him in a low voice that did not carry. Keenan did not reply. He just stood there, staring straight ahead, a blind man on the edge of a cliff afraid to move for fear of falling.

Lukas tightened his grip on the psychiatrist's shoulders once more, then let go. Bending over, he picked up the injector and brought it to Kiley.

"If you think you need to use this, I want you to," he said, holding it out to her.

His eyes were deep gray, as clear and open as she'd ever seen them. She looked into them and saw only what she had always seen: Greg Lukas. Horrifying as she found the concept of an alien being invading his mind, she could see no sign that he was deranged. True, he was upset, but it was their reaction that worried him, not the Quayla. Her eyes went from his to the injector and back. They wouldn't learn anything more if he were unconscious, but they would lose their only real means of communication with the Miquiri.

"I don't think that's necessary," she said. "Not yet."

"But maybe later?" he asked, his eyes searching hers.

"I don't know." She gave him an honest answer. He deserved that much.

He smiled, his eyes so warm that she felt she was standing under the hot summer sun of Everest. He put out his hand, as if he were about to touch her cheek; then he stopped.

"Kiley, I won't let anything hurt you," he said softly. "Not you, not your family, not the ship. I promise."

She nodded, accepting his intention, though she doubted his ability to keep such a promise. There were too many factors outside his control for her to believe he could guarantee their safety unconditionally.

The alien with the scanner gave a piercing cry, and Kiley clapped her hands to her ears in reflex. Both the aliens were making sounds, and the foul odor was back in the room.

"What's wrong?" she asked Lukas, alarmed.

He was already moving toward the door. "Incoming ship!" he said over his shoulder.

He was gone before Kiley could respond, the aliens close behind him. The light followed them. It flowed down the wall, across the floor, and out in the hall, a glowing pink trail shot through with orange and yellow.

She started after Lukas, then stopped when she realized Keenan wasn't following. "Daniel, are you coming?"

"You didn't notice, did you?" he said, still not moving.

"Notice what?"

"Greg. Five minutes ago, he was on the brink of collapse. I was certain he was going to pass out. And then, all of a sudden, he was normal. No, more than normal, he was . . . revitalized."

She hadn't noticed, but he was right. Lukas had not been pale with exhaustion when he had left the room. He'd looked like a man who'd had eight solid hours of sleep. Her heart skipped a beat. "The Quayla?"

"I don't know what else could account for such a change."

"It could do that? Restore a man as easily as it drained him? Affect him physically, as well as mentally?"

"It affected this ship."

"You're afraid of him, aren't you?" she asked abruptly.

"Aren't you?"

"I don't know. If I think about what's happened to him, I am, but if I just look at him, I can't believe he's any different than he ever was. Daniel, what are we going to do about him?''

"More to the point, what *can* we do?''

Lukas and four of the aliens were already on the bridge when Kiley and Keenan arrived. Three aliens held various instruments, some unidentifiable, some apparently communications equipment. They still issued periodic cries, but the intensity had eased to a more tolerable pitch.

Lukas sat at the control board, intent on the bank of functioning monitors and scanners. Jon Robert had apparently restored sufficient power to give them eyes and ears again. The gray alien stood at the pilot's side, the only Miquiri not actively engaged in talking or working some device. It divided its attention between Lukas and one of the visual monitors.

There was a second ship on the monitor, not far from the first one. It, too, was drifting.

"Daniel, she's Horizon class," Lukas said, without looking around. "She has defenses, but she's not a battleship."

How had he known they were there? Their feet hadn't made that much noise, and the cries of the Miquiri should have drowned out the sound of their arrival. Kiley glanced warily at the light that pooled on the control board beneath Lukas's hands and spilled over the edge to form another pool on the floor, where his feet rested. Could it see—or did it have other, equally powerful, senses?

Keenan went to the monitor and studied the image. The incoming ship was half the size of the Delta-class cruiser. She was bright silver, her hull made entirely of sensor plates. She had no external structures, but that didn't mean she wasn't armed. All Admiralty ships carried sufficient firepower to render the *Widdon Galaxy* a memory in milliseconds. All of them.

"You're right," Keenan said. Hope flooded his face. Kiley had known he was upset about Lukas, the Quayla, and the Miquiri, but she hadn't realized how great his tension was until it abruptly eased.

"Greg, Horizon-class ships are only used on courier missions, or as escort ships," he said. "They generally operate directly out of Everest. Admiral Quiller was supposed to send a ship to meet us at Cardos. I think she's the one. If Omanu received our message, he might well have commandeered her to follow us. Have you tried to contact her?"

"No. I've been trying to convince Chirith this isn't a trap.

He's very upset, Daniel. The Quayla disabled her, but it can't absorb energy at this rate indefinitely, and it can't handle both ships if they power up simultaneously.''

"Nice to know it has some limitations,'' Keenan muttered under his breath. "Greg, we have to signal her. If she is from the Admiralty, we may be worrying unnecessarily. Will you ask the Quayla to let her restore power long enough to let her receive a message from us and send a reply?''

"Daniel, it may not be messages she'll send. If she came because Sorseli told her we entered the restricted zone, if she had time to see the alien ship, she may fire on us. The Quayla can shield the *Nieti*, but it can't protect the *Widdon Galaxy*, too.''

"Well, we can't just sit here watching them forever. You said yourself, the cruiser can't operate on emergency power much longer. We have to make a decision. I don't think that ship is from Zerron Base. I think she's from the Admiralty, and if she is, she won't fire on us without cause.''

"We're in a restricted zone. That's all the cause she needs.''

"So is she. That means she had orders to come. She wouldn't have entered Belurian space without them.''

"The orders could have come from Sorseli,'' Lukas said stubbornly.

"You don't really believe that ship is under his command, do you? Greg, were there any Horizon-class ships stationed at Zerron Base when you were there? Well, were there?''

"No.''

"Greg, she's from the Admiralty. She has to be!''

"I don't know,'' Lukas said, his voice trailing off. He looked from Keenan to the ship, then to Chirith. The alien gestured and he replied. Neither one of them appeared happy. Lukas had to repeat his gestures several times; either he was mangling them badly, or the alien needed persuading. Chirith made a final signal, a sharp cutting motion of his right arm, then folded his hands against his body and turned away from Lukas.

"What did he say, Greg?'' Kiley asked, giving the alien a sympathetic look. However bad things were for them, they couldn't be much easier for him. His ship was surrounded by three alien vessels, and the Quayla had joined with a human. He must be as worried and frightened as they were.

"He said he wished he'd listened to his instincts and never stopped us in the first place,'' Lukas replied. "He said I might as well do whatever I wished—that I would anyway and he couldn't stop me."

"Is that true?"

"What? That he couldn't stop me? Not really. They could stun me with one of their weapons if they wanted to, but they'd upset the Quayla if they did. They'd have to believe I was clearly jeopardizing their safety before they'd attack me, and I won't do that. I won't knowingly create any situation in which the Quayla would be forced to choose sides. Unless one side was clearly wrong, it would find choosing impossible. It would cease to function rather than be forced into a decision."

"You mean die?" Kiley asked. "You said it's alive, does that mean it can die too?"

"Not the way we mean death. But it could dissipate itself. That would be the same as death to it."

"What would happen to you if it did?" Keenan asked.

Lukas looked at Keenan uneasily, uncertain where his question was leading. He could have equivocated, but he chose honesty instead. "Daniel, I am linked to it," he said with quiet dignity. "Like it or not, the link is for life. My body might survive a separation, but I do not believe my mind would."

Keenan turned back to the monitor. "I still think we should contact that ship," he said. "I know we're taking a chance, but the only other choice is to leave them disabled and hope we can jump before they restore power. That might resolve our problems, but it won't help the Miquiri and it won't help you, either. You can't be separated from the Quayla. That means we'd either have to leave you behind, or it would have to come with us. Either way, someone will be hurt. Is that a fair assessment of the situation?"

"There is one alternative," Lukas said reluctantly.

"What?"

"The Quayla could separate itself. Part could come with me, and part could remain behind. That would not be desirable, but it would do that if it had to, to protect both the Miquiri and me."

"The Quayla can spread itself to other ships?" Kiley asked sharply.

"Yes."

"Easily?"

"It has no physical body. It is free to go where it will, so long as there is a vessel to contain it."

"A vessel? You mean a ship?" Keenan asked.

"That would be its first choice, but any physical object would do."

"Including a human body?"

"Possibly, but only in an emergency, and then not for long. It is not comfortable attached to biological forms. It prefers inanimate objects."

Kiley looked at the light. "It's already spread itself to this ship, hasn't it?" she asked.

Lukas shook his head forcefully. "No! It's here, but it hasn't attached itself yet."

"Attached itself?"

"Made itself part of the ship. It is onboard, but it is not inside. It hasn't spread itself through the ship: the bulkheads, the engines, the computers."

"But it could?" she asked sharply, sharing Keenan's earlier alarm.

"Yes, but it wouldn't, not without permission."

"Do you want to give it permission?"

He blinked. "That's not for me to do. This is your ship, Kiley, not mine."

"But if you and the Quayla stayed on the *Widdon Galaxy*, it would have to attach itself, wouldn't it?"

"Sooner or later, yes."

"What if we didn't want it? Would you have to go with the Miquiri, then?"

"I suppose so."

"Could you survive on their ship?"

"We seem to be able to breathe the same air, so that shouldn't be a problem."

"What about their food and water—could you survive on it?"

"I don't know."

"Does the Quayla?"

He blinked. Left them for a moment. Came back. "I . . . I think I could."

"For how long?"

"I don't know. A while."

"How long is a while? A few weeks? Months? Years?"

"I don't know. A few months at least. Maybe a few years."

"And then you'd die?"

"We all die, sooner or later."

"Only with you, it would be sooner, wouldn't it?"

He didn't reply, and Kiley sighed. She had been hoping for an easy answer, but there wasn't going to be one. No matter what they did, someone faced a very real danger of being harmed, Miquiri or human.

She turned to Keenan. "Daniel, do you really think that ship is from the Admiralty?"

"Yes."

Kiley studied the ship. Even disabled, she looked dangerous. They would be taking a tremendous chance, letting her restore power. It was not an easy risk to justify, not with all their lives at stake. But the alternative—the alternative was equally unthinkable.

"Greg, I think we should try to contact her, too. Will you tell the Quayla to let her start her engines?"

Lukas hesitated, then nodded. "I need to tell Chirith first, though—to warn him . . ."

"Go ahead. They're at risk too. If there's anything they can do to protect themselves, they should, by all means."

The talk did not take long. Chirith watched Lukas's hands move; then he gave a series of short cries. All but he and one other alien started to leave the bridge.

"Kiley, something's going on," Reese said over the intercom, sounding alarmed. "One minute the aliens were looking at the plants, and the next they were running out the door."

"Another Corps ship has arrived, Reese. Daniel thinks she may be from the Admiralty, but we're not sure. We're going to let her restore power so we can signal her, but if we're wrong about her intentions, she may open fire on us. The Miquiri want to get as many of their people back on their ship as they can, in case things go wrong."

"What about us?" Jon Robert asked from the engine room before Reese could say the same thing. "Do you want me to raise our shields? We have enough power now."

"I don't think you need to bother. They won't do much good at this range."

"Kiley, are you sure—"

"No, I'm not sure. I'm not sure about anything at all."

She had worried she was making the biggest mistake of her life when they hired Lukas on Demarker, but the consequences of that decision did not begin to compare with the ones they faced if she made the wrong choice now. She started to tell Lukas she'd changed her mind, but she was too late.

"The Quayla's letting her restore power," Lukas said before she could speak. "We won't be able to contact her for a while, though. Her captain will restore shields and sensors before communications."

Kiley went to the pilot's seat. If they got out of this alive, she was going to reevaluate her career options. There'd been times lately when she wasn't sure she was cut out to be a ship's captain after all. She was reaching for her headset when a strong, female voice sounded over the intercom.

"This is Captain Ellison, of the Starship *Harlinger*. Are you receiving us?"

"They restored communications first," Lukas said, wonderingly. "They haven't even raised their shields yet."

Kiley scrambled to put on her headset. "This is Captain Michaelson, of the freighter *Widdon Galaxy*," she said. "We're receiving you, *Harlinger*."

"Are you people all right?"

Chapter 24

"We're fine," Kiley replied.

"You appear to have company," Captain Ellison said.

"Affirmative."

"You're talking to us; does that mean they're friendly?"

Kiley glanced at Keenan and Lukas, then at Chirith. The alien had turned away from them, but he watched them out of the corners of his eyes. He no longer had his hands tucked under his arms; they hung at his sides.

"So far," she said.

"Are they wearing protective suits?"

"Negative."

There was a pause on the other end.

"You're sure you and your crew are well?" Ellison asked. "No sign of illness or other adverse effects?"

"No. The aliens were suited when they first boarded. They swept the ship with what appeared to be scanners, then quit wearing their suits. They don't appear to believe there's any concern for biological contamination in either direction."

Another pause. "Captain, we followed you here to offer protection against the *Railion*. We obviously weren't expecting to find aliens. Naturally, we'd like to speak with them, but before we do, we'll need to send over an inspection team to check you and your ship out. We don't want to risk any lives, either—ours or theirs. Will the aliens permit that?"

Kiley turned to Lukas, who looked in turn to the light. It had sent a long streamer out toward Chirith. The streamer was forming symbols on the deck of the bridge.

"The Quayla is asking him," Lukas told her. "It can write faster than I can signal."

"Those are words it's forming?"

"Yes."

The light stopped moving and pooled near Lukas's feet, pulsing slowly, a deep pink marbled with soft oranges and yellows. Chirith looked at the monitors, at his own ship, at the *Harlinger*, and then made a single sign to Lukas.

"He says yes," Lukas told Kiley. His eyes were worried, not about the alien, but for him.

"Captain Ellison, you can send your party over," Kiley said. "The Miquiri ship is docked at our main hatch, but you can—"

"We'll board through a cargo hold."

"—board through the number three cargo door," Kiley finished deliberately. She wasn't sure she liked the officer's brisk assumption of authority. Ellison might be captain of the *Harlinger*, but that didn't mean she could take command of the *Widdon Galaxy*, too. This was *her* ship, not Ellison's.

"*Harlinger*, please be advised we have multiple alien lifeforms onboard," she said. "One of them may be capable of spreading itself to your ship via the shuttle." There, that ought to slow Ellison down a step or two, as well as satisfy her conscience and Keenan's.

The pause this time was significant.

"Captain Michaelson, is this life-form a physical entity?"

Kiley wondered who had prompted her to ask that question. The *Harlinger*'s science or medical officer? Her security chief?

"It's hard to say," Kiley replied. "We can see it, but it might be capable of reducing itself to a level that would be undetectable."

"Reducing itself?" Ellison came back immediately. No one had to prompt her to ask that question.

Kiley decided she'd given Ellison enough to think about; there was no sense magnifying the danger the Quayla—and Lukas—posed. She had warned them; that was all she was obligated to do. "The Quayla looks like a pool of opaque light, Captain. It does not have a body. As nearly as we can tell, it exists as an energy state. It can apparently move between any vessels that are physically linked. It may also be capable of dividing itself. Captain, it is communicating with one of my crew. It has established some sort of mental link with him."

Kiley looked at Lukas as she spoke. His eyes were fixed on a point straight ahead, his shoulders rigid with tension.

"You have a crewman in contact with the alien?" Ellison came back sharply.

"Yes."

"Captain, is he a danger?"

"We don't believe so, *Harlinger*," Kiley said.

Lukas's eyes closed and his shoulders slumped as the tension left them.

"Is he *in* danger?"

"As far as we can determine, no."

"Very well, we're assembling a boarding team now. Be advised, they'll be wearing protective suits and will have orders to go over your ship from top to bottom. Will you let the aliens know they're coming?"

"Affirmative."

"The party will leave in fifteen minutes. You said they could use your number three hold to board?"

"Affirmative. It's empty."

"The team will rig a temporary access tube. They'll seal off the cargo doors and let you know when it's safe to open them."

Unlike the aliens' cursory inspection, the boarding party's took hours. Four hours and twenty-three minutes, to be precise.

They started with the holds, then made their way to the main deck, making frequent reports to the *Harlinger*. Kiley put the exchange on over the intercom, eavesdropping shamelessly. The reports sounded fairly routine to her, and Keenan heard nothing in the instrument readings they relayed to give cause for concern, but that might not mean anything. The boarding party could have preset codes that would sound innocuous to outsiders, but were in fact warnings.

The anonymous, white-suited figures went everywhere: the engine room, the galley and dining room, their cabins. In addition to a visual search, Kiley saw at least six different types of scanners being used. If there was anything out of the norm on the ship, physically, electronically, magnetically, or biologically, the team clearly intended to find it.

They searched the bridge last. They strode into the room, then stopped dead as they caught sight of Chirith, the second Miquiri, and the Quayla.

If they were excited about being among the first humans to meet aliens, however, their voices gave no indication as they reported what they were seeing to the *Harlinger*. They were calm, factual, and meticulous, calling off every reading on their instruments. The Quayla drew one startled, "What the—?" but that was the only sign they were looking at anything remotely out of the ordinary.

"Will you ask them if they mind us scanning them?" the leader of the inspection party asked Kiley, nodding to the Miquiri.

She turned to Lukas and he signaled Chirith. The alien made no objection. He stood still as the team moved their various scanners around him, watching them warily. But there was curiosity in his eyes, too. At least, that's what Kiley thought she saw—it was difficult to know for certain. What appeared as curiosity in a human's gaze might just as well represent rage in the Miquiri's, she kept warning herself. But his looks so closely resembled a human's, and the shock of recognition she felt whenever their eyes met and connected was so intense, that she did not think she was completely mistaken.

The inspection team had no compunction about asking the humans to submit to tests. They went over each of them with scanners, then took blood samples, skin scrapings, throat swabs, and urine specimens. Except for allowing them privacy to produce the urine samples, they did not attempt to separate them from each other, and Kiley was thankful for that. It was bad enough to be surrounded by people who looked at you as if you were contaminated, without being denied the comfort of others in similar straits.

If they made *her* feel like a monster, she could imagine how their treatment was affecting Lukas. They had no difficulty telling that he was the one in contact with the alien life-form, not with the Quayla glowing on the control board behind him and the floor at his feet. If he had been a twentieth-century reactor on the brink of meltdown, they could not have treated him more gingerly.

When they had finished examining the humans, the leader of the team turned to Kiley. "We'd like a blood sample from one of the aliens. Would that one agree to give one?" he asked, nodding to Chirith.

"We'll ask," Kiley said, glancing at the alien, "but it might be better if they decided who should give the sample and let their own medical people draw it."

The team leader looked to one of the others, who nodded. "That would be acceptable," he said.

"Will you ask Chirith if they could have a sample?" Kiley asked Lukas.

He consulted briefly with the alien, then nodded. "One of their medical crewmen will come over shortly."

A reddish brown alien arrived three minutes later, a heavy bag slung over one shoulder. The suited figures moved aside to let it on the bridge. It went to the second alien, reached inside the bag, and pulled out several cylindrical objects, rounded at the base and narrow at the tip. They appeared to be made of a translucent glass or plastic material. It pressed the cylinder against the alien's wrist and the tube darkened as it filled with fluid.

The alien held out the cylinder and a member of the inspection team came forward, moving with exaggerated slowness. Chirith gestured to Lukas.

"He wants to know if you'd like another sample for comparison," Lukas translated.

"That would be very helpful," the team leader replied.

Kiley expected Chirith to tell the medic to take a sample of its own blood, but the alien went to him instead and pulled another cylinder out of its bag.

"Greg, he doesn't have to—"

"He knows that. He says it's only fair. They examined one of us. We have an equal right to examine them to be certain they are no threat."

"Greg, that was *you* they examined," she replied, startled by his casual dismissal of that experience. A day before, he had been virtually unable to speak about his time on the Miquiri ship, and now he was brushing it off as a matter of no consequence? Maybe Keenan was right to be worried about him.

Her words startled the pilot. He looked momentarily confused, and his breathing quickened. His eyes opened wide and his face twisted. The light at his feet changed color, yellows shifting to orange, throbbing rapidly.

"Greg, are you all right?" Keenan asked. Forgetting his earlier fears and reservations, he caught Lukas by the shoulders, his hands tightening until the pilot registered his presence.

"I'm okay," Lukas said, his expression clearing.

"Greg, before Kiley asked her question, you were seeing the Quayla's memories of that examination, weren't you?" Keenan demanded.

He hesitated, then said, "Yes."

"And just now, you saw your own?"

A nod.

"The Quayla looked upset. Didn't it realize how you felt about those tests until now?"

"Not consciously. It has access to all my memories, and I to its, but we haven't had time to explore all of them yet."

"Whose take precedence?"

"Neither of them. I know you're going to argue that the Quayla's did, but that was only because I was concentrating on it so hard, trying to understand what Chirith was saying. The Quayla is not controlling my mind or my memories, no matter what you keep suggesting to the contrary."

"But it has influenced you."

"No more than I've influenced it. Daniel, I wish you could talk to Chirith about me. He could reassure you. Hinfalla, the Quayla's last companion, was his closest friend. He did not lose that friendship after Hinfalla joined with the Quayla. It's true his friend was different, but he was the same, too."

Lukas smiled suddenly, his face so open, so joyous, it took Kiley's breath away. "I know that doesn't make much sense," he said, "but it will. You'll see. There is always a period of adjustment—for the Quayla as well as its companion. I may change, but I will not change that much. The Quayla says you only notice the differences because you are watching me so closely. Soon, you won't see any differences in me at all."

"Because there aren't any, or because we've become accustomed to them?"

"Daniel, we all change, even you. You were quick to tell me that's both necessary and inevitable a few weeks ago. Repeatedly. I seem to recall you saying change is a prerequisite of growth."

"Not all change is growth."

"Well, I guess we'll just have to wait and see if this one is, won't we?"

Keenan didn't reply, and the team leader shifted uneasily, as if sensing undercurrents he did not understand and instinctively mistrusted.

"We've finished our inspection, Captain," he said. "We'll need a good eight to ten hours to evaluate the data and samples we've collected. Assuming they check out satisfactorily, the *Harlinger* would like to send over representatives to meet with the aliens. Will you ask them if they'd agree to that?'' he asked Lukas.

Lukas gestured to Chirith, received a response, then turned back to the team leader. ''He said to return when you are ready. They will talk to you.''

The family should have slept after that, but none of them managed more than a few hours of rest. There had been too much to talk over, too much adjusting to do.

Ellison's official greeting party arrived some twelve hours later, a group of six. Kiley, Keenan, and Lukas met them at the elevator leading to the cargo deck. Jon Robert, Holly, Lia, and Reese watched their arrival from farther down the corridor.

Keenan's face lit up at the sight of one of the men. ''Hal!'' he cried, making no effort to hide his pleasure or relief.

''Daniel.'' Omanu gripped the psychiatrist's elbow and shook his hand. He was shorter than Keenan, with black hair, a round face, and black eyes as bright as Chirith's.

He examined the psychiatrist closely, as if searching for bends, cracks, or other signs of damage. ''Not bad, considering,'' he said lightly. Then his attention moved on Kiley. ''Captain Michaelson, I presume?''

She nodded.

''Allow me to introduce Commander Ibo, the *Harlinger*'s first officer,'' he said. ''This is Dr. Guinn, her chief medical officer, and Lt. Farthing, one of the ship's navigators. The *Harlinger* doesn't have a regular science officer, but Farthing has an undergraduate degree in interdisciplinary sciences, so Ellison asked him to come along. The other two gentlemen are security officers. Captain Ellison insisted they accompany us, but they'll do their best to remain unobtrusive.''

Ibo was very tall and thin, with dark skin and hair. Guinn was about Kiley's height, though twenty years her senior. Gray streaked her hair, and wrinkles creased the corners of her eyes. She nodded to each of them, her eyes keen, her smile assured. Farthing was the youngest. He could not have been out of the Academy more than a few years, and he clearly felt ill-at-ease in the other officers' presence.

Kiley introduced her family, and Omanu said, ''I believe Commander Ibo is anxious to get on with the business at hand. Are the Miquiri here?''

"They're in the common room," Kiley said. "We thought that would be the best place. It's the largest room on the ship."

Ibo glanced at the door, then turned to Lukas. "Our inspection team said you understood their language, is that correct?"

Lukas nodded.

"With any fluency?"

"I can translate almost everything, but it takes time. I still have to rely on the Quayla to tell me what they're saying."

"That should be sufficient for a first meeting. Very well, Lukas. Let's go meet our visitors, shall we?"

With Lukas leading the way, the *Harlinger*'s crew disappeared into the common room. Chirith was there, along with three other Miquiri Lukas said were ship's officers and scientists. He had worried about the meeting, afraid each side would reject the other. Kiley was glad Ibo let him accompany them; if anyone had an interest in furthering relations between the two groups, it was he.

The door closed behind them, leaving the Michaelsons, Keenan, and Omanu standing in the hall.

"Do you have another room large enough to hold us all?" Omanu asked.

"The dining room," Kiley said.

"Why don't we adjourn there? I'd like to hear what happened to you after you left Siddorn. I believe I have some news that will be of interest to all of you, as well."

They gathered around the table, Kiley at one end and Omanu at the other. Jon Robert and Holly sat to Kiley's right, Reese, Lia, and Keenan to her left.

"I assume you know about Lukas's trip to Gynos, his court-martial, and the therapy he received afterward?" Omanu asked when they were all sitting down. They all nodded as Omanu's eyes went around the table, searching each face.

"What you may not realize is how close he came to a complete breakdown," Omanu went on. "Daniel recorded his sessions with Lukas, in case they were needed as evidence in a trial against Renard. He gave the recordings to me when you docked at Cardos. Parts of them were very difficult to watch, even secondhand. Admiral Quiller and I had debated assigning Daniel to Lukas's case. We were concerned that he might have difficulty maintaining his objectivity while dealing with a friend. I'm glad we didn't reconsider. I don't think anyone else could have brought Lukas through intact. You did a good job, Daniel,"

Omanu said as he turned to him. "Admiral Quiller sends his personal thanks, and he's adding a written commendation to your file."

"That isn't necessary," Keenan said stiffly.

"You don't receive commendations because they're necessary," Omanu returned dryly. "You receive them because you earn them."

Keenan's head came up. His eyes were a bright, fierce blue. "I nearly got everyone on this ship killed," he said heatedly. "If I'd listened to you on Cardos, none of this would have happened. The *Railion*'s ambush, the Miquiri's interception of the *Widdon Galaxy*, Greg joining with the Quayla—it was my fault, all of it."

"If you're going to take the blame, you'll also have to take the credit." Omanu's voice was mild, and he was not the least deterred by the psychiatrist's outburst. "And there will be credit, Daniel. Quite a bit, I should think, once the Admiralty's had time to evaluate what's happened here. What's more, you deserve it, all of you." His eyes went around the table again, warmly approving. "I imagine you must have been frightened when the Miquiri ship stopped you."

"The worse part was not knowing what was happening," Jon Robert said. "One minute we were entering transition and the next we were dead in space. We didn't know what happened until we got one of the monitors working and Kiley took a look outside."

"Did they attempt to signal you?"

"No. They scanned us, though. At least, we think the light was some kind of scan," he said.

"The light? You mean the Quayla?"

"No, this light was different. It was deep blue."

"Tell me about it. Did it move around? Did it touch you? Was there any sensation to it?"

Omanu questioned them for nearly an hour. It didn't take Kiley long to realize he was conducting a debriefing. He wasn't taking notes, which meant he was either carrying a recorder, or a transmitter was relaying their conversation back to the *Harlinger*. On the whole, she suspected the transmitter. She glanced at Keenan, who had remained silent except for that one exchange with Omanu. His eyes met hers, then moved on, but that brief exchange told her all she needed to know. He knew what Omanu was doing, too.

Of course he does, she told herself. He must have conducted similar sessions himself in the past. That was his job. He didn't look happy about being on the other side of the process, though.

Omanu asked her a few direct questions, and she replied, but her answers were short and guarded, particularly when the conversation turned to Lukas and the Quayla. Omanu must have noticed her reticence, but he did not press her. She didn't like that. If he wasn't insisting on detailed responses, this was likely only the first of several sessions—and she doubted all of them would be so genial.

She didn't relax until Omanu finally changed topics, saying he had news for them, too, beginning with Admiral James Sorseli's arrest.

"I sent your tapes on to Admiral Quiller as soon as I finished watching them," he said to Keenan. "He decided they contained sufficient evidence to act. The *Harlinger* was already on the way to Cardos to meet us, and he had Captain Ellison intercept my ship and take me directly to Zerron Base with orders to arrest the admiral. A prosecution team is on its way to the base now to lay the groundwork for a court-martial.

"Unfortunately, Sorseli gave Tichner permission to follow you before we arrived. We spent several hours convincing him it was in his best interests to tell us which way you and the *Railion* had gone. He finally did, and we followed as quickly as we could.

"The *Harlinger* is a fast ship, and Ellison pushed her as hard as she could go, but we were worried we'd arrive too late. From the look of things, we would have if the Miquiri hadn't intervened."

"We'd have lost the *Railion* if the Miquiri hadn't kept us from jumping," Kiley said. "They boarded us several hours before she arrived."

"The Miquiri disabled her the same way they disabled the *Harlinger*?" Omanu asked.

"The Quayla did."

"Do you know how?"

"Greg says it can absorb power. If it does so suddenly, a ship's engines overload and the computers initiate an automatic shutdown."

"That's all that's keeping the *Railion* on emergency power now? The Quayla?"

"Yes. We were trying to decide what to do about her when the *Harlinger* arrived."

"Captain Ellison has already sent a team over to take command of the ship. Captain Tichner has been relieved of his duties, pending an investigation of his role in the affair. We'd like to send the *Railion* back to Zerron Base with a message for the Admiralty, reporting contact with the Miquiri. That will be the fastest way to get word to them. They'll want to send an official contact team out. The *Harlinger* is only an escort ship. She doesn't have the specialists the Admiralty will want on hand, particularly the linguists."

"We do have Lukas," Keenan said.

"Yes, we do," Omanu returned neutrally.

So, the verdict was still out on him. Kiley wasn't surprised. The *Harlinger* might be willing to use him as an interpreter, but they weren't going to trust him, or the Quayla either.

"What about us? How soon can we leave?" Lia asked.

"I'm afraid you'll have to stay indefinitely," Omanu said sympathetically. "Under guidelines laid out for a first contact, you must remain at the scene until the Admiralty's medical and science teams give you clearance to leave."

"How long will that take?" Reese asked.

"The *Railion* will need four days to return to base, and it will be at least a week before whatever ship the Admiralty sends out can reach us. You'd better plan to be here at least a month."

"A month!" Jon Robert exploded. "We can't sit idle that long! We have a living to make."

"I know. The Corps is not unsympathetic to your problems, Mr. Michaelson, but orders are orders. No one who's been near the Miquiri is going anywhere until they've been cleared. As for your loss of income, I believe the Admiralty may be willing to consider some sort of compensation, particularly since we'd like to use your ship as a meeting point. Captain Ellison wants all discussions held here to minimize her crew's contact with the Miquiri—with your permission, of course," he added to Kiley.

"Do I have a choice?"

"Honestly? No," Omanu said. "But the Corps prefers to observe the niceties and ask, wherever possible."

"Very well. Captain Ellison has my permission to use this ship as a meeting point."

"That's very accommodating of you, Captain," Omanu replied with a mocking smile. "I'll be certain to mention your cooperation in my report." He stood. "I believe I've kept all of you long enough. I'll have more questions tomorrow, but for now, I suggest you all get a good night's sleep."

They rose and started moving toward the door.

"Daniel, would you mind staying a few minutes?" Omanu asked. "I'd like to talk to you. Alone," he added when Kiley pulled up, too.

She looked at Keenan, seeking confirmation that he wanted her to leave. He nodded. "Go on," he said.

"Very well," she said, and went out, leaving the two men alone.

Chapter 25

The dining room door closed, cutting off Kiley's view of Keenan. She didn't envy the psychiatrist his meeting with Omanu. He had not pressured the family when they evaded a topic or gave less than a complete reply, but she doubted he'd let Keenan off so easily.

"He asks a lot of questions, doesn't he?" Holly said to Kiley. "I thought he'd want to know about the Miquiri, but he seemed more interested in Greg."

"Yes."

"Kiley, what's going to happen to him?" she asked. "Jon Robert and I talked about him after we left you last night. We're worried about him—not because of the Quayla, but because of the Corps. Greg won't hurt anyone—I know he won't—but the Corps doesn't seem to believe that."

"It's their job to worry, Holly," Kiley said. "If the Miquiri or the Quayla are a threat, they need to assess the danger and isolate the risk as best they can."

"But what's going to happen to Greg?" asked Holly. "He says he has to go with the Miquiri, that he can't leave their ship until they find another companion, but if he does, he's going to be stranded out there. I can't see the Corps bringing him back on one of their ships, not when it means letting the Quayla onboard, too. What's going to happen to him?"

"I don't know," she said. She'd spent most of the previous night worrying about that very matter.

"We could go after him," Jon Robert said.

"What?" Lia and Reese questioned in simultaneous disbelief.

"We could follow the Miquiri home and bring him back."

"What about the Quayla?" Lia demanded. "He himself said

he can't be separated from it, even if they do find another companion for the *Nieti*. You aren't seriously thinking of letting it on the *Widdon Galaxy*, are you?''

"Why not?" Holly said. "It hasn't hurt the Miquiri. If they aren't afraid of it, why should we be?''

"How about because we don't know what it would do to us or the ship, for starters," Reese said. "And if that's not enough, there's always the Corps. You said yourself, they don't want to risk letting the Quayla spread. They'd never let us back into human space if we had it onboard.''

"Maybe not all the way," Jon Robert said, "but they might let us go as far as one port. Just because they're worried about it doesn't mean they aren't curious, too. If we let it on the ship, they might be willing to give us permission to dock at one port, under supervision, just to see what happens. They'd want guarantees the Quayla wouldn't spread itself to the station or another ship, but Greg says he can give us that. Besides, even if it wanted to transfer itself, it couldn't unless it found a receptive person on the other vessel who could become its companion. Not many Miquiri can do that; the same may be true for humans.''

"Assuming the Corps would give us permission to visit one port, how are we going to earn a living?" Kiley demanded. "We can't haul goods between there and nowhere.''

Her brother sighed. "Sometimes I think it's no wonder we don't make a profit. You and Reese must be the densest freighter captain and shipping agent in the business. Here we are, the first people to meet another intelligent species, and neither of you even considers the possibility of trading with them.''

"Trade? With the Miquiri?" Reese asked, startled. "What would we trade?''

"Lia's plants, for starters. They're fascinated with them. After that? Anything we could get our hands on. At first, it probably wouldn't matter what we offered. The fact that the goods came from aliens would make them valuable in and of themselves. What's more, even if civilian traders weren't interested in any cargo we might bring back, I'll bet the Corps would be.''

"Oh, they'd be interested," Kiley said. "They'd slap it into quarantine so fast, we wouldn't know what had happened.''

"Naturally, there'd be restrictions on some goods—live plants or animals, certain forms of technology—but there'd be plenty of other items we could exchange. Reese, you must be able to see the possibilities, even if Kiley can't! Any halfway competent trader stands to make a fortune—*and we're the first on the scene*! What's more, we'd have Greg and the Quayla. They can talk to the Miquiri, Reese. No one else will be able to."

"They will be once translation programs are commonly available," Reese said, "and you can bet that won't take long." He wasn't really objecting, though. He was seeing opportunities, too, his mind racing ahead, thinking, planning.

"Even the best translator isn't always accurate," Holly countered, "and they miss almost all the nuances of speech. The Quayla wouldn't, though. It knows the Miquiri. Jon Robert's right—with Greg and the Quayla, we'd have advantages no one else would."

"Don't you think you're getting a little ahead of yourselves?" Kiley asked sharply. "We don't know for sure the Quayla is harmless. We don't know what it would do if it attached itself to this ship, and we don't know what it might do to Greg in the long run. Just because he seems sane and healthy now doesn't mean he'll stay that way. And even if you discount those problems, who's to say he'll want to stay with us? Or that he'll have a choice? The Corps might conscript him to act as a translator. He may not be free to make his own choices. And then there's the Quayla itself—it appears to have a mind of its own. What if it doesn't want to stay on the *Widdon Galaxy*? Have you considered any of that?"

Jon Robert hadn't, but he rallied quickly. "I don't know where else it will be able to go. Greg can't live on one of their ships indefinitely, and where he goes, the Quayla will have to go too— or at least a part of it. Much as the Corps might need interpreters, I sincerely doubt they'll be willing to use Greg if it means letting the Quayla set up residence on one of their ships."

"And you are? You're willing to let it attach itself to the *Widdon Galaxy*?"

"I might be," Jon Robert said stubbornly. "I agree, we'd want to know more about it first, but I might be."

Kiley looked from Jon Robert to Holly, to Reese, and finally to Lia. They were all considering the idea. Even her sister hadn't given a firm no.

"I don't think you've even begun to consider the ramifications of this plan," she said heatedly to Jon Robert.

"I agree, we have a lot of talking and thinking to do," he replied. "But if Omanu is right about how long we'll be here, we'll have plenty of time to decide. Why don't we all give the idea consideration and discuss it again in a few days? Agreed?"

"Agreed," Reese said immediately. Holly and Lia nodded.

"What about you, Kiley?" Jon Robert asked. "I know you feel you have a duty to raise objections, but you can't possibly want to leave Greg behind. We may like him, but you're the one who loves him."

"I never said—"

"Don't bother denying it. We all know you do. And unless Holly heard wrong on the bridge, he loves you too. Do you really think we'd desert him, knowing how you feel about him?"

"My feelings are irrelevant compared to the safety of the *Widdon Galaxy*."

"But if the ship isn't in danger, if we're willing to give this a try, you wouldn't object, would you?"

They were watching her, all of them. She could not deny she cared about Lukas; she could not deny she wanted him to stay on the ship. She had raised the problems, had given them more than sufficient grounds to reconsider. They were all responsible adults. If they were still interested in proceeding, knowing the risks they faced, did she still have an obligation to deter them, to ignore her own wishes and desires?

"No," she said abruptly.

"Good. Let's think things over and meet again in a few days," Jon Robert said. "For now, I suggest we adjourn to the galley and fix some dinner. I'm hungry, even if none of you are."

Keenan joined them just as they were filling their plates, and Lukas came in a few minutes later, the Quayla trailing along behind him.

"How did the meeting go?" Kiley asked.

"All right, I guess," Lukas said. "Everyone was talking at once, and I couldn't keep up with the translations, but that didn't seem to bother anyone. The Miquiri have gone back to their ship for the night; Ibo said his party is leaving, too. They set up another meeting for tomorrow afternoon."

"We were just about to eat," Keenan said. "What do you want?"

"Nothing," he said, making a face at the food on the psychiatrist's plate. "All I really wanted was to go to my cabin and sleep, but Omanu stopped me and said I had to have dinner first."

"He was right," Keenan replied firmly. He put his plate down on the counter. "What do you want? I'll fix it for you."

"I don't care. Anything."

"He can have my plate," Kiley said. "I haven't touched it

yet. I'll fix another one.'' She held her dish out to Lukas. They'd opened a little of everything, and the dish held a reconstituted casserole made up of cheese, potatoes, and a vegetable protein with a smoky taste the package described as ''ham.'' Alongside that were slices of ripe tomatoes and yellow melon that had come from Lia's garden.

Lukas clearly didn't think the meal looked as good as she judged it, but he took the plate anyway and went into the dining room. He sat down, picked up his fork with a long-suffering sigh, and started shoveling the casserole in.

He chewed the first bite and a look of utter astonishment spread across his face. He swallowed, then speared a piece of melon and tasted it. His eyes opened wide.

''It's different,'' he said, amazed.

''What's different, Greg?'' Keenan demanded.

''The melon is different from the casserole. I didn't—'' He broke off, correcting himself. ''No—the Quayla didn't realize food could have so many different textures and flavors. It was so surprised, I forgot myself for a minute.'' He was either too preoccupied to consider Keenan's probable reaction to that admission, or for some reason was completely unconcerned about it.

''Either the Miquiri's diet is very bland, or they can't taste things the way we do,'' he went on. ''It didn't realize food was so—so good.'' He speared another piece of melon, chewed it slowly, then laughed. ''It's like tasting everything for the first time,'' he said. ''This is going to be fun! It will take days, maybe even weeks, to work my way through everything in the ship's stores. I can't wait!''

''It's nice to know someone's looking forward to the time ahead,'' Keenan said dryly.

Lukas wasn't listening. He was lost in a world of sensation and didn't surface until he'd eaten the last scrap of food on his plate.

The *Railion* left at 0500 the next morning, before any of them were up. Omanu and the security guards returned to the *Widdon Galaxy* at 0800. He told Lukas he and Keenan needed to run several psychological and physical tests on him. Lukas gave him an impatient look, then shrugged and nodded.

The tests took all morning, but whatever they revealed must not have been too alarming, for Lukas appeared completely relaxed afterward, and Omanu made no objection when Ibo and a group of officers arrived from the *Harlinger* and asked if Lukas could translate again. They gave him time to eat lunch—he was on his third meal and still enraptured by every new item he tried—and then the group disappeared into the common room.

Five Miquiri arrived a short time later. Kiley thought one of them was Chirith, but she had seen several short gray aliens, and could not tell them apart with certainty. She wondered if they had equal difficulty with humans. The characteristics that made them so different to themselves—sex, size, color of hair and eyes—might not be so obvious to the Miquiri. She wished she could talk to them and ask them questions, but so far Lukas was the only one who could speak to them directly, and he was tied up in official meetings in the common room all day.

The Miquiri had been working on translating the humans' language for months, but they had made little progress. They had asked Lukas to help them compile a list of basic words and definitions. He agreed, and Ellison endorsed the idea. She also suggested that two of her communications officers sit in on the sessions and work on building a list of Miquiri words at the same time. Both sides hoped to have a basic working vocabulary established by the time the Admiralty's ship arrived.

They settled into a pattern after the first day. Kiley, Jon Robert, and Holly went about their usual business, monitoring instruments and running maintenance checks, while Lia worked in her garden and Reese helped whoever needed him the most. Lukas translated, and when he wasn't in meetings he was either in his cabin, sleeping, or in the dining room, eating.

"How can he eat so much and not gain weight?" Kiley asked Keenan incredulously after Lukas left the dining room several afternoons later. "He's going through more food than you, Jon Robert, and Reese combined, but I can't see that he's gained a pound."

"He hasn't," Keenan replied. "I've checked him several times, and his weight hasn't varied an ounce. He's either burning calories faster than normal to maintain contact with the Quayla, or it's somehow regulating his metabolism the same way it would regulate a ship."

"It could do that?" she asked, shocked.

"I don't see how," Keenan said, "but if it isn't, then I don't know what's going on."

"Have you talked to Greg about any of this?"

"Yes."

"What did he say?"

"He shrugged and said, 'I feel fine. If the Quayla is affecting me, it's for the better.'"

"I find it very difficult to believe that having anything control your body or mind could be for the better."

"So do I. So does everyone else. But in all fairness, every test we run—psychological or physical—says he's as healthy as the day he left the Academy."

The phrasing caught her attention. "As healthy as the day he left the Academy?" she questioned. "Did you mean that literally, or was it just a figure of speech?"

Keenan gave her a long look. "I meant it literally," he said at last.

"But you told me before he had changed. You said Renard had done irreparable damage."

"I did."

"And now you're saying the damage has somehow been reversed?"

"Yes."

"How?"

"Greg said the Quayla was struggling with guilt and grief. He said he told it everything I had been trying to tell him. He laughed about that, saying he never thought he'd be using my words to comfort someone else. If he could help the Quayla, maybe it's helped him, too. Maybe joining with it gave him an objective view of himself. If so, he couldn't have missed the scars Renard left—they were obvious. And if he could see them, he might have been able to counteract them, or even remove them completely."

"Do you really think that's what happened? That he and the Quayla helped each other?"

"I can't account for the change in him any other way."

"Daniel, are you afraid of him?" Kiley asked abruptly. "Of the Quayla? Do you think they're a threat to us, either of them?"

"Honestly?" he asked, then said with a sigh, "No. Every bit of common sense I possess says I should be, but I'm not. What about you?"

"I don't know. When I look at him, when he talks, he seems perfectly normal. It's hard to believe contact with the Quayla has been anything but beneficial. But that might only be what it wants us to think. I don't know what to believe."

"Neither do I. I wish I did. Maybe then I could sleep at night."

* * *

On the eighth day after the *Harlinger*'s arrival, Kiley visited the Miquiri ship.

She had been on the bridge, compiling a list of food stores that were running low. Between Lukas's binge and the *Harlinger*'s crew making themselves at home in the galley, their supplies were rapidly running out.

She had mentioned her concern to Omanu and he had called Captain Ellison on the spot. She told Kiley to make up a list of everything they needed, and a shuttle would bring the supplies over as soon as the stores could be loaded. Kiley's wariness of Ellison hadn't eased completely, but she had to admit the other woman was making every effort to be cooperative.

She was transmitting the completed requisition when she heard a sound behind her. She swung around and found a gray alien walking around the bridge, examining the control boards. He touched nothing, but he was looking at everything.

"Chirith?" she questioned, speaking softly so she wouldn't startle the Miquiri.

The alien looked up and made a sign with its hands, the same one it had made when they first boarded the ship. Kiley moved her hands in response, copying the sign the way he had showed her. She had shown Lukas the gesture several days before and asked what it meant.

"It's one of several greeting signs," he said. "They have many forms of greeting, depending on the relationship between the people. The translation for that one would be 'greetings to a respected stranger.' The finger movements at the end indicate a willingness to continue talking."

He no longer hesitated when he translated, looking inward; his answers came immediately. She didn't know if he had learned to recognize many symbols himself, or if he and the Quayla had fused to such an extent that there was no longer a difference between what each of them knew.

Chirith made another sign, his hand touching a spot between his eyes, then moving out toward her, palm up.

What's he saying? she wondered desperately. And where was Lukas when she needed him?

In the common room, of course. Tied up in one of the interminable meetings. He said they actually discussed very little, mostly going over and over the same ground. The Miquiri had told the humans how they came to be there, but they would not say where they came from. They had let the humans examine them with scanners, and they were working on the joint vocabulary project, but that was the extent of their cooperation.

Chirith was watching Kiley. Waiting. Not knowing what else to do, she repeated the sign. His eyes sparkled, as if with laughter. Had she said something stupid? She didn't have time to wonder, because he moved forward abruptly, pointing to one of the boards; then he moved his hand toward his body and away again, his hand turning palm-up.

Was he asking a question? Did he want to know how the boards operated and what the various instruments did? If she were on a strange ship, she would be curious about their controls; maybe he was, too.

She went over to the panel and pressed a button. A visual monitor came on overhead, panning the space ahead of the ship. The *Harlinger* filled most of the screen, light bouncing brightly off her sides. Kiley touched the button again, and the display went off. Then, without even thinking about what she was doing, she pointed to Chirith's hand, then the button, and made a pressing gesture.

He didn't need additional encouragement. He pressed the button and the monitor came back on. He pressed it again and the monitor went off. He pointed to another button and made a pressing motion, then repeated his earlier gesture, which seemed to be some sort of question. Kiley pushed the button and a different monitor came on. She motioned to him and he repeated her action.

She spent the next half hour demonstrating every control on the panel, except the ones that started and stopped the engines. She doubted he understood most of them; many simply called up displays that scrolled quickly down the screen. They went too fast even for her unless she was fully focused on them, looking for specific details or warning signs.

Chirith touched all the controls himself, but he always looked at her first, as if confirming that he could. She let him. Why not? She didn't think the Miquiri were about to take over the *Widdon Galaxy*, but if they did, it might be just as well if they knew how things worked.

He walked around the boards once after she finished the demonstration, as if fixing them in his mind, then went to the center of the room. He stood there, looking at her, then pointed to her and made another gesture, the back of his hand facing her and his arm moving toward his body. She had understood ''push'' immediately, and she understood this one, too—it meant "come."

She walked over to him. He went to the corridor and made the same gesture again. She followed. He pointed down the corridor, toward the access tube that linked their ships. He made the gesture again.

Come.

She looked around wildly, but there was no one in sight to tell her what to do.

There was no one to stop her, either.

Eight days of enforced inactivity were enough to instill a spirit of recklessness in the most responsible of people, and Kiley Michaelson was no exception. She looked at Chirith. He had taken another step toward the access tube. He made the sign again.

Come.

She went.

Chapter 26

The tube between the ships was some twenty feet long and ten feet wide. Kiley stopped when she reached it, looking ahead. There wasn't much to see, just smooth, opaque walls. At the end lay a cross corridor, then a wall.

The tube glowed, a soft pink mixed with even softer yellow and orange. She hesitated, rationality making a last-ditch effort to prevail. Chirith had already reached the far end. He turned around and beckoned her forward. She thought about what lay behind her—a ship filled to capacity with Corps officers and security guards, and most of the rooms under twenty-four-hour-a-day surveillance—and she followed.

Her first impression of the Miquiri ship was the cold. The temperature was at least ten degrees cooler than on the *Widdon Galaxy*, and perhaps as much as fifteen. She shivered in the chill air, wishing she had on warmer clothes. The second thing she noticed was the smell: the scent of spices was much stronger here. There were other, fainter odors as well, all tantalizingly unidentifiable.

Chirith turned left at the end of the tube, and Kiley followed. A corridor stretched out ahead of her. The ceiling was low by human standards, but the passage was wide, and it curved at the end, following the circumference of the ship. There was no one to be seen. Kiley glanced behind her. The corridor disappeared around the curve of the ship in that direction, too. No one walked there, either.

She heard a faint background noise that she took for the ship's air-recycling system. It was quieter than the *Widdon Galaxy*'s, and she could hear the sound of her own breathing over the background *shoosh*.

Chirith was already moving. He turned back to be certain she was following and gestured her forward. She took a few tentative steps and the deck gave slightly, as if she were walking on a semirigid sponge. The substance absorbed sound, and her footsteps were only soft patting noises.

The lack of noise did not disturb her, but the light did. The walls of the ship swirled with color. Most of it was yellow and orange, but darker swirls moved along the walls at what appeared to be random intervals. It was almost like being inside a living being, watching blood circulate. For one hysterical moment, she would have sworn the walls moved out, then in again, as if they were breathing. She stopped abruptly, frightened and disoriented. It wasn't only the walls that were funny, it was the air, too. Whatever the Miquiri breathed, it wasn't quite the same mixture humans were used to.

A hand touched her arm and she jumped. Chirith was standing beside her, his arms moving. What was he saying? *Don't worry, you'll be all right in a moment*? Or *Hurry, leave while you can*?

She took a shaky breath and the disorientation eased. Chirith touched her arm again. *All right?*

Concern. His worry was unmistakable. Kiley took another breath, then nodded. She pointed down the corridor. *Go?*

He made a quick sign, one finger tracing a line across his palm, then started off again. She followed, keeping her eyes on him and off the ship's walls.

They went some fifty feet; then he stopped and put his hand on a section of wall colored mainly orange. She could see nothing to indicate a control panel, but the wall opened. It simply spread apart, as far as Kiley could tell, revealing a large room beyond. Chirith stepped inside and Kiley followed. The opening closed behind her, so completely that she could not see where it had been.

There were three Miquiri in the room, a dark gray one nearly Kiley's height and two brown ones who were several inches shorter. Like the other Miquiri she had seen, they wore no clothes, but each of them carried a round, bluish-silver object about twelve inches in diameter. The smell of cinnamon was strong enough to make her sneeze, and when she did, the aliens all looked up, startled. The dark gray one whistled, a single sharp note that sent Kiley's hands to her ears in reflex. Chirith answered with a single, shorter sound, then gestured to the others with his hands.

The dark gray one gave Kiley what appeared to be a wary

look, then gestured to Chirith again. He replied briefly. The aliens resumed whatever they had been doing, but they gave Kiley frequent sideways glances, as if they did not quite trust her there.

The only furnishings in the room were the chairs the three Miquiri occupied. There were no instrument boards and no monitors, but there were displays. In fact, the walls were nothing but displays. Symbols scrolled down the walls straight ahead and to her right, constant streams running as fast as any on her own ship. The wall to her left displayed what appeared to be a vast star map composed of white dots she took for suns. Superimposed over that was a second image composed of larger dots. The Gynos system? There was a single, bright yellow spot that could have been a sun and ten smaller ones which were in the correct positions to indicate planets. The third dot from the sun was blue, the rest were brown. Tan dots surrounded several of the brown ones. Moons?

Kiley turned to Chirith, wishing she could ask if she was interpreting the images correctly, then forgot that question as she saw the wall behind her.

Where the door had been, there was now . . . space. She was looking at the *Widdon Galaxy* and, in the distance, the *Harlinger*.

She had been outside the ship in a protective suit several times, accompanying Jon Robert on visual inspections, and she felt as if she were making one of those trips now. The picture could not have come from a camera—the vessel was too close to make viewing her in her entirety possible—but the image was so real, so detailed, she could see individual sensor and solar collector plates. Several near the main hatch were dented and scraped from numerous dockings. No matter how carefully you guided a ship in, there was always a bump as ship and station joined. The plates needed replacing—that was another maintenance item for which there hadn't been enough money the past few years.

She was so mesmerized by the display she didn't notice Chirith had left her until she caught a movement at the corner of her eye. He had gone to the wall with the star map. A fissure opened and he reached inside, pulled out a round object similar to the ones the other Miquiri were holding, and brought it back to her.

Kiley took the platter hesitantly. It was very thin and extremely light. Dark green marks stood out against a silvery blue surface. They made no sense to Kiley, but Chirith touched one of them and the picture of the *Widdon Galaxy* disappeared. The wall came alive with symbols. They did not scroll like the ones on the other wall, but they did change periodically.

Status screens? Kiley had time to wonder, and then Chirith touched another symbol on the plate and the picture of the ships came back. He pointed to the symbol he had touched for the displays, as if encouraging Kiley to try it herself. She hesitated, then pressed it. The picture on the wall disappeared and the status display returned.

He pressed another point on the platter and a chair rose out of the floor.

No, not rose—swelled. It seemed as if the floor itself pressed up in a thick column that spread out as it grew, forming a chair. He waited until it had stabilized, then pointed first to the chair, then to Kiley.

Sit.

She didn't want to. There was something about seeing the chair form itself that raised fears it might disappear just as quickly, taking its occupant with it. But Chirith was insistent. He pointed to her and then the chair a second time. She sat.

The chair fit itself to her.

There was no other way to describe it. It moved, fitting itself to her back, sides, legs, and head. When she shifted position, it flowed with her. The sensation was disquieting at first, but it didn't take her long to adjust. She leaned back. The chair resisted, then gave way, moving with her. She lifted her legs. There was an instant's lag; then the substance rose until it touched her legs, changing shape to conform to her altered contours. She pressed down with her legs and it gave way, though more slowly than it had risen. She sat up again and the chair moved immediately, supporting her back all the way up. Whatever technology had gone into the creation of the chair was far beyond anything humans had accomplished.

She spent the next hour pressing symbols on the platter. Most of them resulted in a series of curving lines and dots on the wall, but some displayed maps. She did not recognize the star systems shown, but that did not surprise her. They were already on the fringes of explored space; what lay beyond had not been explored in detail.

At least, not by humans.

Chirith stopped her only when she started to touch a symbol at the center of the plate. He pointed out a black line that ran around the plate about two-thirds of the way in, and made a backward gesture with his hand.

Did he mean don't touch these? Kiley pointed to a spot on the outside of the platter and made a pressing motion. He did nothing. She pointed to a symbol inside the line and made the same gesture. He caught her hand and moved it away.

A definite "don't touch" area, then. Well, she could live with that. She had no desire to cut off the ship's life-support systems, let alone accidentally fire whatever weapons the vessel might be armed with. She nodded to Chirith to show she understood, then went back to trying out the icons in the safe area. When she had worked her way through all of them, she handed the platter back to him and stood.

"Thank you," she said. She was certain he did not understand the words, but he seemed to catch the meaning. He touched the disk, and the chair she had been sitting in flowed back into the floor. After returning the platter to its place inside the wall, he came back to her, touched her arm, and motioned to the *Widdon Galaxy*, floating again on the wall. He pointed to her, then the ship. Apparently, it was time to go.

Kiley wasn't sure she wanted to leave yet, but she nodded. Chirith went to the wall, put his hand against it, and the opening reappeared. Kiley studied the section as they went by, but try as she might she could not see anything resembling a control panel. Nor could she see where the excess wall went. It was just absorbed—the same way the floor absorbed the chair.

Chirith took her back to the access tube, then stopped at the edge. He made the pushing gesture that meant "go" or "back away," but made no move to follow her. Well, he probably had other business to take care of.

Or else he'd had enough of humans for the day.

Kiley had a brief but horrible thought that she'd somehow offended him. As if sensing her sudden apprehension, he patted her arm, then made the pushing gesture again.

"Thank you," she said again, then started back across the tube.

There was little light on the other side. She didn't notice the people waiting for her until she was almost back on the *Widdon Galaxy*. There were five of them and they all wore protective suits. Two of them were carrying disrupters, the weapons pointed straight at her.

"Stop! Right there!" a metallic voice said as soon as she stepped out of the access tube.

She stopped.

They went over her from head to foot with their scanners.

When they had finished, they ordered her to her cabin, where Guinn was waiting. The doctor was not suited, but neither was she friendly. Except to order Kiley to strip, then stand still, lie down, and sit up, she didn't say a word. She put the clothes Kiley had been wearing in a transparent bag, sealed it, then took another complete set of blood, skin, and hair samples. When she finished that, she went over her with two different bioscanners.

"Done?" Kiley asked curtly when she had finished. Guinn might be angry, but so was she. Going to the Miquiri ship without telling anyone first probably hadn't been such a great idea in retrospect, but they didn't have to treat her like she had the plague. They'd been in close contact with the Miquiri for eight days now. If there were any germs to be passed back and forth, the damage had already been done.

"I am," Guinn said. "But you aren't. Get dressed. Omanu and Ibo are waiting for you in the common room."

Debriefing did not begin to describe the session that followed. Inquisition came closer.

Someone had brought a table over from the *Harlinger*. Kiley hadn't seen it come onboard, but it filled the center of the common room, and the furniture had been pushed back to the walls to make room. There were video and audio recorders everywhere, and they were all running.

Omanu and Ibo were sitting on one side of the table, along with two other men and a woman. They were all wearing officer's uniforms. Lukas sat at the far end. He was the only one in civilian clothing, and the only one who did not look up as the door opened. The security guards who had escorted her from her cabin motioned her into the room, then closed the door and took up positions on either side of it. No getting past them, their stances said.

"Sit down, Captain," Omanu instructed.

His black eyes were not friendly today, and the chill radiating from the others on his side of the table made the Miquiri ship seem positively warm. Her eyes went from face to face, but she saw no sign of welcome until she reached Lukas. His head was up and he gave her a long, anxious look, then smiled and winked at her.

They're going to make this as difficult for you as they can, he seemed to say, *but really, what can they do? It's not as if you've broken any laws. Just don't let them get to you, and you'll be fine.*

She held tight to that message in the hours that followed, but it wasn't easy. Omanu made her tell them everything that happened, all she had seen and done. He did not interrupt. Not once. When she finished, he made her tell the story again, but this time he and the others asked questions, jumping on the slightest discrepancy between her current words and her previous recitation. After that, the real questions started, hostile and sharp, coming at her from three directions at once. She would start to answer Omanu and Ibo would break in, asking something totally different. Before she could respond to him, one of the others would ask yet another question. She would no sooner reply than Omanu would demand a response to his question.

It was clear they were trying to fluster her and force her to stumble over inconsistencies, but why? They should have been grateful for anything she could tell them about the alien ship. Instead, they were treating her like a criminal—or like Lukas. Wasn't this the way they'd treated him at first, too? As if he were no longer a trusted member of the human race because he'd been in contact with aliens? She was beginning to understand how he must have felt. *She* knew there was nothing wrong with her. Why couldn't they believe her? For the same reason they hadn't believed Lukas? Because they didn't dare?

She wanted to ask Lukas about that, but she couldn't, of course. She looked in his direction several times anyway, only to find him staring down at the table. He was listening, but he did not speak unless he was asked a direct question, and then he said as little as possible.

"Was she seeing status displays?" Ibo asked him once.

"Yes."

"What did they show?"

"The same things our instruments would: environmental data, engine power, course and speed, the location of other vessels."

"Who really controls that ship, Lukas? The Quayla or the Miquiri?"

"The Quayla operates the ship under the Miquiri's instructions. If they want something done, they tell the Quayla and it carries out their instructions."

"But it is capable of independent action?"

"Yes, but it stays within the guidelines set down for it."

"What if it couldn't?"

"Then it would do whatever it believed best to protect the ship and her crew."

"Including firing on a threatening vessel."

"The Miquiri don't carry offensive weapons, Ibo. I've told you that a number of times."

"But you and I also know defensive weapons can be turned into offensive ones easily enough. Even if you do nothing more than cut off a ship's engines, her crew will die. It may take hours instead of seconds, but they're no less dead."

"The Miquiri don't want to hurt anyone, Ibo. They're traders, not conquerors."

"That's what you say."

"Gentlemen, I believe we've agreed on several occasions this argument is fruitless until we have further data," Omanu broke in. "Let's get back to the issue at hand, shall we? Kiley, I want you to write down as many of the symbols you saw on the wall as you can remember. Lukas, see if you can tell us what any of them mean."

He passed her a computer and stylus. She did not need much time to draw the symbols—she could not recall many specific ones. Lukas got up and took the computer from her when she was done.

He could tell little about them. They were on the order of single letters, he said, meaningful only in the context of the entire word. She wasn't entirely sorry. She didn't think Chirith had shown her his ship so she could turn informant, any more than he had been spying on hers. They had been curious about each other's ships. That was all.

"It's amazing no one stopped him," said one of the officers she hadn't met before. "You don't casually invite an alien onto your ship."

"You might if you were captain," Ibo said, looking at Lukas. "Well, Lukas? Is he? You haven't exactly been forthcoming on that matter either, have you? I think maybe Chirith just gave us the answer, all by himself."

"You can believe whatever you like, Ibo," Lukas said evenly.

"And you won't help us out?"

"Not on that question."

"Nor a good many others," Ibo said. "I sometimes wonder just whose side you're on, Lukas."

"I'm not on any side, Ibo. I told you that, too—or had you forgotten?"

"I don't see how I could—not with you at such pains to make the point every other sentence."

"Gentlemen, that's enough!" Omanu said shortly. Kiley had the feeling he'd said the same words before, and more than once.

"I believe we've learned all we can for the moment. I suggest we adjourn for the day and let Kiley and Lukas have their dinner. They've earned it." He rose and the *Harlinger*'s crew followed suit. The security guards opened the door, and all but Omanu filed out. He waited until the others were gone, then came around the table to Kiley. He put his hand on her shoulder, bent over, and said in a quiet voice only she could hear, "Good job, Captain."

She was still trying to recover from the shock of that unexpected praise when she went to bed that night.

They had two days of relative peace before the *North Star* arrived. A deep-space exploration ship, she had been at Everest refitting and resupplying for an extended mission beyond Zerron Base. She had been just preparing to leave when word of the Miquiri reached the Admiralty, and they had diverted her to Gynos.

Except for the men and women required to operate the ship, her crew consisted entirely of scientists: astronomers, physicists, geologists, chemists, xenobiologists, botanists, and medical researchers—she had them all. Her roster even included an anthropologist, two linguists, and an archaeologist, in case they found evidence of another intelligent species, either living or extinct.

Omanu had guessed the *North Star* would be the ship the Admiralty would send, and he had warned Kiley that she should prepare herself and her family for an uncomfortable week once the vessel arrived. The physical examinations and debriefings they had received so far would be nothing compared to the ones the *North Star*'s crew would conduct.

He was right.

The ship arrived during their sleep cycle, and they woke to find themselves surrounded by men and women wearing protective suits. They were told to dress, then were escorted to cargo bay three, where a shuttle waited to take them to the *North Star*. Only Lukas was left behind. The shuttle had observation ports, and Kiley's first view of the ship was from space.

She was gigantic.

At least three times the size of the *Widdon Galaxy*, she completely blocked off all view of the space beyond. She was all bulges and turrets; there wasn't a straight line to her. Her hull was dull gray—no sensor plates. Instead, concave dishes covered her sides, top and bottom, and long, antenna-like rods sprouted out randomly. Kiley had never seen a bigger ship in her life—or an uglier one.

The shuttle landed in a small bay on the side of the ship, and they were herded across the bay to a hatch some ten feet away. One of the people escorting them opened the hatch, then motioned them into the corridor beyond. The corridor was white, floor, walls, and ceiling. The overhead lights were so bright that the light seared Kiley's eyes.

The *North Star*'s medical staff were waiting for them just inside the hatch. They were separated, and that was the last time Kiley saw the others for six days. She spent the first three being subjected to every test the doctors could dream up. Their tests and instruments might have been more familiar than the ones the Miquiri used on Lukas, but she was willing to bet they were no less intrusive.

The days of questioning that followed the tests were equally unpleasant. Kiley was furious about the medics' refusal to tell her how the rest of her family was doing, let alone see them, and she flatly refused to cooperate.

"There's no cause for concern, Captain," she was told firmly. "In fact, the other members of your family have already been released and gone back to your ship."

"And they're well?"

"They're fine."

"What about Captain Keenan?"

"He's still being debriefed. The two of you were the last to leave medical."

"How long are you going to keep me here?"

"That all depends on you, Captain. We have a number of questions, but if you cooperate, you shouldn't be here more than a few days."

"What do you want to know?" she asked.

Everything, as it turned out. They even asked about Jon Senior's death. They spent a day and a half on Lukas, going over every act, every conversation she could recall from the time he'd boarded their ship until the present.

After they exhausted that topic, they turned to her decision to run before the *Railion*. Why had she been so afraid of a Corps cruiser on an apparently legitimate mission? Why had she chosen to evade it? She did her best to explain how things seemed at the time: being stopped for no apparent reason, being so close to Zerron Base and Admiral Sorseli, Keenan's concern about the lengths to which the Admiral would go to protect himself, her immediate if irrational dislike of Tichner—she told them all that, but she didn't think they believed her.

The *North Star*'s captain and another admiral were present during that questioning, gold braid covering the shoulders of their white dress uniforms. Of all the interrogators, scientific and military, they were the most relentless. It did no good to remember Lukas's wink after her visit to the Miquiri ship. Unlike Omanu and Ibo, these men *could* do something to her. Whatever reasons Kiley and her crew had had for entering Belurian space, they had broken the law simply by being there. Worse, entering a restricted zone was the single violation for which a death sentence not only could be, but still was carried out. Her hands were shaking by the time the admirals left and the questions turned to her visit to the Miquiri ship.

She spent one more day going over that trip. The conference room was filled to overflowing, and it seemed as if every person in the room had a question that needed answering. It was late evening before the inquiries finally stopped coming.

They let her go back to the *Widdon Galaxy* after that, but she was so exhausted from three days of nonstop interrogation that she could hardly summon the energy to care. Jon Robert must have seen the shuttle coming, because he was waiting in the cargo bay to greet her.

"Are you all right?" he asked, looking her over anxiously.

"Yes."

"We were worried—they kept you a long time."

"They had a lot of questions. How about you and the others?"

"We're fine. They gave us every medical test known to man, asked a few questions, then let us go. They haven't bothered us since."

"What about Greg?"

"He's okay, too. They sent two doctors over to examine him, but the general consensus seems to be 'look, but don't touch.' I'm beginning to think the Quayla has its advantages, after all."

"And Daniel?"

"He isn't back yet."

"What?" she demanded, swinging around to face him. They'd reached the elevator and she'd been about to push the button, but her hand stopped in midair.

"He's not back yet," Jon Robert repeated. He looked worried. "Omanu says they're still questioning him. Kiley, he's upset. He won't say why, but it must be because of Daniel."

"I don't understand why they'd keep him so long. He hasn't done anything."

"Except be Greg's psychiatrist and friend. They may not be able to question Greg, but he's fair game."

"Where's Omanu? I want to talk to him."

If Keenan's boss knew any more about him than they did, he was not saying. Still, she sensed he was both concerned and frustrated behind the wall of official briskness.

Kiley waited until the next day. When Keenan still hadn't returned, she called the *North Star* and demanded a status report on the officer.

"Captain Keenan is still assisting our staff with their investigation," she was told. "He will be staying with us until the official inquiry is complete." She pressed for further details, but none were forthcoming.

Nor was Keenan, not for three more days. He came back to the *Widdon Galaxy* on the evening of the third and went straight to his cabin. He slept for nearly twenty-four hours. Omanu checked up on him shortly after his return and pronounced him fit, but Kiley wasn't convinced the senior officer was being completely honest. She was even less certain when Keenan finally emerged. His clothes hung on him as if he'd lost fifteen pounds. His expression was flat, his eyes shadowed. He avoided everyone but Omanu, but the two of them had several long conversations in his cabin. Kiley didn't know what they discussed, but whatever it was, the topic clearly upset both of them.

If she hadn't been so concerned about Keenan, she'd have said affairs on the *Widdon Galaxy* had taken a turn for the boring. The Corps and the Miquiri were still talking, but the dialogue appeared to have reached an impasse. The Miquiri had been disappointed to learn that the humans knew nothing of the barrier. They wanted to resume their search for a way home, but the *North Star*'s officers asked them to stay where they were, perhaps worried that they would leave and never come back. They said the Admiralty would search for a way around the barrier. They were prepared to commit an entire fleet to the effort, and they could cover far more territory than the Miquiri, far faster.

Chirith still wanted to leave. Lukas talked to him for hours and finally persuaded him to let the Admiralty conduct the search. That intercession won him some favor with the Corps, but he was still regarded with suspicion. They might need him, but they didn't trust him.

Kiley rarely saw him. He spent most of his time in the common room, working with Miquiri and human linguists. When he wasn't there, he was either talking to Chirith on the *Nieti*, where their conversations could not be observed, or he was eating or sleeping. He and Kiley managed a few minutes alone on the bridge several times, but even then their conversations were strained. They suspected most of the ship was being monitored and shied away from personal matters. Lukas was hesitant to say much about the Miquiri, either, not wanting to reveal anything about them they did not choose to say themselves.

He did tell her they were some distance from home, though he would not say how far. He said Chirith's ship was an exploration vessel, much like the *North Star*. The Miquiri had colonized a number of worlds, but many of them preferred to live in space. They were intensely curious by nature and loved both trade and travel. And, while they were nonaggressive and preferred to avoid trouble rather than meet it head-on, they both could and would respond forcefully if pressed.

He said they were not unlike humans in many respects, but there were some vast differences between the two cultures. For starters, the Miquiri placed no emphasis on gender. The only time a person's sex became important was during mating. That was another cultural difference he was finding difficulty comprehending. It seemed the Miquiri chose their mates based on scent, not love.

"You're joking," Kiley said in disbelief.

"I'm not," Lukas replied. "Males and females develop strong, sharply different scents as they enter their first season of fertility. From what I gather, there is an escalating chemical reaction between a male and female. Initially, the male may be attracted to several females. If one of them shares his attraction, her scent changes subtly, making her more attractive to him. His appears to change in return, making him more desirable to her and less desirable to other females. The chemical alterations escalate until the pair's mutual scents become literally irresistible. The mating that follows is intense and prolonged. It's also irreversible. Whatever biological changes occur, once a pair has mated, they are not attracted to, or attractive to, other partners for the rest of their lives, even if one of them dies. The really odd thing, though, is that they often live together only as long as the female is in season. The rest of the time, they may not see or even speak to each other."

"They mate, but they don't love each other?"

"They share a special affection for each other, but it's not what we'd call love. That emotion is reserved for the few each one calls *akia*."

"*Akia?*"

"Friend. Literally, sharer of my heart and mind. An *akia* is someone with whom a Miquiri feels very close ties, emotionally and intellectually. Mates are for procreation; an *akia* is the person one turns to for comfort and affection."

"And one's mate isn't an *akia*?"

"Not often, though it can happen. Hinfalla's mate was also his *akia*."

"What about their children? Who takes care of them if the pair doesn't stay together?"

"They become a part of whatever family the female belongs to. That's another thing. The Miquiri differentiate between the family one is born to and the family one chooses to live with after maturity. Chirith considers the crew of the *Nieti* his family, and himself the father of any and all children onboard. All the adults feel that way."

"You like him, don't you?" she asked, catching the softening in his voice she heard whenever he spoke of the gray alien.

"Yes, I do. Very much." He looked at her. "Does that bother you? That I might like one of the Miquiri as much as a fellow human?"

She thought of Chirith, of the pat he had given her arm before sending her back to her ship. If they could talk, would she discover she liked him, too? On the whole, she thought she would.

"No, that doesn't bother me," she said with complete honesty.

The conversation turned to the Miquiri language after that. Lukas told her that the sharp, high-pitched whistles that nearly ruptured human ears were part of their primary language. Because they had only a three-note range to their vocal cords, however, they had evolved a complex, formalized set of hand gestures to accompany their spoken words. The gestures had become the basis of the sign language they used with all non-Miquiri, most of whom found their whistles as painful as humans did.

"What do you mean, all non-Miquiri?" Kiley demanded. "Are you saying there are other aliens out there?"

"Yes."

"How many?"

"Three races they know of. They trade with two of them

regularly, but they avoid the third—they're relatively unadvanced, but they've been hostile on several occasions in the past. The Miquiri are worried about them; they're expanding in all directions and they're aggressively pushing at the borders of space the Miquiri have considered theirs for centuries.''

"Does the Corps know about these other aliens?''

"Yes.''

"I'll bet the news came as a shock.''

"That's a mild way of putting it. It's like going to a room you think is empty and finding a party in full swing. I think they're going to need time before they decide they feel like socializing.''

"The Miquiri don't mind that?''

"The Miquiri are ecstatic. Their worst fear was that we'd be another aggressive species more interested in seizing goods and territory than trade.''

"I trust you reassured them on that point.''

"I did my best, but I'm not sure they believed me, even so. The circumstances of their first contact with humans weren't exactly auspicious. 'Carnage' was the word Chirith had used to describe the scene on Gynos. I've explained what happened as best I could, but they're still leery of humanity.''

"Greg, do you think they'd be willing to trade with us? I don't just mean humans, but us in particular. This ship.''

"Trade?''

"Jon Robert mentioned the idea. He pretty well has the rest of the family convinced we could make a fortune—assuming the Miquiri would agree to exchange goods, of course.''

"You're talking about traveling into Miquiri space?''

"Yes. I don't see why you're acting so surprised. You were the one who said we ought to consider branching out into new territory.''

"I wasn't exactly referring to unknown space.''

"No, but it is a possibility, isn't it? Jon Robert thinks we could sell anything we could bring back—even if no one knew what to do with it—just because it came from the Miquiri.''

"You probably could, but that doesn't mean you have the faintest idea what you're letting yourselves in for—any of you. This isn't the fringes we're talking about, it's alien territory. You'd be surrounded by beings you didn't understand, none of whom spoke your language. You'd be isolated in ways you can't begin to imagine.''

"We've spent large portions of our life isolated. That's the way it is when you live on a freighter. We seem to have survived so far. As for their language, well, we can learn it. We're probably going to be here for some time before the Admiralty lets us go; we might as well put it to good use. We might not be able to duplicate their spoken language, but we could learn their hand signs and written language with your help.''

''It's not just the language that would be a problem—it's customs, patterns of thinking. You could mortally offend someone and never realize what you'd done.''

''Why do you keep acting as if it would be just us? You'd be there too. We'd be counting on you to keep us from making precisely those kinds of mistakes. You would be there, wouldn't you, Greg?'' she asked, suddenly uncertain. ''I know we can't match the pay the Corps would offer, but—''

''Kiley, I can't stay on the ship,'' he interrupted.

''Why not? The Corps can't force you to work for them if you don't want to. You don't, do you?''

''It isn't the Corps that's the problem—it's the Quayla. I can't be separated from it.''

''So? You said it could transfer itself to another ship. Couldn't it come with you?''

''Yes, but if it did, it would have to attach itself to this ship. You wouldn't want that, any of you. It would spread out everywhere—in the engines, the computers, in your cabins. It would make the ship an extension of itself. Even if you could live with that, the rest of humanity couldn't. You won't be able to go back into human space. Even if a station would take a chance and let you dock, the Corps wouldn't. Not with a life-form capable of spreading itself wherever it wanted to go.''

''Jon Robert thinks there's a chance we could go as far as the first station this side of Miquiri space. He thinks the Corps will be so interested in the Quayla and any goods we could bring back, they'd be willing to let us dock at one port.''

''And you could accept that? Being allowed to visit only one station—and one that likely won't offer anything but the most basic necessities, at that? It wouldn't be Aumarleen, with stores and entertainment—it would be a way station that would let you off-load, resupply, and be on your way.''

''Most times that's all we do.''

''But not all the time, and that's what we're talking about. All the time. Forever.''

''No, not forever. A few years maybe, but not forever. Stations at the center of trade routes grow fast, and we're betting this one will be huge within a few years.''

"You really have been thinking about this, haven't you?"

"Yes. We've talked about you and the Quayla, too. We want you to stay on the ship, Greg. Both of you."

She saw the first glimmerings of hope in his eyes, and only then did she realize how much fear he had been concealing.

"I couldn't come with you right away," he said slowly. "I have to stay with the *Nieti* until they find another companion. If the Quayla split now, the part on their ship would be alone. I couldn't do that to it. I couldn't."

"I understand—but later, after they've found another companion, would you come back to us?"

"There's only one thing I'd like more."

"What?"

"To be able to talk to you—really talk—without worrying about who might be watching or listening."

"I'd like that too, Greg."

Chapter 27

Sixty-eight days after the search began, the Corps found a way past the barrier. The exploration had been complicated because their instruments, too, malfunctioned within a hundred kilometers of the invisible wall. The crews could detect no visual abnormalities in the space around them, but they were all forced to turn back before shipwide malfunctions disabled their vessels. Before the search ended, nearly half the Corps's fleet was looking for a way into Miquiri space. They finally found it, light-years from Gynos.

The Miquiri hadn't believed the humans at first. They insisted on seeing their star charts and instrument readings. Once they realized the humans were telling the truth, a flood of thanks poured out, mainly in the form of information.

They gave the Corps the coordinates of their closest outpost and said they would welcome a contact mission. They did set a limit of one Corps ship, but said others could follow after diplomatic relations had been established.

Working with maps the Miquiri provided, the Corps calculated that the journey to the outpost would require five long jumps. The distance was sufficient to provide a comfort zone, without being a true inconvenience. Reaching boundary agreements that would keep the distance between the two groups comfortable would be one of the first tasks the diplomatic missions faced. Clashes happened along borders that lay too close to populated areas, and the Miquiri did not want clashes. Neither did the humans—not when they had a strong suspicion who would come out the victor.

Besides, it was always better to have friends than enemies, particularly when others were out there who might not prove as friendly as the Miquiri. An alliance was in the best interests of both sides.

One of the first conditions of the newfound spirit of cooperation was the release of the *Widdon Galaxy* from Corps custody which the Miquiri requested as a favor to Lukas. He had told Chirith he wanted to rejoin the Michaelsons' ship as soon as he could, and Chirith had agreed to let the *Widdon Galaxy* travel to the closest Miquiri outpost along with the *North Star*.

The *Nieti* could reach the station in three long jumps. The Corps agreed to let her go ahead and warn the Miquiri that visitors were on the way. The *North Star* would follow at her best speed, and the *Widdon Galaxy* would travel one day behind the *North Star*.

Lukas would stay on the *Nieti* until another companion was found; then he and the Quayla would return to the *Widdon Galaxy*.

The Miquiri were not happy about the Quayla transferring itself to a human ship, but there was little they could do. The Quayla had come to them of its own accord. They did not own it; it was not their slave. If it chose to go among humans, they could not stop it; they could only hope it knew what it was doing.

The Corps was as unhappy about the Quayla as the Miquiri. If they could have prevented the *Widdon Galaxy* from going into Miquiri space, or Lukas from rejoining the ship, Kiley was certain they would have. But they couldn't—not with Lukas saying that was what he wanted and the Miquiri backing him. The Corps had given in, perhaps deciding humans would be well advised to hold on to a piece of the Quayla in some manner, even if they weren't quite sure what to do with it. If the Michaelsons wanted to let it onboard their ship, they would let them, and watch and see what happened from a safe distance.

Since the Miquiri had granted the *Widdon Galaxy* permission to travel as far as their first outpost, the Corps gave them tentative permission to dock at the first station their side of Miquiri space. They could travel freely between the two locations, but that would be the extent of their freedom—at least initially.

The family had second thoughts after hearing those limits, then third and fourth thoughts. They held another meeting to discuss their options and vote. It was long and tense.

Taking chances did not come easily to them, and they had taken more in the past few months than in all the years Jon had been alive. They were reluctant to take another one, and finally did so only by convincing themselves the risk was minimal. There would always be time to back out if what they saw on the other side of the barrier proved intolerable. They could change their minds anytime before the Quayla attached itself to their ship.

Lukas made numerous trips to the Miquiri ship as the *Nieti*'s departure neared, settling into the cabin he'd been allocated and seeing to the safe storage of the food and water the *North Star* had provided. They'd given him three months' worth of supplies, and he could stretch them to last five, if necessary. The Miquiri helped him carry them onto the ship. Despite the warmer relations, Lukas was the only human they permitted onboard. Even Kiley was not invited back.

If the pilot had any qualms about leaving with the Miquiri, he did not display them—until the last moment, that is. The family had gone to the personnel hatch to see him off, as had Keenan and several officers from the *North Star*. He said good-bye to everyone, leaving Kiley until last. He made an aborted move toward her, as if he had been about to touch her, but had remembered they were being watched.

"Good-bye," he said.

"Good-bye," she replied, following his cue and keeping her voice level.

He turned to the access tube, started to cross, then stopped. He started forward a second time, and stopped again. He turned around.

"You will come?" he said to Kiley, looking almost desperate, as if the realization that he was about to be left alone with a ship full of aliens had finally penetrated.

"We'll come," she said with all the conviction she possessed. And then, when those words did not ease his anxiety, she did the one thing she thought might. Disregarding her family, Keenan, and the Corps officers, she went to him and gave him a quick kiss.

She had meant it to be a brief gesture, a reassurance only. She would have moved away immediately, but his arms went around her, holding her tightly. He looked at her for five endless seconds, his eyes dark with emotion, and then kissed her.

She forgot about her family. She forgot about Keenan and the *North Star*'s officers. She forgot about the Quayla. Nothing mattered except Greg Lukas, the feel of his hands and mouth, and the desperate need that flared into hunger in the space between two heartbeats. Nothing that had come before in her life had prepared her for the intensity and immediacy of his response. Or hers.

And then, a lifetime too soon, he tore himself away and strode across the access tube. He stopped when he reached the other side. She thought he would look back then, but he continued on, turning to his left and walking out of sight.

Her mother had left her the same way—without a backward glance. She had never understood that before, but she thought she did now. If she had looked back, she would have lost all resolve. So would Lukas.

No one spoke after he disappeared, and she was glad. If anyone had said a single word, she'd have started crying. As it was, she was blinking back tears as she went to the hatch and closed it. The Miquiri ship undocked a short time later. Five minutes after that, they left.

The *North Star*'s officers watched the *Nieti*'s departure until the vessel was out of instrument range, then returned to their own ship, leaving the Michaelsons alone on the *Widdon Galaxy* for the first time in two months. They spent the evening wandering around aimlessly, as if no longer quite sure what to do with themselves. They retired to their cabins early, but Kiley doubted any of them slept long or well. She didn't.

The next day was better—there was so much to do, they didn't have time to think. The *North Star* was already gone when they rose, but the *Harlinger* was still there. She would return to Everest and make a complete report to the Admiralty as soon as she saw the *Widdon Galaxy* off. Jon Robert and Holly ran their systems checks. Four hours later, they pulled out. Six hours after that, they made the first of the five jumps that would take them to the Miquiri outpost.

The intervening weeks were long and brittle. They were all preoccupied and short-tempered. Even Holly's manner sharpened. Despite the vote to follow the *North Star* into Miquiri space, they were not certain their attempt to establish themselves as traders would work, nor were they easy about having the Quayla attach itself to the ship. They had taken the first step toward commitment, but they still had room to back out, and the temptation grew stronger as each subsequent jump took them farther and farther from all they knew.

Kiley wasn't sure what she would do if the rest of the family voted to return to human space. She did not see how she could go with them and leave Lukas behind—not after that last kiss, not after realizing how much he wanted her, and how very much she wanted and needed him. But if she stayed with him, the *Widdon Galaxy* would have no pilot. Working double shifts, Jon Robert and Reese could take the ship back to human space by themselves, but they couldn't run her that way for long. They would have to hire a regular pilot, and that would cost them whatever profit they might be making. There would be no money left over. In the end, they would lose the ship.

Jon Robert was quick to notice she was unhappy, and it didn't take him long to uncover the reason. He and the rest of the family tried to assure her that she would never have to choose; they were determined to proceed with their plan to trade with the Miquiri. She wanted to believe them, but she couldn't stop worrying. She was afraid they would change their minds once they had seen the Miquiri outpost and realized just how far from home they would be.

By the day they were due to exit jump the final time, she was so tense that she could hardly keep her hands steady on the ship's controls. Jon Robert was alone in the engine room. He'd insisted that Holly stay in their cabin, since she was well into her pregnancy. The *North Star*'s physicians had assured him she was completely fit, but they had agreed she would find transition less stressful if she was lying down, and she'd been duly ordered to bed.

Lia and Reese were on the bridge with Kiley for once, too anxious about what lay ahead to stay in their cabin. Keenan was there, too, sitting beside her in the copilot's seat.

He had wandered onto the bridge several days before the *Widdon Galaxy* left Gynos. Kiley had just finished running the morning status checks and was on her way to breakfast. She asked him if he wanted to come, but he didn't answer. He was standing with his back to her, his eyes on the external monitor displaying an image of the *Harlinger*.

"Daniel, what's wrong?" she asked, not wanting to pry, but so concerned about him that she felt she had to say something. "I'd be glad to listen if you'd like to talk."

"I'm leaving the Corps," he said without turning around. "I told Hal I'd made up my mind to resign my commission this morning."

"You what? Daniel, why?"

"I don't want to be a part of . . . of that anymore," he said, gesturing to the ship on the monitor. "I talked to Hal about a transfer several months ago. I just didn't expect I'd want to leave the Corps completely.''

''But you do?''

''Yes.''

''What will you do?''

''Start a practice somewhere, I suppose. That's what I trained to do.'' He spoke with a complete lack of enthusiasm.

''Is that what you really want?'' she asked. ''To have your own practice?''

''Honestly?'' He turned around to look at her for the first time.

''Of course.''

''No.''

''Then what?''

''I don't know. Can you believe that, Kiley? All my life, I've always known exactly what I wanted, and now, suddenly, I don't. I don't seem to know anything anymore.''

''What about the *North Star*? You said you wanted to work on a deep-space ship once. Couldn't you transfer to her?''

''They already offered me a position. I turned it down.''

''Why?''

''All they really wanted was someone to watch Greg.''

''And you didn't want to do that?''

''Of course I didn't!'' he exploded. ''He's my friend. I don't want to spy on him for them!''

''Not even if they're right to be concerned about him? They may be. Greg seems perfectly normal now, but we don't know what long-term contact with the Quayla will do to him. We don't know what it will do to any of us, but we're about to find out.'' She hesitated. ''Daniel, I can understand your not wanting to work for the Corps, but would you consider staying on with us for a while, just in case we do run into problems? It would give you time to decide what you really want to do, and we could relax knowing you were around in case any of us did need help.''

''You're asking me to stay on the *Widdon Galaxy*?''

''If you want to. Would that be so very terrible?''

''This is a working ship, Kiley. You don't have room for non-paying passengers. I wouldn't be much use on the bridge or in the engine room.''

''I wasn't asking you to work, but I expect we could keep you busy if you really wanted to be. Then, too, there's Holly. We're going to be a long way from the nearest hospital, and her baby is due in three months. You may not be an obstetrician, but you're a whole lot more qualified to deliver a baby than Jon Robert.''

''Me? Deliver a baby?''

He sounded so appalled that she burst out laughing.

''I take it psychiatric residents don't see much of maternity wards,'' she said.

''They don't even go close.''

''Well, it was an idea.''

''I could study, though. Almost anyone could handle a normal delivery with a little training. And if there were complications, I could probably cope with them better than your brother could. He's too close to her to stay calm during a real emergency.''

''My thoughts exactly. Well, Daniel? Are you interested? We aren't talking long-term commitment here—just a few months. You'll have time to sort out what you want to do, and we'll be more relaxed knowing you're around. What do you say?''

''I'll think about it.''

So he had come. She was glad he had, even if he had radiated as much tension as the rest of them on the trip out. She was willing to bet even the *North Star*'s crew had experienced an unusually high level of anxiety as they traveled farther and farther from home, not knowing what they would find when they reached their destination.

By now, the *North Star* knew. And in thirty seconds, they would, too.

Kiley took a deep breath. It was too late to go back now—it had been too late for some time. They would exit jump virtually on the Miquiri's doorstep. She had not wanted to come in that close, but Chirith had insisted. The Miquiri were not going to risk them going anywhere but the outpost, not until they'd been officially checked out and cleared.

Twenty seconds. Ten.

She reached for the intercom. ''Coming up on transition . . . now!'' she announced.

The words were barely out of her mouth before her body turned inside out. As transitions went, it wasn't bad, but even so, she came through breathless and shaky.

''Oh, my—'' Keenan exclaimed, eyes going to the monitor before him, copilot's duties forgotten.

Kiley didn't follow his gaze. She was too busy dumping speed and executing a split-second change of course to avoid hitting a slow-moving vessel lying dead ahead. Beyond that were three more ships, and beyond that a large moon orbiting an Earth-sized planet.

"Full reverse!" she ordered Jon Robert.

Rapid deceleration slammed her back into her seat and made breathing virtually impossible. The ship wallowed to starboard and Kiley banked her even more sharply to the right, narrowly missing the other vessel and cursing Chirith the entire time. She had shut off the proximity alarms, knowing other vessels would be in the vicinity, but she had never expected to land so close to so many. She maneuvered around two more, then brought the ship back to port in a sweeping trajectory that would drop them into orbit around the planet's moon.

"If that's an outpost, what do their main bases look like?" Reese asked plaintively.

Only then did she look up at the visual monitor. What was left of her breath went out in a *whoosh* as she bit back an exclamation of her own. The body they were about to orbit was no moon—it was a space station. Moreover, it was unmistakably Miquiri. Yellow-orange ripples swirled across the surface, forming tantalizing patterns that almost made sense. Beyond the station, a blue and white planet basked in light streaming out from a distant yellow sun. The light struck the station as well, and wherever it touched the colors turned incandescent, swirling around each other with a speed that would have caused instant nausea in anyone foolish enough to watch for long.

"There's the *North Star*," Keenan said.

Velocity had taken them around to the far side of the station, and they were about to overtake the exploration ship, which had also gone into orbit. Several Miquiri ships were clustered around her, and one had already docked. Kiley adjusted course, giving the ships a wide berth.

Chirith had warned the humans that the outpost's personnel would insist on boarding their ships and inspecting them before any talks could begin. The *North Star*'s captain had agreed to the visit, but Kiley was willing to bet he didn't like having his ship scrutinized any more than she had—or would again, when the Miquiri arrived to inspect them, too.

They weren't going to take long to do that. One of the ships left the *North Star* as they passed her, accelerating rapidly to match speeds with them. Moments later, it docked. Kiley waited until sensors showed that the air pressure in the tube matched that inside the *Widdon Galaxy* to open the hatch. Then she sent Keenan and Reese to meet their visitors. She stayed on the bridge, continuing to decelerate and watching for other slow-moving vessels in their path.

The Miquiri escorted Keenan and Reese back to the bridge, gestured for them all to stay where they were, then fanned out to conduct their inspection. One group went toward their quarters, one to the engine room, and a third down to the cargo holds. They went over the ship as carefully as the *Harlinger*'s and *North Star*'s teams had. When they had finished, they gathered in the corridor outside the bridge to consult with each other, and then one of them came forward.

You understand my words? it signaled.

Yes, Kiley replied. Lukas had taught them basic hand signals before leaving, and they had continued to study the tapes the Corps translators had prepared.

Continue orbit, the Miquiri said. *Others come.*

The boarding party returned to their ship, and the vessel pulled away. The *Widdon Galaxy* completed another full orbit of the station, overtaking and passing the *North Star* again. They expected another ship to peel away from the group clustered around the exploration vessel, but instead, sensors picked up one leaving the station itself. It rose smoothly and matched their speed without effort. When it docked, Kiley opened the hatch a second time.

Keenan and Reese went back to the corridor. A moment later, Kiley heard startled exclamations. She was on her feet, heading for the hall, before she remembered the ship. Lia was standing, too.

"Go," her sister said. "I can manage here." She slid into the copilot's seat. Kiley gave the boards a quick glance—no immediate problems there—and headed for the corridor with long strides.

She heard his voice before she saw him.

". . . constant bombardment. I'm—"

"Greg?"

He broke off his conversation with Keenan. She wasn't sure afterward which of them moved, or if they both did. All she knew was that a second later, he was holding her as if he would never let her go again, and she was returning the embrace with a fierce one of her own.

His hair had grown and needed cutting badly. His face was dark with stubble and it sagged with exhaustion. He was the most beautiful sight she had ever seen.

"I missed you," he said, his face tight against hers. "I missed you so much."

"I missed you, too," she whispered back.

She was going to cry, she knew she was, but Jon Robert saved her.

"Greg!" her brother exclaimed from behind them.

Lukas let her go and held out his hand to Jon Robert. If Kiley had harbored any doubts about the pilot's welcome from the rest of the family, they vanished as her brother ignored Lukas's hand and gave him a hug nearly as tight as Kiley's had been.

"We were worried about you," he said, breaking away. "Was it a difficult trip? You look worn out."

"It wasn't that bad, but I have to admit, being a Quayla's companion has its drawbacks. I was just telling Daniel and Reese I wasn't prepared for the constant bombardment of information, most of which didn't make much sense for the first week or two. The last couple were better, but I've only had a few hours' sleep since we arrived. Everyone on the outpost had questions. I don't think they've let me sleep more than three hours at a time since I arrived. On top of that, there was the strain of separating. The Quayla found another companion among the station personnel. The joining was—unpleasant. Too many sensations from too many directions. The Quayla separated almost immediately afterward. Most of it stayed with the *Nieti*, but part remained with me. We had to leave the ship. There just wasn't room for all of us. The Miquiri officials wanted me to stay on the station, but Chirith persuaded them to let me come here instead. He said the Quayla and I wouldn't be comfortable until we were on our own ship."

"Where is the Quayla?" Daniel asked, noticing the one thing all the rest of them had missed. "I don't see any light."

"It's still on the Miquiri ship. It didn't want to come across until we were sure you were ready to accept it. The bond between us is strong enough to let us be a short distance apart and remain in touch."

"For how long?" Keenan asked.

"At this distance? Indefinitely. Any farther and maintaining contact would be a strain, but this is no problem. There's no need to rush your decision," he said, turning to Kiley. "You have plenty of time to be certain this is what you want."

"We've already made up our minds," Reese said. "Tell it to come over, Greg."

Lukas looked at him, then at Jon Robert and Kiley.

"He's right," Jon Robert said. "We had a meeting last night. We voted to go ahead. All of us. The Quayla can attach itself to the *Widdon Galaxy*, as long as it agrees not to interfere with the operation of any of the ship's systems."

"It will draw power from the ship," Lukas warned. "Not much, but enough to detect. Except for that, though, it won't interfere with anything, not unless and until you want it to." Lukas was speaking to Jon Robert, but his eyes were on Kiley. The others could give their permission all day, but the real decision lay with her. She was captain. The ship was her command, her responsibility. The final approval was for her alone, no matter how the family had voted.

"Tell it to come, Greg," she said.

"You're sure?" he questioned, his eyes on hers. It wasn't just the Quayla he was asking about. He was asking about himself, too. About them.

She gathered up all the courage and love she possessed and took what she swore would be the last chance of her life.

"I'm sure," she said.

The Quayla came. It was so faint, she wouldn't have seen it if she hadn't been looking for the telltale glow at Lukas's feet.

"What's wrong with it?" Jon Robert asked, shocked.

"I told you, only a small part came with me. The rest stayed behind. It will grow, though. There won't be a place on the ship it won't spread before it's through. You are sure?" he asked again, this time speaking to Jon Robert, who was staring uneasily at the single spot of color.

"Well, I can't deny I have concerns," he said. "But we've made our decision—for better or worse. Don't look so worried, Greg. We aren't going to back out. Just give us time to get used to all this, okay?"

"You can have all the time you want."

Keenan volunteered to sit watch on the bridge so the family could have dinner together that night. Though he still had a great deal to learn, Kiley didn't see any problem in leaving him alone. The ship was in a stable orbit, and moving vessels would be obliged to maneuver around her. She left the proximity alarms on anyway and, much as she wanted to linger, was the first to leave the dining room.

"I have to get back to the bridge," she said. "I'd like to post a twenty-four-hour watch, given the amount of traffic in the area. Do I have any volunteers to relieve me in a few hours?"

"I will," Jon Robert said immediately.

"And I'll follow him," Reese said.

Lia and Holly volunteered for shifts, too. Lukas tried to, but they all overruled him.

"You can hardly keep your eyes open," Jon Robert said. "You'd be asleep five minutes after we left you alone."

"He's right, Greg," Kiley said. "Get some sleep. We'll still be standing watch tomorrow; you can take a shift then."

"If you're sure . . ." he said, his voice trailing off.

"Positive. Go on, we all excuse you."

He walked down the corridor with her, then turned to go to his cabin. He looked back before he went in. She was still watching him.

"Good night," he said softly.

"Good night," she replied, just as quietly.

She stayed on the bridge two hours, watching ships come and go from the outpost. The activity made standing watch more interesting than usual, but even so, she was yawning by the time Jon Robert relieved her.

"About time," she said, standing up and giving him the pilot's seat.

"What do you mean, 'about time'?" he demanded. "I'm five minutes early."

"So you are. Thanks. I'll remember that the next time I relieve you."

She started to leave.

"He's in the galley, Kiley," Jon Robert said without looking around. "I saw him on my way here. He said he was having trouble going to sleep. He was going to fix something hot to drink. If you ask me, he was just waiting for you to get off duty. It might be a good idea if you checked up on him—in case he needs something."

"Thank you, Jon Robert. I'll do that," she said coolly.

His shoulders were shaking with silent laughter. She had a feeling there were going to be times in the near future when having even the best of brothers around might be a severe trial.

Lukas had finished his drink and was putting his glass in the washer when she went into the galley. He glanced up as she came in, then turned back to the washer, closed its door, and started the unit.

"Couldn't sleep?" she asked.

"No."

The unit rinsed and sterilized the glass, then switched to its drying cycle.

"You aren't missing the Miquiri ship, are you?"

"Not at all!" he said, turning around at last. "They were very good to me, especially Chirith, but this is the first time I haven't been cold in five weeks. I'll take a human ship any day."

The washer chimed. He pulled out the glass and put it back on the shelf.

"Greg, you do need to rest," she said. She could see that he was so tired he could barely stand without swaying, but he was trying. He was trying very hard. "Come on," she said with a sigh. "I'll walk you back to your cabin."

The walk was short and silent. He opened the door to his cabin, then stood in the entrance so it would not close again.

"The Miquiri will be back tomorrow," he said. "I told them you were interested in opening up trade with them. They want to talk to you. I think the matter may be open to consideration."

"That's good to hear. It would have been an expensive trip without a return cargo."

"I know." He paused. "Kiley, we never had a chance to talk. I wanted to, but there was never a good time or place. I meant what I said on the bridge the day I joined with the Quayla. I love you. I don't ever want to be separated from you again."

She had not believed him on the bridge. She had even doubted him when he kissed her before leaving with the Miquiri. His sudden realization that he wanted and needed her could have been prompted by his fear of being deserted as easily as by love. But he was not afraid now. Or uncertain. Neither was she.

"I love you, too, Greg," she said softly. "I have for a very long time."

She had worried about feeling awkward around him once they were alone. She shouldn't have. Kissing him then was the most natural act of her life.

She did not know what the future held, but whatever happened, they would face it together. They had each other, and for the moment that was all that mattered to either of them.

About the Author

Margaret Davis is a lifelong resident of Medford, Oregon. She graduated from Southern Oregon State College with a bachelor of arts degree in history, and is currently employed as the scheduling and budgeting coordinator for the customer service department of a local mail-order company. *Mind Light* is her first book.

DEL REY DISCOVERY

Experience the wonder of discovery
with Del Rey's newest authors!

. . . Because something new is
always worth the risk!

TURN THE PAGE FOR AN EXCERPT
FROM THE
NEXT *DEL REY DISCOVERY:*

Ammonite
by Nicola Griffith

Chapter 1

Marghe's suit was still open at neck and wrist, and the helmet rested in the crook of her left arm. An ID flash was sealed to her shoulder: "Marguerite Angelica Taishan, SEC." The suit was wrinkled and smelled of just-unrolled plastic, and she felt heavy and awkward, even in the two-thirds gravity of orbital station *Estrade*.

She stood by the airlock at the inside end of A Section. The door was already open. Waiting. She rested the fingertips of her right hand on the smooth ceramic of the raised hatch frame; it was cool, shocking after two days of the close human heat of A Section.

The sill of the airlock reached her knees; easy enough to step over. No great barrier. The lock chamber itself was two strides across. The far door was still closed, sealed to another sill, like this one. Four steps from here to B Section. Four steps. She had recontracted with SEC, endured six months of retraining on Earth, traveled eighteen months aboard the *Terragin*, spent the last two days on the *Estrade* bumping elbows with the three-member crew, all to take those four steps.

"Well, Nyo and Sigrid say good luck, but they'll be out there for hours yet, fixing the satellite." Sara Hiam unclipped her headset. The slight, small woman with the atrophied muscles and club-cut dark blond hair was matter-of-fact, using her doctor persona. In the two days since she had come aboard *Estrade*, Marghe had learned that Hiam had several distinct facets to her personality, facets she rotated to face any given situation. It was a survival tactic, one way Hiam—and Sigrid and Nyo—had managed to spend five years up here without going mad. Marghe knew there was a great deal of the doctor she had not seen; she wondered what the real Sara Hiam was like.

"Life support is up and running in Section D," Hiam said. "Are you ready?"

Adrenaline, faster than conscious thought, flooded through Marghe and she had to discipline her breathing, decreasing her pulse and respiration rate, slowing blood flow and reducing the sudden over-oxygenation of her long muscles. Her face pinked as the capillaries under her skin reopened; her muscles stopped fluttering. It was a routine learned long ago.

"I'm ready."

"Very well." Hiam's voice was suddenly more measured, formal. "I'm obliged to remind you that the vaccine FN-17 now offered is still considered experimental. I also remind you that once you have taken it and once you step beyond this airlock, you will under no circumstances be allowed back into Section A: nor, whether or not you proceed as planned to Grenchstom's Planet, will you be allowed to enter any other uncontaminated Company installation until you have undergone extensive decontamination procedures." She sounded as though she was reading from a screen prompt. "These procedures consist of—"

"I know what they consist of," Marghe said. She pulled on gauntlets, closed her wrist seals. Was it her imagination or did the air coming from the lock smell different?

"This is a taped record, Marghe. Let me finish. These procedures consist of: isolation; the removal of all subject's blood, marrow, lymph and intestinal flora and fauna and its replacement with normal healthy tissues; reimmunization of subject with all bacterial and viral agents commonly found in Earthnormal human population; prior to return to home planet, further isolation at a location to be decided upon to determine the efficacy of said reimmunization. Do you understand these procedures?"

"Yes." The lock was small but, unlike the rest of what she had seen so far of *Estrade*, blessedly uncluttered.

"Further, I remind you that although FN-17 is a development of the Durallium Company, the Company in no way holds itself responsible for any adverse effects that may result from its use. Nor, though you are to be offered the utmost cooperation aboard *Estrade* and on Grenchstom's Planet, are you to be considered an employee of said Company liable to the financial restitution available to indentured personnel. Is this clear?"

"Yes." She closed her neck seal, hefted her helmet. "That's everything?"

"Yes."

"Will you help me with this?" She should have put the helmet on first; the gauntlets made her clumsy.

When the helmet and shoulder ring clicked together, the suit air hissed on. It tasted hard and flat, not like the warm, re-breathed air of the orbital station. She tongued on the broadcast communications. "Can you hear me?"

"I hear you." Hiam checked a workstation screen. "You're reading well enough." She looked up. "You?"

"Loud and clear." Through the audio pickups Hiam sounded even more remote and doctorlike. And then the only sound was Marghe's own breathing and the faint hiss of the forced air. Blue and purple readouts flickered in the lower left of her vision. Everything worked perfectly. There was nothing else to wait for.

Marghe stepped over the sill. Her boots clumped and echoed in the bare chamber, and her breath sounded loud. She touched the amber light on the control panel; the door slid shut. Hiam, arms folded, was visible through the small observation window.

Marghe studied the variety of lights, then tapped out a command sequence. A display flared red: VACUUM. Her helmet pick-ups were full of a hard hissing, and readouts flickered, then steadied, showing zero pressure, zero oxygen. When she moved, she felt vibration through her boots but heard nothing.

The wall display changed: AIRLOCK SYSTEMS ROUTED TO ES-TRADE MAIN CONTROL PRIOR TO DECONTAMINATION PROCE-DURES. TO PROCEED, INPUT SEQUENCE. Another last minute reminder: once she started on this, there was no turning back. Marghe tapped out the memorized sequence. RAISE ARMS, RAISE CHIN, STAND WITH FEET APART. Marghe did. BLANK VISOR FOR FIFTEEN SECONDS. COMMENCING. Even through her darkened visor and closed eyes, she sensed the flare as the chamber was flooded with radiation.

EXTERIOR DECONTAMINATION COMPLETE. LOCK GOVERNANCE RETURNED TO INTERIOR CONTROL.

Marghe cleared her visor, opened her eyes, blinked away the dancing green spots. Hiam was still in the window, watching. Then, suddenly, she was gone.

Marghe watched the blank window for a moment, then took a deep breath and turned to the second door, the second panel with its red light. She reached out to input the sequence that would open it, that would enable her to take that last step over the sill that marked the boundary between what was understood and controlled and what was dangerous.

"Marghe, wait."

Marghe whirled, forgetting the two-thirds gravity. Hiam was back at the observation window, headset at one ear. Marghe had to breathe slowly, in and out, before she could speak. "What?"

"Turn on your suit comm."

Marghe tongued the channel on. "What's wrong? What have—"

"Nothing." Over the closed channel, Hiam's voice was quiet, intimate. No longer the doctor. "This is off the record."

"I don't—"

"Just listen. All those things I said before, about isolation, about spending time somewhere unspecified before going home . . . that's not what really happens."

Marghe listened to her heart kicking under her ribs. She breathed, seeking calm. *Never refuse information*, her mother had taught her when she was just six years old, *you never know what you might need.* But her mother was dead. She managed a *Go on* gesture.

"If you leave the airlock, if you take the vaccine, you'll never go home. Not ever. I had a . . . a good friend. On the planet. Was one of the initial batch taken off Jeep for study. She promised to be in touch. I think someone else wrote her mail."

"How could you tell?"

"It felt all wrong."

"If she'd been ill—"

"No. Just listen. It seemed fine at first. I assumed she just wasn't feeling good. Decon's not pleasant. Anyway, I didn't pay close attention. But once when I wrote back I put in a private joke we'd shared for a long time. A very long time. When I got her response, I knew. It wasn't her."

Marghe said nothing. She wished she had just taken that last step, not listened to Hiam—this new Hiam. *The real one?*

Hiam watched Marghe intently, then laughed, a short, hard bark. "You don't believe me."

"I'm wondering why you didn't tell me this before. Why you let me get this far."

Hiam stepped right up to the glass, close enough for Marghe to see the pleats of her irises. "Because I couldn't decide whether to trust you. But, Marghe . . . this is real, and somebody has to know. I can't prove any of it, but that doesn't mean it's not happening. You seemed . . . I just thought . . ." She laughed again. "I should have saved my breath."

Marghe did not know what to say. "You and Sigrid and Nyo have all been up here a long time. I know that must—"

"Don't patronize me," Hiam said wearily. "If you don't want to believe me, then that's your privilege, but don't patronize me."

Marghe shook her head. "I'm sorry."

Silence.

To go down to Grenchstom's Planet—GP, Jeep—would be the culmination of years of study that had started when she was just a child, first with her mother, then her father; had continued at Universities, and as assistant SEC rep on Gallipoli, then Beaver. This was the reason she had swallowed her pride and set aside her misgivings about Company, why she had recontracted with SEC after they had betrayed her, why she had traveled vast distances, literally and metaphorically: to come to Jeep and study over a million people who had been out of contact with humanity for two or three hundred years. There would never be another chance like this, never.

"Sara, I have to do this."

Hiam turned away abruptly. "Then you'd better go ahead and do it."

Marghe looked at Hiam's thin back, hesitated. "I'm sorry," she said again, then tongued off the comm channel and turned slowly to face the flaring red panel. Red for danger.

The known dangers she had prepared for, as far as humanly possible. The vaccine would be waiting for her in D Section. As for the unknown dangers . . . Well, they were unknown. Nothing she could do about them.

She stretched out her hand, clumsy in the gauntlet, and tapped out the sequence slowly and carefully. The red panel blinked off and the lights around the door flared green.

The door slid open.

B Section was silent and dark. Ice glimmered in the dim sodium glow of the emergency floor lights. Marghe stepped over the sill and the door closed behind her. It was done.

The lights ran like runway flares down a narrow corridor between stripped, bare beds, each with its entertainment hookup coiled neatly at the head. Marghe's boots glowed orange as she walked. Her breathing was loud. She felt utterly alone.

She was the first person who had walked here for five years; five years since the glittering dumbbell shape that was *Estrade* had been hurriedly converted from an orbital monitoring and communications station to a research and decontamination facility. Five years since the station crew had taken refuge in Section A, leaving Sections D and C for the decontamination of occasional Jeep personnel. B Section, and the long corridor beyond—the shaft of the dumbbell—was the crew's insurance, their buffer zone, with movement allowed one way only: to the dirty sections.

Marghe watched her boots rise and fall through the orange glow; there was no dust.

The lights at the airlock blinked a reassuring green. The door opened and the wall display told her to blank her visor and hold out her arms; she keyed in the sequence on the next door, stepped through.

The corridor seemed a mile long. The familiar orange running lights gleamed on unsheathed metal and exposed wiring. Gravity decreased rapidly as she approached the center of the shaft; her suit automatically activated the electromagnets in her boots and she had to slide her feet instead of striding.

There was another airlock at the center of the corridor. She went through the dictated procedure, familiar now. The micro gravity and her sensitivity to the strong magnetic field under her feet made her dizzy. She closed her eyes and took three fast breaths to trigger a meditative state, monitoring for a moment her heartbeat and electrical activity.

She went on: more corridor, another lock. C Section.

In C Section there were beds, like B Section, but each had a hood waiting to be lowered over an occupant to suck out her blood and lymph, ready to push physical and electrical fingers deep into her intestines to kill and remove the swarm of bacteria and yeasts, eager to sear away the first layers of skin and leave red, raw tissues with colorless fluids until new skin grew back. Tombs for the living. She hated them. They had not been able to save her mother.

She walked faster; she wanted to be out of C Section.

In the lock. *Hurry.* Eyes shut and arms out. *Faster.* Key sequence. *Now.*

Nothing. The panel still flashed red.

Marghe stared at it. If she could not get through into D Section, she was trapped. The lock systems would not permit her to retrace her steps without a record of her having undergone either isolation in D or fluid replacement in C.

Think.

Perhaps she had input the wrong number sequence. She had

been in a rush. Yes. Precisely, accurately, she tapped in the code a second time.

No change.

She tongued on the comm channel. "Hiam, can you hear me?"

Her helmet speaker clicked. "I can hear. Go ahead."

"I'm still in lock three."

"So my readouts say."

"It won't accept the sequence."

"You're sure you got it right?"

"Seven-eight-three-six-nine." Silence. "It's the right one, isn't it?"

"Yes." Another silence. Marghe imagined the *tck-tck* of Hiam's nails on the keyboard. "How much air do you have?"

"About eighty minutes."

"There should be an emergency suit. In the locker to your left."

Marghe opened the left locker, then the right. They were both empty. "Nothing. And all the emergency blow patches have gone."

"I forgot. We had to clear everything, just in case someone infected tried to blow her way out. Let me think."

Marghe stood in the dim light and breathed precious air.